Indomitable
The Viceroy Chronicles
Book 1

Claudia Brooke

SNARKY & QUIP
PRESS
It was a dark and stormy night.

Publisher's Cataloging-in-Publication Data
provided by Five Rainbows Cataloging Services

Names: Brooke, Claudia, author.

Title: Indomitable / Claudia Brooke.

Description: Bethesda, MD : Snarky & Quip Press, 2022. | Series: Viceroy chronicles, bk. 1.

Identifiers: LCCN 2022938936 (print) | ISBN 979-8-9862879-2-8 (hardcover) | ISBN 979-8-9862879-1-1 (paperback) | ISBN 979-8-9862879-0-4 (ebook) | ISBN 979-8-9862879-3-5 (audiobook)

Subjects: LCSH: Vampires--Fiction. | Women--Fiction. | Fantasy fiction. | Paranormal fiction. | BISAC: FICTION / Fantasy / Urban. | FICTION / Fantasy / Paranormal. | FICTION / Fantasy / Contemporary. | GSAFD: Fantasy fiction.

Classification: LCC PS3602.R66 I63 2022 (print) | LCC PS3602.R66 (ebook) | DDC 813/.6--dc23.

To Anthony, my muse, my world builder, and buyer of my chairs—no matter how crazy. Your encouragement, tolerance, and love make me believe I can reach the stars.

To my incredible family—without your snarky wit, unfailing support in the face of ridiculous odds, and perhaps slightly misplaced loyalty, I never would have finished this book.

To Suleiman the Magnificent, Toby, Skylar, Willie, Molly, and all the dogs in my life, past, and present who have inspired me to love harder.

And to James Thurber, whose books taught me to find the humor in any situation.

1

Gracie

Thursday, November 5

Rent was due again.

A problem, considering I hadn't had a job in over a month and didn't want to pay my half out of my savings account. I had almost enough money to buy my cake truck, but withdrawing rent money again meant my dream would recede into an uncomfortably distant future. My family had been pressuring me to quit it with the crappy gigs and find a real job in my field. But working a full-time job would leave little time for polishing my business plan and testing a few final recipes.

My eye twitched. I had to get my cake truck off the ground before my mother and brothers drove me into grad school at Columbia. And that was how I found myself sitting in front of a mansion in Greenwich, Connecticut. Dog-sitting was one of my favorite gigs. I loved dogs, though my father's allergies meant we'd never had one as kids. Aside from the fact that I needed a job, *any* job, this one had sounded promising, and Greenwich was only a few miles from my neighborhood in Port Chester, New York.

The front door opened before I rang the bell. A woman in a

white blouse and black pants examined me like a less-than-prime slab of beef.

"You're small," she said.

I *was* small. Five foot nothing in my size 5 bare feet, I often shopped in the kids department. But I came by it honestly, as my entire family was of less-than-average height—which might account for our collective overachievements.

Choosing to ignore her rudeness, I slathered on the charm and extended my hand. "Hi, Lauren, I'm Gracie."

The woman thawed and smiled, taking my hand and shaking it.

"Hello, Gracie, I'm Marcy, the house manager. Please follow me. Lauren is waiting for you."

House manager? I refrained from shaking my head and followed Marcy down a hall lined with artwork into an enormous kitchen. A tall, slender blonde woman, who might have been anywhere from thirty to fifty, stood staring out a set of French doors.

Hearing our approach, she turned. "Gracie, hello. I'm Lauren. I'm so glad you came." She dwarfed me.

"Hi, Lauren, it's so nice to meet you." I stuck out my hand again.

She took it and held it for a touch too long, examining me much like Marcy had, making sweat prickle in my hairline. Finally, she pulled me up onto my toes and into a hug.

"I think Viceroy will love you," she pronounced, releasing me. Allowing myself a small thrill of promise, I was suddenly glad I'd worn my one interview blouse tucked into dark jeans. I glanced around, not seeing a dog.

"He's there." Lauren pointed outside to a shaggy little tan dog trying desperately to play with a phalanx of gardeners raking fallen acorns from dozens of tall oak trees.

My heart melted. "Oh, he's a cutie," I said. *Wow.* Taking care of a little fun-sized dog would be no trouble at all. "So, you want me to take him to a park twice a week?"

"Yes, but . . ." She paused. "I'm afraid his needs are more complex than a walk in the park, Gracie. He's a special little boy." She picked her words as if they were unknown flavors in a box of chocolates.

"Special how? Is he disabled?"

Lauren burst out laughing. "Far from it. Viceroy is as healthy as a horse and will be for a very long time." She stopped, peering at her perfectly manicured nails before adding. "His needs are more complicated than a bit of exercise."

"I don't understand."

"He needs more than trips to the park and cuts from the butcher, Gracie." She frowned, dragging her gaze to my eyes. "I'm just going to tell you. There's no point in sugarcoating it. I tried that with the first few sitters, and it didn't work out well. He's a vampire, Gracie."

I froze. Less than five minutes in this house, and we're talking vampires? She had sounded so normal on the phone.

"Uhh . . . what?" My brain had frozen right along with my body. "One of the gardeners is a vampire?"

"No. Viceroy." She pointed toward the flying ball of fur. "Viceroy, my dog, is a vampire."

The dog? *She's talking about the dog. The dog I'm being interviewed to sit for.* I struggled to breathe while my brain groped for words. "Do you mean an emotional vampire? Does he take up a lot of your time and energy?"

She pursed her lips. "No, Viceroy is not an emotional vampire. He's an actual vampire. He drinks squirrel blood." She eyed me and, seeing I wasn't about to bolt, continued in a chattier tone, as if telling me her dog was a blood-sucking vampire wasn't oversharing her craziness with someone she'd just met. "He's drained all the squirrels in the neighborhood. He needs new places, places with squirrels, and I don't have time to take him myself." Lauren crossed her arms tightly over her chest, hugging herself. "Listen, I love him, no matter what he is, and I need you to know that."

I backed up a step. Questions swirled, tilting my balance. If I made a run for the front door, would Lauren and Marcy chase me? The prickles of sweat in my hairline bloomed.

Lauren's shoulders slumped. "I can tell you the story. How he got this way, I mean. It might help if you heard it all. Then, if you still want to leave, I understand." She stood still as Lot's wife, waiting for me to decide.

Okay, Gracie, think. If you have this many oak trees, you have squirrels. Lauren thinks she has no squirrels because her dog has drained them all. So who's crazier here? Her, for thinking her dog is a vampire, or me for listening to her. I watched the half dozen gardeners rake acorns. The little dog dashed back and forth between them, nipping at their heels until one of them picked up a yellow tennis ball and threw it across the lawn. The shaggy little thing flew after it, bringing the ball back to the gardener and setting it at his feet. Well, how cute was that?

So, the little dog was adorable, and his owner was bananas. And Bananas was still waiting for my answer. Running like hell would be the rational thing to do. But I needed this job, crazy lady notwithstanding, if I wanted to buy my cake truck and get my emotionally wrought-up family off my back.

That, and I was curious. I wanted to hear Lauren's story. Besides, there were at least six gardeners and a house manager to help me if Lauren's head suddenly did a 360.

"I'll stay," I said.

She heaved an enormous sigh of relief before turning away from the doors. "How about a cup of herbal tea? I have a new one that's quite soothing."

"Um, no, thanks, but water would be great." I wasn't a tea drinker and didn't think an herbal sedative would be a wise choice, seeing as how I should probably hang on to my wits—what few of them I seemed to have about me today.

Lauren pulled a bottle of Pellegrino out of the glass-doored refrigerator for me and busied herself with the kettle.

I tried not to think about the big V in the room, forcing

myself to study the gleaming kitchen instead. It was enormous, and I was instantly envious. The refrigerator stood next to what must be a separate upright freezer. The two giant appliances dwarfed a squat Wolf range. A white marble pastry bench dominated the center of the room. Next to it, a butcher block built for three was attached to a prep sink. An open pantry held a shelf full of professional-grade appliances.

But for all the money spent, the gorgeous kitchen smelled like window cleaner and furniture polish. Not a single food aroma tickled my nose. If this were my kitchen, it would smell like cakes baking, like vanilla, caramel, cinnamon, and chocolate. My heart cracked open like an overbaked cheesecake at the tragedy of it all.

A loud scratching at the French doors interrupted my kitchen lust. Lauren let the little dog in, and he shot right past her, beelining straight for me. He stopped short, stood on his hind legs, and placed his front paws gently on my knee for balance, his tail wagging so hard his entire body rocked. He grinned up at me, panting. I scratched his ears, pulling my hands back quickly when I remembered the vampire thing.

"Don't worry, he never bites people. Do you, Viceroy?" Lauren smiled to reassure me. Viceroy dropped back to the floor and ran from the room. "Oh, perfect." She beamed. "He's going for a ball. He likes you, Gracie. He never asks to play with people he doesn't like."

"Uh, maybe I will have that cup of tea." I needed something more substantial than fizzy water, and since she hadn't offered me a straight shot of anything alcoholic, a hot, soothing cup of tea would have to do.

2

Gracie

Lauren brewed a cup for me and sat down to begin her story. "Maybe this is odd, me telling you all of this when I don't even know you. But I have a good feeling about you, Gracie." She leaned toward me. "You do like him?"

"Yes, I like him a lot. He's . . ." I'd only just met the little guy, but some dogs just put a spell on you with their happiness, and he was one of them. "He's so loveable."

"He is, isn't he?" Lauren smiled. "Okay, here goes. I was living in New York City and working at an advertising agency. That's where I met Michael. He was handsome and sophisticated, a little dangerous, if you know what I mean."

I nodded. I'd dated one of those.

"Michael and I had been together for less than a year when he surprised me with a puppy for my birthday—an adorable, tiny cairn terrier with an engagement ring hanging from his collar!" She shook her head. "I said yes."

I took an exploratory sip of the tea. Minty with a slight undertone of dirt, but not gag-worthy. I took another. I felt calmer. I had watched her make it, so I knew she hadn't drugged me. I just might have to ask her about the brand. Any tea that soothed me through this wacky interview was worth having.

Viceroy had brought me a tennis ball, placing it at my feet. He sat patiently, waiting for me to throw it. I picked up the wet, obviously well-loved ball and tossed it across the kitchen. Damp circles formed every time it hit the floor. Lauren, deep in her story, didn't notice. Viceroy streaked off, toenails scrabbling on the polished wood. He caught the yellow missile on a bounce and trotted back, placing it at my feet again. He was utterly adorable. We were on the sixth round of squishy fetch when Lauren's voice changed, forcing me to look up.

". . . a few days before Christmas, Michael called to ask me to go with him to a party hosted by Felix, a friend of his. I didn't have a sitter for Viceroy and didn't want to go, but Michael insisted I bring him." She got up to refill our cups.

"Then what happened?" I prompted.

"What can I tell you? I was in love, so we went." She shrugged. "When the elevator doors opened, Felix came to greet us, and Viceroy went crazy. He snarled and leaped out of my arms, biting Felix. Then, and I know it sounds crazy, Felix grabbed Viceroy and bit him back. I cried all the way home. Michael, that evil bastard, dropped me off without a word, calling the next day to ask for his ring back."

I felt sick. This woman wasn't odd or a little off center; she was insane. And I was insane for sitting there, drinking herbal tea and listening to her crazy talk. People don't bite dogs and turn them into vampires, because there are no people vampires, and there are no dog vampires. But I stilled myself in a rush of empathy. Michael sounded like a real jackass. I wanted to tell her that she was lucky to be rid of him, but I didn't want to interrupt.

Lauren blinked away more tears. "Once I was upstairs with Viceroy, I checked where Felix bit him and found two small holes. I called the vet."

I PULLED OUT OF LAUREN'S DRIVEWAY AND PARKED
alongside a stone wall across the street. Pendulous oak branches
flowed over the wall from the neighboring estate, brown leaves
swaying in the breeze. My tires crunched over a thick layer of
acorns. I shivered in my thin blouse and light jacket as I punched
my boyfriend Bryan's number into my cellphone.

"Nope, nope, nope. I am not taking that job!" I shouted
when he picked up. "I think I just escaped with my life. That
woman is nuts!"

Bryan barked a laugh. "Hi to you too." He chuckled. "Nuts,
huh? What happened?"

"You're not going to believe this. I can't believe it myself. But
the woman who interviewed me thinks her dog is a vampire."

"What? You broke up for a second. Did you say vampire?"

"Yes! A for-real bloodsucking vampire!"

"First of all, vampires aren't real. Second, even if they were, a
dog could not be one." He stated the last bit with a satisfied final-
ity. "I've seen all the movies."

"Yeah, well, she's delusional. She says the dog drinks the blood
of squirrels, which is why there isn't a squirrel left on 12 Oaks . . ."
I stopped, noticing, for the first time, the too-quiet landscape.

"Hey, babe, I'm sorry, but I gotta go," Bryan said, breaking
my trance. "I've been up all night with a transplant patient, I
haven't had coffee, and I just got a page. I'll see you at dinner,
okay? Dr. Rinelli said it's at his house tonight, and we can talk
about the crazy lady."

It was so cute that Bryan always called my brother Dr. Rinelli.
But I supposed since Bry was a resident under him in Surgical
Cardiology at Westchester Medical Center he couldn't very well
call him Auggie like we all did. I sighed.

"Fine. Vampire dogs can't compete with heart transplants. See
you later. Love you." I hung up, sticking the phone into the drink
holder, still scanning the street for squirrels.

My stomach alternately churned and growled. I'd missed both
breakfast and lunch sitting with my next-door neighbor until his

daughter arrived. He'd stumbled on the stairs, and after helping him into his apartment, getting him ice for his knee, and making him a cup of coffee, I was afraid to leave him alone. I'd barely made it in time to my interview, and now I needed food.

Starbucks. A nice caramel mocha and one of those chicken sandwiches would do the trick. To hell with the calories I shouldn't consume and the money I shouldn't spend; a few dollars wouldn't break the truck bank. I started the car and made a tight U-turn when my cell rang with my unknown caller ringtone, "Stuck in the Middle with You." I pulled over, plucking the phone back up.

"Hi, this is Gracie."

"Hi, Gracie." A woman hesitated before rushing on. "I hope I didn't frighten you. I should have waited until the second time you came to tell you."

Oh, crap. Vampire dog mom. Despite her practically begging, I had told her I'd have to think about taking the job. "Um, hi, Lauren. No, you didn't frighten me, but it's a lot to process. I-I need time to—"

"I'll pay you more," she said, interrupting my budding string of excuses. "Viceroy loved you, and you liked him. You don't have to worry. He has never once bitten a person since Felix. Is forty dollars an hour enough?"

"For—" I dropped the phone and had to fumble for it in my lap before snatching it back up and smacking it against my ear. My beautiful cake truck sparkled before my eyes then faded as I remembered I'd have to deal with ongoing crazy.

"Uh, that's a generous offer, Lauren. Thank you. And Viceroy is adorable . . ." Lauren waited. "But I don't think I'm the right person. What if he attacks something bigger, like another dog? I wouldn't be able to handle that."

"Gracie, please believe me. He is the sweetest little boy. He has never so much as chased anything bigger than a squirrel. He even avoids confrontations with other dogs." Her voice hitched. "He loves you. I know this will work. Please at least try."

It was so much money. And I did have delusional friends—lots of people believed in the supernatural, okay? But not like this. Lauren needed a therapist, and a psychiatrist, and maybe some medication. My psychology degree told me as much.

"Lauren, listen, I'm sorry, I really am." My cake truck vision popped out of sight like a cartoon bubble.

"Gracie, please, take a couple of days to think about it, then call me. If you still don't want to be Viceroy's companion, so be it. I won't hire anyone else until I hear from you."

"Okay, Lauren, I'll call you. But—"

"Please. Just think about it. I'll wait to hear from you. And I hope to see you again. Bye, Gracie." She hung up.

Great. I'd just jumped off the express train to my cake truck because the cute dog's owner was off her rocker.

3

Gracie

Too keyed up to eat once I hit Starbucks, I made do with a latte. I was halfway home, crawling down 95 toward Exit 22. Ongoing roadwork meant traffic was practically unbearable, even off peak. I usually went the back way, but while fretting about the money I'd just tossed down the toilet, I'd accidentally gotten on the highway.

Port Chester had a few things going for it. Not fancy, like its surrounding neighbors, the village had a working-class vibe. I grew up there, and it was still home. We had an excellent library, decent restaurants, a train into the city, a waterfront, and okay shopping. I drummed my fingers on the steering wheel, waiting for the cars in front of me to move. I picked up the phone to call my mom and tell her I'd be late for family dinner when it rang in my hand. "Chariots of Fire." It was Auggie.

"Hey," I said. "What's up?"

"Hey yourself. In case Mom didn't tell you, there's a change of venue for dinner tonight. It's at my house—Alicia's cooking."

"I haven't checked my messages; I was in an interview. But I just talked to Bryan, and he told me."

"An interview?" His voice climbed half an octave.

"Yeah, but I'm not taking the job. The woman I interviewed with was too weird. We can talk about it later."

"Okay, but I want to hear everything. Rob's family is coming too. Mom's already there, so don't go home."

I snickered. "I wish you'd called thirty minutes ago to remind me not to get on the highway. Now I'm sitting in this mess."

"Uh, right. I'm so sorry. I'm a terrible social secretary. You should fire me and hire someone more competent."

"I should." I giggled at the thought of my heart-surgeon brother keeping track of my calendar. Auggie—his full name was Augustine—was my eldest brother. Not only was he a father figure to my three other brothers and me, and father to his own rambunctious family, he was also the head of cardiothoracic surgery at WestMed. My brother had a full plate. That he was calling me during his workday was a testament to how much he worried about us all.

"We'll wait," Auggie said. "Gotta run, or you'll beat me. I have one last patient to see."

Auggie and his family lived in Larchmont. Their house was ten minutes from the hospital on a congested traffic day. He could beat me to his house if he walked backward while blindfolded.

"Wait, what are we having?" I was starving, and my empty stomach growled at the thought of one of Alicia's enormous dinners. I didn't know how my brother stayed so thin. I'd be as wide as I was tall if I lived in that house.

"Your guess is as good as mine. See you in an hour." He hung up.

MY SISTER-IN-LAW, ALICIA, HAD MADE A LASAGNA WITH three-meat sauce, which meant the meats—chicken thighs, beef braciole, and pork chops—were served on a platter alongside the lasagna. She'd made sautéed broccoli rabe; an enormous salad studded with capers, olives, and slivers of parmesan; and a tray of sizzling garlic bread. If it weren't for Bryan, who was eyeing the table with lust in his eyes, I would seriously consider stealing Alicia from my brother.

My second-oldest brother, Rob, beat Bryan to the seat next to me, sandwiching me between him and my youngest brother, Chris. We were all conversationally fluent in Italian, but because I'd skipped as many Italian language classes as I could get away with as a kid, my spoken Italian was the worst. Even my nieces and nephews corrected me. Listening to the chatter in English and Italian, I looked around the table at my family, wondering again how I'd gotten so lucky. While they sometimes drove me crazy, I loved them all to pieces. I held out my plate for a serving of lasagna.

We usually started dinners with a one-minute synopsis of what was new since our last dinner, running from my mom down to me.

"You don't mind if Gracie cuts the line, right, old man?" Chris spoke before Auggie could start his turn. I sent Chris a death glare. He'd just bought a motorcycle and probably figured I'd done something dumb enough to draw attention away from his own asshattery. He offered me up on a regular basis, and I was generally happy to help him out, but only because he was my favorite.

"Not at all. Be my guest, Gracie," Auggie said.

I dug a knuckle into Chris's thigh under the table, hard enough to make him yelp and his fiancée giggle.

"Gracie, that's enough," my mother admonished as she lifted a forkful of braciola. "We have something we want to share with you, and now is as good a time as any. But you first."

I gulped my bite of lasagna fast enough to choke myself.

"Chris, why don't you go so Gracie has time to recover?"

I shot Auggie a thank-you smile through my coughing fit.

"Uh, sure," Chris said, giving me the evil eye and draining his wineglass. "Well, everyone, guess what? I bought a motorcycle!"

My mother's fork clattered onto her plate, and the table fell silent. Even Auggie and Alicia's twin babies stopped burbling.

And just like that, I was off the hook while my mother shrieked at Chris, and everyone chimed in, attacking his idiotic decision to kill himself on the Devil's machine.

Or at least I was, until dessert, when my mother held out a manilla envelope topped with a fat red bow.

I eyed it, hands in my lap, until Bryan took it from her and handed it across the table to me. "Open it," he said in a stage whisper.

"It's not my birthday. What are you guys up to?" I asked, dread pooling atop the heavy meal resting happily in my stomach. Everyone was grinning at me, even Chris. I shook the envelope, but nothing rattled. I folded up the two metal wings and slid a sheaf of papers out. The first page was a bank statement. Underneath was the Columbia University catalog and a handful of brochures.

"What did you do?" I gazed around the table at the delighted faces of my family. I loved them so much, but right then, I wished they would all disappear in a puff of smoke.

Auggie cleared his throat. "We deposited the tuition for a graduate program at Columbia into an account for you."

BRYAN HOPPED DOWN THE STEPS AND LEANED AGAINST the hood of his ancient Jeep, turning to grin at me. "I love how supportive your family is. It's incredible that they all chipped in to do that for you." He shook his head. "They're pretty perfect."

I stared at him like he was a pot of custard that had just curdled. "Bryan. I am getting a cake truck. Remember? I never said I was going back to school. In fact, I believe I said, as plainly as possible, in as many freaking ways I could think of, that *I am not going back to school!*"

His eyebrows folded inward. "Yeah, I know. But they want what's best for you—"

"Wow. I don't even know where to start with that one." I shook my head, my temper simmering. "My career path isn't up to them. The fact that they think they can force me into school by paying a ridiculous amount of tuition is nuts. Don't you see that?"

He scuffed a toe against the pavers in the wide driveway. "I see that they care about you, and they worry about you."

"And you? What do you think I should do?" I was winding up.

"Well, I think you should have your truck. But I also think you should go to school so that if the truck fails"—Bryan put up a hand to stop the explosion he knew was coming—"you have a day job to go back to."

My lips thinned, but he forged on. "Gracie, listen. Having a great education is never a bad thing. Lots of people get degrees and then end up working in fields entirely unrelated to what they studied. Or they try something else first and go back to their original field. Think of it as a great tool to have in your toolbox. Or a fallback plan."

My heart sank. Bryan might not be wrong about having the degree. But he was wrong about what made me who I am. And no amount of screaming at him in my brother's driveway would fix that. So, even though my emotions wanted war, I bit my tongue.

"You have a point. I'll think about it," I said to forestall the argument that would ensue if we kept talking about school. "In other news, I'm going to turn down the dog-companion gig."

"Oh, that's probably for the best, seeing as how she sounds delusional."

"Yeah, well." I sighed. "She offered me forty dollars an hour."

His eyes went wide. "Did you say forty?"

"Uh-huh. And the dog is adorable. It kind of killed me to say no."

"Yeah, I would have had a hard time refusing that much money myself, crazy lady or not." Bryan opened his arms, and I leaned against him while he hugged me.

"Are you done for the day?" I asked into his chest.

"No, Jack is covering for me so I could sneak over here for dinner, but I have to get back. Barring any highway pileups, I get off at six a.m."

I heaved a sigh, and he leaned back to search my face.

"I'm sorry, I thought I told you."

"I don't remember you mentioning it, but it's fine." I stretched up, wrapped my arms around his neck, ran my fingers through his overgrown hair, and kissed him. He was an exceptional kisser, and I kicked myself for letting him off so easily.

"You have garlic breath. Yum," he whispered. "I could find someone to fill in for me."

I breathed into my palm and sniffed. "Ew. Nope. No shirking doctor duties on my account. I'm going home, taking a hot shower, and collapsing. We can talk tomorrow after you finish your shift and get some sleep." I shooed him toward his car and turned to my own. "Go. Doctor people."

"Gracie, wait."

"What?" I stopped at his expression. It was his intent face.

"My mom is coming into town next week. She'd like to meet you."

I froze. We'd been dating for two years, but I'd never met his mother. Mostly because, according to Bryan, he rarely saw her himself. And I was okay with that. She was a busy neurosurgeon at Boston Children's. The woman operated on kids' brains, and here I was about to throw the opportunity to get an advanced degree back in my family's face so I could run a cake truck.

"Stop it." Bryan grasped my arms and shook me gently. "She's going to love you as much as I do."

I pasted on a smile. "I can't wait. Your mother is an amazing woman, and she made you. I'm going to adore her."

"You will. My mom is the funniest person I know, and you two will get along like a house on fire."

Or she'd burn me to the ground. But Bryan was so excited I couldn't rain on his parade even if I was terrified of the magnificent Dr. McLaughlin.

"It's a date." I touched his cheek. "And your breath is just as bad as mine."

He breathed into his hand and sniffed. "Yikes, I'd better brush. And gargle." He blew me a pungent kiss and got into his car just as my mom appeared in the doorway.

"Are we going, Gracie?" she called to me, waving to Bryan as he pulled away.

"I'm ready, Mom," I said as she stepped down the stone stairs. Trim and athletic, her energy belied her sixty-three years. She had taken an Uber to Auggie's, as her car was in the shop, and so she'd asked me to drive her home.

My mother gave me a side-eye as she opened the passenger-side door. "I want to talk to you about Columbia," she said.

"I know, Mom, I can't ever thank you all enough. And I want to talk to you about something too."

"You're going to refuse," she said, narrowing her eyes.

I started the car and pulled out of the driveway. "Not that. Bryan just asked me to meet his mother."

"Oh, Gracie, honey, that's wonderful!" she cried, clapping her hands together. The second-best thing to happen to an Italian mother's daughter, after an excellent education, was a wedding. And talking about even a potential wedding trumped arguing about Columbia any day. She peppered me with questions about Bryan's mother all the way home.

Columbia and my truck never came up.

4

Gracie

Friday, November 6

I woke the next morning to a text from Bryan saying he would be at the hospital for the long haul. I pulled up the news. There had been a multi-car pileup on 287.

Offering up a short prayer for the poor souls Bry was treating, I brushed my teeth, washed my face, and wrapped my hair in a messy bun. The garlic was still coming out of my pores, so I spritzed on some of my dad's Acqua di Gio.

It was one of the things I'd taken when I moved into my apartment. He'd always put it on after his shower on days he wasn't at the restaurant, and it made me feel, for the briefest second, like he was standing next to me.

I threw on running gear and let myself out of my apartment. Running in my neighborhood meant sidewalks, but if I was early enough, I'd manage to get in a couple of miles before I had to slow down to avoid pedestrian collisions. I was outside the bagel bakery on the corner in twenty minutes flat. Manny was alone at the counter. A line stretched between us.

"Hey," I said when it was my turn to order. "Where's Susie?"

"She's sick again." He shrugged, shaking his head. "You want a job?"

"Really?" I asked, perking up.

"I know you're starting school in January and all, but I could use your help until then."

"Wait, what?"

"Your mom was here picking up a breakfast tray for a meeting. She told me about Columbia. Congratulations."

My head exploded, and it must have shown on my face.

"What? What's wrong? Isn't that a good thing?"

I stepped out of the line to duck under the counter and stripped off my jacket. "Let me help you out, at least for this morning. My mother was misinformed. I'm not starting school in January—I'm not going back to school, ever. NEXT!"

By 9:30, the crowd had thinned to the point where Manny could take over. He tried to pay me, but I declined, asking the grill cook for a bacon, egg, and cheese on a toasted everything bagel instead. I had slipped into my jacket and gathered my bagel and coffee when Manny put a hand on my arm.

"So, you want the job?"

"Thanks, Manny. Ordinarily, I'd jump at the chance, but I just got offered a job, and I'm going to accept."

"Just my luck," Manny grumped.

"You should ask Sylvie. She'd love to work for you."

Sylvie was my roommate. We were high school friends and had lived together for the past six months. She was in grad school and always looking for part-time jobs to supplement her parents' contributions. She'd also been crushing on Manny ever since he'd become single again.

His wife had left him for a real estate salesman, screaming as she stormed out of the deli that she was sick of smelling like a hot griddle. Rumor had it she shopped in Scarsdale now.

Manny was too cute for his own good, even though he had to be close to forty, and just dark enough to suggest secrets in that recently wounded way, and Sylvie had fallen hard. I suspected he was equally gaga for her, as he consistently spent precious extra minutes chatting with her. That she was usually falling out of the V-neck T-shirts she favored in all but sub-zero temperatures was just the icing on the cake.

"Really? Do you think she'd be interested?" Manny asked, his eyebrows rising about an inch.

"Yep, I do," I said. "Call her." I scribbled her number on the green receipt pad and pushed it back to him.

Manny took a fresh black-and-white cookie, folded it into a square of waxed paper, and handed it to me with a flourish. "Thanks, Gracie. I'll call her today."

I grinned at him, waving my gratitude over my shoulder as I wove past the line and out the door. Breakfast and bonus cookie in hand, I made my way across the busy street to a bench facing a little triangle-shaped park. I usually ate my breakfast on that bench in all but the worst weather, usually while reading a novel.

This time, I just sat, counting at least fifteen squirrels romping in the thin, browning grass. They were legion. Well, my neighborhood was a little far from Greenwich, but I could always bring Viceroy here.

I pinched my arm. Hard. Lauren's crazy was seeping into me, and I hadn't even called her to tell her I'd take the job yet. I tossed a chunk of bagel over to a waiting squirrel not eighteen inches from my shoe. "Here you go, beggar." It snatched up my offering and ran up the closest tree trunk.

I'd return my family's deposit next week at dinner. Standing, I brushed crumbs off my lap and headed back to my apartment to call Lauren and start my newly affluent vampire dog-sitting life. It was a good thing rich people didn't walk their own dogs.

LAUREN HAD ASKED IF THERE WAS ANY WAY I COULD start immediately. So here I was, sitting in her driveway, gathering myself.

"Viceroy is just a cute little dog. Viceroy is not a vampire," I whispered to myself as a tan streak from around the corner of the house resolved itself into a wiggling Viceroy. I got out. Barely able to contain his joy, the little guy bounded about my feet. I dropped my bag and bent to greet him.

"Hi, Viceroy," I whispered. Pushing my fear at being bitten aside, I scrunched my fingers through his shaggy coat, massaging him all over while his tail continued to wag his body before attempting a command. "Sit." Viceroy promptly sat, looking up at me with an adoring expression, his tail still going at full speed. "Well, you are a good boy! Where's your mom?" I said to him just as Lauren appeared around the corner of the house.

"Hi, Gracie!" she called. "Come. The sun is warm on this side of the house. Let's sit on the patio and talk." Viceroy ran back and forth between us as I walked toward her.

"Sorry I'm a little late. There was—"

"Oh, no worries. I'm so happy you came." She dismissed my apology with a wave of her hand, leaned in, and hugged me. I hugged her back hard. Despite her conspicuous wealth, she seemed lonely, and I felt sorry for her. Lauren broke away and smiled at me. I followed her to a beautiful, old wrought-iron dining set. I was glad to sit outside; that kitchen made me sad. And she was right. There was no wind on this side of the house, and the sun was pleasantly toasty. A pitcher and two tall glasses sat in the middle of the table.

"Please." Lauren pointed to the chair opposite her.

I had to struggle to pull the heavy thing out without scraping the flagstone.

"Oh, aren't they awful? They weigh a ton." She sighed. "Cider? We just pressed it."

Right. Of course they had.

"Thanks. That would be great. Your house is so beautiful," I said. Accepting a full glass, I took a long drink of cider that tasted exactly like a freshly picked apple. Delicious. It would make a wonderful apple cider caramel.

"I grew up here. It was my parents' house. I used to come up on weekends when I worked in the city, but after what happened to Viceroy, I thought living here full time would be easier for both of us."

She had quit her job to take care of her dog. Crazy or not, I was starting to really like her. I looked past her at the beautiful old house, white with indigo shutters. Shiny-leaved bushes and manicured flower beds surrounded the foundation. I could see beyond the oak trees to a miniature orchard. That would explain the cider.

"I've been thinking," Lauren said, "three days a week, at least. Three to four hours a day to start, and I'll need you to take Viceroy farther afield. Down into New York, perhaps?"

Viceroy, who had been sitting at my feet, began thumping his tail. I reached down and fondled his ears, looking up to see Lauren leaning across the table, staring at me. "Gracie, do you understand?"

I sat back. "Yes." I understood that she believed her dog was a vampire, and whether Lauren was loony or not, I was more than willing to take the little guy to a few parks for forty dollars an hour. "I know of some perfect places," I said to cover the pause of my adding up the hours and dollars.

"They need to be quiet parks with not too many people—and no children. Playgrounds won't work at all."

Viceroy's tail stilled, and his ears fell at this pronouncement, as if he understood the no-kids rule. He yawned his stress up at me.

I leaned over and whispered to him, "Don't worry, little man. I know of some great parks with lots of room to run. We'll have so much fun!" He looked reassured and thumped his tail again.

"Oh, I almost forgot," Lauren said. "I have a tote bag of things for you. There's a water bowl, Fiji water, jerky treats, leashes, a raincoat, a quilted coat, dog wipes, and a towel."

Viceroy was all set for a cruise to Alaska.

"Enough for a play date!" she finished with a wave of her hand.

A man in a plaid flannel shirt and gardening hat appeared from the back of the house, carrying an enormous tote bag. He walked up to us, nodded politely, and set the leather bag down next to my chair before turning and heading back across the lawn.

"And about your salary. If you give me your checking account information, I'll have Marcy deposit your paycheck every Friday for you."

"Um, don't you want to wait until I get back to make sure it went okay?"

"I assumed you'd have to get that information from home, so I believe it will all work out perfectly."

Right. Duh.

Lauren stood, so I followed suit, taking a last long drink from my glass. "Do you have any questions?" she asked.

"No, I think I can take it from here. Viceroy?" I looked down at the little dog. "Do you want to go for a ride?" He was running for the car before I had even finished my sentence. "Well, I guess that's a yes," I said, following him. "See you later," I added over my shoulder to Lauren.

"Oh, Gracie, one last thing."

I stopped, turning toward her.

"He's fast and strong. And he has terrible recall."

My mouth dropped open. "But—"

"Don't worry. He always comes back eventually." Lauren turned and practically ran around the back of the house. Her "bye" floated back to me, but she was out of sight.

I froze, looking back and forth between the now-empty lawn and Viceroy, who was running in circles around the car. He yipped at me. "Well, I guess it's too late to back out now," I muttered. Hefting the twenty pounds of dog stuff to my shoulder, I walked across the lawn to my old Toyota and opened a door. Viceroy jumped in and settled himself in the front passenger seat.

"So this is how it's gonna be, is it, little man?" I asked him. He gave me a doggy grin. He hadn't seemed to notice my garlicy undertone, which, if you believed the legends, meant he wasn't a vampire. Even if Sookie Stackhouse of Southern Vampire Mystery fame disagreed.

I pulled out of the driveway and headed toward home, choosing Route 1 instead of the highway so I could open the window for Viceroy's pleasure. Though I shivered, he had a grand time, not at all minding the rushing wind.

I thought through the end of Lauren's story as I drove.

Upon getting home from Felix's party, she had taken Viceroy for an emergency visit to a top Fifth Avenue vet. The vet cleaned the bite and gave Lauren an antibiotic cream and pills in case of infection. He warned her that if the wounds were infected, Viceroy might have a couple of rough days before the antibiotic fully kicked in.

Lauren had said that Viceroy was not himself for most of the following week. He was listless, refusing to get out of his bed, sleeping most of every day, and staring at nothing when he was awake. Saturday morning, Viceroy woke her by licking her face and leaping around on the bed. He'd jumped down like nothing had happened at all and ran to scratch on the apartment door to go out. She took him to Central Park where, in full view of a family of four, Viceroy yanked the leash out of Lauren's hand and got his first squirrel.

I sighed and looked over at him. He still had his face out the window, his chin resting on the top edge of the door, but sensing my attention, he turned to glance at me, wagging his tail briefly in affirmation.

Well, here went nothing. If I believed Lauren, I was about to take a vampire dog on a blood-sucking jaunt through Pemberwick Park. But for forty dollars an hour, I'd pretend he was Dracula himself if she wanted me to. I pulled into the parking lot. The park was quiet on weekdays—the perfect place for a trial. I was looking forward to getting some exercise.

Hopefully Viceroy liked to run.

5

Gracie

Viceroy was beside himself. He had started yipping in an eardrum-piercing register as soon as I found a parking spot, and my eardrums ached already. I wiggled a finger in my ear and stretched my jaw to ease the ringing. "Wait a sec," I said, holding up a hand to him as I got out of the car.

Opening the trunk, I rummaged around in the bag Lauren had given me and pulled out a leash and whistle. It was substantial. Far thicker than was necessary for a fifteen-pound dog but made of soft rolled leather that probably cost more than my car. Next was an equally expensive harness.

"You're one lucky little boy." I opened his door, slipped his harness on, and clipped him to the leash. Viceroy sat patiently, tongue out, waiting for me to finish. "Okay. Let's go."

He jumped down and sat at my feet. Keys in hand, I crouched down next to him to adjust the harness, holding the leash close to the clip in my hand, letting the length of it trail on the ground.

A rustle at the edge of the woods bordering the parking area caught my ear, and something in the bushes moved. Viceroy stiffened for half a heartbeat before exploding on a tear toward the trees. He rammed into my bent legs as he shot past me, flinging me backward. I landed with a jarring thump on my butt, crying out as my tailbone struck the asphalt and my keys flew into the grass. The leash whipped through my hand, scoring my palm, as I tried uselessly to grip it.

Viceroy was gone. Stunned, I curled up, groaning at the pain in my tailbone and clutching my burning hand to my chest. I lay there for a few precious seconds before realizing I had to get up and find Viceroy.

"Viceroy?" I shouted, levering myself upright and touching my backside with my uninjured hand. "Ow!" The dark red burn mark on my palm hurt like holy hell. I shook my hand in the air in an attempt to relieve the stinging. Blinded by tears, I searched the grass for my keys, finally locating them and shoving them into my hoodie pouch.

"Viceroy," I called again. He was nowhere in sight. I'd lost him on our first outing.

I jogged across the grass, my tailbone blazing, and stopped at the place where he had disappeared into the bushes matting the tree line. The trees were sparse, but the bushes and weeds blocked any entrance into them. I heard a rustling. "Viceroy!"

A woman with an enormous white poodle on a leash called to me from the parking area. "Are you hurt? I saw you fall."

"My dog bolted after a squirrel," I called back to her. "But I know where he went. I'm fine." I gave her a thumbs-up before turning to push my way through the best opening.

The scraggly branches tore at me, my palm throbbed, my butt was on fire, and my hair, yanked loose from my ponytail, kept getting caught in the brush, collecting dead leaves as I went. I pushed them out of my face and shoved farther in, finally spotting Viceroy. He was lying in the leaves, his back to me. His head was bent to a gray squirrel draped over his two outstretched front paws. He didn't turn around when I stopped, though I knew he could hear me.

"Viceroy?" I said. He wagged his tail but didn't turn his head to look at me. I took another step toward him, directly into a massive pile of . . . "Shit!"

I looked down at my running shoes. One green and black and one now green, black, and brown. By the time I stopped cursing, he was at my feet, wagging his tail and doggy-smiling. The shriveled squirrel, motionless and forgotten, lay a few feet away. I gagged, both from the sight of the desiccated squirrel and the smell of my shoe. Viceroy sniffed at the giant stinky pile I'd stepped in, sneezed, and backed up.

I tore my gaze from the dead thing to glare at him. "Oh, perfect. This is all your fault, and you don't want any part of it?" He cocked his head. "Okay. Fine. Let's go home." Pushing back through the brush snagged my knit hoodie past redemption—I'd never be able to wear it out of the house again.

With Viceroy right at my heels, I walked slowly back to the car, dragging my foul shoe through the dry grass to scrape off as much poop as possible. But thanks to my ridiculous efforts, I'd only managed to smear the poop up to the laces. My palm was sizzling, and my tailbone was a flamethrower sending fiery bolts up my back and down my legs. Viceroy plopped himself down next to the passenger-side door, stretched out on the asphalt, and fell asleep.

I leaned against the car and stared back into the trees. I'd barely been able to dog-sit Viceroy for twenty minutes. How was I going to survive three to four hours three times a week?

I chewed my lip. Maybe Lauren and her horror story of how Viceroy had become a vampire wasn't crazy. What the hell had I gotten myself into?

THE X-RAY WAS CLEAR: MY TAILBONE WAS INTACT. Bryan stood next to the narrow bed in the emergency room, picking bits of leaf debris out of my hair while a nurse—who, to her credit, hadn't once snickered at my pink sparkly-eyed bunny slippers—bandaged my palm.

"Nice one, Evel. Do you sell tickets?" He was referring to Evel

Knievel, the motorcycle daredevil. We had watched the 1971 movie a couple of weeks ago.

"Honest, Bry, I just can't . . ." I shook my head. I had stopped crying over an hour ago, but a hot flush in my eyes was threatening to spill a few more tears. "I can't figure out what the heck happened. It was like he had superpowers. I've never known a dog to be so fast or so strong. He barely weighs fifteen pounds."

"He just caught you off guard," Bryan said, angling me on the gurney so he could reach my back.

"Oh," I groaned as he began to massage my shoulders. "That feels . . . oh, don't stop." He kneaded while the nurse, grinning, finished up and left.

"You were just surprised."

"Yeah, I guess so." For some reason, I hadn't told him about the squirrel. I shifted on the hard pad that passed for a mattress, trying to find a less painful spot.

"Hold on, I have something that'll take care of that," Bryan said, hands leaving my back. He disappeared through the curtains.

I sat alone in the cubicle, arguing with myself. I had fallen hard for Viceroy, but he'd literally knocked me off my feet, and I'd seen what he'd done to that squirrel. Could I handle him? Should I even try?

I had put him back in the car at the park and changed into a pair of old slippers I kept in the trunk for niece and nephew-babysitting emergencies. It broke my heart, but I'd dropped my ruined runners in the trash. Not even my mom would have been able to get the poop out of the fabric. I managed to drive him back home without crying more than a few tears, but Viceroy sensed my distress.

After pulling up to Lauren's front door, I'd ruffled Viceroy's fur and told him that everything was okay, that I was okay, to reassure him. But he climbed into my lap to stretch up and lick my face, and I hugged his little body to me, bending my head to whisper soothing sounds into his neck until he relaxed enough for us to get out. The poor little guy followed me, ears and tail down, up the path to the imposing front door. He peered up at me, eyes huge, as it swung open. I reached down to take his little face in my hands.

"It's okay, Viceroy. I'm okay." I stopped short of promising to return. He rubbed his body along my leg as I gave Marcy an abbreviated version of what had happened. Viceroy hung back, reluctant to go inside. When he looked up at me once more before disappearing into the house, I saw something I hadn't noticed earlier—blood on his chin.

Bryan pushed back through the curtain with a blue square. Unfolding it, he blew it up. "Voilà! Madam's donut throne." He presented the little pool ring to me with a flourish.

I blushed furiously but leaned to one side, slipped the squeaky blue plastic under my butt, then rolled on top of it. "Hey, this thing works." My embarrassment faded as I wiggled around to find the perfect spot. "Okay, I might be able to get home without crying again. You're amazing," I said.

"Yep, I am. At least, that's what everyone tells me." Bry bent his head toward me.

"And so humble." I kissed him. "How can I resist?"

My phone rang. "Stuck in the Middle with You." Despite the generic ringtone, I knew who it was, and I couldn't deal with her right now.

"Aren't you going to—"

"Nope. It's Lauren. She can wait until tomorrow." I reached for my phone and turned off the ringer. "I have a dinner date with Rachel tonight, and I need a shower and maybe a nap first."

Rachel was an old friend and a librarian at the Port Chester-Rye Brook Public Library, where I got my books. We chatted whenever I went in, but I hadn't been out with her for weeks.

"I remember having enough time to eat dinner every day," Bryan said morosely, eyeing me for sympathy.

"You ate enough for three dinners last night," I reminded him. "I doubt you'll starve any time soon in our family." That came out more hinty than I had intended, but he didn't pick it up.

"Here." He fished in his pocket and pulled out four small packets. "Advil." He tore two open and shook three of the tablets into my palm. "Take these now." He handed me a cup of water from the tiny sink. I tossed them back while he checked his watch. "And take another three about half an hour before you go out. "At about six?"

"Yeah, about."

"You'll be fine, but you'll be sore for at least a week to ten days. Sit on the cushion so you don't bruise it any further."

"Thanks, Doc. Will do." I fired off a snappy salute before easing myself to the floor. Picking up my bag, I slid the blue donut into the crook of my elbow. I should have probably been embarrassed with my rat's nest hair, snagged hoodie, pink bunny slippers, and the blue donut. But after what I'd been through, my appearance was the least of my worries. I gave Bryan major points for not laughing out loud at me. "This year's hot accessory," I said, wiggling the donut.

"Hey, don't knock it. I'm sure the hospital charges a pretty penny for those," he said, pretending to be miffed.

"What about the weekend?" I asked. We had planned a date for Sunday: a leaf-peeping drive and lunch.

"All things considered," he said and nodded toward my lower half, "you should be somewhat better by then, but perhaps additional bed rest at my place is in order?"

"Hmm. Well, you're the doctor," I said. "Bed rest, delivery Thai, and some old movies? I could do that. Pick me up?"

"Of course." He pushed back the cubicle curtain and paused. "Maybe you should think about not going back. I mean, there are other jobs out there." He left the statement hanging in the disinfectant-scented air.

I stared at him, unwilling to hear the undercurrent beneath his innocuous words.

"I'll think about it," I said before giving him a parting peck on the cheek and leaving him to heal people.

THE DRIVE HOME BEGAN UNCOMFORTABLY BUT BECAME less painful as the Advil kicked in. I should have talked to Lauren, but I hadn't wanted to shout over the din in the emergency room, and I wasn't ready anyway. I'd failed, and I felt like crap about it. I knew she'd be worried, but I couldn't juggle my phone and wobble on the squishy donut while apologizing for my inadequacies.

I pulled up to my building to see my mother standing on the sidewalk. She had walked the four blocks between her house and my apartment to wait for me. Bryan must have called her. I needed to have a serious talk with him about tattling. My family loved him, and he had become one of us, so his calling my mother was not entirely out of left field. Still, my mother was the last person I wanted to see.

"You need to call that lady and quit that job," she said, opening the passenger door and sliding in before I could stop her. "The dog is dangerous."

"What—"

"Don't park. You're coming home with me so I can take care of you."

"I'm fine, Mom. It was just a bump. All I need is to go upstairs and rest a little."

"Absolutely not. You're coming home." She slammed the car door. "Let's go."

There was no sense arguing. My mother might be fit, stylish, and educated, but she was still old-school Italian.

I pulled back into traffic, drove the short distance to the house where I grew up, and turned off the engine. She hurried to my side to help me as I fumbled my way out of the car. Reaching behind me, my mother snatched the blue donut from the seat. I stepped carefully, trying not to jostle my tailbone.

"Look at you!" she fumed as I righted myself. "And your hand? That dog could have crippled you."

"Mom . . ."

"Don't 'Mom' me. Into the house," she ordered.

I stumbled onto the sidewalk and turned to reach for my bag from the backseat, but she beat me to it, wrinkling her nose. "Grace, this bag is falling apart." She shook her head. "I'm surprised you haven't lost your wallet. I'll buy you a new bag this week." She grabbed the donut, shut the car door, and held a hand at my back as I walked carefully up the front steps. "Where are your shoes? Did you go into the hospital like that?" She had stopped on the sidewalk and was staring at my slippered feet.

"I'll tell you inside."

With her interruptions, it took me half an hour to spool out enough of the story to convince her to leave me alone to nap on the couch. A blanket, a heating pad, a pillow for my head, another for under my knees, the donut under my butt, my phone to call Rachel—these things appeared one by one, each accompanied by more questions, which I answered with only minimal evasion.

She had been less than thrilled when I told her my plans to go out, suggesting I invite Rachel to the house for dinner instead.

"I'll make chicken cutlets," was all she had to say. My mother's cooking was legendary in our neighborhood. I was convinced that our neighbors feigned illnesses just to have her bring over a covered dish of whatever they smelled wafting out of the kitchen window.

Rachel was thrilled, of course, loving my mom's food even more than my baking. Finally, I was left alone, swaddled in a cocoon of pillows and blankets.

I drifted into a dreamless sleep almost immediately, waking to the chime of the front doorbell. I struggled to free myself, only managing to twist the blankets tighter. My mother got to the front door while I was still wrestling with them. I craned my neck to look out the front window to see our local florist's van parked in the street.

"No one answered at her apartment, Mrs. Rinelli, so I figured I could leave them with you?" My mother appeared after closing the door, hidden behind a gorgeous flower arrangement. She set it down in front of me, where it dwarfed the small coffee table.

"Wow," I said.

She plucked a card in an envelope from a green plastic fork. Raising an eyebrow, she held it out. I took it from her.

I AM SO SORRY, GRACIE. I HOPE YOU'RE OKAY. PLEASE CALL ME WHEN YOU CAN. —LAUREN

I looked up to see my mother glaring at me from the other side of the extravaganza. "They're from *her*."

"Yes, Mom, they're from Lauren. And I'm not quitting." The words were out of my mouth before I realized I had made a decision. I was about to backtrack but stopped myself. Rachel's imminent arrival would divert her attention, at least for a couple of hours. Besides, going back to Lauren's wasn't completely crazy.

Even though I had seen blood on Viceroy's chin, I hadn't actually seen him suck it out of the squirrel.

"One day. You work one day with this little dog, Gracie, and you end up in the hospital. What happens after a week? Will I be at the funeral parlor picking out your—"

I cut her off before the yelling started. "Viceroy is a fifteen-pound sweetheart, Mom. You'd love him if you met him. The whole thing was my fault. I can't go around quitting great jobs because I'm clumsy."

My mother heaved a gusty sigh. I came by the drama honestly —it was genetic.

"Well, Gracie. You're twenty-three. I can't tell you what to do, only what I would do in your situation. A dog-sitting job is not what anyone would call a great job. There are plenty of part-time jobs you could do without putting yourself in the hospital. Or better yet, you could move back home and go back to school. I honestly don't understand what is so important about living four blocks away."

I couldn't tell her that her relentless pressure had finally driven me to distance myself. I hated fighting with her, and those four blocks had provided some relief.

"And I still don't believe anyone would pay forty dollars an hour for a dog walker," she continued.

"A dog companion, Mom. And she has more money than she can spend."

My mother blew a breath between pursed lips. "She didn't get rich by throwing her money around. None of this makes sense."

I opened my mouth to argue but closed it. My mother should have been a trial attorney. I wouldn't win no matter what I said.

"I would quit, Gracie. I have a bad feeling about this." She raised her eyebrows at me. It was at least her fifth eyebrow lift since we'd walked into the house. She wasn't going to let it go.

I had worked hard at any job I could get, using every spare moment while in high school and college and since graduating, saving every cent possible. Between my own earnings and graduation gifts from family meant to go toward grad school, I had nearly twenty-eight thousand dollars saved. I only needed another five to seven to buy a used truck and get it cleaned up, equipped, painted, and running.

My mom and my four brothers all thought I was certifiable. They wanted me respectable. And respectability, by their definition, meant a JD, a PhD, or an MD and a thriving practice. We would never agree on my future. But despite any misgivings about this job, hers or mine, I couldn't turn down forty dollars an hour when my goal was so close.

Crap. She'd been talking the whole time and I hadn't heard a word of it. When I didn't respond, she sat down, not ready to cede the battle quite yet.

"Gracie, I've talked to your brothers. I know I just said that I can't tell you what to do, but what kind of mother would I be if I didn't try to help you. You need to get your life on track. Injuring yourself by taking unnecessary risks is not acceptable. You can still have your cake truck as a hobby if it means that much to you. Hobbies are healthy."

She stood. "Your future is not a joke, Gracie. You were meant for bigger things than running a cake truck." She bit her lip. "I'm sorry. I've said too much. I'm just worried about you." She turned and strode into the kitchen before I could yell at her.

I snatched the newspaper off the coffee table, tearing it in my frustration, and sank back into the pillows. Every mother thinks their kids are exceptional, but forcing me into grad school because I was "meant for bigger things" was just too much. I scanned for the "cars and trucks for sale" section, and there, three ads down the page, was my truck.

6

Felix

My mother had been a whore, and not the fancy kind. Not like the women I'd just left who preened, sparkled, and starved themselves for the wealthy men who didn't notice or care about them. The women at Michael's party were paid in Birkin bags and summer houses in the Hamptons. My mother had been paid in soiled dollar bills, free drinks, and me: the baby who killed her.

I stared up at the historic Dakota. For two hours, I had watched successful, well-dressed men drown themselves in the hippest new bourbon drinks and wolf down tasteless hors d'oeuvres while the women anxiously faked interest and engagement. A total waste of time. There had been nothing worth nicking. Worst of all, I had skipped a VA meeting.

Now, I stood, shivering, on the corner of Central Park West and 72nd Street. The temperature had dropped, and the weatherman had promised snow flurries. Full-blood vampires were impervious to weather, though for some reason, they still hated the cold. Half-bloods like me, on the other hand, felt every damp chill.

A cat yowled from the alley behind me, interrupting my mental droning. Damned cats. I ground out my black cigarette butt with the heel of my new Ferragamo boot and began walking, turning my collar up against the chill. I didn't smoke often, but tonight I needed a cigarette. The aroma of cloves usually summoned my precious few pleasant memories of home—New Orleans in the twenties—but this time the aroma did little to dispel thoughts of the mother I'd never met.

Michael preferred blondes, and his party had been full of them. My mother's customers had described her to me as fair, her hair naturally flaxen. That must have been why she lingered in my thoughts now.

But I'd never managed to learn anything else about her, not even so much as her last name. Much less why, if she had been as beautiful as they said, she'd needed to resort to prostitution. Her regulars cried into their beer about how much they all missed her while I stood on my stool, wiping down the bar and trying to ignore them. More likely, those drunks missed the freewheeling days of Storyville, New Orleans's official red-light district.

I sighed. I had no right to complain. My lot in life could have been so much worse. The bar owner had folded me into his family. And though my adoptive brothers and sisters never acknowledged me as such, I had a bed, food, a roof over my head, and some schooling in exchange for keeping the bar as clean as I could manage. I didn't mind the work, but I hated every minute I had to listen to the alcohol-fueled stories about my mother.

I scowled back up at Michael's windows. After the dog incident, he had asked his fiancée, Laura or Lauren, whatever her name was, for his ring back, claiming she was overly sensitive and that he'd begun to find it exhausting. That was Michael to the core. Tonight's party was a parade of new hopefuls. I'd left before he could ask my opinion, which was probably for the best. Friend or no, I needed to stop going to his parties before I told him what I thought about the women he chased.

I shook myself. This train of thought only stopped at one place—misery. A little pick-me-up, a snack to quicken my step and lighten my mood, would banish my gloom. So I started walking.

I hated winter. All half-vamps did. Something about the virus we carried, a virus that would die once we became full-bloods, sensitized us to the cold. But I had spent the last fifty-odd years searching for a sponsoring vampire willing to turn me to no avail, so I suffered. Though not enough to leave New York for New Orleans. The city I was born in might be home, but too many vampires, both full-blood and half-blood like me, meant we'd started queuing up for snacks. It was humiliating.

New York was a comparative behemoth, the winter temperatures making the city far less attractive to a cold-hating half-blood population, so fewer vamps overall meant uncomplicated hunting. I shivered again. Although I had recently relieved a snack of a rather spectacular sheepskin overcoat, it barely kept the chill from seeping into my bones. I should bite the damned bullet and wear warmer clothes. And heavy wool socks. *Ugh.* I imagined hives rising on my feet. The thought of rough wool touching me made my skin crawl.

"And what the hell is it with all this Paul Bunyan shit?" I muttered aloud as I stalked across Central Park West and into the park proper.

I hated checks, plaids, and tartans like most people hated rats and roaches. And every store, including my beloved Barneys, which, heartrendingly, was about to close, seemed to be filled with the hideous fabrics. Sartorial elegance was truly dead and buried under a mountain of buffalo check shirts. Bah. It was all ugly.

I walked faster, as if speed would keep me warmer. The Strawberry Fields memorial, created in memory of John Lennon and named after the Beatles song "Strawberry Fields Forever," was a few minutes of shivering ahead. I couldn't understand everyone's fascination with the Beatles, but tourists were attracted to that spot, and there might still be a few people there. The nights of effortlessly finding willing men to snack on and rob in the vicinity of the Ramble were long gone.

Even given the cold, the disappointing party, and the unpleasant memories, I was crankier than usual. Coming into the park had been a mistake. I wasn't starving, and the weather was too miserable for effective trolling.

A man stepped out of the shadows. "Got a light?" I'd seen his cheap motorcycle jacket and dismissed him as a snack before he'd so much as moved a muscle. I had standards.

"Fuck off." I spun on a heel and stalked back to the street. Snowflakes had begun to fall fast, sparkling in the lamplight. Staring at my water-droplet-dappled boots, I raised my arm for a cab, hailing one uncharacteristically fast.

"Where would you like to go, sir?" the turbaned driver asked too politely. This guy was new to the job.

"Whole Foods. Bowery." One of my favorite hunting grounds. And, as it so happened, my grocery store of choice. I was out of saline nasal spray.

"Yes, sir. Right away, sir." The driver grinned at me in the rearview mirror. "Do you live here, sir, or are you visiting?"

Jesus! Was there no rest for the weary? "I live here, and I have a headache, so please, stop talking." I didn't wait to see his face in the mirror, leaning back against the cracked vinyl seat and closing my eyes. My chest felt tight; I was probably coming down with something. I stretched both arms up to encourage my lungs to open and yawned, then rolled my head, first one way, then another, to loosen my neck.

The cab was warm. Feeling marginally better, I stared at the traffic. The swirling snow thickened, obscuring my view enough to make me close my eyes again. I opened them as we pulled over. My spirits rose at the sight of the Whole Foods doors. Convinced that I would find the snack I craved, I gave the driver a generous tip. His open-lipped smile at my generosity displayed two gold teeth. I didn't know they did the gold teeth thing in India or wherever he was from—you learned something new every day.

I SLAMMED THE DOOR AND MADE MY WAY THROUGH THE accumulation of slush and into Whole Foods. The sloshy gray mess on the sidewalks had all but the appropriately booted tucked safely in their overheated apartments. The pickings would be slim.

I brushed past a young woman in a worn dark hoodie loitering at the entrance. A bit disheartened, I made my way toward the store's grocery section, searching for a well-dressed man of my approximate height and build, ideally wearing an expensive overcoat I could convince him out of after I'd had my fill. Of course, with my luck tonight, the store was practically devoid of appropriate men. But plenty of hungry, lonely women roamed the aisles.

Oh well, desperate times called for desperate measures. One woman lingering over the cheese counter smiled at me as I stopped next to her, pretending to peruse the cheese. I detested cheese.

"Miserable weather," she attempted. "I'll never find a cab." She smiled at me.

I knew the smile. It said: talk to me, like me, go to dinner with me, fall in love with me, drink my—no, wait. Not that last part.

I smiled back at her and began to walk away. I didn't like to snack on the needy, but there were no men in the store, and I needed a lift, just a sip. I paused. I could lower my standards or go home with a steak. But I wasn't in the mood to grill, so lowered standards it was. I took the few steps back to the now disconsolate woman at the cheese counter.

"Did I hear you say you would be interested in sharing a ride?" I beamed at her.

"Oh, well . . ." She was suddenly hesitant, stepping back to look me up and down. Her gaze paused on my water-stained Ferragamos. *Damn it to Hell!* I'd worn the wrong shoes. No wonder no one at the party wanted to talk to me. And now, after wading through icy puddles, they were a mess.

I gave her a rueful smile. "No point ruining the handmades in this weather."

She brightened. "Oh no, you are so right." She nodded down at her boots. "I keep these at the office for snow days."

Yech. I hadn't noticed her feet. Her hideous green plastic boots nearly made me opt for the steak. Still, she was attractive. Probably thirty. Clear skin, a straight nose, blue eyes, shoulder-length dark-brown hair. She looked professorial. Just my type. No swag, but what the hell. At least I wouldn't have to cook.

After determining we both lived below Houston, we separated to shop, agreeing to meet at checkout. I hadn't come in to shop at all, but I figured I might as well pick up a few things while I was there. I selected two steaks for the next day at the butcher counter and made my way to the health and beauty section for nasal spray. My loft was so damned dry in the fall and winter, my nose bled. I picked up two squeeze bottles and a package of zinc throat lozenges.

The woman, Kate, was in the same section picking out soap. She had insisted upon learning my name was Steve. It was the name I'd started using with snacks after watching the movie *The Tao of Steve*. She added she didn't usually share rides with strangers but allowed that lousy weather made for strange bedfellows, after which she promptly blushed. She was charming. We smiled at each other across the aisle.

I picked up more items, accepting a basket from a clerk along the way. The last thing on my list was protein powder. My favorite was Garden of Life's RAW Vanilla Spiced Chai. It had twenty-six different organic sprouts, seeds, and greens and mixed well with whatever else I felt motivated to add. Plus, I had a coupon.

Finished, I checked out to find Kate was waiting for me on the other side. She eyed my paper bags. "Want to borrow plastic?" She held out two spare reusables. This woman wanted me.

"No, thank you. I'm double-bagged."

"If you say so," she said, doubt in her voice.

"Ready?" I asked.

"Yes. Let's go."

We pushed through the doors. The cheaply dressed young

woman was gone. Out on the sidewalk, the snow was falling thickly now, and traffic had slowed to a crawl.

Kate furrowed her brow. "We'll never make it home." On her frustrated exhale, a cab pulled up to let two passengers out. I held the door open and leaned in.

"Two stops?"

"Okay. But it'll take a while."

"We're not in a hurry," I assured him. I got in, pushed my bags ahead of me, and slid across so Kate wouldn't have to.

"A gentleman," she said. "Not many men do that." She slid close to me, making room for her single bag, which she placed on her opposite side, wedging us together. After giving our addresses to the driver, we settled in. I learned Kate had grown up in Bedford and had two sisters. She'd gone to Columbia, worked at Deutsche Bank, and lived on Sullivan, half a dozen or so blocks from me. She learned I had grown up in New Orleans.

"Really? I've always wanted to go!" she gushed. "Give me the Lonely Planet overview?"

We were thirty minutes from her apartment, so I needed to move things along. Timing was critical in cabs. I inclined my head toward her.

"Oh, New Orleans. How do I begin? She's a hot, sultry, enticing place." I lowered my voice and slowed my speaking pace. "Everything is low and slow, and the night there is hypnotic. The jazz, the cocktails, and the incredible food, they feed your body and ensnare your heart." I paused for effect. "She flatters you, she loves you, and ultimately she slides so deep into your psyche you'll never be free of her. No matter where you go, how hard you try, or how many stellar experiences you may have, you will belong to her. You will dream of her. You will hate her for making you crave her."

Kate was rapt, hanging on every word. It was all crap. New Orleans was a nightmare. But my marketing spiel reeled women in every time—like a catfish on a safety-pin hook.

We didn't have to bite necks; that was all Hollywood and

vampire books. Any vein would do. Though the larger ones meant a faster feed, they were dangerous. Vampires were electrified by the river of blood pulsing just beneath the surface of the skin. A new full-blood or an inexperienced half-blood could quickly drain a victim dry in the orgasmic throes of bloodlust.

But even for the experienced, unless death was the intended ending, taking blood from the neck presented difficulties. The jugular was painful to access, frightening even the most willing donor. Smaller veins were less complicated, and a bite into one of them could go unnoticed under the right circumstances. I liked a spot above the wrist, particularly if long sleeves would temporarily cover the evidence.

I glanced at Kate's hand. She was wearing gloves. I gently touched the left one as I continued describing my birthplace. Women often complimented my deep, melodic voice, as well they should. In another life, I might easily have been an NPR program host. She was enraptured and did not respond as I lifted her hand to slip off her leather glove.

"The flickering gaslights in the French Quarter make you believe nothing has changed in centuries . . ." I paused to judge my effect and our location. Two blocks away from her place. Perfect.

She was leaning back, eyes closed. I turned her hand over, bent my head, gently kissed her palm. She sighed deeply. I kissed the place where her thumb joined her wrist. I pushed the sleeve of her coat and sweater up slowly, following the motion with a trail of kisses until I reached my sweet spot. I looked up at her.

"More," she whispered.

I brought my teeth together lightly, not breaking the skin. She pushed her wrist into my mouth, and my fangs reflexively descended just enough to pierce her skin. I bit. She gasped but did not pull her arm away. Her blood flowed in a small, steady stream, pulsing with her heartbeat. A couple of ounces would be enough. The minutes lengthened, as they always did while our hearts synchronized. The blood was a high better than a double Pappy Van Winkle bourbon—an awful name for a superior sip. I had about a minute before I'd have to seal the wound and release her. Finished, I pushed the tip of my tongue fast and firm against the punctures. The movement released additional saliva, which would numb the pain, make her drowsy and forgetful, then coagulate the blood and seal the wounds. The cab pulled over.

"Kate." I shook her.

"Mmm . . . are we home?" She had fallen asleep, as often happened in cabs, in those last seconds.

"You're home safe and sound!" I sounded a bit like a lunatic, enough that the driver frowned at me in the rearview mirror. I could afford to be cheerful. Her blood had given me the clean buzz of an organic eater—the key reason I shopped at Whole Foods. Not to mention, that particular Whole Foods had beautifully aged steaks.

I got out and carried her bag up to her front door. Though her drowsy eyes asked the question, she was too overcome to suggest coffee or a drink. We said our goodbyes. She would drag herself into her apartment and collapse into a deep sleep. By tomorrow morning, she would have forgotten the ride, puzzling over why she hadn't unpacked her groceries and was still wearing her coat. She'd chalk it up to exhaustion from overwork. If she found them, the faint marks on her wrist would be an easily forgotten mystery.

The snow had stopped, and the cab pulled back into the street, heading toward my loft. I started humming "Cool," from *West Side Story*. The evening hadn't been so bad, after all.

7

Felix

Saturday, November 7

The remnants of last night's energy lift still invigorated me. In the shower, I belted out songs from Sweeney Todd, ending with "Pretty Women." Stepping out, I wiped the fog from the mirror and stuck out my tongue: a rosy shade of pink. I combed wet hair back from my forehead and peered at myself. I was born in 1910, but thanks to a steady diet of sips, I looked thirtyish. No crow's feet or laugh lines. Excellent, at least from my perspective. I'd catch hell for my unlined skin at tonight's VA meeting, though.

Moira, my sponsor, would be all over me for my bright, pore-less complexion—again. I hated those godforsaken meetings. I hated Vampires Anonymous; an organization formed by full-bloods to maintain control over half-bloods. And, more than life, I hated Moira. There was no being in all of creation as nasty as an abstemious, female half-vamp who was wrinkling like a time-lapse film of grapes shriveling into raisins.

All half-vamps were required to attend the meetings, and full-blood vamps ensured we did. Most of the half-vamps I knew—except for Moira, who took it all very seriously—only went to meetings to avoid the alternative: a very human death at the hands of a furious vampire. Attending meetings helped us "refrain from overindulging" and calling attention to ourselves, thus endangering the entire vampire community. Or so the party line went.

We were supposed to age, which meant abstention, and I had sipped a bit too much lately, so no sobriety coin for me this month. Three coinless months in a row meant attendees didn't have an opportunity to attend any month after that. I'd had a friend disappear that way.

But Moira was hours away. First, I was in for a delightful afternoon of shopping. I had slept soundly, another benefit of having a warm-blooded snack right before bed, and I looked marvelous. I wrested myself from my reflection. My hair was drying in tufts, so I pulled out my hair products and blow dryer and went to work on my head.

An hour later, after a lovely cup of tea and a bowl of muesli—one needed fiber to keep all systems working smoothly—I made my way uptown. The sun was out, the flash snow had melted, and the streets were as shiny as fresh licorice. Late fall meant an early Christmas in the stores, and the windows were all appropriately decked out. It was the best time for shopping. Holiday merchandise was out, but people were not yet thinking about buying presents for others and were still busy gifting themselves for the upcoming flood of seasonal parties. I consistently scored this time of year, and a Saturday late afternoon was a prime time in the men's department at Barneys.

Exiting the cab, I recognized the same girl in the hoodie I'd seen outside of Whole Foods last night. I dismissed the creeping suspicion that she was following me. Thousands of people in dark hoodies must wander this city. And what on earth was the attraction of that hideous piece of clothing anyway? Hoodies and plaid. This country was going to the dogs. I pushed through the glass doors and made my way to the menswear, still slightly spooked.

I scanned for and instantly pinpointed an impeccably dressed man in my size. Shadowed by a fawning salesman, the man was obviously a regular who spent actual money in the store. Keeping him within my peripheral vision, I perused the sports jackets. Ordinarily, I'd have to cruise around for half an hour or more, waiting for a mark. When I found one, luck would have him going straight for the dressing room, where I would follow with a random pair of pants to judge his size, and things would move right along. But if he dithered, I might end up having to buy a tie, handkerchief, or a pair of socks so I wouldn't appear to be loitering. It took all the joy out of the experience. The whole point of my version of clothes shopping, after all, was not to spend any money.

But this time, it looked as if I wouldn't have to buy a thing. I watched the man, who was coatless and appeared to be precisely my size, pick a gorgeous black suit, then a gray one, and a dark-blue pinstripe, from the rack and hand them to the salesman. I busied myself perusing inconsequential things while the man declined the store's tailoring services and paid for the soon-to-be-mine suits, congratulating myself on my unbelievable good fortune. I trembled with the thrill of the chase, trailing him to the exit. We turned west on 61st Street toward Central Park. He turned into The Pierre, and I followed a few yards behind. Hopefully, he was going to the bar, where I could easily talk him into following me to a quiet place where I could snack on him and retrieve my suits. I nearly clapped my hands in delight, already planning to celebrate with a Sazerac and a selection of oysters.

But once inside, I couldn't locate him. On any other day, I might have given up the chase by now, but I was in high spirits, and those suits were gorgeous. I was loath to let them go without putting a bit of effort into it. I stepped through the men's room doorway, figuring there was no harm in checking.

"What took you so long?" my mark asked, leaning against a sink, facing me.

Oh shit. All sensation drained down to my feet.

He smirked. "You can't have my suits. I happen to like them."

I shook myself out of my cataleptic state, closed the door, and leaned my back against it to keep anyone else out. "What . . . what are you talking about?" I stuttered.

"Felix. You're a kleptomaniac, and not a particularly talented one," he said, crossing his arms and making himself comfortable. "You seldom purchase anything yourself." He regarded me from under lowered lids. I flushed, fingering the Whole Foods receipt from last night in my pocket.

"That's not—"

"But while your thieving poses a problem, my friend, your snatch-and-grab habit is not why I lured you here."

The door I stood against bumped my posterior. "Closed for cleaning," I shouted over my shoulder. "Who are you," I hissed, "and what are you talking about? I am not your friend, as we have never met." My voice rose. "And I most certainly do buy things, although I don't see how that is any of your business." Despite the chilly room, a rivulet of perspiration trickled from my armpit to my waist. Who the hell was this guy?

"You are my business because you are drawing attention to yourself, and by extension, to all the vampires in New York. And I need you to remain under the radar to be successful at the job I am about to assign you."

Oh fuck. This asshole was a vampire. How had I missed the clues? His skin was pink. I looked closer—good makeup, and a lot of it. Crap. I opened my mouth to protest.

"Be quiet and listen," he ordered. "You will stop stealing immediately, or we will stop you."

"Fine." I held my hands up. "You win. I'll stop whatever it is you think I'm doing." I had nothing to gain by arguing with a full-blood vampire more knowledgeable about me than I was about him. Besides, though we were in The Pierre, we were still in a bathroom, alone. That, and as fancy as it was, it smelled. I wanted out. He raised an eyebrow.

"Can I buy you a drink? There's no reason we can't talk over libations," I offered, at a loss as to what else to say.

He showed all his teeth in a smile that could freeze the Hudson River. "Why not?"

I shuddered as I edged backward through the door and turned toward the lounge. We sat, and while the vampire motioned for a waiter, I studied him.

He appeared to be about forty, but he was undoubtedly considerably older. Like me, he was slim and tall, but the resemblance ended there. I was dark while he was fair. I looked more the part of a sophisticated, movie-style vampire than he did but for the eyes. My eyes were almost gold, shot with dark hazel. His eyes were a hypnotic pale blue with a darker blue rim—impossible to look away from.

Shit . . . he was attempting to enthrall me; I tore my eyes away from his and focused on the waiter just arriving with our drinks.

My temples throbbed, and I shuddered. Having never been enthralled, I had no idea what it was supposed to feel like. But I knew it made the victim compliant. I felt anything but.

"Well, well," the vampire said, "it appears there may be a bit more to you than meets the eye. But never mind that. You have agreed to stop stealing. Yes? You are of no use to me as a petty thief drawing attention to himself in public." He stirred his drink while I gaped at him. "Come on now, Felix. Close your mouth, be a good minion, and say yes."

My face burned as I clamped my mouth shut and recklessly barreled toward fed up, which was maybe better, but possibly worse, than being frightened. "I will not agree to a single thing until you tell me who the hell you are, why the hell you are following me, and why the hell you think I should work for you when I don't need to work, period. And I am not your minion."

He may have been faster than me and powerful enough to know all about me, but we were in a public place, and I had nothing to lose as long as I was sitting among all these people.

He regarded me for an overlong moment while I broke into a full sweat. Finally, he sighed. "Since we'll be spending quality time together soon, we may as well become better acquainted. My name is Robert Jameson."

"Bob? Your name is Bob? Vampire Bob?" I had leaned in and taken the first mouthful of my Sazerac. I almost sprayed him.

"Lower your voice." I didn't know it was possible to bellow in a whisper, but he did. Shocked into silence, I mopped a dribble of the bourbon cocktail from my chin. "And I am the new King of New York."

"You're insane. What the fuck is this, *Gangs of New York*? Since when the fuck is there a vampire king? We don't have kings." *Much less a king named Bob.* But I wasn't stupid enough to say that part. Picking up my drink, I took a sizable mouthful to block my view of him. When I put down my glass, his face had hardened to granite, constricting my nether region. Unable to swallow the burning liquor, I shifted in my seat, trying to release the pressure down there.

"We do now," he said, examining manicured fingernails before nailing me to my seat with a glare. "You know, Felix, for a handsome man with a degree of sartorial polish, a reasonable life span, and a slightly more than modest bank account, you truly are an embarrassment."

I flushed again and swallowed.

"And to you, I am Mr. Jameson, but my lord, or my liege, is also acceptable."

I choked on my current swallow, sitting on my hand to keep it from clutching my throat, coughing like I was going to eject a lung. I needed another drink, many more drinks. I waved to the waiter.

"I'll have a plate of oysters—mixed is fine—and another Sazerac," I wheezed through my burning esophagus, tipping my head toward Vampire Bob.

"Another Jameson Vintage Reserve, please."

"Yes, sir!" The waiter blushed with pleasure. I hadn't paid enough attention to the vampire's surname or to what he had ordered the first time. Now I did a double take. The Vintage

Reserve was a $250 bottle. I knew because I had nicked one once. I didn't want to imagine the price by the glass.

"You're *that* Jameson?" I yelped loud enough to turn heads at the next table.

"Shut up, you idiot," he whispered. "Holy Mother, you are a child. Control yourself and listen carefully."

THE CONVERSATION WENT DOWNHILL FROM THERE. According to Bob, the city of New Orleans had increased their police force in an attempt to protect drunken tourists—making it toilsome for a vampire to find a decent meal. The vamps were leaving in droves, having learned the northern cities offered richer pickings. Vampires from all over the South were emigrating, en masse, to Chicago, Boston, and New York.

And guess who was to be the new vampire concierge, assisting them with the move from the Big Easy to the Big Apple? That would be me, Felix Belloquot.

But none of it made sense. A creature as old and powerful as Vampire Bob didn't have to lure me. He could have grabbed me off the street anytime he wanted. He was playing with me. But why bother? True, I had excellent taste and knew all the best restaurants and shops, but I was a half-blood, a nobody. My head spun as I clutched my new suits to my chest in the hopes of blocking at least some of the wind. Bob had handed them over as a symbolic parting gift from my old ways. A nice touch, but the cheap bastard had stuck me with the check for three platters of oysters and eight drinks, four of which would have paid for a ruby facial at Alana Sovigne. I had never figured out how to steal services.

"Damn it," I swore aloud. I had been too unnerved to think clearly, and couldn't remember if I had agreed to anything else. My stomach churned, the now-nauseating combination of oysters and whiskey churning me into a cold sweat as I tried to make sense of what had just occurred while searching in vain for a taxi.

Here was what I knew:

- Vampire Bob of Clan Jameson had installed himself as king of New York, head of the local chapter of the vampire cartel, in a blood battle that, somehow, while caught up in my own life, I had missed.
- The previous ranking full-bloods had met untimely ends via meat grinder.
- The cartel was in complete control of the city, including some of the underground parking garages, and was wealthy beyond measure.
- Disobeying would end badly for me.
- Vampire Bob was an asshole. Oh, and I would most likely have to ditch my parking garage because I wasn't going to put another dollar into Bob's pocket, which fucking sucked.

I stood on the corner of 61st and Lexington in the fleeing light, clammy and freezing, desperate for a taxi. My head spun, and I was in imminent danger of losing the contents of my stomach.

Bob's words played like an old TV show rerun blasting in my ear: I was a "liability." Snacking was dangerous, and it was only a matter of time before I was "outed, drawn, quartered, and set afire in Central Park by a screaming human horde. With pitchforks." He had actually said that. My teeth chattered.

So, I was supposed to quit being freewheeling Felix, go work for Vampire King Bob, and be a loyal member of his army of darkness. I would share in the wealth if I did this, which was nice but not particularly enticing. You don't live for as many years as I had without learning a few tricks. I had plenty of money—I just didn't enjoy spending it.

The riveting part was that I would win a sponsor if I

complied. A full-blood vampire who would take me under their wing. A vampire who would school me, turn me, and become my master, finally granting me full-blood status.

But—and this was a potential deal-killer—according to Bob, I'd have to tie up loose ends by draining everyone I'd snacked from in the last three months. Three months because that was how long it took for any shred of memory of a feeding event to disappear from human consciousness.

Oh, and I needed to find the fucking dog, the one I had bitten. Because apparently, the dog was now a vampire. And I had somehow turned him. It was the first time a half-vamp had instigated, much less completed a transformation. Both firsts in vampire history. That it had been me, Felix, who would go down in the history books as a first anything was just mind-boggling. Which, now that I thought about it, was why Bob was interested in me. So, I was to bring the little dog to him, and in doing so, also deliver myself.

Failing that, I would visit the meatpacking plant in Queens. As meat.

8

Felix

By the time I found a cab, my headache had me dizzy. I sank into the armpit-scented seat and fished around in my pocket for an antique silver pill box I had picked up at an estate sale years ago. I swallowed my last three Advils dry. Traffic was unexpectedly light for this time of day, and the cab pulled up in front of my building in record time. I crossed the lobby, rode the elevator, and dumped my suits and overcoat across an armchair before collapsing on the sofa.

The second I was horizontal, searing bolts of pain shot around inside my skull, forcing me upright. "Fuck!" I yelled. My head sizzled in response. "Well, Bob is right about one thing: I do have a foul mouth," I muttered and massaged the back of my neck.

I got off the sofa and headed for the kitchen and my migraine medication. There was one tablet left. My physician had recommended against taking ibuprofen with any migraine medication, much less on a stomach full of alcohol. I took the pill anyway, upset stomachs and strokes be damned. I stood still for two minutes, willing the drug to take effect. Nothing happened.

Tea. Tea would help, and I had a new one. Traditional Cures' Cup of Serenity. The ingredient list included passionflower, chamomile, lavender, and catnip; the soothing name was a bonus. Serenity was precisely what I needed. That and a suit of vampire-proof armor.

I had taken a lot of ribbing for my tea-drinking over the years, but I'd never developed a taste for coffee. Likely because chicory coffee tastes like a cross between tar and swamp water.

Growing up in New Orleans, if you weren't drinking alcohol, you drank the dreck that passed for coffee. Or you drank the water, unsafe until boiled. Since I already had to go to the trouble of boiling it, one day I made tea. The habit stuck.

The steeping brew smelled heavenly, the aroma dissolving some of my tension. I added a dollop of Manuka honey and carried my cup to the bank of windows overlooking Broadway. The street bustled with people out for the evening. My headache was lifting enough to make me think of food. I was hungry, as all I'd had since my breakfast bowl of muesli were oysters and whiskey. But I had no desire whatsoever to grill the steaks I had purchased at Whole Foods.

"Fuck," I muttered, cursing the closing of Dean & Deluca. I could have used some plain crackers to settle my growing upset stomach. A significant other who would lovingly trot down the street to get me crackers and a prescription refill would come in handy right about now, but I was all out of those too.

I watched the movement on the street below and sipped my tea. Broadway channeled a churning mass of humanity, people walking purposefully through the damp chill—except for one man leaning against a lamppost in front of the shoe store across the street. The lights from the storefronts threw his face into shadow. He watched the cars, trucks, and buses stream past. I took another sip when the man stepped forward into the light and looked directly up at my window. Vampire Bob.

The intercom chimed as I sprang back, sloshing tea all over myself and the floor.

"Go away!" I shrieked at the unit, forgetting Bob couldn't possibly have crossed the street and talked to the doorman so quickly. It chimed again. I could go out onto the back balcony and climb down the fire escape—it worked in the movies. Avoiding the tea puddle, I stalked over to the intercom and pushed the button to talk.

"Tell whoever it is to go home!" I yelled at the speaker and disconnected. It rang again and I poked the button hard enough to crack a nail.

"Mr. Belloquot, I have Michael here. He says he needs to see you."

"Oh. I'm sorry for yelling. Send him up," I said to the doorman.

"Shit, Michael," I groaned when I opened the door. "I thought you were someone else. Come in." I stepped aside, still agitated, to allow Michael to edge past me. *Why the hell is that freak watching my loft?*

"You look like crap," Michael said.

"Hello to you too. I feel like crap. I've had a frightful day."

"Pour me a drink. My day sucked too, but you first." Michael tossed his coat on top of mine.

I got a dish towel and blotted my shirtfront before mopping up the spilled tea as he collapsed onto the couch. Michael was one of my closest friends. We'd met in my early days in New York. He had a thing for alternative lifestyles back then, and we'd run into each other at a party full of half-bloods. He'd been sloppy drunk, and three women in various states of dishabille were snacking on him at once. Though I wasn't as prudish then as I am today, the sight was just too Dracula. I'd dragged him from underneath the three women and gotten him into a taxi. We'd been friends ever since.

I walked to the bar cabinet and blanched. The bottle of Jameson was front and center. I reached for the Lagavulin 16, poured two glasses, and carried them to the couch. Handing Michael his drink, I peered at him. His complexion, usually a healthy tan, was white. Tiny droplets of sweat beaded his forehead.

"You look embalmed. What the fuck happened?" I asked.

He wiped his face on a shirtsleeve. "I need to tell you something." He bobbed his foot. "But you first."

"Me? A terrifying vampire who says he's the king of the vampire cartel of New York is stalking me."

He tossed back the contents of his glass and studied its bare bottom before answering. "Oh?" His shoulders rose in a shrug before he forced them down. I wanted to slap him.

"That's all you've got? 'Oh?'"

Michael leaned toward me. "Is his name Robert Jameson?" he asked, his voice low.

I stared at him, my glass leaden in my hand. "How—?"

"Let me get this out, okay? Two days ago, I met a prospective client named Robert Jameson. He said he was expanding his fine liquor company's presence in the US and needed a new ad agency. I don't have to tell you that my brain practically exploded. The Jameson account? I launched into my pitch, and he was receptive, so I kept going." He scratched an ear. "Even though he gave me the fucking creeps."

Michael paused, holding out his glass for more. He paused while I walked back to refill both our glasses. "He was wearing makeup, for Christ's sake." He shook his head but went on. "He said he'd had his eye on us for a while, loved our work, and wanted to move forward. I nearly wet myself. Then he got chatty, and we started talking about people we had in common. You know, the usual name drops."

Michael picked up his drink, swigging it again in one swallow, and coughed. "Then, out of the blue, he asked about you. And here's the weird thing. I got the idea that he knew we were friends. So I said yes, we'd been friends for a long time."

He took a shaky breath. "And then, shit, Felix, the thing went totally off the rails. He asked me about my girlfriend and her dog, if I knew where they were." Michael banged his glass down on the table. "And I swear to god, Felix, I don't know what the hell was

wrong with me, but I couldn't stop answering his questions."
Michael put his head in his hands.

"This happened two days ago?" I sputtered. "Before I saw you
at your party? Why the fuck didn't you tell me? Where the hell's
your brain been for two whole fucking days?"

Eyes now red-rimmed, Michael shook his head. "I-I don't
know. I guess I forgot. It was like I'd had a friggin' blackout. And
then this afternoon, I went to the office for a meeting. I walked
into the conference room, and bam! It all came back. That asshole
glamoured me, or whatever the fuck it is you vampires do to
people."

I blanched as Michael began to cry.

Ignoring my expression, he swiped tears off his cheeks with a
sleeve and went on. "I told him, Felix. I told him where they are."
He looked around for a tissue, and I handed him my clean handkerchief. "I tried to get through the meeting, but . . . I walked out
on the client and came here. You didn't answer your bell or your
phone, so I've been walking around waiting for you."

I stared at Michael. It was one thing for Vampire Bob to
threaten and stalk me, but to go after my friend and his ex-girlfriend? I remembered Bob's eyes, the thrall he'd put me under,
and the frightful headache he'd given me merely by talking. If
Michael's ex-girlfriend stood between Bob and the dog, she was
food.

Fuck. I had put the target on her back by biting her ridiculous
dog, and I hadn't even gotten a snack out of it.

I felt my forehead. Either I was coming down with something
or I was having a stroke from mixing meds. It was the only explanation as to why I cared what happened to Michael's ex and her
damned dog. I shook myself to clear my head of the maudlin
thoughts but only managed to make myself dizzy.

I picked up Michael's glass and went to the liquor cabinet for
a fresh bottle, grabbing the Jameson. I poured us both doubles
and held his glass out to him.

"You'll need this." I took another gulp of my drink and told

Michael the entire story. He listened, tears leaking down his face. He mopped them up, sipping his whiskey while I spooled it out, up to and including the meatpacking threat. But while telling the story to Michael didn't shed any new light, it did spark a memory. Bob had said there was more to me than met the eye, or something to that effect. And he'd said it after he'd tried to enthrall me. *More of what?*

"So what are you going to do? Go on a killing spree to eliminate all your snacks? Go on an outing to Connecticut to kidnap a dog?" He looked incredulous.

Mired in thought, I didn't answer. The New Orleans community, at least, differed vastly from the New York community. NOLA half-vamps were clubby. We minded each other's business and at least tried to respect each other's territories. It was too small a city not to. While I lived there, I had visited San Diego, Miami, Savannah, Atlanta, Chicago, Minneapolis, and New York, looking for a ripe hunting ground. And I'd done so through NOLA vamps who had emigrated to those places. We did that for each other, whether we still socialized or not.

There were only a handful of former NOLA vamps in New York City. We were all friendly enough. They had helped me settle here. If there had been, or would be, an influx, word would have spread like blood on the Hudson. There were no vamps flooding New York from down South. Vampire Bob had lied.

"Felix. Did you hear me?" Michael snapped his fingers in my direction. "What the hell are you going to do. Are you going to Connecticut?"

"Not me, Michael. You. You need to take care of your ex and the dog. Hide them somewhere safe."

He flushed an unattractive shade of red. "I can't—"

"You can." I stood up and frowned at him. "You have to. You should have done it two days ago."

Michael was a narcissist and too self-involved to fret about current girlfriends, much less ex-girlfriends. We argued about it through another drink until he finally consented to get Laura, or

Lauren, whatever her name was, and the damned dog. He left grumbling. A lack of concern for others was understandable, given my proclivities, but I was irrationally afraid for Michael's ex and the dog who was . . . my child?

Technically, turning another vampire invoked a master–child relationship. But I wasn't a full-blood vampire. Which meant I shouldn't be able to turn anyone, much less a dog. Or maybe half-bloods could turn animals? I pressed a hand against my churning stomach as I stood at the window, watching Michael cross the street. There was no sign of Vampire Bob. Michael looked up at me from the corner before disappearing into the crowd. He might be a cold-hearted bastard, but he was the closest thing I had to a brother—and I knew my ersatz brother, no matter what he said, wouldn't go check on his ex. I'd bet a snack on it.

I lifted my glass to my lips, only to find it empty.

9

Gracie

Saturday, November 14 – One Week Later

The smell of freshly brewed coffee enticed me awake. Beads of water on the screen sent sparkles into my old bedroom. I stretched among the lights dancing on my white chenille bedspread, levered myself up, grabbed the inflatable donut, and made it down the stairs with less pain than I had been feeling since the accident.

I'd spent the past week supposedly nursing my bruised tailbone at my mom's. But one day lying on the couch, reading and watching old movies, had been enough. I wasn't feeling creative enough to work on new recipes, so I called the animal rescue center at which I often volunteered. They were always short-handed, and begged me to come in. I spent four happy days on light duty taking care of the cats, dogs, and parrot that allegedly cursed in Greek, though no one understood him. And as the icing on the cake, my mother had decided to shelve the school discussion.

Lauren had deposited my paycheck plus $500.00 in hazard pay to replace my ruined shoes and hoodie, so I walked over to my apartment on Friday to leave a rent check for Sylvie, plus a note, on the kitchen table, before carefully descending the old stairs to go to Manny's.

Peering into the window, I saw Sylvie happily waiting on customers. She waved me in. As soon as I was close enough, Manny leaned over the counter and pulled me into a hug tight enough to mash my thighs against the rack of chips. Several bags cascaded to the floor. A guy waiting for his order grinned at us and picked them up, tucking them back into place once Manny released me.

"Hey, thanks for sending bagel breakfasts to my mom's," I said.

Sylvie had brought me a bacon, egg, and cheese bagel each morning. It was like room service, only better. Manny's bagels were legendary in Port Chester.

"No, thank you." He blushed and added, "She's amazing!"

I looked over at Sylvie, who was pretending not to listen. She was glowing.

"I'm so glad it's working out for you two," I said, grinning at him. I meant it. Sylvie was in grad school for criminal justice, struggling to make ends meet and dating one loser after another. She didn't love school, but it sure looked like she was loving bagels. And Manny.

"Can I have a black and white?" I hadn't been baking the week I'd spent at the shelter and was dying for a sugar hit. He stepped to the case, folded one into a square of waxed paper, and handed it to me. I fished for my wallet, and he waved a dismissive hand.

"Gracie, this is a token of my appreciation. If you ever need a favor, anything, you call me." He jotted a phone number on a receipt pad, tore the sheet of paper off, and pushed it across the counter at me.

I wrinkled my forehead. "Manny, you don't have to do that. I just wanted you two to be happy."

"I never take affairs of the heart lightly, and neither should you," he scolded, tapping three fingers over his heart. "Remember that. You've given me hope that I will love again. That's worth more than"—he swept his arm in an arc—"everything else I have."

I was speechless for a heartbeat. Sylvie was a lucky girl. "I'm glad I could help. And thanks for this. You never know when a favor will come in handy."

He winked at me. "Just remember, I *can* help. And it won't cost you a favor. Don't lose that." He nodded at the slip of paper.

"Don't be silly. You know I'm always happy to help you out. By the way, I've been meaning to ask. What's the secret ingredient in your black and whites? No-one else's are as good as yours."

"It's an old family secret. I can't tell you."

My face must have fallen because he barked a laugh.

"But since I like you, I'll tell you. Flowers of Sicily."

"I frowned. Flowers?"

"Fiori di Sicilia extract, just the tiniest amount on the batter. It reminds me of my family's village. The scent of lemon blossoms." He grinned at me. "It isn't really a family secret; I don't even know if they have it in Sicily. But it does amazing things for the cake."

I grinned at him and stuck my hand into the neck of my T-shirt, tucking his number under my bra strap and against my heart.

"Thanks for the tip. I'll have to get some. And I won't lose your number." I waved the cookie. "Thanks again. I needed this."

Manny chuckled. "Not as much as I needed her." He nodded his head toward Sylvie. She was full-on listening now and grinned at us.

"Oh, and you don't need to bring me any more breakfasts. Bryan is coming by tomorrow morning, and I'm pretty sure he'll stop here first!" I called to her as I walked out the door with my cookie, leaving two radiant people in my wake.

I spent the rest of the day with my mom, baking cupcakes for some of our senior neighbors. I even got to test a new pumpkin spice buttercream I'd been wanting to try. Feeling flush, I convinced her to let me treat her to dinner at Luigi's, our favorite local Italian restaurant. Dinner was delicious, and we talked about a couple of movies we both wanted to see, the book she was reading, my sister-in-law Alicia's upcoming birthday party, and Bryan's mom, who neither of us had met. We didn't argue once.

10

Gracie

Sunday, November 15

Morning brought an overcast sky. I was making my way into the kitchen for coffee when the doorbell rang. I detoured to open the door to Bryan.

"Hey, you," I said. "Get in here." I drew him inside as a few crisp brown leaves blew in around him. I hugged him hard, inhaling his scent. He smelled like snow: clean, cold, and damp, even though the little bit we'd gotten on and off the last couple of days had melted almost immediately.

He pulled off a knit hat, tousling his fine-textured, sand-colored hair. A cowlick made it flop onto his forehead. I reached up—pretty far since he was 6'3"—and pushed it back.

"Hey yourself." He held out a brown bag. "Bacon, egg, and cheese on a toasted everything. Your favorite."

"Did you see Sylvie?"

"I did. She looks like she won the lottery." He followed me into the kitchen, shedding his jacket on the way. There was a note on the table saying my mother had gone shopping for a book bag. A pot of fresh coffee, still hot, sat in the coffeemaker. I poured two mugs and added half-and-half to both. Bry carried them to the table, unpacked the breakfast, and dropped onto a chair.

"Was that you?"

"Sure was. Manny needed help. Sylvie needed a job. The rest, as they say, is Gracie's magical matchmaking history." I patted myself on the shoulder and bowed. "Thank you, thank you. No applause necessary—I'll be here all week."

He burst out laughing. "If I remember correctly, not all of your matches worked out."

"Hey, the broken windows were not my fault. Those two—"

Bryan waved a hand. "No worries. Both parties have forgiven you. Besides, Henry never would have met Cecile if he hadn't come to the ER for stitches. Now they're happy as clams. So—"

"So I think I'll quit defending myself while I'm ahead."

"I would if I were you." Bryan snickered, unwrapping his sandwich. I huffed at him, even though he was right. My matchmaking attempts were generally epic failures and had descended into chaos on more than one occasion. "How's your hand? And your butt? You up for a car ride?" he asked, unwrapping his bagel.

I sat on the donut, opened mine, and took a bite. "Mm." I swallowed. "My butt is perfect, if I do say so myself." I quirked an eyebrow at him. "My tailbone, on the other hand, is still a little sore. But my hand is as good as new." I waved my un-bandaged palm at him while taking another bite.

"Well, as your doctor, I should probably check that tailbone when we get to my place." He raised an eyebrow suggestively. "I'll drive. You can ride donut." He chuckled at his joke and tucked into his chopped liver and egg on a toasted poppy seed just as I leaned over the table to kiss him, my pajama top gaping. He leered into my cleavage. "Keep it up, and we won't make it out of the kitchen." He grinned. "It's been a whole week."

"Not my fault doctoring takes up all your time. I've been right here, in bed." I wiggled the collar of my pajama top suggestively at him.

"Do that again, and you'll be reheating your breakfast in the microwave." He rose a couple of inches out of his chair. "On the other hand, this sandwich is pretty darn tasty." He plopped back down and picked up his second half.

"Seriously? You're picking chopped liver over me?" I wrinkled my nose at him. "Fine. Eat your liver, see if I care," I said with as much drama as I could muster.

As we ate, Bryan caught me up on hospital news, and I filled him in on the new cats and dogs at the shelter. Not wanting to get into the school thing, I didn't tell him about the truck.

I washed another couple of Advil down with the last of my coffee, leaving Bryan downstairs reading the paper while I went upstairs for a shower. I had forgotten about Manny's phone number, only finding the receipt paper stuck to my skin when I peeled my clothes off before bed last night. I had, unfortunately, slapped it on myself ink side down, and my body lotion must have transferred the ink to my skin. I'd tried to get it off, with no results other than a sore red spot from my vigorous scrubbing.

I stared at my chest in the mirror. Great. Manny's number was tattooed backward over my heart for who knew how long. Explaining that to Bry would be fun. But if I were being honest, he'd probably be distracted enough by what was below the number to not care.

"Hey, did you catch this story in the paper? They found some guy dead in Central Park."

I shrieked, my eyes closing against a face full of conditioner. "Don't do that! You scared the crap out of me! I thought you were still downstairs. No, I haven't read the paper yet. You brought it with you, remember? But some guy is always being found dead in Central Park."

"Yeah, well, they found this guy with two small puncture wounds to the neck and no visible blood," Bryan said.

"And . . .? What?"

"Two small puncture wounds. How do you suppose the victim got two small bloodless puncture wounds?"

I finished rinsing and shut the water off, stepping out of the shower sideways while angling the number away from him. "I give up."

"A VAMPIRE!" he yelled, grabbing a towel and wrapping it around me in a bear hug.

"Now who's nuts?" I pushed him out of the bathroom. "Can't a person have any privacy around here? My mom could walk in at any minute. And the holes could be from anything. Maybe someone stabbed him with a meat fork after he was dead, so, no flowing blood. You're supposed to be the doctor. It totally could have been that, right?" Clutching the towel, I shut the door firmly in his face.

"Yup, it absolutely could have been a post-mortem meat fork in the neck. But I don't know, it could have been a vampire. *Woooo.*" He made a ridiculous horror-movie sound from the other side of the door.

"You're not as funny as you think you are," I said, pressing my mass of hair between the folds of the towel. "Give me a few minutes to dry my hair and get dressed." Thanks to my mom being more than willing to store my overflow wardrobe, I was all set for clothes.

"Okay. But you'd better hurry. A man has needs, you know."

"Bry, wait. Can you grab the box from the chair next to my bed? It's preemie hats and blankets from my knitting group's charity project. Can you take them to Maternity for me next time you go in?"

"Sure. They'll be thrilled to have them."

When I heard his footsteps retreating down the stairs, I pulled out the blow dryer and began detangling my wet curls, my thoughts going back to the dead guy in Central Park. It was a coincidence. Plenty of lunatics roamed the streets of New York. None of them were vampires. I was not ruining a perfect Sunday with my boyfriend worrying about something that didn't exist. Period.

Light traffic meant the drive to Bryan's apartment was quick. He probed my tailbone gently, and then the rest of me a lot less gently, until we exhausted ourselves and fell asleep tangled together. I woke to a kiss on my forehead.

"Gracie, I'm so sorry, I gotta go. A heart is coming in for—"

"Say no more. Who wouldn't jump at their first transplant? Go. I'll be here."

He grabbed his jacket and keys, blew me another kiss, and was out the door before I could say "have fun." He had picked me up, so if I wanted to go home, I'd have to call a relative. Scratch that. A relative ride would come with questions and lectures. Uber would be a better choice. But I was perfectly content in Bry's tiny third-floor apartment in White Plains. Around the corner was a decent Thai restaurant that delivered, and I could always walk a couple of blocks to the mall if I got bored with TV.

Hmmm. Thai. That sounded perfect. I padded into the kitchen and plucked the Thai menu from beneath a magnet on the fridge. I perused the menu every time, though I almost always ordered the pad thai. Not because I didn't like anything else, but because it was one of my favorite comfort foods. That and my mother's carbonara. I was in the mood for a yummy plate of pad thai with extra veg.

After calling the restaurant, I wandered over to the kitchen window to spend a few minutes watching the street below. The weather had shifted while we were sleeping, the sky now an even darker gray that threatened imminent rain or snow. The few people on the street didn't linger. I rethought my idea of walking to the mall and wondered about Viceroy. He'd looked heart-broken when I left. Without squirrels, what would he eat? Lauren had said he ate regular food, but would dog food give him all his nutrition?

Gracie, get a grip. Viceroy does not drink squirrels. He'd gotten along just fine without me all this time; he'd survive another few days. But worry itched between my shoulder blades, and I stewed.

After a few minutes, I shifted position to pivot from the

window and my fretful thoughts when I noticed a man standing on the street, looking directly up at me. I leaned closer to the glass to peer down. Dark haired and too well dressed for this neighborhood, he might have been waiting for someone and looking at random windows. Dismissing him, I decided to turn on the TV when he waved. I stumbled back and ran to the door. Bryan had locked it when he left, but I slid the chain into its groove and snapped the deadbolt. Bry's building didn't have a doorman, so anyone could get in. I crept back to the window and sidled up to it from along the wall. He waved at me again.

"Frak!" I yelped, going back to recheck the locks. The buzzer rang. "Uh, nope," I said to the door. But it was most likely my lunch. I couldn't leave the delivery guy with my food—it would probably come out of his pay. The buzzer rang again. I pressed the button. "Hello?"

An unintelligible stream of Thai came through the speaker.

"Okay, okay, come up," I shouted. It wasn't as if a well-dressed man would rush the door. I was being totally paranoid. He was probably waving at someone else anyway. I fished in my bag for my wallet, unbolted the door, and yanked it open. The man from the street stood on the landing holding a folded brown paper bag.

"I bought your lunch," he said, raising an eyebrow and one side of his mouth in a lopsided smile. I didn't wait to hear what he said next—I slammed the door and twisted the deadbolt back into place.

"GO AWAY!" I screamed. "I'm calling the police! You'd better get the hell out of here!" I yelled, pulling my phone from my pocket and dialing 911.

"What's your emergency?" a bored-sounding woman read from the script.

"There's a man trying to get into my apartment!"

"I wouldn't do that," the dark man said, his voice muffled through the door. "I have things to tell you—"

"I don't know him, and he broke into my building," I continued into the phone.

"Things about the little dog." He raised his voice to be sure I heard him. I nearly dropped the phone.

"Ma'am, ma'am, your address. Can you give me your address? Where are you calling from?"

I gulped. "Uh, I'm sorry. It's my brother. He's wearing a mask and playing a practical joke. I'm so sorry." I hung up. "What did you say?" I demanded through the door.

"Can you open up? Your lunch is getting cold, and this horrid landing smells. My coat is getting dirty just standing here."

"Not on a bet. Start talking, or I call 9-1-1 back." Silence. "Start *talking!*" I yelled. "Or I'll call—"

"I know, I know, I heard you the first time," he fumed. "How about this? You open the door, let me in, offer me a cup of tea, which I will drink while you eat this disgusting mess you call food, and I'll tell you how you can save that little rat from the pain and suffering of an impromptu vivisection performed by a man you *should* fear."

I hesitated, my finger on the 9.

"I am not here to hurt you!" He was furious.

"Who the hell are you? And how do you know Viceroy?"

"My name is Felix, and since you know the dog, I'm assuming you know about me."

My death would probably be reported in all its grisly detail in the *Post* the next morning, and Bryan would have a huge mess to clean up. I opened the door anyway.

"Well, was that so difficult?" He swept in, smacking my lunch against my chest and letting go of the bag so that I had to clutch at it.

He stepped into the kitchen, slipped his overcoat off, and delicately draped it over a chair. "Now, how about that tea?"

11

Felix

Grace Rinelli was a tiny thing. Barely five feet tall in her sock feet. She brushed past me in a huff and filled an electric teakettle from the tap. I settled myself in one of the kitchen chairs to watch her. She had dark hair that fell in tight curls about her shoulders, dark-brown eyes, a gap between her two front teeth, and a sprinkling of freckles. Pretty, but too small. And very young. And her behavior was off. Why had she let me in? I wouldn't have let me in. I would have kept talking to 911 until the police arrived. But not only had she opened the door, she was also making me tea. It was just my luck—she was a lunatic.

"You'd better not touch me," she said, looking over her shoulder. "I'll scream, and these walls are thin."

"Screaming won't be necessary, I promise. I have no desire to touch you." I sniffed, deciding not to tell her that it was unlikely anyone would come to her aid, even if she screamed her head off. People rarely stepped up. She frowned and opened her mouth to say something. I cut her off. "I need your help."

Grace turned from the kettle and leaned away from the counter to peer closely at me. "You need my help? How can I possibly help you? And why would I?"

"Because it's in both your and the dog's best interests."

Something passed over her face. "I don't see how any of this has anything to do with me, but get on with it. I don't have all day. I'm not afraid of you, but I have things to do, and they don't include entertaining weird men."

"Well, perhaps you should be afraid of me," I exploded, furious and frustrated at this ridiculous situation. "I know who Lauren is and where she lives. I know where you and your mother both live."

She leaned back. "Maybe you're right. Maybe I should be terrified, but if you wanted to hurt me, you'd have done it already," she answered, mirroring my tone. "And not that I'd let anything happen to Viceroy, but why is he in danger?" The teakettle whistled, and she reached back to turn it off. "Well?" she demanded.

"What kind of tea do you have?" Now that I was sitting in her boyfriend's kitchen, I hesitated. Stepping in to locate this ridiculous person had been idiotic, and I hadn't really had a plan other than to find her. Spycraft wasn't my strong suit. I didn't even like spy movies. Waving at her from the street and then bringing her lunch up had been spur-of-the-moment insanity. It had paid off in that I might be able to solicit her help, but I hadn't been prepared to talk to her yet. I needed to think fast unless I wanted to end up somewhere in Queens as a plastic bucket of ground Felix.

We stared at each other for a long minute before she turned to pull a lone box of tea from a cabinet.

"This is all he— *we* have." She presented me with a faded, dented box of Lemony Lilt. I sighed and plucked out a slightly musty-smelling tea bag.

"Fine," I said, watching her pour boiling water into a mug and bang it in front of me. The water sloshed onto the old Formica tabletop, barely missing my hand. She ignored the puddle.

"Now that you are certain I'm not going to eat you, why don't you open your lunch? It's rather a long story."

She hesitated and frowned. "Do you want some?" She was far from pleased with me but had clearly been raised to be polite to guests.

"No. I hate Thai." I remembered my own rusty manners. "But thank you."

"Well, if you don't mind, I'm hungry." She pulled out a chair opposite me. "Hold on . . ." She trotted out of the room and returned with a plastic pool float, plopping it onto the chair and arranging herself on top of it. "I can't sit without it. And if I believed in fairy tales, my bruised tailbone is all your fault." She glared at me and picked up her fork.

"Don't people usually use chopsticks with Asian food?" I asked.

She forked in a mouthful, chewed, and swallowed before replying. "Seriously? I can hear you, even over the sound of the wrong utensils. Just get on with your story." She clinked her fork against the rim of her plate for emphasis. What a little smartass.

I studied her while she ate, puzzled at the fact that she could eat and even seem to enjoy the stringy brown pile of mushy noodles with a highly suspect stranger sitting not four feet away. I sighed. She should not have let me in. I was tall, dark, better dressed than anyone in a ten-mile radius, and dangerous looking.

I couldn't help myself. "Didn't anyone ever tell you not to trust strangers?"

She raised her eyes from her plate. "You're not a stranger. Lauren told me all about you and Michael, her loser fiancé. She believes that you bit her dog and turned him into a vampire. Even though she's sweet and pays well, she's off her rocker." She filled her fork. "Is it possible you bit her dog? Sure. You were probably high. But the rest of it? All crazy talk." She shrugged, put a forkful of noodles into her mouth, chewed, and swallowed. "Also, I have an overdeveloped sense of curiosity. And I am armed." She pointed over a shoulder to a rack of sharp knives on the wall behind her.

I swallowed a laugh. I'd be at her neck before she could put down that damned fork.

She lapsed into silence while inhaling her lunch. I looked around the tiny kitchen so as not to stare at her, my gaze settling on the knives.

"Wait a minute," she said as she froze, fork in the air. "If Lauren's crazy, and you're not a . . . a vampire, which you can't be because A: there are no vampires and B: even if vampires do exist, and you are one of them, you're here in the middle of the day. So that pretty much means you're a creepy stalker."

"I am not a stalker," I hissed.

"Then why the hell would you look for me in the first place? How, and why, do you even know about me?" She scraped her chair back a few inches, edging closer to the knives on the wall, fork hovering, waiting, still as stone. "Well?" She pointed the fork at me.

"I'm here because Lauren's loser fiancé," I said, "who is a friend of mine, didn't do what he was supposed to do, which was to go to Connecticut and take care of this problem himself. I found you because . . . Listen, it's a long story and a lot to take in."

"I'm angry, not stupid," she said through gritted teeth. "Tell me."

"Not here." I looked around. If this was how most people lived, humanity was doomed. "This place is giving me claustrophobia. Let's go for a walk."

"So you can drag me into your car and disappear me? I don't think so."

"I don't have a car," I lied. "I took the train and a taxi."

She raised her eyebrows. "No car? What kind of rich guy are you?" She eyed my vicuna overcoat. "Okay. Let's go to the mall." She ate one last forkful of noodles. I bit my lip to keep my eyes from rolling. Of course she wanted to go to the mall. Where else would a twentysomething want to go?

"Fine. Anywhere but here, and as long as we stay far from the food court."

"What's wrong with food courts?"

"They're terrible places. They smell, the food is barely food, and I had a life-threatening experience at a food court. Does that answer your question?"

She shook her head. "I don't want to know."

"Good, because I have no intention of telling you." I stood up, brushing nonexistent crumbs from my lap. If we had to go to a mall, I might at least find a mark. *No.* I mentally slapped myself. None of that, not on this trip. I picked up my coat and slipped it on, wishing I had worn a hat. It was damp and getting colder, and it felt like more snow. I shivered in anticipation. I might have to buy one so as not to catch a chill on my way back to my car.

"Gracie. My name is Gracie Rinelli." She stood in front of me, zipped herself into a criminally ugly winter jacket, and stuck out her hand. "Since we've come this far, we might as well be properly introduced."

I took her small, sturdy hand in mine, only to yank it back when I felt a sharp spark.

"Hey! That tingled. Did you get a shock? It must be this polyester carpet," I said, frowning down at the cheap Persian knockoff.

"Yeah, that happens sometimes. It's just static electricity."

"Of course." I rubbed my palm on my leg to ease the sting of her touch. My last close human contact for activities other than snacking had taken place several years ago, but as I recalled, it hadn't hurt. For the most part, I was satisfied with my single status. I sometimes wished for more, but I could generally fend off the ache by shopping, dining out, or cruising.

But talking to this tiny young woman, who was equal parts charming and infuriating, and holding her warm hand, even for a few painful seconds, brought my occasional loneliness into sharp relief. That, and her misplaced trust and bravery fed a new and uncomfortable protective urge. I must be feeling this way because I had put her in harm's way by biting that damned dog. The fact that she could end up as my massive fuck-up's collateral damage made my skin crawl.

"Felix Belloquot. At your service." I bowed low to cover my confusion and straightened to see her eyes sparkle.

"Well, then, Felix, I suppose we should go. Don't bite me while my back is turned." She chuckled at her joke, opened the door, and stepped out onto the landing.

I followed, stepping aside so she could lock up. The unpleasant aroma of Thai food and anxiety that had clung to her in the tiny apartment dissipated, and I could smell a hint of her perfume. Something cool and mossy. I inhaled deeply and followed her down the stairs.

She was pretending I didn't have bad news for her. I was pretending that I wasn't the one who had to tell her that vampires were real. But I supposed pretending together was better than pretending alone.

12

Gracie

I was going to get myself killed with my idiotic impulses. And seeing as how I had left our dishes on the table, I would be a sloppy dead girl. I shook my head at myself as I exited Bryan's building, Felix at my heels. We turned left toward The Westchester Mall. It was a couple of blocks farther than The Galleria, but it fit Felix better, and the extra distance would give me time to think.

I snuck glances at him as we walked. Though not my type, he was still handsome enough to make me go out on a limb if I wasn't madly in love with Bryan. Tall, with a long, straight nose; clear skin; full lips; dark, almost black hair; hazel eyes that appeared to sparkle; and a faint Southern accent I couldn't place lent him an exotic air. He was also shivering despite his gorgeous overcoat.

"Are you cold?"

"I'm always cold."

"Hm." I picked up the pace. "Walk faster. It helps."

He sped up but quickly overtook me.

I broke into a jog to keep up. "I suppose that's what comes of being a Southerner?"

"I'm from New Orleans."

"Oh. I went there once, during my last year of college." I didn't add "for Mardi Gras." The memory didn't bear dredging up.

He said nothing, slowing his stride when he noticed my jogging. We walked in silence.

"The mall is just ahead," I said. "We can go to Tea Nirvana and get you a better cup of tea and Starbucks for coffee for me."

I frowned. He had stalked me, talked his way into Bryan's apartment, and gotten me to make him tea. And I had let it all happen, like the coming together of an Italian meringue. On the surface, I was an idiot. But I'd seen Viceroy kill that squirrel, even if I didn't want to believe he had sucked its blood, and I needed to talk to someone who didn't dismiss me as delusional. That, and Felix said Viceroy was in danger.

We made it into the mall. Once we were in the center court, Felix stopped to survey the stores.

"Not bad for a mall," he allowed.

"Yeah, this is the fancy one. People call the other mall The Gonorrhea."

Felix barked out a laugh. "I'm glad we didn't go there."

I led the way to Tea Nirvana. He trailed behind me, scanning the stores and the people crowding the walkway.

"Come on, keep up." I stopped at the tea boutique's entrance. Not watching where he was going, Felix ran into me, pushing us both into a table holding a tower of tea boxes. The tower wobbled. "Yikes!" I reached to steady the trembling tower, glancing over my shoulder to find him staring open-mouthed into the store. "Haven't you ever been to a tea store?"

For a moment, he couldn't answer me—he was rapt.

"This is tea heaven," he chortled.

"No, it's Tea Nirvana. They sell tea. Come on." I grabbed his lapel and dragged him inside, where a saleswoman closed in. I stepped back and let her have at him. "I'm going to get myself a cup of coffee. I'll be back for you. Stay here." He ignored me, but I could tell he wasn't going anywhere.

I headed across the walkway to Footlocker for a new pair of running shoes. I looked back to see how Felix was doing. Two saleswomen were fawning over him, offering him sips of the sample teas. He'd be fine.

I found replacements for my trashed Nikes. Lucky, too—since I wore a five, it wasn't always a given I'd find my size. I checked out and ran back to the tea store to find Felix, eyes glazed, standing out in front with an enormous shopping bag in one hand and a tall cup of something in the other.

"Okay, shopaholic. This way." I led him to the Starbucks, parked him at a table out front, and went to get my coffee. When I got back to the table, he was sipping his tea.

"This is delicious." He sighed. "They're right. It is truly an enlightened leaf. Why have I never heard of this company? I need one in my neighborhood."

"I give up, Felix. I guess you live in the wrong part of town." He gave me the stink eye over the rim of his cup but didn't take the bait. I took my jacket off and arranged it into a cushion on the wooden seat before settling myself. "I'm glad you're happy, but I need answers. What the hell is going on?"

He stared into his tea, silent for a beat too long. When he looked up, his eyes had darkened.

"Gracie, I have no painless way to say this, and believe me, I've been trying to think of one." He searched the surrounding tables to see if anyone was listening, but they were all involved in their conversations. "I'm just going to tell you," he rushed on. "Vampires are real. I'm a vampire and, though no one seems to know how, Viceroy is a vampire too."

Time stopped as I gaped at him.

"I knew you'd say that," I whispered. It had all become real somewhere between letting Felix into the apartment and sitting across from him with my coffee. What other explanation had him showing up at Bryan's front door?

I sipped from my grande breve latte to forestall having to say anything more, burning my tongue before remembering it was still too hot. "Ouch!" I yelped. I touched the burned spot with a fingertip and popped open the top off my coffee cup to cool it faster.

"Well?" he prompted.

"Well, what? You're a vampire. Viceroy is a vampire. Is Lauren a vampire? Who the heck besides me in this story isn't a vampire?" My voice raced toward hysteria. My weird calm was wearing off, and realization bloomed like a molten chocolate cake in my chest.

"Shhh . . . keep your voice down." The people at the next table were staring. "She's working on a screenplay," Felix said to them. They smiled, and the man gave me a thumbs-up.

I lowered my voice. "So, if you're a vampire, why didn't you drink my blood when we were alone, huh?" Part of me was still hoping the whole thing was a practical joke.

"Look, it doesn't work that way. First, I'm not a full-blood vampire. Yet. At this stage, we don't need blood to survive. If we ingest small amounts regularly, we age slowly, live longer, and have somewhat heightened senses. The more we drink, the stronger the effect. If we don't drink—and many half-vamps do not indulge— we live normal lives, aging and dying like any other human." He coughed lightly and blushed. "There's even a twelve-step group— Vampires Anonymous."

I raised my eyebrows at him. "VA? You've got to be kidding!"

He didn't respond, and I flushed beneath his cold stare.

"Sorry. So?" I scratched at the seam of my cup with a fingernail. "Were you born this way? Is it hereditary?"

He smiled with his lips. "No. No one is born a vampire. Vampirism is a virus transmitted through an exchange of blood. There are two phases to becoming a vampire. The first happens when a vampire bites you and injects their blood into the wound. It can be intentional or accidental. A blood exchange of this type creates a half-blood vampire." Felix looked away. "Someone I trusted, someone I thought was a friend, bit me in the alley behind the bar where I lived and worked. I don't know if she intended to turn me or not. I was fifteen." He sniffed. "But she wasn't kind enough to stick around, become my sponsor, and complete my transformation to full-blood. I was—"

"So you're only a half-vampire," I blurted.

He flushed, blotching pink, like scattered rose petals across his cheeks.

I bit my tongue right where I'd burned it—served me right.

"Precisely."

Seeing his pain, I had to look away. Crap. I felt sorry for him when he should be feeling sorry for me.

"Gracie, knowing this changes nothing in your world."

I shook my head. "You're so wrong, Felix. This changes everything. How am I ever supposed to sleep again knowing real vampires are lurking in the streets waiting to bite me?"

He didn't answer.

"Okay, nope, I'm done. I can't talk about this. I need to think. I need to go."

He closed the space between our hands, hesitating for a fraction of a second before grasping my wrist gently. "No. You need to stay. If you leave, your brain will fill in the blanks, and it won't fill them with anything positive. Let me tell you everything, so at least you'll have the facts."

I gritted my teeth, determined not to give in to the panic simmering beneath my bravado. Felix took it for permission and continued where he'd left off.

13

Felix

She looked lost, and I was overreacting to her distress. Why on earth did I care? I had come to this crappy White Plains neighborhood to see who she was, not to make a friend, much less fold a little bird under my wing. I was glad she hadn't pressed me for how I'd found her. I didn't want to tell her about the investigator and frighten her even more.

The last decent thing Michael had done before leaving my loft was to tell me Lauren's last name. The problem hadn't been finding her house; it was the degree of her wealth. I had parked on the street in front of her driveway only to see several gardeners. The house was big enough to have indoor staff as well. There was no way I was walking up to the house without alerting someone. That, and Lauren would slam the door in my face the minute she saw me. There was no way I'd be able to convince her to hide herself and the dog.

But I thought perhaps there was an in with the staff. I hired an expensive investigator, who had given me, among others, Grace Rinelli, the new dog walker, and her boyfriend, Bryan McLaughlin. Addresses in hand, I'd driven to Grace's apartment first, and then the house she'd lived in just prior, which, judging by her age, probably belonged to her parents. After eating a rather tasty bagel sandwich at a place called Manny's, I'd driven to White Plains to find Bryan's building. I had been leaning against my Range Rover when she spotted me, ultimately landing me in my present predicament.

But on the plus side, I had some delicious new teas.

"Where do you want me to start? Viceroy? Or the history of vampirism?"

She narrowed her red-rimmed eyes at me. "How about you start with why Viceroy is in danger? Then we can move on to whether or not I need to help him."

I swallowed. "Well, in short, Vampire Bob, Robert Jameson, the self-proclaimed vampire king of New York and head of the local vampire cartel, ordered me to find, collect, and deliver Viceroy. He wants to learn how I turned a dog . . ." I trailed off, realizing how terrifying this must sound to an outsider.

She crossed her arms over her chest and sat back, staring at me. "The king of a vampire cartel wants Viceroy, a little dog. Is that what you're saying?" She puffed air out of her cheeks and shook her head. "Do you have any idea how completely insane you sound? Don't answer that; it was a rhetorical question. And you are supposed to deliver him, which means you are supposed to kidnap him, either from Lauren's house or from me. Right?"

"In a nutshell."

"And if you're supposed to kidnap him, you're warning me because . . . ?"

"Fuck all!" I pushed back from the table, rocking the two half-full paper cups. She didn't move to still them. "I don't know. You weren't supposed to show up at the window! I wasn't prepared to talk to you today. I don't want anything to do with you, or that dog, or Vampire Bob. I have a fabulous life, and I want to live it. Alone and undisturbed." By the end of my outburst, all the people at the surrounding tables were staring.

She leaned forward to shush me. "Keep it up if you want to get kicked out of here," she hissed. "We're rehearsing a scene from a screenplay," she called out to our listening neighbors, who broke into applause at Felix's performance. He blushed as a chorus of "great performance, congrats" and "nice soliloquy" rang out.

"Thank you, it's going to be a great show," he said to his audience before turning back to me and whispering. "Listen, Gracie, none of this is going according to my original plan, which was to have my friend Michael go up to Connecticut and take Viceroy and Lauren away. But as I can't reach Michael, I can only assume that plan failed. I couldn't very well knock on Lauren's door myself, so that left you. I was going to tail you and take the dog— if you had him. But it seems I'm warning you instead. I bit a dog one night by accident. I didn't mean to do it. And as preposterous as it sounds, that dog is now my child."

I ran a hand through my hair. "My maker abandoned me, and while I may be doing the same thing, the least I can do is refuse to sentence the dog to death." I paused. "But if I don't produce him, Bob will send someone else. And that someone won't go to the mall and have tea with you."

Her eyes filled with tears.

"No. No crying." I rose. "Look, Gracie, I've done all I can for you. I don't have the energy, nor, frankly, the desire to sit here for two hours and give you the entire vampire backstory. And I cannot protect you. I'm as serious as death. But you can help all three of us, Gracie: hide the dog." I picked up my overcoat and loaded shopping bag. "This was lovely, and thanks for showing me the tea store."

What remained of her anger crumbled along with her face, then something hit her. Her eyes grew wild.

"Wait." She shot out of her seat. "If there are vampires"—she whispered the word—"what else is out there?"

I stared at her for a long moment. There was no way in hell I was going to tell her about the vast variety of supernatural beings bumping elbows with her right here in this mall. I spun and wove my way through the tables. It took every ounce of self-control I possessed not to go back and take her with me. To what? To protect her? I couldn't even defend myself. I would drain a couple of my past snacks to make Bob believe I was on a roll, report that I could not find the dog, and run. I had a connection in Portland, Oregon, which was rainy as all fuck, but on the other side of the country. I'd regain my freedom and start over in a new city. It was a miserable plan, or rather, I'd be miserable in Portland, but wet and alive was better than dry and dead.

It could work, and I had Gracie—and the fact that she had momentarily softened my heart—to thank for it. I should have been relieved, but my lungs felt like lead weights as I trudged back through the depressing White Plains streets toward my car.

THE DRIVE BACK TOOK TWICE AS LONG AS THE DRIVE out, it being Saturday night, when the hicks flooded the city for an evening of whatever it was they did when they finally escaped their horrid little towns. I sat in traffic, the windshield stubbornly reflecting Gracie's pleading, distraught face at me. I called her twice. She hung up on me both times.

Finally making it to SoHo, I drove around searching for street parking. I wasn't about to park in a cartel garage ever again, even if I was paying a small fortune monthly. If my plan worked, I'd be gone soon anyway. But I had a bad feeling about Gracie. I'd failed to make her understand just how dangerous Bob was. I called her again.

This time she answered, but only to yell at me to leave her alone, hanging up for the third time. I needed to get through to her, but it wasn't going to happen tonight. Finding a spot I could fit the Range Rover into on Thompson, only a couple of blocks from my loft, I parked and walked around to the passenger side to retrieve my Tea Nirvana shopping bag from the seat. I opened the door and leaned in when a hand landed on my shoulder. I jumped, banging my head.

"Ow! What the—"

"Slowly . . ." a familiar voice whispered. I spun to find a man silhouetted against well-lit storefronts. Bob.

"What's wrong with your garage?"

"Don't you have anyone else to pester?" My voice shook despite my misplaced bravado.

"Not at the moment," he said brightly, leaning closer.

I elbowed him backward, grabbed my shopping bag, and slammed the door, beeping it locked.

He fell into step beside me as I headed home. "You saw the girl. Where is the dog?"

"You followed me?" I frowned at him. "Then you know she didn't have him."

"I had you followed," he corrected me. "And obviously, or you would have handed him to me, and this chat would be unnecessary. Did the girl tell you where he is?"

"I didn't ask. I assumed he was home with his owner. The girl's going back to work next week." I dodged a child running down the sidewalk, then his mother, right at his heels.

"So you plan to do what, exactly?" Bob asked, keeping pace with me as I walked toward Broadway.

"I plan to go home and pour myself a triple shot of bourbon and grill a steak. After dinner, I'm going to brew myself a cup of tea and watch an old movie. Want to join me?"

"For steak? Seriously?" He wrinkled his nose. "Unless you want to pour some decent Irish whiskey and go out on a hunt with me?"

I nearly said yes. I desperately wanted a relationship with a full-blood—any full-blood who might then be willing to sponsor and turn me.

"Thank you, but no. I'm tired, and I like steak. Perhaps another time." I stopped in front of my building. Bob stepped closer.

"Felix, either you find and deliver the dog, or I'll get him myself. And you can imagine what will happen to you if I have to find him."

I stepped back, a nasty retort bubbling to the surface. I caught myself, possibly avoiding a gruesome death right on the street, before it came out of my mouth. "I'll get your dog by the end of next week."

He studied me as if I were a bug. "Let's hope so."

I stepped up to the glass door of my building. "Last call for *My Man Godfrey*. And I only have Kentucky bourbons."

He didn't answer, stepping back to melt into the nighttime Broadway crowd, leaving me alone, shivering, and wondering why, if he had so many minions, he didn't already have the dog. It hit me as I waited for the elevator. Michael must have gotten them away in time. If I was Bob's best hope of finding that damned dog, he was fucked.

And because he was watching my every move, so was I.

14

Lucy

This last collection had taken a while. Though rampant cancer and excruciating pain had rendered the man's body uninhabitable, he hesitated when I beckoned. I sat by his bed for the better part of an hour, waiting until he was ready and thinking about Felix Belloquot.

I'd been following Felix for the past week, ever since my boss Deathy's call. She'd released me from most of my collections so I could keep tabs on him, refusing to answer when I asked who he was and why he was so important. And I'd slipped up. Felix had seen me outside Whole Foods, and he might have seen me outside Barneys. But in my defense, I had never followed anyone before. And average people didn't generally remember us.

As reapers, we guided souls that were assigned to us, and that was as far as it went. We didn't tail people. But Deathy—her real name was something unpronounceable in ancient Aramaic—had been insistent, so I followed Felix.

Back out on the sidewalk, after guiding the man's soul out of his hot, cramped apartment, I gulped cold air. I was glad to be done. There wasn't a taxi in sight, so I started walking. A passing truck sprayed me with dirty slush, soaking my feet. Fortunately, this new-to-me body was still healthy, so aside from frozen toes and a pair of ruined boots, I'd be fine.

I picked up my pace. I needed to change before heading back out to meet Deathy for dinner. She had, as usual, ignored my request to eat at a restaurant of my choice, this time my favorite fried chicken place up in Harlem. So, in addition to hearing her elaborate on this year's fiendish plan to keep me in her service, I'd have to eat cardboard food and drink her cocktail of choice, which would contain enough sugar to jump-start a diabetic coma. My self-pity kept me company all the way home.

Finally, in front of my brownstone, I pulled my keys from my pocket with numb fingers and unlocked the heavy front door as Felix, full-blood vampire wannabe who, as far as I could see, didn't deserve to die before his time, nagged at me.

Once inside, I peeled off my soaked boots, leaving small puddles on the polished hardwood. They had been brand-new, glove-soft, red Spanish leather just this morning. Now they were the color of old blood and misshapen past recognition—two thousand dollars down the drain. Tossing my coat neatly onto the coat rack, I almost sighed. From the look of Felix, he'd know exactly how I felt. It was a shame we'd never meet.

I climbed the stairs to the third floor and my private suite. My new body was fit, and I had pushed it, arriving at my front door with enough time to spare for a shower. Shrugging off the rest of my clothes, I stopped to examine myself in the full-length mirror. The young woman whose body I possessed had been twenty-two and a ballerina when she died. She was also precisely the same size as my current wardrobe, down to the shoes. Convenient, as it meant I wouldn't have to shop. The dancer had been beautiful, with long red hair, large green eyes, clear pale skin, and a good nose. She was a bit too thin, breasts smaller than I'd like, but I wouldn't quibble. It meant I could dispense with a bra. I smiled broadly at the overall effect and continued into the bathroom.

Thirty minutes later, hair dry and wrapped in a loose bun, I pulled on an indigo wool dress and matching tights. Eyeliner, mascara, a dusting of blush, and a red Chanel lipstick that complemented my fair complexion finished my face. I added a pair of pearl earrings, a Birkin bag in Bleu Nuit to match my dress, a Marc Jacobs puffy coat with a fur collar, and I was ready. One dressed for Deathy.

As I ran down the stairs carrying a pair of waterproof black leather boots, I heard the front door's opening and subsequent slamming.

"Luce? Is that you?" The voice belonged to Marco, one of my two housemates. He came into view as I took the last curve on the staircase.

"Yes. Patience is at the hospital. She'll likely be a while," I said, smiling at him.

"Oh! Does she have a body in mind?"

"She does. I talked to her this morning. She's going to do the usual guide and claim late today, by the looks of the woman's condition. She said we probably wouldn't see her till sometime tomorrow."

Patience, at ninety, was our third housemate and the youngest of the three of us. A baby, as reapers go. Marco was 145, and I was the oldest. At 423, I was, in fact, the oldest reaper, period, which was why Deathy wanted to hold on to me even though I desperately wanted my humanity back. Since the day I'd declared my wish to her, ten or so years ago, she'd put one stumbling block after another in my path. The annual challenges grew more difficult each year, and her phone call last week told me I probably wouldn't regain my humanity this time either.

Marco unlaced his boots and set them carefully in the boot tray, moving my ruined red boots to the tray to sit next to his. "Tsk. You really should put wet shoes into the tray, Lucy. I'll get a towel and clean up this water."

"Sorry." But he was already around the corner, reappearing with a kitchen towel to soak up the mess I'd made. I didn't want to discuss why I'd been in a hurry and left my wet boots on the hardwood floor, so I pivoted back to Patience.

"I hope she's picked a suitable one this time," I said. By suitable, I meant less ostentatious.

"Me too." Marco grinned at me while he divested himself of his coat, hat, and gloves. "Her last one was a humdinger!"

Patience's parents had been devout Baptists, and she grew up in the church. As a reaper, with the freedom to do whatever she wanted and be whomever she chose, she invariably picked strippers and showgirls. Each new body was flashier and better endowed than the last. We both hoped for something less this time, but neither of us would have bet money on it.

"Sorry I can't stay in with you tonight. I need to run, or I'll be late." I didn't tell Marco where I was going. I didn't have to. His current body had belonged to a perfumer from Grasse, France. He smelled my apprehension.

"Good luck." He touched my shoulder. "You'll need it."

Now I sighed. "Yes. Yes, I will." I slipped past him and out into the damp chill.

The snow had stopped, but the temperature was still dropping, and a crust of ice edged the slushy puddles. I made my way down Morton Street toward 6th Avenue and a taxi. I didn't watch the dark for danger. Humans avoided me instinctively. Even the least intelligent among them seemed to know better than to confront me. Lost in thought, I was caught off guard by a faint heartbeat.

Someone or something was near death. Human? I sniffed the air. Nope. Supe? I stopped walking. It was an animal—a cat. I searched the immediate area, stepping down an alley I'd just passed. Though I didn't have night vision, I did see auras in those close to death. This one was a pale, sickly yellowish-green. I walked into the dark, following the faint emanation, and bent down to find a thin wet feral cat huddled in a pile of old rags at the back of a shop. It opened its eyes, purring feebly at my approach. Animals did not fear us. They accepted death as they did life, with either joy or equanimity.

"There, there, sweet love," I murmured to it, reaching out to stroke its wet, matted fur. It pushed itself into my warm hands, happy to be touched, finally.

"Are you ready?" I asked in a whisper. The little cat nuzzled its bony head deeper into my palm and notched its purr down a full octave. Then it stilled and stretched its face up to look, eyes suddenly bright and wide, into mine. "Yes, yes, you are so ready, little one," I continued in a whisper. "Walk where the sun is warm, the grass is green, and the air is fresh."

The cat's eyes were now radiant. "Run, and play, and be forever free from pain and hunger." I pressed my right index finger to the cat's tired third eye. It let out a last exhale, rested a paw on my wrist, and slipped away.

A shimmering tendril of light rose in front of me and disappeared into the dark sky. A bright spark illuminated the lower cloud cover and winked out. I wrapped the cat's body in the rags and tucked it into one of the empty boxes—the best I could do under the circumstances.

People arrogantly assumed only humans went to Heaven. All animals went to Heaven. Their paradise, far more complex than the human version, had existed for eons before the first pre-humans were even a wrinkle in the primate timeline.

I smiled as the light and sounds of traffic from the busier streets ahead enveloped me. The cat did not need me to complete its journey, but I had spared it suffering in the end. The memory of the little head signaling deep gratitude tingled in my palms. Helping the innocent, forgotten creatures of this world had always made my job feel particularly worthwhile. And lately, it had been the only thing that eased my frustration.

Reclaiming my humanity would strip me of this ability. Grief gripped my chest, halting my forward momentum. That would hurt. I loved animals and wished for a cat or a dog. I often stopped to play with dogs on the street or kittens at adoption events to fill the ache for a little warm body to snuggle with. But I kept long days and late nights, and so did my housemates. It wouldn't be fair to burden them with the responsibilities that came with pet ownership.

I thought back to Deathy's phone call. There must be something unsavory, or perhaps dangerous, about Felix. I just had to find it. If I did, and I was able to justify what I suspected Deathy would ask of me at dinner tonight, if I could make peace with the horror, maybe next year when I was human, I would adopt a dog.

A cab appeared just ahead, and I sprinted for it.

15

Felix

Willem, the doorman, was talking to an overwrought woman when I entered my lobby. Sunday evenings in SoHo were usually quiet, but tonight was a free-for-all. The lobby was full of confused tourists and irritated residents. Willem waved at me to wait, but I was too worried and tired to talk. I had steaks to grill and a lovely Bordeaux to drink. Then, a bath with hinoki bath salts, a cup of tea, and *My Man Godfrey* might distract me just enough to allow me to sleep.

I continued into the elevator and keyed it for my loft. The doors slid open, and I stumbled backward in alarm. My lights were on. And sitting on the floor facing me, tail wagging, was the dog—the little tan dog I had bitten—the dog Bob wanted.

We stared at each other until the doors began to close. I reached to still them but stayed inside. "What . . . How . . . How are you . . . How did you get here? Who brought you, and where are they? Hello?" I shouted into my loft. There was no answer.

"You don't have to yell—I ain't deaf, and nobody brought me. I came by myself," the dog said with more than a hint of irritation.

His mouth wasn't moving. I was hallucinating.

"Dogs don't talk, Felix," I said aloud to myself. The dog stared at me and smiled. Someone down the shaft yelled for the elevator.

"Come in, for cryin' out loud. I don't bite. People, anyway," he chuffed, which sounded like a snicker, and backed up a few paces.

Stepping out, I edged around him, clutching the shopping bag of tea to my chest. The dog started to wag its tail again—more forcefully this time. The hallucination was making me slightly nauseous. He tilted his head at me. He had the upper hand, and he knew it.

"Listen, Felix; this ain't a long story. You bit me, I got turned into a vampire, and you're my master, which is most likely why you can hear me. In a nutshell, that means you gotta take care of me. As for how I got here, I walked." He lifted and licked at a paw before putting it back on the floor. "If you're asking how I knew where to go, I can't tell you 'cause I don't know. I sort of felt you, like you were always right in front of me but just out of reach. No matter how fast I ran, I couldn't catch you until I got to this building. I scratched on the door, and that guy let me in. I thought about you, and he brought me up here."

He drew his eyebrows down in what looked like a frown. "I'll take more questions later. But right now, I gotta piss. Bad. I been locked up in here all afternoon. I coulda peed on a couch leg, but I didn't want to start off on the wrong foot, or paw, if you get me."

To drive his point home, he began to whine. Loudly. I didn't move. What the fuck? Dogs don't talk. And if they did, they didn't speak with atrocious accents.

"Are you dim or what? You hear me talking, don't you? Well, lemme re-say that. I don't 'talk,' I think stuff, and some people can hear me. You can hear me. That guy downstairs in the funny suit can hear me too—he's not human. I told him I lived here and got lost from you, and he brought me up. Nice guy." He paused. "But his weird suit's gotta go."

Wait. Willem wasn't human? Crap, I'd missed that. I stared at the talking dog.

"Yeah, you missed it, alright. Hey, Felix, snap out of it, or I'll let loose right on this carpet." He lifted one hind leg. That did the trick.

"No. Don't you dare." I dropped my crushed bag of tea. "Fine. Let's go." He didn't move. "What? What's wrong?"

"I need a leash, or people will look at us weird."

I threw up my hands. "I don't have a leash. Why in the hell would you think I have a leash?"

"Do you have a belt? Some cord? Maybe a tie you don't like?"

I stalked to the bedroom and fished in a dresser drawer for a length of brown grosgrain ribbon I had saved from a Hermes gift box I'd nicked while out shopping a few weeks back. It was only about five feet long, but it would have to do. I found the dog standing in front of the elevator. He had a rolled leather collar with two dangling tags. I tied the ribbon to the brass ring and read the tags. One was a rabies tag from Greenwich, CT; the other bore his name—Viceroy, a Greenwich address, and a phone number.

"Viceroy." Gracie had called him that.

"In the flesh. You got a problem with my name?"

"I . . . uh . . . no. No. Not at all." I swallowed a retort. I didn't want to irritate him when he was full of urine. I pushed the button, and he smiled. Dogs smiled; that was news to me. We made our way through an empty lobby. Willem was nowhere in sight, but I stopped dead at the reception desk. If Bob was having me watched, I couldn't waltz out the door in plain sight with Viceroy. I spun and led him to the service entrance that opened onto Spring Street. We walked to the middle of the block, where it was darker. He hopped off the curb and did his business. Both parts. Stepping back up onto the sidewalk, he looked at me expectantly.

"What?"

"Did you bring a poopy bag?"

"A *what*?" I asked. Then it hit me. I had seen people picking up their dogs' leavings with little printed plastic bags. Viceroy shook his head slowly back and forth while I worked it out. "Listen, you little cretin. I am not picking up your shit."

I pulled at him, and he trotted reluctantly after me. We approached a couple who abruptly crossed the street to avoid us. I frowned at them. "What's their problem?" I muttered to him.

"Well, for starters, you left my wad in the street. Then you talked to me out loud like I was talking to you." He chuffed and snorted.

"Are you laughing at me?" I shouted at him. The couple broke into a run. He chuffed harder. "Well? Are you?" He heaved a sigh too gusty for his body size.

"You don't have to talk out loud. I can hear you think."

"Oh. Wait. What? What do you mean you can hear me think." I was shouting again. Several more people crossed the street.

"You're still doin' it. Stop screaming, or someone will call the cops. *Think at me!*"

This was bad. The little rat could read my mind.

"Hey, I am not a rat. For your information, I am a pure-blood cairn terrier. I have a lineage and papers to prove it. And yup, I hear everything. So far you're not all that interesting. In fact, you're kind of a . . ." He stopped and glanced up at me, ears drooping. "Let's just go."

I didn't argue, as I didn't know what else to say, and I didn't want to think anything I didn't want him to know. I forced myself to consider how fast lower Broadway was gentrifying as I tugged on the service entrance door, only to remember I'd have to ring the bell to get in from the outside. I didn't want to wait for Willem. Great.

"I'm going to pick you up and hide you under my coat in case someone is watching the building." I didn't wait for an answer. I unbuttoned my overcoat, scooped him up, and yanked my coat closed over him as best I could while rushing around the corner and into my building. Willem was waiting.

"Good evening, Mr. Belloquot. I see you two are reunited!" he said brightly. A little too brightly.

I dropped Viceroy to the floor. "Hello, Willem. Yes, and thank you for letting him in. I don't know how he got away from me."

The doorman narrowed his eyes, and I stepped back. "Perhaps you need a better leash. There's a fancy pet store on Broome at Broadway, just down the block. They'll be open in the morning." He frowned slightly. "When did you acquire him, Mr. Belloquot? I can't seem to recall you having a dog."

I peered at Willem. He had a faint accent I'd never noticed before. Irish? Viceroy claimed he wasn't human. Why hadn't I seen that? And what the hell was he, if not a vampire? A warlock, a shifter, a leprechaun?

I was a deft liar, but I had no idea what kind of creature I was dealing with, and I was breaking into a telling sweat. "Oh, several months ago. Viceroy's been with my sister, upstate," I said smoothly.

Viceroy pulled toward Willem, wagged his tail madly, stood on his hind legs, and put his front paws up onto the doorman's knee. Willem obliged by leaning over to give him a scratch behind the ears. "Well, hello there, Viceroy. Nice to meet you properly." Standing, he added to me, "He's a great dog."

"Yes, yes, he is. Have a pleasant evening, and thank you again." I tugged Viceroy toward the elevator and waited until the doors closed and we were ascending.

"We have some talking to do," I hissed. "And I have some thinking to do—without you listening in!" I frowned down at the little mutt. "And what the hell is Willem?"

He smiled, his feathery tail wagging jauntily. The little shit wasn't going to tell me.

16
Gracie

After sitting in the food court for the better part of an hour while I tried to make some sense of what Felix had said, I dragged myself out of the mall and toward Bryan's apartment, my tailbone aching. I couldn't believe Felix had left me in the mall after the bomb he dropped. What kind of person did that? Oh, wait, he wasn't really a person. He was a blood-drinking, dog-biting monster.

Bryan was going to lose it when I told him I had let a vampire into his apartment, made the vampire a cup of tea, and then taken the vampire to the mall. Crap. I *couldn't* tell him. I had only said that Lauren believed Viceroy was a vampire. I'd never claimed to believe her story myself. How was I supposed to tell him that the head of a vampire cartel might come calling to kill me and steal Viceroy? Yeah . . . nope. He'd either think I had lost my mind or, worse, if he believed me, he'd be furious I was in danger. That, and he'd tell my mother.

Pulling my keys from my pocket, I realized I'd forgotten my new Nikes under the table at the food court. Rats! I pivoted to go back and shrieked when I slammed into a solid wall of man.

"I'm sorry. I didn't mean to frighten you." The man stepped far enough back for me to see that, at 6'7" or 8" and I had no idea how many pounds, he was enormous. I bumped my back against the door just as it began to open, forcing me to step aside. It was Fay, Bryan's downstairs neighbor.

"Hello, Gracie. How nice to see you! Phillip, I see you've met Gracie. Her boyfriend lives above me." I moved farther to the side to let Fay slip out. She held a brown paper bag out to the man, who took it with a grin.

"Hi, Gracie, I'm Phillip." He held up the bag. "Fay made me a dinner sandwich. Her roast beef is incredible." Then he looked directly at me, and my mouth dropped open. He had gorgeous blue eyes—the color of the Caribbean Sea. They were bright and clear beneath a set of bushy brown eyebrows. My mouth dropped open, and I clamped it shut as Phillip peered at me.

"You . . . you look like my sister, Hilda. Your hair is darker, but . . ." He searched my face with those glorious eyes. "You could be her." His eyes reddened, but his smile returned. "I'm sorry, I just . . ." He stepped farther back.

Fay moved to Phillip's side and laid a hand on his arm.

"Phillip lost his sister several years ago. You must look quite a bit like her," she explained. "Phillip is a good friend. We've known each other quite a long time." She tugged her sweater across her narrow chest and tightened the belt against the chill. "Aside from being frightened nearly out of your wits, how are you? It's been a while."

I'd helped Fay with her groceries a few times. She'd made me coffee, and we'd occasionally played cards while Bry was stuck at the hospital. She held out her arms, and I stepped into them.

After a quick, tight hug, she released me. "You're fine. How could you not be?" Her peculiar sideways grin made me remember that I did really enjoy her company.

"It has been a long time. I've missed you." I smiled at her and turned my attention to Phillip, who stood silent, his dinner in one hand.

"Hello, Phillip. It's very nice to meet you." I held out my

hand. After a long moment, he enclosed my small hand in his huge one and shook it solemnly.

"It's nice to meet you too, Gracie." He smiled directly at me, and the world lit up like a Christmas tree. He had an accent, perhaps Scandinavian, and his features, though warm and kind, might have been chiseled from an old oak. With his flannel shirt and insulated work jacket, he looked as though he belonged in the forest, not on the streets of White Plains.

I could stare at his face forever. But I needed to get my shoes from the food court before they became someone else's shoes.

"Um . . . I'd love to stay and chat, but I need to get back to the mall. I left my new running shoes at a table in the food court." I frowned. "I hope they're not gone."

Fay creased her brow. "Phillip can walk with you. This neighborhood isn't the safest place for women at night." She beamed up at Phillip without even waiting for my consent.

He nodded his giant head. "Of course."

I looked up at Phillip's gentle face, and we turned to go back the way I had just come.

"Hey, are you busy tonight?" I called to Fay over my shoulder. Sitting in her plant-laden apartment and chatting about anything but vampires would be great.

"I'm heading out to check on a friend who just got out of the hospital. Nothing serious, but I want to make sure she has dinner. I should be home by eight if you want to come down."

"Okay, thanks. Maybe I'll see you later."

"Have a good night, Gracie." Fay headed back inside.

"And thank you for the escort, Phillip," I said to the big man.

He glanced down at me. "I work in shipping and receiving at the loading dock, so I'm going in that direction. But I would have walked you anyway." He blushed as we headed toward the mall.

"Do you live near here? Have you worked at the mall for long?"

"I live in the building next door to Fay," he said softly. "And I've worked at the mall for a few years now. After my sister, Hilda,

died, I was lost. I met Fay in Iceland, where I lived, at a conference. She talked me into moving here. She thought a change of
scenery might help with my sadness."

"Has it?"

"This place is so different, it takes my mind off what
happened."

"I get it. Sometimes you just have to move away." I thought of
my four-block separation from my mother.

"Did I share too much?"

"No. Not at all," I said, feeling his pain. "Losing my dad broke
my heart. Sometimes it helps to talk to friends about what we're
going through, about the people we lose."

The rational part of my brain screamed that walking the
streets in the dark with a guy who could be a giant for all I knew
—since vampires were real, why not giants?—was even crazier
than taking a vampire to the mall. I told it to shut up. I had
already let a vampire into Bryan's apartment, and I liked Phillip.
Besides, a new friend was an unexpected gift during an otherwise
crappy afternoon. I was so lost in thought that I didn't notice
Phillip had stopped walking.

"What?" I asked.

"We can be friends?" Phillip seemed shocked that I would
even consider it.

"Why not? Do you play cards? I play with Fay sometimes. You
can join us."

"I do. And I would love that, Gracie. I'm so glad we met."

"Me too, Phillip."

I gave Phillip my phone number, which he carefully typed
into the contact list on his phone, though I had no idea how he
managed it with his thick fingers. I did the same with his number.
We parted at the corner, Phillip only agreeing to go to work after I
assured him I would take an Uber back to Bryan's, and agreeing
that we would get together soon. He went left, heading to the
mall's loading docks. I went right and walked through the front
doors with a lighter heart.

I broke into a jog, as if running the last few hundred yards would guarantee my shoes' safety. But my bag was gone. The upside was that Lauren had given me enough money to buy several pairs. With that cheery thought in mind, I made my way back to Footlocker and picked up the shoe I had just lost. The same kid who had helped me before came up to me and did a double take.

"Hey, you're the size five."

"Uh, yeah, I am. How did you remember that?" He must have helped at least a dozen people since me.

He tapped his forehead. "I have a good memory. And not too many people wear your size," he admitted.

"Right." I nodded. "Can I have another pair?"

"You bought the last pair in that size. But believe it or not, we have your shoes!" He looked delighted at my confused expression. "Some weird guy brought in your bag. Said he found it at the tables and maybe the person who lost it would come back looking for it. Wait here." He made his way to the front counter and came back with my bag. The box inside still held my shoes.

"Wow." I hesitated. "But why did you say the guy who found them was weird?"

The kid scratched his head. "I dunno. Too well dressed for this store, obviously not a trainer or hiker-wearing guy. I suppose he could have been a good Samaritan, but people like that don't usually take the time to return lost stuff to stores. It's always people who understand how financially painful it can be to lose something, ya know?"

I nodded and reached for my bag.

"And something else—he was wearing makeup. I'm into horror movies, and if I was a director, I would totally cast him as a vampire. Or the devil, or a demon or something. But hey, at least he brought your shoes back." The kid grinned.

"Yeah, lucky me. Thanks." Grabbing my bag a little too fast, I walked out of the store.

It took two tries to hit the right numbers for my mom, my

hands were trembling that hard. I stopped at the railing over-looking the first floor while I searched among the people for a vampire, devil, or demon in makeup.

"Mom, I hate to ask, but I ate sushi, and I don't feel so good. I'm at the White Plains Mall. Can you pick me up?"

Listening to a lecture on the dangers of sushi all the way back to her house was a small price to pay for the ride. But after several doses of Pepto Bismol and a cup of my mom's homemade herbal blend of worm-killing tea to take care of whatever she was convinced was crawling around in my stomach, I wasn't so sure I'd called the right person.

17

Lucy

Five minutes to seven. I was right on time. Deathy hated to be kept waiting, but even if I had been a few minutes late, what could she do, take away my birthday? I'd been dead for hundreds of years.

I exited the cab and wrestled my thoughts to focus on Felix. Who did he see when he looked at me? Reapers are mutable to all humans. Each person perceives who they need to see, though most don't notice us at all. In Felix's case, I hoped that I appeared ordinary and forgettable.

I hesitated on the corner, the Lotus Club entrance just yards away. I hated the place. Uptight, snobby, and decorated with plaster statues and musty drapes. But Deathy was on the board, so we ate there more often than not. Despite the tragic setting and pending disaster, I was hungry, and thinking about any food at all made my stomach grumble.

The opening of the envelope was supposed to be a celebration, but the ritual was a sham. Deathy preferred to keep her older reapers close at hand, as training initiates was time-consuming, and she grew lazier by the year.

Any senior reaper in their right mind despised playing her cruel game, but few of us were anymore. Insanity claimed us all eventually. It had something to do with living too long and seeing too much. The task Deathy wrote on the card was invariably so distasteful or immoral that most of us declined—unless we were too far gone. And by that time, we were no longer of use to her anyway. It was torture. After so many years of service, we deserved the right to ascend or become human again. I ached for my humanity, and year after year, Deathy made it clear I'd never win it.

The game went like this: Deathy, trembling with anticipation, would hand me the thick cream-colored envelope. I'd smile back and open it, removing and reading the handwritten card inside. If I accepted, I'd place the card face up on the table. If I refused, I'd place the card face down. The urge to tear the thing to pieces, drop them on the floor, spit on them, and stomp the mess into the hideous carpet grew harder to fight each year. But giving in to my inclination would make my existence more of a living hell than it already was.

So, for more years than was fair, I'd placed the card face down.

She always accepted my refusal with a satisfied smirk, and we ate an unpalatable dinner.

I suffered a recurring dream about opening the envelope over a Styrofoam plate of hot, juicy, crispy fried chicken, a generous helping of collard greens, and a dollop of mashed potatoes. Inside would be a claim I'd be happy to accept. But I always woke up. In reality, year after year, I'd open the envelope over the Lotus Club's monogrammed porcelain plate upon which rested the equivalent of three scant tablespoons of hysterically wrought flavors garnished with a dollop of tasteless mushroom suds. The meals were all challenging to get down on the best of days but impossible after reading the inevitably revolting claim written in some poor unfortunate's blood.

"Madam." A polished doorman opened the door to the club as I dragged my feet up the steps. By the expression on his face and servile tone, he must behold a princess. Suppressing a lunatic giggle, I swept through the doors, surrendered my coat to the young man at the coat check, and made my way into the dining room. There, waving a slender, elegant hand at me, sat Deathy.

The dining room was packed, but no one sat at any of the adjacent tables. Wherever we ate, Deathy paid for the ring of tables surrounding ours so we would not be disturbed or distracted.

"Hello, darling!" She rose from her seat to give me a warm hug.

"I can't believe a whole year has passed!" I gushed, lying through my teeth.

"I have so much to tell you," Deathy said, "and yes, it has to do with what I asked you to do last week. But let's order first."

I took stock of her as I picked up the menu. This year, she wore her hair red and looked suspiciously like the actor Julianne Moore, only thinner, paler, and garnished with better jewelry. Above the perfect neckline of an ivory satin sheath, an emerald the size of a robin's egg sat nestled in the hollow of her throat. Refined, elegant, and frightening in her perfection, Deathy drew every eye in the too-quiet room.

"They're looking," I whispered.

She raised a hand to adjust a small diamond-encrusted bobby pin holding the hair over an ear. All eyes turned away from us and back to their menus, plates, or companions. The music, conversations, and clinking of silverware on plates resumed.

"I love doing that." She laughed, a low, liquid sound.

"I hate it when you do that," I said lightly, frowning at my menu instead of at her. "Does the restaurant have a new chef?"

"Surprise!" she cried, ignoring my slight and enjoying my shock at the menu items. "Oh, darling, whatever is wrong?" Her face fell. "The new chef is from that little restaurant you love in Harlem! I got him just for you!" She clapped her hands in delight.

I stared at her, open-mouthed, then back at the menu. The first item listed under entrees was the fried chicken with mashed potatoes and collard greens. The very dinner I loved.

She was desperate for my cooperation.

Deathy waved to a waiter, who disappeared to return in seconds with two cocktails on a tray. He placed them reverently before us, and I leaned over mine to catch the unmistakable scent of a proper Sazerac. Still shaking, I ordered the fried chicken. She ordered shrimp and grits.

I took a sip of the perfect cocktail. "Did you get a new bartender too?"

"Why, yes, I did. Do you approve?" She tossed her head, and her gems sparkled.

The room tilted, and I grabbed at the table's edge. Deathy drew her eyebrows together, reaching over to pat my hand, and I clicked my teeth together to keep them from chattering.

"There, there, dear. You'll feel better in just a minute." She produced the cream envelope, sliding it across the table at me. "I think you'll be pleased for once."

I took a couple of deep breaths, and the room righted. I reached for the envelope, but Deathy stilled my hand with hers.

"Lucy, can I be frank?"

Only if I can be anywhere but here. I'd fallen down the rabbit hole, but I nodded.

"This task I am assigning you will guarantee your humanity, and yes, I will give it without reservation. I will also grant you the option of forgetfulness, allow you to choose your own time of transference, allow you to choose your body, and anything else you ask."

I slipped my hand from under hers. "Deathy, please excuse me, I, ah, need the ladies' room."

"Oh, my dear, I hope you're not losing this body—I do like it!" Her smile fell from her face, and her voice dropped a register, freezing me in place. "Lucy, you'll not only gain your humanity, but you'll be helping me." She gazed up at me with an expression I'd never seen on her face before—hope.

My throat closed. Something was very wrong with my boss. I stumbled to my feet and, without waiting for permission, lurched through tables to the back of the restaurant, somehow managing not to bolt through the front doors as I passed them.

Alone in the ladies' room, I leaned over the marble sink and splashed cold water on my face. Being a reaper didn't mean immortality in the physical sense. During the process of transference, the bodies we took over were miraculously healed of whatever had killed them. And to some degree, they were rendered stronger. But they were still human bodies, and reapers experienced every illness a human could contract.

But since a new body was instantly animate upon possession and couldn't easily die of illness, injury, or disease, Deathy didn't consider sick days necessary to the practical completion of our duties. So no matter how exhausting the process of body-switching or how feverish you were with the flu, you went to work. I hadn't had a sick day in over 400 years, and the way things were going, I'd never have a day off again.

I straightened and stared at myself in the mirror, momentarily thankful for waterproof eyeliner and mascara. I'd kept this body the longest of any I'd inhabited since my own body's death 424 years ago—as of tomorrow. Still, I'd been watching for signs of deterioration. Eventually, the nervous systems of borrowed bodies degraded, making them difficult to control. If you found yourself unable to whistle or snap your fingers, you switched bodies before you became unfit for polite company.

My expressive green eyes peered back at me while runnels of water soaked into the neckline of my dress. I should have gone back, but the sink's cool marble soothed my fevered palms, and my feet were rooted to the immaculate tile floor.

Deathy wasn't usually emotional, so her display at the table was a red flag. Was she losing her mind? Could that even happen to her? My fear over what she wanted was suddenly eclipsed by my fear over what she was becoming—an insane goddess of death.

"There's fried chicken out there," I coaxed myself. But my feet remained planted, so I tried a firmer tack. "The sooner you go out there, the sooner you go home!"

That did the trick. I pushed back from the sink, picked a soft cotton hand towel from the top of the stack, and wiped my face and hands. I pressed the cloth around the wet neckline of my dress to remove some water.

"You're okay," I muttered to my reflection before turning away to drag my feet to the door. I had a crawling suspicion that I wasn't, but I had to go back to the table, and to the Sazerac I desperately needed.

Once seated, I smoothed my napkin back onto my lap and slowed my breathing before reaching for the envelope. I ripped the seal open, not bothering with manners, and tossed the empty envelope onto the floor. Deathy's disapproval at my irreverence hit me like a blast of frigid air. I held the notecard, which was inscribed in blood, in my hand.

"Are you sure you want me to read this?" I asked.

What little color she had drained down her neck as her face morphed into its true visage: a writhing gray cloud. She threw what had been a hand into the air, and the waiter carrying our steaming plates froze in place.

"Deathy, if I read this, we may make a terrible mistake neither of us can undo."

The cloud boiled on itself as her entire body dissolved, twisting within her dress and sending tendrils into the room. I reached out and grabbed one as it gyrated past me toward the waiter.

"Stop! Please, Deathy, maybe if you tell me what's troubling you, I can help—"

"Help?" She touched her bobby pin and laughed, a tinkling sound that rose into her spectral voice, a high-pitched nasal whine not unlike the sound of a wood planer on steroids.

I resisted the urge to release the tendril and clap my hands over my ears, but the finger of Death I held back allowed the waiter to keep his soul. I had guessed at least some of what was on the card, piecing it together from the phone call and her bizarre behavior tonight.

I'd known Deathy for over 400 years. The Angelic Council, the group that oversaw life and death, had stripped her powers away one by one until all she had left was assigning souls to reapers. To be fair, she had caused her own demotions along the way through her abuse of those powers. But she'd cried on my shoulder each time it happened.

We'd been through a great deal together: plagues, wars, drought, and crop failures. I'd always been there for her, so it made sense that she'd turn to me for whatever it was she had planned. What didn't make sense was that she wasn't willing to tell me what it was she needed.

"Darling, I need you to do your job and complete the task." Her voice returned to the human range as she reabsorbed her tendrils and solidified into her human form.

I glanced around the room, sighing in relief to see that no one had fallen over dead. Frozen in time, they had not seen the monstrous form sitting across the table from me.

Deathy's eyes shone in a manic fever. "All that remains is for you to accept the challenge. Lucy, please. You will be doing the world a service, ridding it of an abomination." She leaned across the table toward me. "I know it hasn't seemed so lately, but I love you, and I want you to be happy. Do this for me, and regain your humanity."

She patted the pin above her ear once more, and the reanimated waiter placed steaming plates before us. I looked down at the card to read what she had written, and the delicious aroma of perfectly fried chicken soured in my nostrils.

It was the final slap in the face. Deathy had ruined my favorite meal.

18
Viceroy

After doing my business, I stood next to Felix in the elevator. He pretended to be irritated with me, but he was scared. I could smell it. That made two of us. Three days ago, I had watched my poor Lauren die by vampires, vampires that were more animal than me. I had wanted to kill them all, but I was only one dog against six of them, so I hid until they were gone. Getting here from Greenwich hadn't been a load of laughs either. It had been a long, cold walk with a broken heart. Tired and dirty, I hadn't expected Felix to welcome me with open arms, but a pat on the head and a "nice doggie" wouldn't have sucked.

"So, what's for dinner, boss?" I played up the Boston Southie accent I'd picked up from my birthplace, knowing it annoyed him.

Felix stared at me like I had three heads. "Dinner? You expect me to feed you?"

"Well, you walked me. Next comes feed me." We traded stares. I drooped my ears and let out a sad little whimper. He hmphed, but I won. Dogs always win that game.

"Fine." He stalked to the refrigerator and pulled it open. I ambled over to check the inside with him. It was empty except for a box with a cow picture on it, something in brown paper that smelled like meat, bottles filled with yellow stuff, long green things like fingers, and *blood*!

"Blood!" I yelled into his head. "I'll have the blood!"

"That's not blood, it's ketchup. It goes on french fries." He shook his head at me and slammed the refrigerator door. "Don't you dare judge me. There's nothing wrong with ketchup on french fries." Then he shook his head, hard. "You're dreadful—you can't stay here. I can't do this."

He sat on a stool, and I sat down at his feet and stared up at him. "That hurts my feelings. I'm staying right here with you. You made me, you're my master, and you're responsible for me."

He sniffed. "I don't care if I made you. I don't care if you are the only vampire dog in the entire history of vampires. I don't care if the whole fucking world thinks you're adorable. If I had a dog, it would be a great dog. One of those tall gray ones. Not a hairy, dirty little nothing like you! Besides, that rule only applies to humans. You probably have fleas." He made a face and scratched himself. "I can feel them. You need to go. Now."

He shot off the stool to head for the door, but I beat him to it. I raised my hackles and growled for real, thoughts screaming. "You did this to me, and I ain't gonna let Gracie get killed too."

Felix backed up. "What, what? What do you mean *too*?"

I hadn't wanted to tell him like this. I was gonna be kind and gentle and explain what happened, but he was an ass, and he had hurt my feelings.

"What, what, what . . ." I mimicked him. "Lauren's dead, Felix. Vampires killed her, and everyone else in the house, because they were looking for me, and it's your fault."

Felix's mouth fell open.

"Did you hear me? I said Lauren is dead! And you know who's next? Gracie. Then you and me."

He stared at me. "And you're just telling me this now!" Felix yelled so loud my ears hurt.

"What was I supposed to do? Call you on the phone?"

To be fair to the dimwit standing in front of me, I'd had the whole time I was walking to ache through my own broken heart and try to work out what to do next.

The smartest thing would be for me to live alone, somewhere in the woods. Feeding myself on squirrels and mice would be no problem. But that would leave Gracie and this self-centered asshole to fend for themselves. Gracie, I had loved immediately, almost more than blood, and Felix, however bad he sucked, was my maker. So that was out. I sat down and licked at a sore front paw.

Felix sat on the stool again. His face was white, and he looked like he might get sick. "But—"

"But nothing. We have to stick together. And it's better if Gracie sticks with us too." I went back to my paw, too red in one spot and stinking of sick.

"But what . . ."

"You said that." I put down my paw. "Listen, Felix. Finding out that I can talk and learning about Lauren's murder is a lot to take in, and you're not that quick or bright. But you gotta understand it's life or death. While I was hiding under the sofa at Lauren's, I heard one of the vamps talkin' on the phone after my pack died. He kept sayin' 'yeah, boss,' and then told the others there was a new plan, and they were to quit tracking me because Mr. Jameson had another way to find me. That was three days ago."

Felix sucked in air. "Lauren's dead." He looked at his shoes and shook his head. "I suppose it's my fault. If I hadn't bitten you, Bob would have no reason to go after her." He was silent for a minute. "I can't fix it." His voice cracked.

I didn't think anything at him, letting it sink in.

When Felix finally looked at me again, his eyes were red. "Wait a minute. Bob doesn't know you're here or he would have come upstairs with me. So we have at least until he figures out where you are." He stared off into nothing.

"Bob again? Who's Bob?" I thought at him.

Again with no answer. This guy was probably a couple of dog biscuits short of a snack. He was still staring at nothing.

"Felix, hey, Felix, I've got something stuck in my foot." I held up my injured paw. "And I need a bath. Bad."

That snapped him out of it. Felix jumped off the stool like he'd just bitten into a string of Christmas lights.

"One question: was Michael there?"

"You mean the asshole who dumped Lauren after you bit me? No. Though I wouldn't be sad if he had been a vampire's lunch."

Felix's face got red, but he didn't yell at me.

"Okay, good, right—food first. I'll grill the steaks. Wait. Do you eat food? Or are you a full-blood vampire who needs to hunt?"

I stared at him. "What do you mean? I'm a vampire kind of vampire. I hunt and I eat food. Isn't that what you do?"

"Yes, but . . . listen, it's complicated. I can't go through it all with you right now except to say that you're an anomaly. I'm not a full-blood vampire, so I can't turn anyone or anything. So that makes you . . ."

"I'm not a nomaly, whatever that is, or a thing. I'm a dog." I looked away. The SOB had hurt my feelings again.

"Listen, Viceroy. I'm sorry. That was a poor word choice. I'm sorry I bit you, and calling you a dirty little nothing was cruel." He said it stiffly, like he wasn't used to saying sorry. "Can we talk about all this later? I'm hungry, and I know you are too." He pulled the brown package out of the refrigerator. He stopped and bent down, so his face was closer to mine. "I truly am sorry, Viceroy."

He was pretty good-looking when he wasn't being a shit heel. "No sweat. We both said some stuff. Let's eat," I thought at him. There was no point in staying mad.

He cooked the meat he called cave-aged steaks and didn't even blink when he put my portion on the same kind of plate as his and put me up on the table so we'd eat together. Maybe it was because he didn't know better, but I felt the loneliness in him.

Lauren had been gone a lot, and the other people in the house were too busy to play with me. I knew how much it hurt to be alone all day. I ate until my belly was too full. I figured both steaks were supposed to be for him, so I gave him points for sharing.

I got a running stream of everything in his head while we ate. He was thinking about taking me and hiding in Portland. Then he thought maybe New Orleans. Now he was thinking about voodoo. What the heck was *voodoo*? His thoughts stopped making sense, so I tuned him out to think about city squirrels. I would have to try to teach him how to think to himself. But not yet. I still didn't trust him all the way.

"Okay, Viceroy, time for a bath and that foot problem," Felix said once we'd finished eating.

He lifted me off the table, carried me to the bathroom, and put me on a white fluffy animal skin in front of the bathtub. I wanted to bury my face in it, but I had my pride.

"Now what?" he asked.

"Didn't you ever wash a dog?" I asked, sighing when he shook his head. "Jeez. Okay. First, do you have any non-stinky shampoo?"

He reached into a shower stall and popped a bottle open for me to sniff. I smelled the woods on a damp fall day, with a fire off in the distance and crunchy dry pine needles. Under that, a hint of apple, like at poor dead Lauren's orchard. And something else, like the curved wood thing one of the gardeners smoked? The only thing missing was rival dog urine. I fought back the great sadness about Lauren and let myself bliss out over being cared for.

"Yeah, I guess that'll do."

He rolled his eyes. "Do you have any idea how much this shampoo costs?"

"Nope, and I don't care. Soap me up."

When I was dry, Felix looked at my paw. He took a tool out of a cabinet and used it to pull a thorn from my pad.

"Done," he said, proud of himself. He held up the same medicine Lauren had used on me a couple of times while I licked the sick leaking out of my burning pad. "Do you want Neosporin and a bandage?"

"I need to clean it myself some. Tomorrow you can put the medicine on." I yawned. "Can we sleep now?"

Felix grinned at me before he caught himself, and I smiled back. In my exhaustion, I thought he might be enjoying me, just a little bit.

19

Felix

Monday, November 16

Viceroy had woken me at the ungodly hour of six a.m., demanding to go out. And it was a good thing too. He'd relieved himself of enough liquids and solids to fill a Great Dane. Where it had all been stored in his tiny body was beyond me. After leaving yet another message on Michael's phone, I ran to put more money in the meter. I returned to the loft with a bag containing egg sandwiches with extra bacon on fresh crusty kaiser rolls from an excellent deli and bakery I frequented.

Viceroy and I ate a surprisingly companionable breakfast, and now we were both settled. Me with my laptop and a cup of linden tea with honey, and Viceroy on the windowsill in the living room. With a full belly, he was content on his windowsill, watching the people flow beneath him. He didn't seem to be listening in, for which I was grateful. The chair and blanket I had placed under the sill—his idea, not mine—looked dreadfully out of place, but I had to admit I was happy to have him play guard dog.

I sipped my tea, my teeth chattering against the edge of the cup. Breakfast had been a good distraction from overwhelming panic, but now that I had nothing to do but sit and sip, dread was setting in. Lauren was dead. Bob wanted Viceroy, and it was only a matter of time until he realized I had him, grabbed us both, and subjected us to endless rounds of agonizing testing to discover how the two of us were even possible.

I shuddered. I needed to warn Gracie before he found her and tortured her for information. I had tried to call her again this morning, but she'd hung up on me twice. If I wanted to talk to her, and I did, I'd have to drive to fucking Port Chester. And I'd have to bring Viceroy along to convince her to listen to me.

That made me realize that leaving the little beast alone all day while I ran around like a lunatic trying to run too many errands would have him using every chair leg and Persian carpet in the loft for his unmentionable needs, just to spite me. And it was looking like I couldn't tap Michael for that task, as he didn't seem to want to talk to me. Frankly, I couldn't blame him.

First, I needed dog-care things, and we had nothing for dinner tonight. If we lived long enough to eat dinner. I sighed.

"Are you okay, Felix?" Viceroy thought from across the room.

"How could I be? My life is in ruins, I could die, painfully, and as a bonus, I have a sore throat."

"And?"

"And," I snarled, "this is all just too fucked up and I don't know where to start."

"You're not the only one up shit creek without a paddle. Me and Gracie are in as much trouble as you."

I glared at him. "Clearly. I never said you weren't." He eyed me and turned back to the window.

I pinched the bridge of my nose in the hopes of preventing a sinus headache and broke into a shout. "SINUS!"

Viceroy whipped around. "Sinus? What the heck is sinus?"

"SINUS is the Supernatural Inter-Species Unification Guild," I said as Viceroy wrinkled his nose. "Exactly, it's a rather unfortunate acronym. But terrible name aside, there are benefits to being up to date on one's dues—library access and the ability to consult an expert in a particular lore being two of them."

Viceroy's ears shot up. "Oh. Okay, let's go!"

"No. I go alone. You're staying here."

Viceroy jumped from the sill to the chair to the floor and trotted over to stare up at me. "No way. Where you go, I go."

"You have to stay here. No dogs allowed."

"I'm not just some dog. I'm a vampire. Vampires can go in, can't they?"

My headache erupted, flashing across my face like wildfire. "How about this. I'm going to take something for the headache you gave me, then you and I will go to the dog store together first. Then, we'll come back here with our purchases, and you will wait for me while I go to SINUS and the grocery store. Then we'll both go and find Gracie. This way, you'll also have another walk, and I'm sure the dog store has treats. You'll have a car ride, and you'll see Gracie."

"First, it's not my fault you have a headache. You think too much. That's a personal problem. Second, does the dog store have squirrels?" he asked in all seriousness.

Thirty minutes later, we were at the dog store, and $415.78 after that, we were back home. "I'll give you this," I thought at Viceroy while we made our way through my lobby, "you have expensive taste for a dust mop."

Viceroy sniffed and jumped out of the tote to sashay around the large service desk as if he thought Willem might be hiding behind it. But the lobby was empty. Odd, as there were usually two doormen on duty. I was hoping one of them might take Viceroy—who was now smartly tricked out in a red plaid wool coat and a black leather harness, his choices—and all the packages up to the loft, freeing me to hurry over to the SINUS library before it closed for lunch. No such luck.

We were waiting for the elevator when a girl wearing a hoodie pushed through the lobby doors. The elevator doors slid open, and I practically fell inside, yanking a yipping Viceroy into the car as the doors slid shut. My heart pounded against my rib cage. It was the same girl who had been at Barneys and Whole Foods. She was following me. And Viceroy knew her.

Upstairs, I dumped the packages inside the door and picked him up. Stalking to the kitchen counter, I plopped him down.

"Okay, who the hell is she?"

"I don't know who she is." He was practically vibrating. "But I know what she is. She's a reaper."

"A reaper? That doesn't make sense." I leaned down so we were eye to eye. "Reapers can't collect vampire souls because vampires have no souls. And they don't reap half-vampires, either, because we technically belong to our sponsors." I swallowed hard. Without a sponsor, I was fair game.

Viceroy sighed. "Someone owns you? Wait—don't tell me. I don't wanna know." He shook his head. "I got no clue why she would be following you, Felix, but we love reapers. When they can, they take us before the worst of our pain. It's a great kindness." He narrowed his eyes, and the sound of his thoughts descended a full octave. "You can't hurt her."

"Hurt her? She could reap me! And anyway, I couldn't hurt her if I wanted to—which I don't. She's already dead. Killing the body she's animating only means she moves to another body. But I need to find out why she's following me." I removed Viceroy's harness and coat and carried him to his window perch—the girl was nowhere in sight.

The intercom chimed while we searched the street. I sprinted to the door and punched the button on the intercom. "What?"

"Mr. Belloquot, there's a girl here who wants to talk to you," Willem said, reverence in his voice.

"No, I don't want—"

"Felix. We've never met, but—"

I disconnected. It chimed again.

Viceroy materialized at my feet. "Talk to her! Let her in!" He was trembling again. "I want to see her!" Now he was bouncing up and down on all fours. How the hell was he doing that?

"No. I don't want to talk to her."

"Answer, answer, answer!" he shouted into my head. "SHE WON'T HURT US!"

"Okay, *okay*. Just please, SHUT UP!" I shouted.

He sat immediately, ears down, the very image of ashamed, but his wiggling back end and tail gave him away.

Still, I hesitated. All a reaper had to do was touch you—she could have reaped me on the street if that was her intent. I pressed the button to talk and told Willem to send her up.

"Felix, please. Let me in. We need to talk," the girl said.

Seconds later, the elevator door slid open, revealing the girl in the nasty hoodie.

"Well, you may as well come in," I said.

Viceroy and I moved backward in lockstep, and the girl stepped inside. We all three stared at each other until Viceroy broke the silence.

"Hey, can you hear me? My name is Viceroy!" he directed this at her, tail wagging, a big sloppy grin on his face.

The girl crouched down and pushed her hoodie back, revealing long black hair with rich purple tips caught in a thick ponytail. She was older than I thought at first. She stretched out a hand to Viceroy, and he flew at her, knocking her onto her ass.

She laughed un-self-consciously. "Yes, Viceroy, I can hear you," she said, looking up at me. Her face clouded, then cleared. She folded her legs beneath her and drew Viceroy into her arms, burying her face in his expensively shampooed fur. "Penhaligon?"

"Opus 1870. I have it blended into an organic shampoo."

"Levantium is my fragrance of late, though I have loved most of the Penhaligon line at one time or another."

Levantium? On a street urchin?

I stepped closer. The complex notes of the reaper's chosen fragrance rose from her in faint tendrils. Amber and oud. Rose. Cardamon and violet. The headnotes were soft, but a hint of saffron was still strong. I shook myself. Something about her was wrong.

She watched me over Viceroy's belly. He had flipped himself over onto his back to give her access to his abdomen.

"All right. That's enough chitchat. Who are you, and why are you following me?"

She stood up, leaving Viceroy panting for more. "My name is Lucy. Perhaps we might sit." She rubbed her hands together. "Do you have anything hot? Maybe tea or coffee? I'm a bit chilled."

I stared at the reaper, who looked nothing like Gracie, but the way she stood there, unafraid, raised visions of Gracie in her boyfriend's attic apartment, the terrible tea she had served me, the mall, the tears she fought so hard to keep inside.

"I do," I said and wheeled about to go to the kitchen, the reaper trailing me, Viceroy at her heels. I filled the kettle and tapped the lever.

"And perhaps something stronger too? I'm afraid you're going to need it."

"Hold that thought," I said. Without turning my back, I grabbed my phone, scrolled through recently dialed numbers, and called her. Oddly, this time she didn't hang up, and I explained why, for her own safety, she needed to join Viceroy and me at my loft.

20

Lucy

"What kind of tea would you like, Lucy?" Felix asked. Having finished his phone call, he opened a cabinet to display an impressive collection of teas. After brewing our selections, we sat. I fiddled with stirring honey into my cup as he watched me over the rising steam for a long minute.

"Okay, I've been as polite as can be expected given the circumstances. Who the hell are you, why the hell have you been following me, and what are you doing here? It wouldn't have anything to do with Vampire Bob, now, would it?"

"Who is Vampire Bob?" I asked.

"His real name is Robert Jameson," Felix snapped.

"I've never met a Robert Jameson," I answered evenly, carefully shielding my thoughts from Viceroy.

He knew. Not about why I'd been following him, or he would never have let me in. I glanced down at Viceroy, who was busy self-petting by rubbing his entire body along my leg before making a U-turn to continue rubbing with his other side. I reached down and stroked his head. He didn't pause but wagged his tail.

"How long have you had him?" I stalled. For the first time in too many years to remember, I was in unfamiliar territory. Deathy had asked me to break a centuries-old agreement between reaper and vampire. And despite everything I thought I understood about the nonexistence of good and evil, right or wrong, reaping Felix would be murder.

"I saw you at Whole Foods, and before that, at Barneys. How long have you been following me?"

"A few days."

Another problem. Felix recognized and remembered me. Reapers were mutable, not memorable. We appeared differently each time to those who could see us, and they forgot us immediately afterward. Only indomitable spirits—highly evolved, enlightened souls who perceived reality unfiltered—could remember us. And the indomitable were immune to vampirism, so why did Felix remember me?

Three drinks into my argument with Deathy about the claim written on the card, she had explained that she was doing an old friend a favor. She claimed that Robert Jameson had learned about the creation of a vampire dog named Viceroy. And that Felix Belloquot, a half-blood, had somehow managed to turn him. It was a historical first, and Jameson wanted to learn how it had happened. So I was to find Felix, watch him, and determine whether or not I could bring them both in alive. If not, I was to reap Felix and collect Viceroy.

In the face of Deathy's clearly dwindling sanity, I hadn't had the nerve to ask what she was getting in return. I'd only managed to escape the Twilight Zone meal by promising to consider her repugnant task. But I'd spent the week since I'd watched her nearly de-soul an entire restaurant full of people, wondering why I hadn't seen the signs of her decline earlier.

I had followed Felix, almost on autopilot, while trying to figure out what to do about Deathy. I hadn't planned on finding Viceroy being not only loveable and adorable, but conversational. I sighed. There was no way I was going to subject him to whatever Jameson had planned. And I certainly hadn't expected to feel any empathy toward a half-blood vampire.

But sitting at Felix's kitchen counter, I knew I had to tell them everything.

Felix wiggled his eyebrows at me, waiting for an answer. I inhaled slowly. Now or never. *Why had Felix let me in?* My control over my thoughts must have slipped because Viceroy jumped up, leaning his front paws on my leg.

"Because of me. I told Felix you were okay. You help animals," he thought at me. "We love you guys." He gave me a doggy grin, and my heart skipped a beat. "I'm right, right? You won't hurt us." I stroked his head when he abruptly let out a sharp whimper, sitting to lick at a paw.

Felix practically fell off his stool to crouch down to the shaggy little creature on the floor, and my heart clenched. Telling them what was coming for them wasn't enough. I needed to help them. My insane boss be damned.

I crouched down alongside Felix to look at Viceroy's paw. One pad was red and slightly swollen. It looked like an infection. I looked down into his soft brown eyes. "No, Viceroy, I will never hurt you. Either of—"

"This needs medical attention," Felix cut me off. "We need a vet."

I left the rest unsaid. No one else would hurt them either.

"I know someone we can call." My next-door neighbor was a vet at Gotham Veterinary Center on the Upper West Side. "She'll see us without an appointment." I pulled out my phone and googled the address.

Fifteen minutes later, we bumped uptown in a cab with Viceroy tucked into a large leather tote bag between us on the seat.

Felix gave me a side-eye. "Don't think this means you're off the hook."

"I'll tell you everything, just not here and now," I said.

The cab driver glanced at us in the rearview mirror. "It's

gonna be a while. Traffic is bad," he offered. "I ain't listenin'. Go ahead, tell him."

"Thank you for the offer, but the story can wait," I said to his reflection.

His face fell. Stories were the entertainment currency of cab drivers, and I was cheating him out of a big juicy urban legend. He turned on the radio in retribution, and we rode the rest of the way to an oldies station, each staring out our respective windows, caught up in our misgivings.

21

Gracie

My building was being fumigated, so come Monday, I was still at my mom's. She'd invited Sylvie to sleep over until the smell dissipated, but Sylvie said she had a place to go. I suspected she meant Manny's. My mother was babysitting at Auggie and Alicia's for the day, so I had the house to myself. I should have worked on my new Swiss meringue recipe, but I couldn't summon the focus. I watched movies instead, trying to distract myself from what Felix had told me at the food court, and I fell asleep on the sofa during *Fried Green Tomatoes*.

In my dream, I looked out of a high window to see Felix striding across a lawn, stopping just under my window.

"Don't worry, Grace, we're going to rescue you. Leave the room!" he called to me through cupped hands.

"Rescue me from what?" I said.

"Look behind you!" Felix yelled.

I turned to find a bedroom full of fancy furniture. Someone was opening the door.

"Felix! Someone's coming!"

"Leave the room, Grace. You have to get out."

"Felix, help me!"

But Felix didn't answer; he started whistling.

Why was he calling me Grace? And what was the song? I knew it.

"Come on, Grace, you know what to do. Get moving!" Felix yelled again and whistled louder. He raised his hand and beckoned to me as I identified the song: "Stuck in the Middle with You."

I woke up with a jerk—my phone was ringing. Still groggy, I answered just as my mother unlocked the front door.

"Hello," I mumbled.

"Gracie, please don't hang up! If you can't talk, just listen," Felix said.

I glanced up, waving to my mother as she hung her coat in the closet and slipped off her boots. "Hi, Rachel, what's up? Is game night still on?"

"Rachel? Oh, you aren't alone. Listen, I'm sorry to have to tell you this over the phone, but Lauren is dead, and I have every reason to believe that the people who killed her will come after you next."

"*What?*" I croaked. "So, no game night?" I managed. "Oh, that's too bad. But he's okay?" I added for my mother's benefit. There was no way she wasn't listening.

"Viceroy is with me, and he's fine. I don't think the vampires who killed Lauren know where you live, so I believe your mother is safe."

"And you think that because . . .?" I whispered.

"Because you'd be dead or worse already. I'll text you my address. Take an Uber, so you don't have to look for parking. I'll pay you back for it. Gracie, do you hear me? You must come now."

"Yeah, sure, I can go with you." I raised my voice as my mother stuck her head around the corner. "It's Rachel's brother. He fractured his leg. I'm meeting them at the hospital in Stamford."

"Gracie, are you listening? Straight into an Uber." Felix hung up.

Twenty minutes later, after answering all of my mother's questions with lies, I had changed clothes and was waiting at the door for my Uber—my mother still protesting.

It was a good thing I had six tablets of the pink stuff in my new bag because if I wasn't sick yesterday, I was full-on bilious now. I texted Felix.

Me: *On my way. In Uber*

Felix: *ETA?*

Me: *Driver says just over an hr*

Felix: *Ask for me at desk*

I sat in the Uber with my eyes closed, thinking about Lauren. While the money had been the reason I had taken the job, my fondness for Viceroy and her love for him were the reasons I hadn't quit. Or were they? I'd been so desperate to gain my independence and prove myself to my family and Bryan that I had gotten myself into this mess. Maybe they were right. Maybe I couldn't be trusted to take care of myself.

I opened my eyes and stared blankly out of the window until my phone rang. "Kiss Me." It was Bryan. Oh crap. I'd left food and a teacup out at his apartment. I let another few notes play while I took a deep breath.

"Hi! Is your surgery over?" Crickets. "Bry?"

"Yeah, I'm here. I just made it home. Where are you?"

"Stamford Hospital."

"What happened? Are you okay?"

"I'm fine. I'm here for a friend. I'm so sorry. I went to the mall to replace my ruined Nikes, and . . ." My face fevered, and my eyes filled as I repeated the same lies I had told my mother. "Then I came to Stamford Hospital from my mom's. I had to fight her tooth and nail to get out of the house."

He laughed out loud. "That's the mother I know and love." The tension dissipated, at least on his end. Bryan's life of abandoned meals, sleep deprivation, and insane schedules meant he wasn't judgmental about most of my crazy. "Well, just as long as everything is okay." He yawned. "How's your stomach now?"

I grinned into the phone in relief. This much, at least, would be true. "Fine. Mom dosed me with enough Pepto and worm-killing tea to kill a plague. You sound exhausted—you should sleep. You can tell me about the surgery tomorrow."

"Worm-killing tea, huh?" He chuckled. "The surgery took longer than planned, but the patient is doing well. I have early rounds, and I'm scheduled for another surgery after, so I probably won't call you until tomorrow night. I'm passing out now."

"Okay, have fun tomorrow. I love you."

"You bet, and take care of your friend. Love you too." He hung up as we hit a traffic jam.

22

Felix

In my anxiety about going up to the vet to have Viceroy's foot examined, I had utterly forgotten Gracie was Ubering to my loft. She texted again while we were still uptown to say that traffic was bad and she'd be delayed by half an hour. Once Viceroy's exam was complete, I rushed us all out of the vet's office, throwing cash at the desk on my way out and yelling at the receptionist to bill me for the rest. Magically, we managed to hail a cab almost immediately. But the worse-than-usual traffic had snagged us as well, and we missed her by five fucking minutes.

Four of us—me, Lucy, Viceroy, and Willem the doorman—stood in my lobby, staring at each other. Or rather, Willem stared at his hands while Lucy stared at me, and Viceroy glared at the ceiling, muttering a stream of curses, some of which I had never heard.

Willem had explained that Gracie had arrived, asking for me, as he was talking to a man about a misdelivered package. He'd told her I'd gone out but should be back soon if she wanted to wait. He heard the two talking while he went to search the package room, coming out to see Gracie and the man step into the street. Assuming they knew each other, he'd thought nothing of it.

I assured a doleful Willem yet again, out loud, that he was not at fault. Viceroy, on the other hand, wasn't letting my other-worldly doorman off the hook so easily. I listened to Viceroy's side of the mental back-and-forth for a minute, finally cutting in after the little ass claimed that someone of Willem's persuasion should have smelled trouble.

"It's not Willem's fault; it's mine, Viceroy. I could have called him and told him to let Gracie into the loft, but it didn't even occur to me that she'd be snatched right from the lobby. It's all my fault."

I apologized for Viceroy's behavior and language to a slump-shouldered Willem and took Lucy's arm. "There's nothing more we can do down here. We'll figure out what to do upstairs."

She nodded. She had remained silent, not knowing Gracie or of my call to her, or why Viceroy and I were so upset.

Once inside the loft, Viceroy jumped out of the tote bag, landing neatly and painlessly on his injured foot. "Hey, my foot doesn't hurt anymore!"

"Who is Gracie?" Lucy asked simultaneously.

I looked between them, deciding to address Viceroy first because the Gracie explanation would take longer. I held up my index finger to Lucy. She nodded assent and took a knee, lifting Viceroy's paw in her hands.

"It doesn't hurt at all!" he chortled. Seeming to forget his anger over Gracie's abduction, he thumped his tail in jubilation. Lucy picked at the tape the vet had applied and unwound the gauze.

"Lie down, little guy," Lucy said, "so that we can see underneath."

Viceroy flipped sideways and extended his leg. We both leaned in to peer at a nonexistent wound. Fresh, pink, perfectly smooth skin lay beneath the ointment. The swelling, pus, and incision from where the vet had extracted the bit of thorn I had missed had healed over.

"Well, I'll be damned. You *are* vampire. Thorns must be

considered wood, which in a vampire, prevents healing." I sighed and stood up.

Viceroy danced around in a circle, stopping abruptly to look up at us. "What are we going to do about Gracie, Felix? Gracie, remember? We need to go get her!" The last bit came across as a low growl.

"I know, I know. But I have no idea where she is." I slumped onto the sofa, still in my coat, scarf, and hat.

"Who is Gracie?" Lucy said.

"She's my companion," Viceroy thought. "And we need to rescue her. I told Felix this could happen, but he didn't listen to me." The little shit glared at me.

"I did listen to you! I called her! She came! What the hell else was I supposed to do?"

Viceroy let out a low grumble.

"That's enough. Fighting isn't going to help, but maybe I can," Lucy said, stepping between us.

"I'm not fighting, that was my stomach." Viceroy lifted an eyebrow.

"How can you think of food?" I leaned around Lucy to frown at him.

"I'm a dog, it's one of the only things I think about."

"Can we eat while we talk?" Lucy asked.

Viceroy gazed at her, avoiding my side-eye. "Steak. That's what I eat. And squirrels."

"Don't listen to him. Like me, he can eat anything. He probably needs the occasional blood meal to remain healthy, but he can eat."

"Quit talking about me like I'm not here," Viceroy grumbled.

Lucy grinned. "Fine, little man. Steak it is." She raised her eyebrows as the little beast practically somersaulted.

"I'm out. I didn't make it to the market—I've been a little busy."

She ignored my snide tone. "No worries. I'll run to Pino's. Is there anything else? I can stop at another store."

I stared at her. She was being entirely too helpful for someone we didn't know. "Why are you helping us?" I blurted.

Lucy stared at me for a long minute. "I can't answer that, Felix, other than to say it feels right. Whoever this Gracie is, she probably doesn't deserve"—she glanced at Viceroy—"whatever you think is going to happen to her."

Viceroy yipped to get my attention. "Lucy is helping us because she's good, Felix. Don't you know a good person when you see one?"

That was the problem: I didn't. I hadn't grown up with very many "good" people, and while I had a couple of friends whom I trusted not to knife me when I turned my back, I wouldn't rank them head and shoulders above the general population on the good/evil scale. And Lucy looked more like a pickpocket than a resourceful and trustworthy woman of any means whatsoever. So, no, I didn't know a good person when I saw one, and I had no reason to believe Lucy was one.

"She called a vet for me," Viceroy thought. "And I'm sorry your life is so sad, Felix," the little rat added.

"Stop trespassing in my head," I muttered at Viceroy, jumping off the sofa to pace back and forth, stopping directly in front of Lucy. "Is the dog right?"

"In a nutshell," Lucy said.

I paced back and forth a few more times while they both watched me. "I don't know you," I said to her, "and you still haven't explained what you're doing here."

"And you still haven't told me how Viceroy's companion is involved in all this."

"And I'm not telling you another thing until you explain yourself, and I know whether or not to trust you with the information."

She sighed. "Let me get the steak for Viceroy, and then we can sit down and tell each other everything. And I'll go first, okay?"

Viceroy thumped his tail hard in agreement, but I knew there was a reason she hadn't just spit it out. Complicated stories take longer to tell, and most of them, at least in my experience, had unhappy endings. The thing was, I didn't have anyone else to call for help with Vampire Bob. So it was Lucy or nobody.

"Yep," Viceroy thought at me. "That's pretty much it in a nutshell. I just learned that line from Lucy. I like it."

"Shut up," I hissed at him. "Fine," I said to Lucy. "Get the steak. Then you're talking."

"Sounds like a plan," she said with a feeble smile.

The loft felt oddly empty after her departure. It was almost like she had taken my slim hope of getting through this alive with her. I shook myself and stalked to the bar cabinet. No matter, I had a cure for that. Bourbon was the cure for everything.

23

Gracie

I never made it up to Felix's loft. The minute the doorman left the desk, the man he had been talking to came to sit next to me. I slid sideways, and he slid right along with me. Before I could get up and say something nasty, he explained that if I valued my life, as well as Felix's and Viceroy's, I should accompany him to his car. His argument was compelling.

My hair standing on end, I slipped my hand into the crook of his proffered arm and, nerves screaming, walked out of the lobby with him. The car was less than a block away, and once inside, I was wedged in the backseat between two very large men. Two more sat in the front seat.

"So, my guess is we're not going for ice cream?"

The man behind the wheel snorted, and the one in the front passenger seat hissed at him. *Like a snake*! I was in way over my head.

I gritted my teeth and resisted the urge to scream and kick. There was no point. There were four of them, and I was small, unarmed, and struggling to keep from hyperventilating. I'd never even taken a single martial arts class. Who in their right mind wants to get hit for fun? But now I was rethinking that decision. If I ever got out of this, I'd sign up for Krav Maga.

"No, though we do have ice cream at the house, and if you behave nicely, I'll get you some," my kidnapper said.

"Why me?" I asked, struggling for composure but failing miserably.

"Because you may be able to lead us to the dog." He kept talking about Viceroy and what a special dog he was and how I'd be helping everyone if I told them where he was. Though he was ordinary looking, his gray eyes seemed to glow as he stared into mine. His voice was low and hypnotic. He was trying to glamour me! Once again, I knew about glamouring from the Sookie Stackhouse books.

And it wasn't working.

My thoughts churned. It would probably be better for me if he thought his glamour was working, so I forced my shoulders, which had been up around my ears, down and sank back in the seat. He smiled, lips stretching a little too wide.

"Good. Now that that's settled, we're going to go for a little ride." The car pulled into traffic, and I felt the monster squad relax. I played along. I might have been close to peeing my pants in fear, but I wasn't stupid. We drove for what felt like hours, but that was probably because I spent the entire ride trying not to tremble. The car finally slowed, winding through a few streets in Riverdale before turning into a drive blocked by a high iron fence.

The driver lowered his window and tapped a few numbers into the keypad. The gates swung open, and we drove through, crunching across fresh gravel before parking in front of a gorgeous house. My kidnapper led me inside, up a broad set of carpeted stairs and down a long hallway lined with nearly identical doors. Stopping in front of a door near the end, he tapped another keypad and opened the door, motioning me inside. I walked past him into . . .

Wait. I was in the bedroom from my dream.

My head buzzed as I staggered sideways. My kidnapper reached an arm out to steady me, but I snapped myself out of my shock before he could touch me.

"You'll find everything you need here. Someone will send up a tray with dinner. Do you have any food allergies or particular dislikes?"

Confused by the familiarity of the room, I stared at him before remembering I was supposed to be glamoured and softened my expression.

"I eat pretty much everything." I added a smile for effect.

"Good. We have an excellent chef. If you need anything"—he indicated a phone next to the bed—"just call. The phone only calls inside the house. You will reach housekeeping. The sooner you tell us where the dog is, the sooner you go home."

I must have frowned. His smile evaporated, and his eyes flashed. He was in my face before I could blink. I stumbled backward, sandwiched between him and the bed.

"Hmmm." He leaned so close I could smell his breath, peering into my eyes before stepping back to examine me as if I were a morsel of meat. "Interesting. You're not compliant. Well, well, well, it looks like we've gotten more than we bargained for." The smile was back but broader, stretching his face unnaturally.

A shudder shook my body and rose into my mouth to set my teeth chattering. I clamped them together for a heartbeat before opening my idiot mouth.

"You really should get some breath mints. It's much easier to make friends with fresh breath," I said.

He barked a short, humorless laugh. "My dinner never seems to be overly concerned by my breath before it dies," he said, running a finger down the side of my neck before stepping back. I scrambled up onto the bed to put some distance between us. "Listen, sweetie, I'm not going to eat you. We just want the dog. Tell us where he is. If you don't, we won't be able to trade you for him."

He examined a cufflink, the brittle smile fading. "On the other hand, we could just convince you to talk and then keep you. Your indomitable blood will help us with our research. Won't that be fun?" His face stretched into the creepy smile again, and he glided toward the door, barely moving his feet.

"Wait. I don't have indomitable blood. I'm AB Positive."

He shouted a real laugh. "Well, isn't that delightful? Indomitable *and* delightful. You're a prize all by yourself."

I watched his face, which, when he didn't show all his teeth, was just average. He didn't look anything like the spawn of Satan.

"Are you in charge here?" I blurted and promptly bit my tongue. *Let him go, Gracie!*

"Enjoy your stay," he said, leering at me before the lock clicked shut behind him.

I rushed over and yanked at the knob—a reflex—leaning my feverish forehead against the cool wood when it didn't open. I turned to look around. The room would be gorgeous if it weren't a prison. It had expensive dark-wood furniture, ivory walls that looked like the kind of plaster I'd seen in Italy, and the same blue-and-white jar lamps one of my sisters-in-law had. But why had I dreamed of this room?

I walked to the bathroom to find an enormous shower, a deep tub, and recessed lighting. The sink counter held top-shelf supplies, though there was no hair dryer, razor, or anything I might use to injure myself or use as a weapon. Back in the bedroom, two windows overlooked a back lawn and garden. The same lawn where Felix had been in my dream. The glass was thick, the latches fitted with a keyed lock.

They had kept my bag. Without a phone, I couldn't call my mother. I couldn't call Bryan. I stalked to the bed and reached for the phone. It began to ring as soon as I picked it up. Dropping the receiver back into the cradle, I leaned over, giving in to a tearing panic.

24

Lucy

I stepped into the elevator, slumping against the back wall the second the doors closed, and massaging my temples. Gracie was deeply involved and in grave danger, judging by Felix's fear and Viceroy's anger. The elevator stopped, and a tall, thin couple with an equally tall, thin borzoi got on. The dog immediately buried its face in my crotch, tail thumping.

"Oh my," the woman sputtered, pulling the dog back. "I'm so sorry! She never does that. She doesn't like anyone!"

"Please, don't worry. Animals love me. It happens all the time." I took the dog's long face between my hands and whispered, "Live a long and healthy life, beautiful girl." I leaned over to kiss her forehead as the elevator doors slid open, stepping out as the tall couple hung back, staring at me. "Have a good evening," I called to them as I hurried through the lobby to the street.

New York, lovely during Christmas and beautiful in the spring, was spectacular in the fall. After enduring a miserable summer of garbage strikes and brownouts, the crisp, clear air was a relief. People had a sense of purpose. Reanimated and remembering why they loved their city, they strode instead of trudged.

I stopped at the corner of Prince and Broadway, waiting for the light to change, when I felt a liquid cold sluice through my veins—a full-blood vampire was too close. Without turning my head, I opened myself to the emanations of the surrounding people. Nope, nope, nope, nope . . . bingo.

In my peripheral vision, I saw him. He stood to my left, separated from me by two teenage girls giggling over a phone screen. He smiled and nodded as I turned toward him. The light changed, and the crowd at the corner streamed between us and across the street, leaving us face-to-face.

He was far from my first vampire encounter. I'd come across many of them over the years. Without exception, being devoid of souls, they were all savages—however cultured, educated, and elegantly dressed they might appear—killing not only for sustenance but for sport. The vampire continued to watch my face as people brushed past us, hurrying to cross the street before the light changed again. I stepped into the flow.

"If you'll excuse me, I have some shopping to do," I said over my shoulder, only to find him right beside me, his arm brushing mine.

I wasn't afraid. There was no way for him to kill me, as I wasn't alive in the traditional sense of the word. He could drain my body, but drinking its blood would make him ill, as it was technically dead. He could snap my neck, but no harm would come to my spirit, and while it might take a few days, I would move into another body. If he was as old as I suspected from the degree of cold I was feeling, he knew this as well as I did.

I strode down Prince toward Pino's on Sullivan, the vampire at my shoulder. People parted as we approached, stepping into doorways or the street to make way for us. We reached the meat market in record time.

I put out a hand. "Please stop here. Whatever it is you want or need, I cannot help you."

He took my wrist in a gesture too fast to comprehend. "Oh, but I think you can, my dear lady. I have someone your friend Felix desperately wants back. I have Gracie."

I froze. "And you are?"

"Robert Jameson at your service, madam." He swept into a bow, grinning at me as he descended. Vampire Bob.

"I am very sorry to disappoint you, sir, but I do not know anyone by that name. Now please, allow me to continue on my way." I tugged my trapped wrist.

Still holding me firmly, Bob stepped back, away from the doors. I followed as if we were slow dancing. He narrowed his eyes and laughed aloud.

"Well, how interesting. I believe you are telling the truth. So Felix hasn't told you. Well, no matter. The messenger does not need to understand the message to deliver it properly." He released my wrist, and I stuck my hand into my coat pocket to keep from rubbing it to restore circulation. "So you will do this for me. You will purchase your food, go back to Felix's, and tell him that I have Gracie. Then you will explain that I will trade her, safe and unharmed, for him and the dog."

I said nothing.

"And you can oversee the exchange. You can be the . . . What do they call it in spy movies? You can be the handler. The handler in a situation about which you know nothing. How delightful!" He clapped his hands together like a child opening a birthday present.

"And if I refuse?"

"I will kill the girl, draining her to near death first, then I will take her on a scenic drive to my meat-processing plant in Queens, where she will *meat* her end while still aware enough to enjoy the process." He chuckled. "I made a joke. See what I did there? Meat her en—"

"I get it," I snapped, stepping backward.

"And then I will acquire Felix and the dog myself. And you will not regain your humanity this year, or ever. Though, frankly, I have no idea why you would want to become little more than vampire food in the first place." He picked a speck from the sleeve of his expensive overcoat. "Your chances of becoming human improve dramatically if you agree to help me."

I stared at him, revolted.

"Don't you see? It's so much easier my way. No one is hurt." He tilted his head. "Well, except for the dog just a bit, and Felix. That sniveling moron needs to die when I am finished with him."

So it was true. I had hoped Deathy was lying about, or at least exaggerating, her relationship with this vampire. But he'd just confirmed everything she'd said. My bones ached, and I shivered, both from a flood of foreboding threatening to drown me on dry land and from Jameson's coldness seeping into my bones. I needed to get out of his presence, but curiosity won.

"Why on earth do you need me? Why not just collect them yourself?"

Jameson trailed a finger down my arm. "Where's the fun in that? Food isn't worth eating unless you get to play with it first," he murmured. "Too bad I can't play with you."

I shrank back.

"I'll deliver your message. Is there anything else?" I said through teeth clenched against the cold of his touch.

"He has twenty-four hours, until six thirty tomorrow evening." He handed me a card bearing only an embossed phone number, bowed slightly, and strolled back up Broadway toward Houston. A lightly accented chuckle floated back to me on the evening breeze, fading as quickly as my good mood had when he'd first appeared.

I purchased a steak for Viceroy and worried my way back to Felix's door. He buzzed me in, freshly showered and shaved. Reaching for the bag, he frowned. "I wasn't hungry when you left, but I am now. Did you buy anything for us?"

"You won't want to eat when I tell you who I met downstairs." I handed him the card.

"Whose number is this, Lucy? Whose card is this?"

"It's Robert Jameson's."

Felix's face paled, and he let the card fall to the floor. I picked it up and held it out, but he spun on a heel and strode into the kitchen. I followed him, watching as he grilled Viceroy's steak with his back to me. Lifting Viceroy up onto the table, he cut the steak into chunks and served it to the little dog before settling himself at the other end.

"Okay, Lucy, start talking."

"He has Gracie, Felix. Which we figured. And he claims he'll trade her, unharmed, for you and Viceroy." I watched as a series of emotions flicked over his face, ending with fear.

"But why not just—"

"I asked him that, and . . . and got a nonsense answer. I don't know why he hasn't just collected you both himself."

"He tried to get me," Viceroy thought, "at Lauren's. But I hid."

I frowned. "What?"

"I'll explain in a minute," Felix said. "I don't think he knows Viceroy is here."

"Perhaps not. It would certainly explain why he didn't just enthrall his way in here and take you both himself."

Felix ran his hands through his hair and left the table. Returning with a bottle of bourbon and two glasses, he poured us both triples. "You still haven't told me your part in all of this," he said.

I drank my bourbon in one go and gently set the empty glass down. "Jameson is involved, somehow, with my boss, Deathy. They've made an agreement, and you and Viceroy are part of it. I was supposed to bring you both to Deathy. Viceroy alone if you refused to come."

Viceroy stopped eating to stare at me. "You were going to kill Felix and turn me over to Vampire Bob?" he thought.

"No, Viceroy, I never agreed to that."

"But you came here anyway?"

"At first, I just wanted to meet you two, to see what Deathy had gotten herself into. Then, after meeting you, I thought maybe I could help."

"Like I said, Felix, she's good." Viceroy, having apparently decided the subject was closed, turned back to his plate and care-fully selected another morsel of steak.

"So wait a minute. Death is after us?" Felix said.

"As far as I know, she's only sent me."

"Should that make me feel better?" He crossed his arms over his chest.

"Well, seeing as I'm the only reaper here, Bob said you have until tomorrow evening, and no one else is storming your eleva-tor, I think it's safe to assume you and Viceroy are safe for the time being."

Felix poured himself another double and tilted the bottle over my empty glass.

"No, I'd better not. This body is a lightweight." I wished I could. I'd almost rather be drunk in the street than sitting in Felix's loft, wondering how to help these two. I rolled the hem of my sweater between my fingers, briefly wondering how it appeared to Felix.

He stared at me and his eyebrow twitched. "Death is after us. Vampire Bob is after us. And since you're the only one who has offered to help, I guess you'll have to do," Felix said, pouring his double down his throat. It seemed to calm him.

"Felix, what does Gracie have to do with any of this? Aside from being Viceroy's companion, who is she?"

I listened while Felix spooled the entire story out, from his accidentally biting Viceroy to Gracie's involvement, Lauren's death, and Viceroy's appearance. Draining his glass, Felix ended with, "And for the life of me, I can't figure out why I care about what happens to Gracie Rinelli other than to keep myself out of Bob's clutches. As far as I can tell, she's just a random young woman who accidentally got herself involved in a mess far beyond her understanding or capability."

"So she just happened to take a job that may end up getting her—"

"Gracie is not going to die!" Viceroy thought. He walked

down the table to stand between us. "We're going to help her, right?" He licked my hand.

"Yes. We're going to help her," I said more confidently than I felt and scratched his ears.

"And we'd better get busy. Jameson said we have twenty-four hours before he—"

"Don't say it," Felix said. "I can't think about that." His head dropped onto the table, barely missing his empty glass.

"Felix!" I leaped up and ran to him, but he only lifted his head slightly to bang it onto the table again.

"Felix! Stop it!" I grabbed his shoulders and hauled him upright while Viceroy pressed his front paws against Felix's chest to make sure he remained upright. "I'm a reaper. I can pinpoint Gracie's exact location in our system. Then all we have to do is free her." Two heads swiveled in my direction.

"Then what are we waiting for?" Viceroy thought. "Let's go! Put me on the floor!"

I held a hand against Felix's chest and lowered Viceroy toward the floor until he could jump to the ground.

"I'm okay," Felix muttered. "How do we . . . Where do we have to go?"

"My house. I need my laptop. But you might want to put a cold cloth on your forehead first."

Felix got up, his forehead redder than the flush suffusing his cheeks. "And don't you dare tell anyone about . . ." He touched the red spot on his forehead. "I have a reputation to uphold."

I grinned at him. "Cross my heart and hope for cake," I said, crossing my heart with a finger.

He frowned at me. "Doesn't it go 'and hope to—'"

"Not when you're a reaper."

"Oh. I suppose that would be awkward in your circles."

Ten minutes later, we were on the way to my house. Felix was silent, and I spent the ride calculating our odds. Viceroy lay sound asleep in my lap, his rumbling snores the baseline to the rapid staccato of my beating heart.

25

Gracie

Exhausted, I'd crawled under the covers for lack of a place to hide, as the bathroom door had no lock. I must have fallen asleep. Now, I struggled out from under them, still fully dressed, with an urgent need to pee. I must have cried in my sleep because my eyes were pasted shut. I rubbed at them on my way to the bathroom.

A soft knocking at the door stopped me midway. The knob turned, and I lunged for the bed, expecting one of the goons who kidnapped me. Instead, a Talbot's model stepped inside, carrying a tray. I couldn't tell how old she was, but she was tall, thin, and blonde in that horsey New England way. The Talbot's woman crossed the room and set the tray on the table. Smiling at me, she set two places with silverware and sat, indicating that I should take the other chair. I didn't move.

"I won't hurt you," she said in a clear, soft voice. She had no accent, though that probably meant she was a New Yorker, and she just sounded normal to me. She beckoned to me again. "Please join me for dinner. The food here is excellent."

She lifted the lid on one of the dishes, and the aroma shot straight to my stomach, triggering a low growl—the traitor. I slipped from the bed, embarrassed that I still had shoes on, and eyed the food as she uncovered the second plate and set it at my place.

"Don't worry," she said, ignoring my feet. "They won't poison you. That would be counterproductive."

"Don't go anywhere. I have questions," I said, holding up a finger and sprinting for the bathroom.

Back at the table, I eyed her persistent smile. Not seeing any weird vampire grin in the making, I sighed and sat. She was just a woman sitting down to dinner, and I could probably take her in a pinch. Roast chicken, grilled Brussels sprouts and baby carrots, an open baked potato with a small pool of herbed butter in the center, and a small salad with a pretty Parker house roll lay before me. My stomach growled again, loud enough to hear.

I desperately wanted to dig in.

"Just so I have the basics, who are you, and why the hell am I here?" I asked in the tone my mother hated.

She flushed. "Oh, please forgive me. I'm Elaine, the mother of one of the residents of this house." She held out a hand, which I reluctantly shook. "And you are?"

I eyed her. "You don't know my name?"

"No one told me, though I do know a bit of your story. As for where we are, we are on Robert Jameson's estate in Riverdale."

Nothing new there. I knew we were in Riverdale, and I knew who Robert Jameson was from my conversation with Felix.

Elaine stared into her lap for a long moment. Then she looked up at me, and as if reading my mind, she said, "I can tell you because this house is a fortress. You, we, cannot escape."

"But—"

"Why? I believe you're here as the ransom for the first vampire dog, and as such, you are valuable."

There was no point in being rude. "My name is Grace Rinelli. Please call me Gracie. And I knew that part. What about you? Why are you here? Are you a Renfrew, a vampire's servant? Do you work for Jameson?"

Elaine flushed. "I'm here to protect my son."

"Your son?"

"Please forgive me, but I need to keep my strength up." She picked up her fork. "I'll explain while we eat."

Kidnapped or not, I was starving. I attacked the roast chicken first. Elaine was right; it was delicious. We ate in silence for a few minutes before she continued her story.

"My son, Ben, is ten. Last summer, a vampire bit him. He was in our front yard with friends when it happened. A Saturday night. It had just gotten dark; they were playing hide and seek." She shook her head, tears forming. "It was Ben's turn to hide. I guess he hid too well. By the time the other boys came to tell me they couldn't find him, it was too late." She cleared her throat and took a small forkful of potato. "I'm sorry, I still can't talk about it without crying."

I swallowed the lump that had formed in my throat. "Your son is a vampire?"

Elaine held up a hand. "Oh, no, Ben isn't a vampire. He didn't transform when the vampire who bit a kid for fun tried to turn him." She shivered at the memory. "We're here because they're trying to—" She broke off. "It's too complicated to explain in detail, but Ben has an indomitable spirit, which means, among other things, that he is immune to vampires."

I stared at her as she put a forkful of chicken in her mouth. "Indomitable spirit? Like a ghost?"

Elaine barked a laugh. "Oh, no, he's as alive as you and I. It's hard to explain without sounding crazy, but essentially, he was born with a type of enlightenment."

I sat back. "You believe in that? Enlightenment?" I asked, my food forgotten. I knew what it was from my class in comparative religion, but I had written it off as superstition.

"Oh, yes. It's real, and there are many forms of it. The indomitable spirit is only one."

I chewed the inside of my cheek, debating what to ask first. "And he's fine? He didn't get sick or die when he was bitten?"

"Yes. He's fine. He was barely aware of what happened to him, which was a blessing."

"Oh, well, that's good." Relieved for the little boy I'd never met, I took a sip of water. "Did you know? About his spirit? Before the vampire bit him?"

Elaine dabbed her lips with her napkin. "I did. Two angels visited me on the day he was born. At first, I thought it was a hallucination brought on by exhaustion. But when they didn't go away, no matter how many times I blinked or pressed the call button for the nurse, I let them talk. But despite everything they said, I still thought I was crazy. I even stopped going to church, thinking it would feed my delusion." She frowned. "As Ben got older, I couldn't keep denying that there was something different about him. The angels, if they were angels, were right. Ben was special."

"Special how, exactly?"

"It's hard to describe without sounding like I'm bragging." She shrugged. "He's inherently good, always trying to help everyone he comes across. He gave his brand-new cleats away to a classmate in need so the boy could play soccer too. He's been volunteering since he learned what the word meant. And he has lucid and prophetic dreams." She sighed. "Too many things to list. That's not to say that he's not an average child in every other respect. He's pretty clumsy and tells terrible jokes." Her face lit up.

"So does having this indomitable spirit thing mean vampires can't glamour Ben?"

"I think you mean enthrall. And yes, that's what it means. Ben is immune to all supernatural forms of enthrallment, which is why Mr. Jameson has imprisoned us here. Ben, because he has a special spirit, and me, well, because I serve multiple functions."

I gaped at her. "What the flying f—"

"Please, Gracie, don't pity me. If I'm honest, the vampires are not unkind, at least to us." She put another forkful of chicken in her mouth. Her animatronic expression of pleasure was straight out of *I, Robot*.

I shivered despite the warm room. "Elaine, should you be telling me all of this?"

"No, but I'm telling you because I think it will make you at least a little less afraid. I overheard one of the bodyguards whispering that you were immune to his enthrallment. Gracie, listen, I spent my first month here under a thrall. All humans are susceptible to the mental and emotional manipulation of supernatural beings—unless they possess an indomitable spirit."

"Wait, you think I have one? Is *everybody* crazy? First Lauren, now you." I shook my head at her quizzical expression. "If there was such a thing as an indomitable spirit, wouldn't we have learned about it in school? And if I had one, my mother would have told me."

But even as the words left my mouth, I knew they weren't true. My mother hovered over all of us, but me in particular, like a mother bear on crack. There was no way she would have told me I was different from other kids. That, and as a kid I had given my allowance away so often, my mother had started putting it into a bank account for me instead of handing me cash.

But so what? Everybody dreams, and lots of people have overprotective mothers, are generous, and do volunteer work, me included. Nope. I wasn't buying it. I didn't know Elaine from Adam, and I had no way of knowing just how far off her rocker she was. There was nothing special about me.

Elaine gave me a minute to think it through before continuing. "I didn't tell Ben until we were here and I had no choice. I didn't know how to tell him, or even if I should." She took another bite.

Watching her eat everything on her plate as I floundered around in my head, I suddenly realized what she'd meant by "keeping her strength up" and "multiple functions." The vampires in this house fed on her. I jumped from the table, knocking my chair over, barely making it to the toilet before I vomited my dinner. I retched twice more until my stomach was empty.

Elaine materialized at my side, holding a cold wet washcloth. I sat back onto the cool tiles and took the cloth from her, pressing it against my face. She held out a hand, but I ignored it, scrambling to my feet on my own. I flushed my dinner, rinsed my mouth at the sink, and blew my nose.

"Gracie, I know this is a lot to take in. You should lie down." She led me to the bed, pushing me onto the edge and kneeling to remove my shoes.

The room wobbled at the fringes of my vision while I looked down at her bent head. My mother had lied to me my whole life, and now a vampire's dinner was untying my shoes. Had she fed someone before eating with me?

Elaine stood and walked over to a large wardrobe, opening the doors and pulling out two drawers. "You'll find a nightshirt and other clothing in here. They gave me your approximate sizes, and I picked up a few things I thought might be comfortable."

I peered into the wardrobe. A *few* things? She'd bought me an entire wardrobe.

"How long am I going to be here?" I was meeting Bryan's mother for the first time tomorrow night! And I had an appointment to see what might be my new-to-me cake truck in New Haven. And Alicia's birthday party was on Friday. My head pounded, and my tailbone, forgotten until now, began to throb in time with my head.

"Oh, Gracie, I'm so sorry, but I have no idea. No one tells me more than I need to know to complete my tasks," Elaine said, her voice soft. "And I don't ask."

I bit back a retort. She couldn't or wouldn't tell me no matter what I said.

"Is there any Advil in here anywhere?" I asked as the room began to undulate faster.

"Yes. I'll get them for you." Elaine disappeared into the bathroom, reappearing with a small bottle. She brought my water glass from the table and handed it to me, shaking three tablets into my hand. I swallowed them and lay back on the pillows, shifting to relieve the pressure on my backside while Elaine placed our plates back on the tray. I thought of Felix, and the ceiling began to rotate.

"Elaine? What's going to happen to me?"

She opened her mouth, but I never heard her answer.

26

Felix

"Viceroy and I will wait here," I said to Lucy, ignoring the driver's glare.

"You should come inside. My house is the safest place in the city for both of you," Lucy said. "No one knows you're here."

Viceroy clambered off her lap to scratch at my overcoat.

"Stop that." I pushed his paws down and brushed at the scratch marks he'd left in the fabric.

"Let's go in. You heard Lucy: it's not safe out here. Come on, Felix." He bounced up and down on the seat.

I peered out the cab's window and up at the façade of the building, a well-appointed brownstone row house. Two perfectly trimmed boxwood shrubs in large urns flanked the foot of the steps. Lucy tapped her foot on the sticky floorboard and gathered Viceroy into her arms.

"Which apartment is yours?" I asked, still looking away from her and out the window.

"Apartment? The whole house is mine," Lucy said.

I spun back to her so fast I nearly gave myself whiplash. She opened her door, slid out, and walked around to open my door.

"Are you coming?"

"Wait, what? You own this whole house?" I tipped my head back, counting five floors. She lowered her voice to a whisper, though the driver was obsessing over the radio dial.

"I've been around a long time, Felix. I bought this house in 1855. Be safe inside, or take your chances outside. Up to you. But Viceroy is coming with me."

Well, death house of horrors or not, I certainly did not want to die on the sidewalk. And now I wanted to see the inside. If she owned this whole house, she must be rolling in it. And there just might be an opportunity to acquire something.

What was wrong with me? I chastised myself with a mental recitation of Bob's insults and got out. Lucy and Viceroy were at the door before I finished straightening my coat and adjusting my hat. I peered into the cab window as it pulled away from the curb. I did cut a dashing figure.

"Felix," Lucy called to me, holding the door open. Viceroy had already disappeared inside.

"Coming." Gulping down my uncertainty, I took the stairs at a clip and walked past her and into the house, stopping short in the foyer. The place was gorgeous. No, not gorgeous, stunning. A brilliantly polished hardwood floor, dark paneled walls, and an enormous mirror set the stage for a U-turn staircase that swept past a large backlit Tiffany window. The stairs, carpeted in a red Persian, led to a second-floor balcony, obviously fronting a hallway that faced away from the front door but directly toward the Tiffany window. All the woodwork was pristine.

"How did you . . . do you . . ." I stuttered.

Lucy unzipped her hoodie. "I made some very beneficial marriages along the way and a few even better investment decisions."

"Marriages? But how, you, who—"

Her laughter rang off the walls. "Reapers can marry, and we generally marry other reapers who are either still in service or just out. It's the only way it would work."

"But you're dressed like a—" I stopped short of insulting her clothing choices.

"Let me guess. I look like a squatter to you. Right? What am I wearing? A hoodie? Maybe I have piercings? Green hair?"

"Black and purple." I shrugged myself out of my coat, but instead of taking it, she slipped her hand into the crook of my elbow and led me to an enormous mirror. I stared at us and swayed, swept by vertigo. The hoodie-wearing urchin was gone. An elegant woman, impeccably dressed, stood in her place. I turned back to gaze at the person next to me—a waif with purple hair. I leaned forward to peer into the mirror again, but the same elegant woman looked back at me. She dropped my hand.

"A mirror's reflection filters your perception, so you see me as I am, not as your psyche directs. How I appear is personal to those who can perceive reapers."

"You're saying I needed to see you as a . . ." I was about to say homeless person, but her gaze intensified, so I stopped talking.

"Felix, most average people don't perceive us at all, much less remember us. I don't know why you can, or why you needed to see me in that particular way. That last part is between you and your psychiatrist," she said, her voice mild in contrast to her sharp gaze.

Viceroy chuffed.

"I don't have a psychiatrist," I exploded.

"You might want to find one," Viceroy thought, chuffing harder. He fell onto his side and rolled onto his back, sounding like he was having an asthma attack.

I forced myself to ignore him in favor of watching Lucy's graceful movements in the mirror as she hung our coats on a Victorian coat rack. "You're a dancer!"

"I'm a reaper. I am wearing the body of a dancer who lost it far too young." She paused, hands still on the coats. "You'd think, after centuries, I would be used to inhabiting the bodies of women who died before they lived," she said almost too softly to hear. "But it's never fair, and it never gets easier, and I am never at peace." When she finally turned to me, her face was flushed. "I'm sorry for oversharing. I shouldn't burden you—it's not your problem."

I agreed with her. I had plenty of problems of my own, and hers didn't seem to involve imminent death, so I changed the subject. "Viceroy. Where are you?" I called.

He trotted in from another room, something small and gray dangling from his mouth. Fuck! I hadn't even seen him leave the room. He laid the little carcass at Lucy's feet.

"Hey, thanks for the snack! That was nice," he thought at her and licked her boot, leaving a streak of blood. "Oh, sorry. Do you want me to hide it?"

"No," Lucy and I cried simultaneously.

"Leave it there. I'll get it." I scowled at him.

Lucy burst out laughing. "Don't fret, little man. You're more than welcome to eat all the snacks you can find, anytime you want. My house is your house." She reached down and scratched him behind an ear. Predictably, he melted.

Watching them, it hit me—Lucy was immortal, and for all I knew, Viceroy might very well be the full-blood dog vamp version of immortal. And I, at least in my current state, was neither. Lucy could provide what the pet store clerk had called a forever home, whereas I would eventually die, no matter how many snacks I consumed, unless I attained full-blood status. I might even die before I could pick up my dry cleaning if we failed in our attempt to get Gracie back without exchanging her for Viceroy and me.

"Felix, you're white as a sheet," Lucy said, interrupting my downward spiral. She took my arm and led me to the kitchen. She put on a kettle and opened a cabinet door to reveal mugs and a display box of teas. "Make us tea while I go and get my laptop," she said over her shoulder before disappearing.

Viceroy had trotted in behind us and plopped himself down next to the enormous and expensive Aga range. "I like it here," he thought. "Let's stay."

"Don't be ridiculous. You can't just move into someone's house uninvited," I said aloud.

"But Lucy said—"

"Lucy was being polite," I snapped, grabbing a handful of paper towels to retrieve the mouse. I dumped it into the trash bin under the sink before washing my hands and taking two mugs and a display box of tea down from the cabinet. I flipped one of the delicate blue and white porcelain mugs over to read the imprint. Royal Copenhagen. I studied the kitchen while I waited for the water to boil. Any chef would be at home here—everything was well used, so someone must cook.

"She wasn't being polite. She likes us. She'd let us move in." The dope quirked an eyebrow at me. "And who cares who cooks it? As long as it's good food! Hey, is there anything else to eat around here? I could go for—"

"You're exhausting, and you just ate, you little pig. I'm the one who's starving."

He flopped on the floor and glared at me as the water came to a boil. A heavenly aroma rose around my face as I poured water over the London Fog tea I had selected.

My stomach growled as Lucy entered the room carrying a slim gray laptop under her arm. She had changed from the cashmere twinset and pencil skirt she had been wearing into an oversized soft red sweater and jeans, shearling slippers on her feet. I stifled a whistle, expressing a loud sigh instead.

She smiled, her green eyes sparkling in the light from the kitchen window. "Oh. You're still seeing me as I am. Sometimes, a mirror sighting shifts your view permanently. That explains the leer." She gave me a side-eye, but the corners of her lips stayed up.

"I am not leering. I just . . ." I huffed, but she was gorgeous in that underfed model way.

She didn't press me but placed the laptop on the giant wooden table and walked to the refrigerator. "You're hungry. That, and seeing two different aspects of me is why you felt light-headed."

Pulling open a refrigerator door resembling nothing less than a solid steel slab, she took out a tray of ham followed by condiments, olives, and pickles. She opened a long box on the counter and took out a baguette, squeezing it to determine its freshness. "Food will help."

The ham looked delicious. "Did you . . .?" I nodded at the platter.

"No. We have a chef come in three times a week. None of us has time to cook, though I love to. But even reapers have to eat, so why not eat well?"

"We?"

"I have two roommates, and yes, they are also reapers."

I shook my head to clear it of the questions swarming in my brain. I didn't need to be asking about her living situation. "We need to rescue Gracie from a monster, and we're sitting here having tea and sandwiches?"

"Felix." Lucy sighed. "I reap souls every day, and sometimes it's heartbreaking, but I still eat. We can't do a thing until we at least know where Gracie is, and then we need a plan. None of that happens instantaneously. I promise, as soon as we have at least a little sustenance, we'll get started."

I glanced around the beautifully appointed kitchen with regret. If Lucy wasn't going to open her laptop until she'd eaten, and I wasn't going to steal anything, I might as well join her.

27

Lucy

Felix looked a bit better after finishing half a sandwich, but his face clouded as I fed Viceroy bits of ham.

"Felix, what's wrong?" I asked.

"Nothing," he snapped. "Can we get on with finding Gracie?"

"Of course. Is that all that's bothering you?" I pushed my plate and mug aside to make space for my laptop.

Felix tapped his long slender fingers on the table. "If you must know, I was thinking that you should take Viceroy when this is all said and done."

My hand paused halfway to my laptop. "Where is this coming from?"

"The master of a scruffy little dog is not who I am," Felix said, his tone clipped. "He's entirely too much work, and I have better things to do with my time. I've decided. Once we free Gracie, Viceroy is yours."

Both Viceroy and I gaped at him. I stifled a smile.

"Oh, okay. I get it," I said.

"Well, fill me in," Viceroy thought. "I don't get it."

"Tell him, Felix." I sat back and crossed my arms.

"There's nothing to tell." He brushed crumbs from the table

into his hand and dumped them onto his plate.

Viceroy and I stared at him until he exploded.

"Fine! You and Viceroy are immortal." He stopped to consider his next words. "If I were worried about him, which I am not, I would be concerned about my ability, as a half-blood with an unpredictable life span, to protect him. You, on the other hand, are immortal, so you are far better prepared to protect the little weasel than I am. Will you take him or not?"

"Wait!" Viceroy shouted his thought before I could answer. "You can't just hand me off like a stale donut, Felix. We've been over this. I'm yours, and there's nothing you can do about it." Viceroy grumbled to himself before continuing. "Lucy, you're great, and you have a nice house that I'd love to live in with Felix so we could all be together, but me and Felix get each other, you know? We're the same." He dipped one eyebrow. "We're like brothers."

"We are most certainly not brothers," Felix snapped, and Viceroy growled again louder.

I put a hand up. "Okay, that's enough. Felix, if anything happens to you, anywhere, anyhow, during any activity, I will take Viceroy. I promise. Are we done?"

Felix glowered silently while Viceroy retreated under the table.

I opened my laptop. "And anyway, no one is going anywhere except to rescue Gracie," I said firmly.

Felix maintained his pique for another minute, but his curiosity got the better of him, and he walked around to watch over my shoulder as I closed my browser and email tabs and opened HELL.

"What the hell—"

"Precisely. HELL, in this case, is an acronym. It stands for our Human Echo Live Locator program."

"That's not creepy at all," Felix muttered.

A chill chased itself up and down my spine. Usually, the acronym made me chuckle, but today it felt portentous. I pushed my misgivings down deep.

"Unfortunate acronyms aside, its creation vastly improved our ability to collect a soul before it experiences the distress of its body's death. The system's AI tracks and messages the reaper closest to a soul about to depart. Sometimes we get a heads-up a couple of days in advance, sometimes a few hours."

I glanced up at Felix, but he was staring out the kitchen window. "Felix? What are you thinking?"

"I'm thinking that we don't have a fucking clue what we're doing. I'm thinking that if Vampire Bob is working with Death, we don't stand a chance. And I'm wondering what kind of deal Death and a vampire could possibly make." He huffed a sigh. "We are truly and royally fucked."

I put a hand on his arm. "No, we're not. I have a friend on the inside. I wanted to talk to him before talking to you about any of this, but circumstances being what they are, that wasn't possible." I twisted the edge of the tablecloth. "It is likely that Deathy and Robert Jameson, Vampire Bob, have made a deal. He gives her something in exchange for you and Viceroy. But that can't be all of it. Bob could too easily collect you himself. I suspect you and Viceroy are an amuse-bouche, an appetizer for the meat of the bargain," I added for Viceroy's benefit. "I believe, and this is just a guess, that Deathy has agreed to give living souls to full-blood vampires . . ." I shuddered and gulped a breath. ". . . in exchange for something for herself."

"That's ridiculous. We have souls," Felix said, skipping right past the horrifying part to the bit about him. He got up and began pacing back and forth in front of the sink.

I fought a sigh. "You do now, as a half-blood. You kill your soul when you drain your first victim to death. It's part of the ritual of the Turn."

"No, that's not true. Our souls go free when we become full-blood. *We don't kill them!*"

"I don't know who lied to you, Felix, but it is most definitely true. You kill them." I held up a hand. "That's not the point here. I'd be happy to argue about vampire souls after we get Gracie." I took the last sip of my now-cold tea. "Look, Deathy is not on Vampire Bob's side, as such. She needs something from him, and killing you both means she doesn't have you as a bargaining chip, which means she might lose the thing she desperately wants, whatever it is."

He stared at me while he mulled it over.

"Felix. It makes sense. Deathy is not our immediate problem. Vampire Bob has Gracie. We deal with him first. Are you still in?" I asked.

He paused mid-stride, frowning hard enough to dim the room.

"He's still in," Viceroy thought, emerging from beneath the table. "Don't be a shit, Felix. Sit down."

To my utter amazement, Felix sat.

"I don't know what Vampire Bob could give her that she couldn't get on her own, and I don't know why they didn't just collect you two themselves, but judging by how hard Deathy tried to convince me that I was doing 'the right thing,' she stands to gain something consequential," I said, chewing a lip. "All of that aside, if Vampire Bob wasn't lying about having Gracie and giving us twenty-four hours, we have a window. So let's find her."

That I would appear on the map as a red spark once logged in gave me more than a moment's pause. It would alert Deathy to my activity, and if she happened to be in the system at the same time, she would be able to watch what I was doing. I tapped in my password anyway. The likelihood that she was actually working was slim.

None of it made sense. Deathy had incredible power. What could Vampire Bob possibly give her? The only thing he had to offer was eternal life, and she already had that.

I cast through memories of the past few years. Deathy had been training fewer and fewer new reapers. She had been increasingly uninvolved, mostly MIA, when a newbie had a problem or the system developed a bug. I knew because I had been the one fielding those calls and dealing with the demons when Deathy bailed on IT meetings. Deathy's behavior had been deteriorating for close to a century. She wanted out, like me. And she'd wanted it for a very long time.

"No," I whispered. "That can't be it."

"What? Can't you find her?"

"No, it's not that. I know what Deathy wants."

Felix shrugged his hands into the air and waited expectantly.

"She wants to quit her job."

"So what? So do most people. What does that have to do with finding Gracie?"

I pressed the heels of my hands against my eyes to ease the sudden throbbing in my forehead. "Nothing." But it had everything to do with me. If Deathy wanted out, she'd have to give up the power she wore, the Mantle of Death. And as the oldest reaper, I was her most likely successor. I swayed in my chair.

"Lucy!" Felix yelped, rushing to prop me upright. "Lucy, are you okay? What the fuck just happened?"

My ears were ringing, my skull feeling as if it wanted to burst through my face.

"Water," I croaked.

Felix handed me a glass, and I drained it, stumbling to the sink to soak a dish towel in cold water, wring it out, and press it to my face and neck until the shock and pain began to recede.

Felix tapped my back in a clumsy attempt to comfort me before leading me back to the chair. "What, Lucy? What is it? Are we really fucked? Are you fucked?"

I sat, pressing the wet towel against my face for a minute before answering. "You? I don't think so. Me? Maybe."

Viceroy jumped into my lap, whining in distress.

"Don't worry, Viceroy. We'll figure it out," I said, massaging his little body with tingling fingertips. "We'll figure it all out." I gathered him up and hugged him to my chest, loosening the tightness there. I took a deep breath. "First, let's see where Gracie is. What's her last name?"

"Search for Grace Rinelli," Felix said, then spelled her last name.

I crossed my fingers and knocked once on the wood of the tabletop for luck. The software, which crashed regularly, desperately needed an update. DOS-based programs had been dead forever, and the hideous gray boxes were a nightmare to navigate. Deathy either hadn't gotten around to negotiating a price for a new system, or she was hoping it would fail.

"Wow, that dinosaur still works?" Felix muttered, jumping back up to watch the screen over my shoulder. He gasped when an address appeared in the Active Location field. "That's where she is? In Riverdale?"

"Yes." I opened Google Maps and typed in the address. "She's right here." I pointed to the red teardrop.

Viceroy danced about, wagging his tail. "Yippee!!!" he thought at us, adding a series of little yips. "Let's GO!" He raced for the front door.

"Viceroy, wait, come back," I called to him.

He raced back in and ran in circles around the table. "GO, GO, GO!" he shouted.

"Hold on, little guy, calm down. We need a plan," I said.

"Right. Two of us—three, if you count a dog small enough to step on—against the vampire king of New York and his hundred or so minions," Felix said, shaking his head. "Hey, can the software tell us how many people are in the house?"

I glanced up at him. "People, yes. Full-blood vampires, no. I'm afraid it only tracks souls, so we'll have no idea how many vampires there are."

He grimaced. I tapped a few more keys, copied the address, pulled up another screen, and pasted it into the location field.

"There are five humans, including Gracie, in the house." I closed HELL, then my laptop. "Ezekiel, the friend I mentioned, might be able to help us get to her and help me figure out what Deathy is up to."

Viceroy was scratching at the front door before I finished the sentence.

28

Felix

"What are you so happy about?" I asked Viceroy. He was trotting jauntily between us as we walked toward the parking lot that housed Lucy's car. "I'm about to die, and none of this is my doing." I hunched my shoulders into the cold.

"All of this is your doing, Felix. You bit me. You called Gracie. It's all on you," Viceroy thought, sniffing at me.

"That's what I get for stepping up and attempting to help? Disrespect? And a death sentence? Next time I'll know better."

"Next time?" Viceroy chuffed.

"No one is dying," Lucy said. "If you were about to die, as the reaper closest to you, I would know. And since I haven't received a notification—"

"Don't patronize me," I muttered.

"No one is patronizing you," she said and smiled. "I'm trying to reassure you."

Viceroy wagged his tail. "But if you do die, I'll miss you, Felix. You buy great steaks!" the crazy mutt thought. "Anyway, Lucy said you're not gonna die. But if you were gonna die, I'd protect you. Like I said, it's you and me." He rubbed himself against my pant leg, leaving streaks of hair.

I couldn't think of a nasty reply, so I ignored him.

He veered toward Lucy, giving me an eye over his shoulder. "Are you done feeling sorry for yourself?" he trotted just out of my reach. I ignored him, wondering if Lucy's claim that full-blood vampires murdered their souls when they turned was true.

Lucy turned into a small lot. The man in the booth stepped out, a big grin lighting his unshaven face. "Lucy! It's been ages! How the heaven are you?"

"Ezekiel, it's wonderful to see you." She hesitated, flushed a bright pink, and frowned slightly. "What are you doing here?"

"Well, the guys are all out on errands, so I'm filling in. Just a working stiff."

He grinned, displaying perfect white teeth, and opened his arms. Lucy stepped into a bear hug. She lingered there long enough to make me suspect there was more than a casual friendship between them. It gave me time to examine the man. Though sporting a two-day beard, he wore a casual but expensive dark suede insulated bomber jacket, expensive jeans, and hand-stitched leather boots. His hands were far too clean for the grubby little parking lot. He was, in fact, immaculate. And not a vampire.

Lucy stepped back, and an eddy of fresh, clean air swirled from between them. It smelled like snow and rain and like nothing you'd ever smell in Manhattan, even on a good-air-quality day.

Ezekiel turned his grin on me and Viceroy, who had gone rigid. "Don't worry, little one. You're safe," the man said as he dropped to sit on his heels. He did not stretch out a hand but gazed intently into Viceroy's eyes.

The little beast was silent as he stared back, shuddering slightly and back-stepping against the leash. His mouth hung open, and he began to pant, his tail wagging furiously.

"You're an Angel!" Viceroy croaked in my head.

It was my turn to step back. "You're an . . ."

"Angel," Ezekiel provided, his smile dying as he stood and studied us. "And you three are in trouble. Lucy—"

"Forgive me for interrupting," I said. "Let me get this straight. Vampires run the underground parking, and angels run the aboveground lots?" I rubbed my cold-numbed hands together. "What a cliché." When in doubt, be rude. It was my go-to attitude.

Viceroy head-butted my leg. "Don't be a jerk, Felix. He's an angel! We can't do any better than having him on our side." He whistled out a snort and wheeled away from me to peer up at Ezekiel. "You *are* on our side, right?"

"I'll do whatever I can to help you," Ezekiel affirmed.

Lucy put a hand on my arm. "Felix, Ezekiel and I are old friends. I was hoping to get a message to him, asking for help. But we're in luck"—she put her other hand on Ezekiel's shoulder—"because not only is he here, he's also willing to help us."

I looked up at the sky. "Lucy, aside from the fact that he is a celestial being who, according to everything I've ever heard, isn't supposed to interfere in the business of humans, you have been hiding critical information—like that we were going to see an angel. Meaning Viceroy and I should not trust either of you in the least." I crossed my arms and shivered furiously. It was fucking freezing. "Viceroy, let's go," I snapped.

"I'm not going anywhere except to rescue Gracie," Viceroy huffed over his shoulder.

I was desperate to go and be done with this mess, but I'd gotten myself into it and couldn't see an easy way out. Suddenly weak in the knees at my lack of options, I cast about for a place to sit. An old metal folding chair leaned against a sign affixed to a chain-link fence. I stomped over to it and dropped onto the creaky thing before twisting to read the words behind me. "Celestial Parking? Oh for—" I looked up to see Ezekiel wagging a finger at me in warning. "—fudge's sake," I finished, slumping against the backrest and glaring at all three of them in turn.

"Felix, if Lucy kept something from you, she had a good reason. Perhaps you ought to find out how I can help before you walk away?" Ezekiel said, gazing at me. He waited for an answer, but even I could admit it might be in my best interest not to piss off an angel, so I said nothing. "Here, let me help you with the cold." He took the few steps over to me and, leaning in, put both hands on my shoulders.

Heat radiated from his hands, down through my body. I stopped shivering. Warm without wool—miraculous. I scowled up at him and shook his hands off.

"I have a particular gift," the angel said, stating the obvious.

"Clearly," I sniped.

He chuckled. "Felix, Lucy would not have come to me unless she believed I could be of use. Can we at least talk about it?"

He held out a hand, and woozy from the sudden warmth, I took it. A jolt of pure energy shot up my arm and exploded like fireworks in my brain. It was beautiful and terrifying. I yanked my hand back and stuck it inside my coat the second I was on my feet. My palm was tingling. "Don't you dare enthrall me!" I yelped.

Ezekiel eyed me, his eyebrows folding. "That wasn't a thrall—angels don't do that. I'm sorry. Are you okay?"

I wasn't. I had seen the angel's soul in that flash of pain, and it was brilliant, a flawless diamond, awe-inspiring. I didn't want or need to compare myself to that.

"Let's go inside and talk." Ezekiel lifted his chin toward the booth.

I stood, avoiding any chance contact, and marched toward Lucy and Viceroy, who were standing in front of what appeared to be a battered outhouse with windows.

Unless that booth was a TARDIS, Ezekiel was two pieces short of a three-piece suit. But at the angel's invitation, Viceroy trotted over and jumped inside, Lucy right behind him. Ezekiel and I reached the door simultaneously. He gestured forward, indicating I should go first. I stepped up and into . . .

A sitting room? The wood-paneled room held an overstuffed couch, two leather wing chairs, a massive oak table surrounded by

ornately carved wooden benches, oriental carpets, and a blazing
fire in an enormous stone fireplace. A coffee station and a tea
samovar sat on a sideboard, along with a Bundt cake and a snack
assortment.

I peered back out the door to the parking lot. "Well, why the
hell not," I muttered. "We're already three stops past Crazytown."

"Not hell, heaven," Ezekiel corrected me. "Spending one's
days and nights battling evil is exhausting, both to the bodies we
inhabit and our souls. Here, in this room and the bedrooms
beyond, we address the body." Ezekiel looked up at the high dark-
blue, gold-star-speckled ceiling. "They take care of the soul."

I did an actual double take. "They? I take it you are refer-
encing God. Is there more than one?"

"Oh, no. There's only one."

"But . . . They?"

"Every faith visualizes a different personification—He, She, It,
and yes, sometimes They, occasionally in the plural. Using They
encompasses almost everyone's beliefs. It's just simpler, and
polite."

"Almost everyone? Never mind, I don't want to know." I
turned to Lucy. "So, what are your pronouns? Do you use
they/them too since people see you differently?"

Lucy grinned. "I'm she/her, and that's how most people
perceive me. Reapers rarely change gender when we take on new
bodies. It's easier to stay with what you know. I have heard of a
few switches recently, so I imagine pronoun shifts will come
soon."

My sinuses began to throb. "Right. So to clarify, God is technically a . . ." I twirled my hand round and round, hoping Ezekiel
would put me out of my misery.

"Whoever or whatever you want Them to be—He, She, It—
they are all the Creator. How you perceive Them is up to you,"
Ezekiel said. "When I reference God to myself, I use He/Him
because that's who I see. But when speaking aloud, I use

They/Them. It doesn't matter, as God is an infinite being who encompasses all beliefs and can support all personifications."

I sighed. "Why can't anything ever be simple? Like my pronouns."

Lucy's eyes flew open. "What are yours, Felix?"

"I prefer yes, sir; right away, sir; and as you wish, sir. Now, where shall I hang my coat?"

It took Ezekiel a full minute to stop laughing before holding out his hand.

"What? I identify as royalty. What's wrong with that?" I sniffed.

Ezekiel swiped tears from the corners of his eyes as I handed him my coat. "Not a thing. I'll try and remember your rank, Felix. And not to belabor the point, but it honestly is simple. Each to their own. What do you call God?"

"God is a man. Everyone knows that." I harumphed, irritated. "He/Him."

"Well, there you have it!" Ezekiel said as if he'd just pulled a rabbit out of a hat.

Lucy sighed. "You know perfectly well that not everyone believes God is a man, Felix. You're just upset." She handed Ezekiel her coat, and he shrugged out of his, draping all three over the back of one of the chairs.

I turned on Lucy. "Don't trivialize my opinions. I'm entitled to them. They're no less valid than yours. And anyway, we came here to get help finding Gracie, not to debate God's pronouns. Furthermore—"

Viceroy began to sing "Cheek to Cheek," cutting off a perfectly good diatribe. The batty little dog ran in a few circles before flopping down on the carpet in front of the fire to roll over and wiggle his legs in the air.

Lucy and Ezekiel burst out laughing, and despite myself, I joined in, short-circuiting my increasingly foul mood.

I walked around the sofa to stand over the little beast and gaze into the crackling fire, allowing the warmth to smooth out my jagged edges. Irritated though I might be at Viceroy for co-opting my moment and softening it with his ridiculous charm, I was warm and safe. And if I chose to believe Lucy and Ezekiel, I might continue in this vein for the foreseeable future.

29

Lucy

Seeing Felix relax and Viceroy roll in front of the fire jarred me. They expected me to come up with a magical solution to save Gracie. But I was so far off script I couldn't even see the stage. Damn Deathy, and damn Vampire Bob.

I wanted to kick myself for not seeing through her at dinner. Though, honestly, I don't know what good it would have done. I would still have had to pretend to consider her request to turn them both over—or murder Felix and turn Viceroy over—to get out of the restaurant. And while I might have followed Felix and gone to his apartment blindly, at least I now had a shot at keeping them safe.

I gazed at Felix as he made himself comfortable. Deathy wanted me to murder him and kill a piece of my indomitable spirit in the process just so she could quit her job. I had thought she was at least marginally fond of me after working with me for over four hundred years, the last hundred of which I'd spent picking up her slack. The truth was she didn't think of me at all. I was nothing more than a tool, and that was all I ever had been. I was such an idiot. And worst of all, for the briefest second, I had been tempted to do it.

"But you didn't," Ezekiel whispered, reading my thoughts

and laying a hand on my shoulder to rouse me out of my stew. The panic evaporated at his touch.

"Don't do that," I hissed.

"Sorry," he said, retracting his hand.

"Not the touch, the mind-reading." I sighed, relenting at his sheepish expression. "It's fine, and you're right. I didn't do it. But now here we are, in a real mess."

Ezekiel gazed into my eyes until I broke the connection. "Do you want to tell me?" he asked, his voice gentle.

I nodded at Felix and Viceroy. "I told them what I suspect, but there was no point subjecting them to the details until I talked to you."

"Felix, Lucy and I need a few moments to work some things out. Why don't you have a cup of coffee or tea and something to eat if you're hungry and sit by the fire for a bit while we talk."

Viceroy flipped onto his feet at the suggestion of food, trotted over to the sideboard, dropped his tongue, and waved his tail in anticipation. After admiring the samovar, Felix made a plate for Viceroy, setting it on the floor before serving himself. Once Felix was seated with a cup of tea and a slice of cake, I tugged Ezekiel to the far end of the table and told him what I suspected about Deathy, along with Felix, Viceroy, and Gracie's part in it, and where Gracie was now. He listened without interruption.

"Well, we knew she was planning to abdicate. The Mantle of Death is restless and has been telegraphing its concerns."

I frowned. "You knew? And you didn't tell me?"

"Yes, I did know, and I couldn't talk to you about it until you found out on your own. Telling you would have changed the course of events in unpredictable ways." He sighed through his nose. "We're still debating a course of action."

I knew him well enough to know that was all he was going to say. I gazed at him, drinking in the sight of him before shaking myself.

"Coming here was a mistake," I said.

"Lucy, of course you had to come." Ezekiel took my hand,

and electricity raced back and forth between us as tears sprang up and rolled down my cheeks. "It will be okay. We'll be okay," he whispered, his voice soothing.

I nodded, tears still streaming. Placing my hand back on the table, he plucked a pink-and-green polka-dot handkerchief from thin air and handed it to me. I giggled through my tears. It was an old trick, and it never failed to delight me. I had a collection of his magic hankies in a satin box in my closet.

"I assume you don't want the Mantle," Ezekiel said.

"I'll take it if I have to." I hesitated. "But I don't want to."

"You would rather remain a reaper than accept the power?" His face creased with concern.

"Among the two choices? Yes. I'd rather remain as I am."

"Even under new and untested management?"

He had me there. As the oldest reaper under an inexperienced Mantle bearer, I would end up as Death's counselor. For all practical purposes: a slave, without even the satisfaction of guiding souls—I'd no longer have time for that. I would have to live with the new Death, accessible at all times, leaving my house and friends behind.

I dropped my head into my hands. "All I want is my humanity, Ezekiel. Why can't I have it?"

It was a rhetorical question. Deathy was the only one who could grant it, and she never would. Nor would a new Death, who would need me close at hand. I laid my head on my arms. "I want to be a woman, to have your . . ." I needed to stop talking. I wasn't going to solve this right now, and neither was Ezekiel.

He didn't reply until I lifted my head to gaze up into his gentle, careworn face. "I want that too, Lucy."

Regaining my humanity was the only way we could be together, and we both longed for the few short years we'd have before my human death. Still, year after year, as Deathy continued to throw boulders in my path, I had given up hope—until two days ago. But now, the bright spark of possibility that encompassed Ezekiel fizzled out of existence with the realization that, regardless of what I had been willing or unwilling to do to Felix, I would have to accept the Mantle of Death.

My vision blurred as my face flushed with too much blood, and my head pounded. I took several deep breaths in an effort to control my surging emotions, until Ezekiel placed his hands on my shoulders, and a deep calm spread through my body, cooling my face and clearing my vision.

"Thanks," I whispered.

"We'll figure something out. I promise."

My gaze sharpened. Ezekiel didn't make promises. There was something he wasn't telling me.

I leaned away from him slightly, shaking myself hard. "We need to work on freeing Gracie. I haven't the slightest idea how to get her out of Vampire Bob's house unless we walk up to the front door, ring the bell, and ask for her back. I was hoping you could do some angel magic, like the hankies? Or smiting? Can you smite the vampires?"

Ezekiel chortled before lowering his voice. "Vampire Bob, huh? I don't know that I'd humanize him with a nickname, but name-calling aside, yes, technically, I could vaporize him and his minions. But that would spark a war between angels and supernaturals, the result of which would be untold human suffering." He scratched at his chin. "So in the interest of preserving the greater peace, I will not 'smite' them. No one wins in that war."

"Oh." My slender thread of hope frayed to the breaking point.

"But maybe we don't need to kill anyone to free Gracie. What if the vampires fall asleep?"

"Oh!" I gasped. "A sleep reverie. I do those all day long." I paused. "But you do know it isn't a true sleep? And I've never done it to anyone who might wake. Wait . . . would it work?" I shook my head, trying to parse it. Ezekiel waited for me to work through the process. "They're soulless, but they have a functioning brain, so they should fall asleep, then wake. What I do is essentially the same as a vampire's enthralling, a force of my will."

I picked at a speck on the tabletop, chagrined. "Why didn't I think of that?"

"Because it's a problem outside your sphere of experience. Besides, if you had, I wouldn't be sitting here with you. It's been fifty years, Lucy."

"I know," I whispered, not adding that I had missed him nearly every single one of those 18,000 days. But I didn't have to say it aloud. He knew. He had missed me too.

"So . . . have you ever performed a reverie at a distance or on multiple people?" he asked, breaking the spell. "Let's try something. Do two at once."

"To them? No. I could be dangerous." I glanced at Felix and Viceroy, chatting in front of the fire.

"I'll fix anything that goes wrong. Go ahead."

"Mm, okay, if you're sure. I'll try." He nodded his encouragement.

I had to fiddle about a bit to release two sleep tendrils at once and direct them at two separate beings. Felix's head tipped forward, but he caught himself with a snort, his head snapping back up. And Viceroy was still thinking at him, so it hadn't worked on the little dog either.

I sighed. "Well, so much for my powers."

Ezekiel pursed his lips. "Perhaps I can help amplify your will. Try it this way."

He held out his hand for mine, and my heart jittered. His shirtsleeve lit up from the glow infusing his arm. Warmth spread from his hand, through mine, and up my arm, kindling a ball of fire in my chest. I looked away from him, centered my will on Felix and Viceroy, and released two new tendrils of sleep. Instant snorts erupted from both Felix and Viceroy. Felix's head was canted at an odd angle against the back of his chair, and I stood to see Viceroy lying on his side. Both were deeply asleep, snoring louder than bulldozers razing a building.

I cringed. "Yikes. Okay, then. It looks like we've got the first part of a plan, though I feel terrible for having used them as test subjects."

Ezekiel grinned. "Oh, come on now. You don't seriously think I'd harm either Felix or Viceroy, do you?"

"Of course not. Should we wake them?"

"No, let them be," Ezekiel said. "They should rest."

I walked over to tuck a pillow beneath Felix's head to prevent him from getting a stiff neck before sitting down to open my laptop.

Two hours later, thanks to Google, a payment of $19.95 to findem.com, and Ezekiel's subscription to *Architectural Living* —probably used as inspiration to create sanctuaries such as this one—we had the floor plans to Robert Jameson's house.

I glanced over at Felix and Viceroy with a pinch of envy before shaking off the exhaustion and changing the subject from Gracie to Deathy. "Grappling with the machinations of Deathy's plan to shift the course of human history is way beyond my pay grade," I muttered.

Ezekiel peered at me, frowning. "We're still okay on that end. Nothing will happen until Jameson gets the dog. Viceroy seems to be the lynchpin of the bargain he's struck with her—as long as we have Viceroy, we still have time."

I tapped a finger on the table. "But removing Gracie from the equation will make Bob desperate. And even more dangerous. We'll need to hide. Do you know of a place?"

"We have a camp upstate, but the catacombs are closer. You're familiar with the section beneath lower Manhattan. Angels maintain a section in the Bronx that also serves as a gathering place. I've already reached out, though I haven't had an answer yet. It should be perfect for us."

"Oh." I sat back in sudden understanding. "That's why you're here at the lot instead of one of your minions. You knew I was coming."

"I did," he said. "And they're angels, not minions. I'm not a villain, and they don't report to me."

I quirked an eyebrow at him. "Maybe, but they look to you for guidance just the same. You need to watch *Despicable Me*. It has a happy ending—right up your alley."

He mimed writing it down in a notebook. "Noted. Now, what do we do after putting the house's occupants to sleep?"

We moved to the sofa, sipping cups of coffee and debating our too-few options as the night wore on. We ran out of possibilities at about one a.m., falling silent as the fire crackled, each lost in thought, no ideas on the horizon, while the other half of our raiding party slept. I must have fallen asleep too because I woke to Ezekiel shaking my shoulder.

"Lucy, wake up. I think you were right. We can walk up to the front door and ring the bell."

"What?" I jerked upright so fast a nerve spasmed in my neck. "Ouch!" I rubbed at the sore spot as he pushed my hair aside and massaged my shoulders. I stifled a groan. "I wasn't serious."

Ezekiel, showered, shaven, and in clean clothes, was raring to go. "We'll knock them into sleep as they appear," he said as I ran my tongue over my teeth. "There are toothbrushes for you both in the bathroom. What do you think?"

I escaped his kneading hands and got to my feet. "About what?"

"About ringing the front doorbell."

"Well, since it's the only plan we seem to have, I think it's a great one—as long as the vampires don't have guns. A human body, remember?" I pointed to my chest, turning to face him.

"I'll go first. Angelic body, remember?" He pointed at his chest, then, throwing his hands up in the air, shook them, fingers spread in a spot-on jazz hands impression, but I was too worried to laugh.

"It's absurd. We'll never pull it off. And even if we do . . . won't you get in trouble?"

"Probably. But it's always better to ask forgiveness than permission. And doubt before a battle, if there is a battle, is dangerous, so don't be a naysayer," Ezekiel scolded. "I have moves and I know how to use them." He crossed his arms over his chest and began to glow, spikes of white fire spiraling outward from him. He grew a good two feet.

"Okay, okay. I take it back. With you looking like a literal avenging angel, we may stand a chance."

He uncrossed his arms and reverted to his ordinary, if far-too-attractive, form.

"I knew you'd see it my way." He flashed me a wicked grin and walked toward the fireplace to wake Felix and Viceroy. A shaft of morning light spilled across the carpets from the windowed door.

Time to go to Riverdale.

30

Gracie

Tuesday, November 17

I woke with hot, swollen eyes; a dry, sour mouth; and a dull headache. If I didn't know better, I'd have thought I was hungover. Either those pills Elaine had given me weren't Advil, or the water was drugged. Most likely the water, since I'd blacked out so fast.

I lay there, summoning the energy to crawl out of bed as my dream surfaced. It was about this house. In the dream, I walked freely, looking into rooms, wandering from floor to floor. None of the people I passed seemed to see me. And then, before I could descend the basement stairs, I woke up. Or had I been awake when I walked about the house, and now I was dead? I snaked a hand across myself and pinched my arm hard. Ow! Nope, that hurt too much, and I was too miserable to be dead.

The room was dark, a faint light showing beneath the bathroom door. I crabbed to the edge of the bed and tried to stand, immediately sinking to the floor on spaghetti legs. Tears burned, but I was mad enough to get the hell up. I levered myself back onto the bed. I could do this—I didn't grow up wrestling and roughhousing with four brothers for nothing.

I massaged my thighs and calves to jump-start my circulation. It was slow going since my hands didn't want to work right either. That bitch *had* drugged me. I wanted to scream, but attracting attention and more drugs were the last things I needed. Some sensation was coming back to my legs and feet, and a fierce prickling replaced the numbness. Pressing one foot to the floor sent a Fourth of July sparkler of pins and needles up my leg. I yelped and rubbed harder. A minute or two later, I felt stable enough to risk standing.

After swaying for a minute, I managed to remain upright. Good. I stumbled to the bathroom. A flip of the switch turned a nightlight to full brightness. The face that peered back at me in the mirror was a horror-movie version of myself—puffy and blotchy. My hair stuck up in a cloud around my head as if someone had dragged me by it. I ran my fingers over my scalp. Nothing hurt. No pain anywhere except for my tailbone as I ran my hands over the rest of me. I checked my neck. I could find no marks, though my fingertips were still slightly numb, so at least no one had sucked my blood. But I hadn't seen any scars on Elaine's throat either.

I washed my face and brushed my teeth with a new toothbrush and an organic toothpaste. I wanted a shower, but that would make me entirely too vulnerable. I scrubbed my armpits, applied the deodorant, and did what I could with my hair. Looking saner, if not altogether lucid, I used the toilet and climbed back into bed to think. I had to get out of here before my family went crazy with worry. But I was pretty sure it was too late for that. My mother would have tried to call me when I hadn't come home. She would call each of my brothers, the police, and probably the FBI, the CIA, and INTERPOL.

My mother. The mother, who, if Elaine was right—and there was no way she could be because I was about as far from exceptional as a person could get—had lied to me my whole life. But I hadn't been glamoured when that vampire tried it on me. And I'd just had a whopper of a lucid dream. *Fuck!*

"Mom, you're in so much trouble if Elaine isn't lying, and if I ever get out of here," I muttered to the room. If I did have an indisputable spirit, or whatever it was Elaine had called it, it wasn't doing me a damned bit of good right now.

I was too itchy with worry to stay put, so I walked around the room, turning on all three lamps, searching for a potential weapon. They had fastened everything down—the lighting fixtures, the phone, and a decorative tissue box. I rocked the tissue box back and forth, trying to loosen it, wondering how they got the fresh tissues in. I opened all the drawers and the closet. The hangers were attached to the rod, hotel style. The entertainment center held a newer TV, but the remote was bolted to an end table next to an armchair. It was the same in the bathroom. Only the toiletries and two giant square French-style bars of soap, one at the sink and one at the tub, were loose.

I could always wash the vampires to death.

Picking a sweater from the wardrobe, I pulled it over my head before settling in the overstuffed chair to examine a pile of books and magazines. The top book was a well-worn copy of *Harry Potter and the Sorcerer's Stone*. I tossed it aside; I liked the movie better. Beneath it was a tattered copy of *The Tibetan Book of the Dead*. Eww. That one went to the floor too. Under that was the *Betty Crocker Cookbook*.

The magazines, though current, were even weirder. *Garden and Gun*, *Reader's Digest*, *Stereophile*, *Birdwatching*, *Forbes*, *Food & Wine*, *Midwest Living*. Who were these people? The last one gave me chills: *Young Rider*. The rumpled cover and dog-eared pages meant it had been well-read, most likely by Ben, Elaine's son. My breath hitched thinking about a child in a house full of vampires. I covered it up with the other magazines and books.

TV might be better. I clicked the remote, grateful the vampires at least had cable. I scrolled through the channels, stopping on *The Grifters*. Angelica Houston, Annette Bening, John Cusack. Bry and I had watched it one snowy Sunday last year, and we'd both loved it. I got as far as the scene where Bobo threatens to beat Lilly with a towel full of oranges. Oranges. Heavy, solid oranges.

Wait. The soap. In a pillowcase, those huge bars could do some damage. My heart pounding, I ignored the rest of the movie, trying instead to figure out how to escape using an old grifter con.

31

Gracie

L ost in thought and the movie, I jumped at a knock at the door and shrank deeper into my chair. But the knock came again. And again. I turned off the TV and waited.

"Please," was all I heard, the rest too soft to make out through the thick wood. The voice belonged to a child. I dashed to the door.

"Hello?" I whispered back.

"I can't get in. I have the code wrong. But I'll be back."

"Wait! Who are you?"

"Someone's coming. Be asleep," the whispery voice said.

I didn't need to hear it twice. I ran to the bed and jumped in, scrambling out again to turn off the TV before jumping back in and covering myself up to my ears. I reached up, mussed my hair, and tried to slow my breathing, which was impossible since I was terrified. I settled for shallow Lamaze breaths. I would thank Alicia for that if I ever got out of here. I'd been the only family member to answer her call while my brother performed a heart transplant, so I'd ended up as her person when the twins were born. I'd sworn off having kids for a whole year after seeing that.

It was a long couple of minutes before I heard the door open, jump-starting my trembling. When was my usual tough-girl thing going to kick in? Now would be good.

The door opened to the smell of bacon.

Elaine carried a tray. Behind her was a man I had never seen before. He was tall and fair with piercing blue eyes. He cast a stone-faced glance around the room, stepping over to peer into the bathroom before his gaze settled on me.

"How do you feel?" he asked in a strangely cultured voice. Irish, from the lilt of his accent.

"I'm fine, considering I'm here against my will. Thank you so much for asking." It came out before I could stop myself. Elaine's shut-up glance had come too late. "The breakfast smells wonderful," I finished.

He examined me as if he could see through my clothes, and I shrank back instinctively.

"We have an excellent chef. Do enjoy it."

I waited for him to add "because it will be your last meal" or "it's the last thing you'll ever eat," but he didn't, so I figured I wasn't going to die right that minute, and it was okay to get out of bed. The tall man backed out of the room as if we were royalty, or more likely, to keep from exposing his back, and pulled the door shut behind him.

"Who the hell was that?" I demanded, my arms crossed over my chest.

"Robert Jameson. He owns this house," Elaine said in a whisper as if he could hear us.

"So he's the one who ordered my kidnapping?"

"Yes, he sent some of his men. And he doesn't usually visit his captives."

Elaine glanced at me with a look I couldn't decipher, placing the tray on the table and laying out our place settings in silence.

I got up and settled myself in the chair across from her. "I guess I should be flattered."

Elaine didn't take the bait. She uncovered the serving dishes to reveal two omelets, bacon strips, gorgeously browned link sausages, fresh scones, butter, jam, and a small bowl of what looked like thick cream. There was also orange juice and coffee. My disloyal mouth watered.

"Did he come to see if I'd recovered from the drugs you gave me?" I said. "And I hope you used the same drugs in this food as you did in last night's meal. They were fabulous!" I rolled my head around on my neck, blinking my eyes and sticking out my tongue. That got her.

"What do you—"

"Don't even. I thought I was dying." I picked up a strip of bacon and waved it at her. "Is this drugged?" I tossed it onto my plate and picked up a juicy sausage link before dropping it; it was hot. "Is this poisoned?" I pointed at the bowl of cream. "How about that?" I waved a hand over the table. "Is anything here safe for me to eat, because—"

"Gracie, no one drugged you. There are no drugs of any sort in this house except for Advil and antacids. They didn't drug you because they didn't have to. You can't get out, and you can't fight them." She looked away.

"And?"

"And drugs spoil the blood."

My appetite evaporated.

"You can eat and drink anything here. Nothing is adulterated in any manner whatsoever. In fact, it's all organic." She glanced at me before reaching for the pitcher and pouring orange juice into both of our glasses. "Gracie." She looked up at me again, brows furrowed. "Please. Eat. You need your strength."

"What do you mean I need my strength? I know why you need yours. Are you saying that—"

"I just mean that starving yourself won't help." She didn't look up from her plate.

I swallowed hard and surveyed the food. I was hungry, and what Elaine said made sense. I cut a sausage link and lifted a bite to my mouth before pausing. The aroma hit my nose, and in it went. I speared another bite and examined it. Small chunks of pork were bound together by rice, herbs, and spices. I saw flecks of black pepper and pine nuts. I put the forkful of sausage into my mouth and chewed slowly, savoring the swirl of flavors.

"You have a butcher too?"

"We do. I think it's somewhere in Queens."

We ate in silence. All I could think was how much my mother would love these sausages. I wondered if I could get the butcher's location before mentally slapping myself—sausage recipes were the least of my concerns. I moved on to the scones. The cream was clotted, which sounds disgusting, but it was delicious. I couldn't help filing the combination away for future reference—if I had a future.

What the hell was wrong with me? How had I gone from cowering terrified in bed, to fury at being drugged, to gastronomic ecstasy in the space of a few hundred heartbeats? What the hell happened to me last night if it wasn't drugs? My weird soul doing weird things to my body?

Elaine smiled at me, unaware of the tempest building in my brain. After explaining how clotted cream was made, she had fallen silent and continued her hearty attack on her food. I suddenly felt light-headed from the zigzagging emotional riptide. Shoving my chair back, I leaned down to get my head between my knees, promptly throwing up all over the carpet. So much for breakfast.

Elaine leaped up and rushed to my side. I hiccupped twice and sat up, wiping my eyes and then my mouth with my napkin. Elaine put an arm around my shoulders. I clung to her and started crying in earnest.

"Oh dear, oh, sweetie, I'm so sorry this is happening to you." She hugged me hard with both arms.

I buried my face in her side, tears and snot mingling on her neatly pressed cotton shirt. She wasn't my mother, but she was a mother. She had this.

She let me cry it out before disengaging gently and getting a hot washcloth from the bathroom. She pressed it into my hands and waited while I wiped my face. After pouring me a glass of water, which I drank gratefully, she led me to the armchair and covered me with a throw before picking up the phone and speaking softly to someone on the other end. I leaned my head back and closed my eyes.

I heard Elaine running water in the bathroom, then the door opening. I opened my eyes to see a short, round woman in a flowered cotton housedress and a pink apron dusted in flour. She carried a small pail and some cleaning supplies. Pursing her lips, she gathered the bulk of my mess in paper towels, then pulled out a sponge, sprayed the spot with a carpet cleaner, and went to work.

Elaine came back to me. "I'm running you a bath. It'll help." I opened my mouth to protest, but she cut me off. "Trust me on this, Gracie. No one will attack you, and you'll feel better." She paused. "Or at least cleaner." Elaine watched the woman scrub the carpet. "That's Maria. She speaks mostly Italian."

A flush of familiarity animated my voice as I broke out my underused Italian. "*Ciao, Maria, mi chiamo Gracie Rinelli. Grazie mille per il vostro aiuto. Mi dispiace di aver fatto questo lavoro spiacevole per te.*" I was pretty sure I'd just said "thank you, and I'm sorry."

Maria looked up so quickly that she banged her head on the underside of the table. She let out a stream of mumbled curses in Italian that I had no trouble understanding. Tossing her sponge back into the pail and wiping her hands on her apron, Maria got to her feet, rubbing the bump and swirling her graying hair into a halo in the process. Her eyes crinkled, and she grinned at me like only an Italian nonna can, rushing over to pull me to my feet and envelop me in a bear hug. About my height and twice my weight, she smelled of yeast and flour—she had been making bread.

"Oh, beautiful one, it is I who am sorry. Sorry for you that you are a prisoner of these monsters," she said in rapid Italian as she released me.

I tumbled back into the chair. She smelled like my mom's

kitchen and sounded like my memories of visits with both my grandmothers.

I drew a shaky breath. "Maria, why are you here?"

She nodded at the door. "I have not much time to tell you the whole story." She jerked her chin toward Elaine, who watched us with fascination. "I am like her. They took my son. I came to take care of him, and now, I have been here so long . . ." She paused and pulled a worn cotton hankie from the pocket of her apron to swipe at her eyes. "This is all I know. They made my son a vampire, and he is here, so I am here. They call me chef"—she shook her head—"but I am just a cook. I have to go back to my bread. I will see you soon."

Maria patted my shoulder, picked up her supplies, and slipped out the door with a backward glance and a smile, taking all the warmth in the room with her.

They could kidnap me and eat Elaine, but nobody made a slave out of a nonna. I gritted my teeth and faced Elaine, newly determined to get down to business.

"Okay, so if I do have this thing, an . . . indomitable spirit, what good is it? Is it like a superpower?" I leveled my gaze at her, saying the next part slowly. "Can I use it to get us out of here?"

32

Felix

That angels ran errands was news to me. But Ezekiel left to take care of them while the rest of us got cleaned up and had some breakfast. By noon, forty-five minutes after leaving the parking-booth TARDIS, we were still creeping and honking our way uptown along 10th Avenue.

"I hate to bring this up, guys," Viceroy thought, wiggling around in the seat next to me, "but I could eat." He thumped his tail in the kind of hopeful anticipation appropriate only to dogs and small children.

"Well, isn't that too bad for you?" I said. "It seems we didn't think to bring a rodent."

Lucy snorted and rummaged in her purse. "I've got you covered, little guy." She brought out a chunk of roast ham wrapped in waxed paper. She stripped off a piece and handed it over the seat to me.

"I don't know what's worse. That you're always hungry"—I frowned at Viceroy—"or that you"—I pointed the ham at Lucy—"apropos of nothing, brought ham to a rescue." I scowled at Viceroy before handing over the tidbit.

He swallowed it whole and wagged his tail, whining to Lucy for more.

She handed over another strip, rewrapping the rest and stowing it for later. "Not 'apropos of nothing,' Felix. We have a special dog with us. We need to keep the little guy fed. And honestly, do you want to find out what happens if he goes too long without food?" Lucy handed me a wet wipe for my greasy fingers then cleaned her own and held out a hand to collect my used one, glancing meaningfully at me.

I heaved a sigh and stared out the window at the bright sunshine.

It was a myth that full-blood vampires caught fire if exposed to sunlight. Once a vampire made the final transformation, the body, deprived of the direct source of vitamins and minerals that humans got from food, developed a sensitivity to the sun. Skin pigment faded, and the skin thinned, leaving the vampire's veins —and the secondhand human blood that ran through them— with no protection from ultraviolet rays. The unfiltered UV caused the blood to coagulate and eventually clot—an excruciatingly disabling event.

While full-bloods often went about their lives wearing thick stage makeup in the daylight, the slightly coagulated blood rendered them slower and weaker. I would miss feeling the sun on my bare skin if and when I managed to find a sponsor to turn me. But that was the price, and I'd pay it.

"We're about five minutes out," Lucy said, startling me. "Remember what we decided? Viceroy, you stay in the car." She raised her eyebrows pointedly at him as he rose to his total, if miniature, height in the seat. "If we lose you, it's game over."

He cocked his head and glared at her.

"Okay?" she prompted.

"I can stay in the car with him to make sure he doesn't get out," I offered.

This time Ezekiel twisted around to add his glare to Lucy's.

"What? I'm just trying to help," I muttered.

"There it is." Lucy indicated a tall brick wall with a gate across the driveway.

Ezekiel pulled into a spot across the street and cut the engine.

"There's a gate. That wasn't on the architectural plan," Ezekiel said.

"No, it wasn't," Lucy said. "Now what?"

"Now I need to pee," Viceroy thought. I unfolded his leash and snapped it to his harness, opening the door.

"Don't go far," Ezekiel said.

Viceroy trotted to the front bumper and relieved himself against a tree. He stepped away and stopped abruptly, raising his head and sniffing the air.

"I smell her!" he thought loud enough to ring my ears, though he hadn't made a sound. "Felix, I smell Gracie."

"Where?" Ezekiel asked, getting out and circling the car to us.

"Gracie is hundreds of feet away, behind a wall and inside a house," I said, pursing my lips. "Viceroy, are you sure you're smelling Gracie and not someone wearing the same perfume?"

"Yes. No. Wait." He stood on his hind legs and sniffed the air again.

Half a block away, a woman emerged from a Volkswagen Beetle. I stepped sideways to get a better view, and Viceroy took off in a blur, yanking the leash out of my hand and giving me a fat leather burn across my palm.

Lucy jumped out to join Ezekiel, racing after the flea-bitten little rodent sucker. Shaking my hand to cool the burn, I started walking toward the small group, aggravated as fuck, as Viceroy danced about the woman's feet. The woman wasn't Gracie, but they must be related. Sisters? No. As I drew closer, I realized she was Gracie's mother—and she was beautiful.

Enchanted, I strode to the middle of the group, displacing Lucy and Ezekiel, and extended my hand.

"Felix Belloquot, madam. Allow me to introduce Lucy, Ezekiel, and Viceroy." I indicated each in turn. "You must be Mrs. Rinelli, Gracie's mother."

Mrs. Rinelli hesitated, then took my hand. I bowed slightly

over it, rising to see her blush most attractively. Her handshake was warm and firm, like Gracie's.

She leaned toward me and looked me in the eye. "How do you know my daughter, Mr. Belloquot? And why are you all here?" Before any of us could answer, an oversized man unfolded himself from the passenger seat to stand, towering over the tiny car. An older woman slipped from the back seat and joined him. They watched us warily.

"Well, Mrs. Rinelli, I'm afraid that's a rather long story. But we're here for presumably the same reason you are—to rescue Gracie. May I ask how *you* knew where she was?"

"Find My Friends." She smiled. "When Gracie didn't answer her phone and didn't come home last night, I called Bryan. When his calls went to voicemail, I drove to his apartment, ran into Fay, and asked if she'd seen Gracie. While we were talking, I remembered that I still had the app on my phone. It was just luck that Gracie had never deleted it either." She shrugged at my expression. "Her brothers and I used it to keep track of her when she was younger. Anyway, Fay called Phillip, and here we are."

I realized I was still holding her hand and regretfully released it.

She motioned to the two standing by the car. "Let me introduce you."

33

Gracie

Elaine left with the breakfast tray after explaining that my indomitable spirit—*spirit* being another word for *soul*—didn't have super powers as far as she knew. She told me the rest of what she did know, which was next to nothing. As far as I could tell, this soul thing I had was good for protecting me against vampires, which, considering my situation, was a bonus, and lucid dreaming, which if I understood it correctly, might be useful in some situations.

But if that was all, what was the point, really, of having a special soul? Most people didn't know about vampires and would never be attacked by one—there must be more.

I was so going to kill my mother. I climbed into the enormous tub Elaine had run for me, my muscles relaxing one by one as I floated, boneless. I sank and remained underwater until my lungs burned for air, bobbing to the surface only when they were about to burst. I tucked my chin to look down at the inky number on my chest—still there. Sitting up, I slicked water from my face to examine the collection of small plastic bottles and tubes arrayed next to my head. I picked them up one by one, reading the labels. Most were Kiehl's: shampoo and conditioner, grapefruit body wash, and body scrub. A plastic jar of a different brand, now half empty, contained a lavender-mint bath soak. I unscrewed the lid and sniffed. That's what was in the water. A shower cap, a scrub puff, and a giant bar of charcoal soap made up the collection. They had thought of everything. Or at least, Elaine had.

With my hair wrapped in an absorbent terry hair towel—another weird amenity—I flipped through the wardrobe for clean clothes, slipping into beige pants the exact shade of a file cabinet, a white T-shirt, and a pullover sweater. Unwrapping my hair, I settled for towel blotting and finger detangling.

Elaine was right. I felt better. I occupied myself scrolling through TV channels, settling on a season of *Supernatural*. Maybe I'd learn something useful. I'd gotten through three episodes before my stomach let out a roar of protest. Having vomited last night's dinner and my recent breakfast, I was suddenly and painfully hungry. Where the hell was lunch?

Stalking to the bedside, I downed the rest of the water and picked up the telephone. I let it ring for a couple of minutes, banging the thing back onto its cradle when there was no answer.

"What the heck is going on around here if you can't manage to feed the people you feed on?" I said to the ceiling in case anyone was listening.

I turned off the TV and pressed my ear against the solid wood of the door. Every previous attempt to listen had been fruitless, but this time, I heard a faint but persistent bell ringing and distant pounding footfalls. A sudden tapping on the keypad made me scramble back, but not fast enough.

The door flew open and knocked me onto my rear, sending shock waves of pain up my spine. I looked up, expecting a vampire, grateful to see a small boy instead.

"Hi. I'm Ben. Can I come in?"

"Hi, Ben, your mom told me about you. Come on in," I said from between gritted teeth. My backside felt like an explosion had gone off in my pants.

Ben peered down both sides of the hallway before stepping inside and pushing the door nearly closed. He held out a hand. I took it, feeling a buzzing sensation, almost as if he were wearing one of those handshake shockers. He grinned, nodding at me to encourage me up. I winced and scrambled to my feet.

"I'm sorry I knocked you down," he said. His ears stuck out beneath a shock of wheat-colored hair, making him look elfin. "Are you okay?"

"I'm okay," I lied. "I'm Gracie. I'm pleased to meet you." I held out my hand to him, hesitantly this time, and he took it. The same gentle buzzing flowed from his palm to mine, but now I seemed to send it back to him.

He released my hand, stepped back, and studied me.

"How did you know I was in here?" I asked.

"I know everything about this house. Nobody cares what they say in front of me, 'cause they think I'm just some dumb kid." He eyed me. "Gracie, you and me are the same."

"The same? You mean the indomitable spirit thing?"

"Yeah. I have one, and so do you!" He grinned from ear to ear. "Did you feel it when we held hands?"

I nodded, dumbfounded at how casual he was about himself and his situation. "So the vampires can't control you?"

He snorted and hopped onto the bed, swinging his legs over the side. "No. And I can't be made into one either."

My eyebrows shot up.

"That's why me and my mom are here. Vampire Bob wants to figure out why he can't make me like him," Ben said, pulling up a sleeve to show me healed puncture wounds in the crook of his elbow. "They keep testing my blood—"

"Ben!"

"Don't worry. It doesn't hurt too much." He fished around in his pocket, giving me a conspiratorial glance. "I came because I had a dream about you, and I brought you something to eat because we won't get lunch. Everybody's busy." He handed me a wrapped and slightly smushed granola bar.

I took the proffered snack gratefully, unwrapping it and taking a bite. "A dream? About me?"

"Yeah, I dreamed we get out today." Ben looked at his commando-style watch. "Almost now."

I stared at him. "What? What do you mean we get out? How?"

I jumped at a noise outside the door, but it was just Elaine.

"We have intruders," she whispered.

Ben jumped off the bed, and Elaine put an arm around his thin shoulders, hugging him to her side.

"It's most likely neighborhood kids. They're always curious about what's inside the walls. But any intrusion puts the house on lockdown until they resolve the situation." She appeared only slightly less calm than usual. "Ben, honey, what are you doing in here? How did you get in?"

"Mom, I was just telling Gracie about my dream last night—"

"Ben," Elaine interrupted him, rubbing his shoulder, "you know you're not supposed to tell people about your dreams. And where did you get the code to this room?"

"I know, I know, they can use me for bad things if they know I can see the future," he recited in a singsong voice while staring at the ceiling. "Gracie's different, Mom. She's like me. I don't have to hide stuff from her. And the dream was about her and us. We escape. Now."

He pumped his fist into the air, and I couldn't help but grin. He reminded me so much of my nephews.

Elaine kneeled at Ben's feet. "Honey, you know we can't leave."

"We get out, Mom. I dreamed it. We have to go, or they'll do things to Gracie, too. They already started." Agitated, he pointed at my neck.

Thoroughly freaked out, I reached up to rub the area and felt a slight depression I'd missed earlier. My knees buckled, and I sank toward the floor. Elaine lunged toward me and caught me before I hit my head. She pulled me upright and guided me into the chair. I ignored the burst of pain from my tailbone and leaned forward, grabbing hold of her arm.

"Did that bastard bite me?" I shrieked.

They both shushed me.

"Yes," Elaine admitted. "Robert bit you last night and transferred his blood through the wound to turn you. But it didn't take, and that—"

I gagged and struggled to stand. She pushed me back down, coughing at the effort.

"Gracie, listen to me. They won't hurt you—you're too valuable to them." She kept talking about divinity and souls, but her words stopped making sense. Time slowed to a crawl.

Sometimes, a situation is just too much. Sometimes, things people say to you don't register. It was like that when my dad died. It took me weeks to admit to myself that he was gone. Neither his funeral nor his burial made his death real. It was his razor that did it.

My dad used an old-fashioned razor that took two-sided blades, and he was ritualistic in its care. After shaving, he'd open up the top wings and remove the blade, drying it gently on a square of toilet paper. He then wiped the razor and set both the razor and blade at the same angle, on a glass shelf to the left of the bathroom mirror. It drove my mother crazy that he refused to store the razor and blade in the cabinet. He claimed they couldn't dry properly, and the blade would rust faster. They argued about it for as long as I could remember.

My mother never prevailed. She had waited for exactly one month before putting the razor away. That morning, as I was washing up, I'd noticed it missing from its customary position on the shelf. I opened the mirror door of the cabinet, and there it was. That was when it hit me. He was dead—and I lost it.

Elaine telling me about my spirit, soul, whatever, was like that, but without the wailing. Was I even really human? Ben looked human enough. I felt human.

The lyrics to the song "Human" by Rag'n'Bone Man started playing in my head. I nearly started humming along. Elaine and

Ben waited, watching me. When I said nothing, he sidled up next to me and touched my shoulder.

"Gracie," he interrupted my mental babbling, tugging on my sweater. "It's good if you're like me. We can talk about how cool it is after we get out of here. Now, we have to go."

I stared at him, his words finally registering, then at Elaine. "We're leaving?"

"Ben, you need to tell me right now. How did you get the code to this door?"

"From Maria." He flushed. "I didn't want to tell you because she's my friend. She gave it to me. She has all the codes and all the keys." He brightened with the satisfied smile that came of knowing something the adults didn't.

"And in your dream, you saw us escaping safely?"

"Yes, Mom! We go out the front door. But we have to go now. That's what happened in the dream."

Elaine straightened and hugged Ben to her before releasing him. "Well, this might work. If Ben saw it, it's true. Let's go."

I shot to my feet. "Hold on." I yanked a pillow out of its case and grabbed both bars of soap, dropping them inside. "The only weapon we have," I said with a grin. I swung the pillowcase in an arc and slammed it down hard on the table. Elaine jumped at the explosive bang, but Ben didn't even flinch.

"I knew you were going to do that," he said and opened the door.

34

Felix

The big guy, Phillip, turned out to be a troll raiser, whatever the hell that was, and the old woman, Fay, was an elemental witch. Lucy and Ezekiel welcomed Fay and Phillip to the mission. I, however, was skeptical. Why on earth would these people want to risk their lives after meeting Gracie once? Okay, according to Fay, she'd known Gracie for at least a year. But still. Ezekiel shot down my muttered protests by pointing out that I was doing the same thing. The angel was getting on my last nerve.

Considering our increased numbers and newly acquired talents, we decided to scrap our original plan of ringing the front doorbell in favor of luring the vampires outside into the daylight so Lucy could put them to sleep. While everyone else was doing that, I would go in through the kitchen door—it was the most likely to be unlocked, according to Lucy—to retrieve Gracie. As a plan, it was even more suicidal than ringing the bell. But as I wasn't fighting, I figured it wasn't my place to tell them what idiots they were.

Mrs. Rinelli, who had no powers I knew of, would wait in her little red Beetle with Viceroy, which was where I would be if I possessed a shred of sanity. At this news, Viceroy growled, his vampire voice loud enough to carry across the street.

"Shut up!" I hissed at him. "Are you trying to get us all killed? We should have left you at the parking booth."

He cut off mid-growl to glare at me before turning his back on us. Gracie's mother looked terrified as she scooped him up and got into the car.

We gathered at the wall, and Phillip boosted us, one by one, over the top. I heard landings into crunchy autumn leaves. Well, so much for a silent approach. Phillip motioned to me. I was last, having hung back to shush Viceroy. He lowered two hands locked together as a cradle.

I hesitated, looking at my feet. These were very expensive loafers.

"Felix?" he asked.

"I'm going," I muttered. "But I don't have to like it."

I placed my stylishly shod foot into his hands. Phillip hoisted me as if I weighed nothing, and I found myself atop the wall and slithering down the other side before I could bemoan the fate of my coat, which caught on the rough brickwork. I came to rest behind a thick stand of shrubbery with Lucy, Fay, and Ezekiel. Phillip dropped down next to me seconds later.

We made a motley crew. We had no weapons, and our instruction from Ezekiel was, "If for some reason Lucy's sleep reverie fails, we may be forced to fight. But I'm hoping I don't have to kill any vampires."

I tried to explain how fast and vicious vampires are—how we didn't stand a chance, our powers as an angel of God, a witch, a reaper, and a troll raiser notwithstanding. I peered from face to face, and except for Lucy, the only one smart enough to be frightened, all exuded a ludicrously calm determination. I was breaking into a vampire stronghold with a bunch of suicide bombers. I wanted to cry, and my face must have shown it.

"Felix, if you want to save Gracie, this is what we have to do," Lucy swallowed audibly and touched my arm. "And remember, some of us have fought battles greater than this." She lifted her chin at Ezekiel. "We can do this. We'll get Gracie and whomever else needs rescuing."

I took in a gulp of air. Lucy's pep talk didn't make me feel any better, but it was probably more for herself than for me. I forced myself to stand straighter, grateful that there were more than three of us.

"For Gracie," I said, sounding like an idiot.

Lucy lifted her chin again, this time at me, and grinned. "For Gracie. Let's go."

She stepped out of the shade of the shrubbery and onto a perfectly manicured lawn. We walked silently on thick grass, keeping to the shade, circling the perimeter of the garden until we came to the back of the house. From the plans in *Architectural Digest*, we knew the locations of all the doors. But we hadn't accounted for the security cameras.

A set of glass doors opened, and two vampires stepped out. One walked away from us, crossing a patio to head toward the kitchen door. The other one walked directly at us. We fanned out, and I took two steps back, tucking myself behind Phillip, who was sizable enough to handle himself and protect me. The short, slender vampire sauntered toward us, expecting to usher us back onto the street. Then seeing something he didn't like, he froze. Opening his mouth too wide for the size of his face, he tilted his head back and howled a high-pitched, ear-splitting sound that raised all the hairs on my body. My knees weakened, and I sank to the ground while Ezekiel, Lucy, and Phillip strode forward.

Ezekiel's arms began to glow. He placed his hands on Lucy's shoulders and shouted, "Lucy, now!"

Lucy held out her hands, but the piercing ululation only increased in volume.

Fay yanked me to my feet. "Felix, I need you to close the circle so I can cast a spell," she said and grabbed my hands.

"Who, me?" I was numb with shock, barely registering that I was touching a witch. They'd always given me the creeps.

"Yes, you! Buck up!"

She dropped one of my hands and slapped me.

"What the fuck!" I reached for my burning cheek, only to see her feet grow tendrils of root that wormed their way into the ground. I yanked my hand back, but her fingers were turning into vines that wrapped their way up my arm. She grabbed my free hand, and the same thing happened. I shrieked before I could stop myself.

"Felix! I'm not going to hurt you! Repeat after me. *Sanguisuga, conticeo, obticeo, taceo.*"

I stared at her, snapping my mouth shut.

"Felix!" she shouted in my face. "With me! *Sanguisuga, conticeo, obticeo, taceo!*"

I joined in. "*Taceo. Sanguisuga, conticeo, obticeo, taceo!*"

The earth beneath my feet rumbled. As we shouted the chant, a shock wave rippled from the ground, through Fay, me, then outward through the air. It passed through Phillip and Ezekiel and hit the vampire in mid-howl. His ululation cut off like someone flipped a switch. His head was still back, his mouth still stretched open, but no sound emerged. His head snapped down, black eyes fixed on us, and he charged. I nearly wet my pants.

Ezekiel shoved Lucy behind him, and she ran to stand with Fay and me. Phillip stepped forward. I watched, my eyes straining to pop out of their sockets, and he grew in height and girth, rising to at least nine feet tall. I stumbled on the Latin badly enough that Fay's vines crushed my hands to alert me.

"Ow! Stop it!"

"Felix. Focus or we all die," Fay shouted.

"*Don't watch,*" I heard Lucy's voice in my head. What the fuck? Now Lucy could get into my head?

I stopped chanting. "Don't watch what?" I asked as the vampire, moving too fast to stop, smashed into Phillip, his face hitting Phillip's belt buckle.

He bounced off and fell to the grass. Phillip reached down with one enormous hand and lifted the vampire into the air by the head. He encircled the snarling, flailing vampire's throat with his other hand. *Oh, fuck!* I whipped my head away from the sight just as I heard a loud, squelching pop.

Gagging, I refocused on Fay, who was grinning like a Halloween jack-o'-lantern. The dead vampire hit the ground with a thump, his head rolling to land three feet from my shoe. I gagged again, and another half dozen vampires poured out of the house, heading directly for us.

"No need for silence now. But maybe this will help," Fay said with a nasty smile.

I swallowed the bile rising in my throat and nodded at her.

"Sanguisuga, lutum, limus, dilabor, prolabor!" she chanted.

I focused on her face, now wild with glee, and picked up on the second round. *"Sanguisuga, lutum, limus, dilabor, prolabor!"*

Our voices rang in my ears, impossibly loud. As before, the earth shifted. This time, the wave flowed up through us and back down into the ground, spreading outward. I stumbled on the suddenly trembling turf, but Fay held me upright as, hands linked, we continued to chant. *"Sanguisuga, lutum, limus, dilabor, prolabor!"*

The charging vampires began to sink, running in slow motion as their legs descended into the turf as if into quicksand, struggling until they were shoulder deep. Fay stopped the chant, and the ground solidified beneath us. I gaped at Ezekiel and Phillip, not understanding why they hadn't sunk too. Lucy stepped from behind us, closed her eyes, and extended her hands, palms out toward the sunken vampires. Nothing happened. They opened their mouths and began to ululate.

"It's not working. I can't put them to sleep," Lucy cried.

Ezekiel frowned at the trapped vampires. "If they keep howling—"

But Fay had already started the silencing spell. I picked it up, and the unearthly wailing ceased.

"Let me take care of them," Phillip said.

Ezekiel shook his head. "We can't. We shouldn't have killed the first one."

"You can't," Phillip clarified. "We can't leave Fay and Felix out here chanting while we go inside looking for Gracie."

One of the vampires broke an arm free of the earth as Phillip spoke. The others began to worm their upper bodies free.

"I'm sorry, Ezekiel," Phillip said and strode toward the vampires, putting a foot on the nearest vampire's shoulder and reaching for its head. "This is the only way."

I couldn't watch, so I broke the chant and ran for the house.

35

Gracie

A goosebump-inducing howl flowed down the hallway as we made our way toward the stairs. The howl cut off, and I stopped, but Ben tugged me forward. I hadn't realized he'd been holding my hand.

"I'm fine," I assured him as Elaine looked back at us, a finger to her lips.

Hugging the wall, we crept to the railing of the staircase and peered down to an empty entryway. We ran down the stairs, ducking into a darkened room that might be a library, judging from shelves I could scarcely make out. Elaine ushered us behind a large object, a sofa.

"Get down and wait."

"No, Mom!" Ben cried out.

"Shhh. I'll be right back. I'm going for Maria." She didn't wait for an answer, disappearing into the dark.

"Gracie?" Ben whispered, tears in his voice. Despite his bravado, he was still a kid, and this was too much for any ten-year-old. I didn't care how vampire savvy he was.

"We're okay, Ben. I'm here. We're safe." I hugged his slender body against me. Like hell we were, but I wasn't going to tell him that. I swallowed to control the jolt of bile rising in my throat.

Throwing up now was not an option. "Your mom will be right back," I whispered. And then the lights went on.

"Well, well, well, borrowing books, are we?" A cultured voice preceded the face that materialized on the other side of the sofa— Robert Jameson.

Ben let out a small involuntary yelp. I rocketed to my feet, the bile I had just swallowed finding its way out of me and onto the center cushion of a lovely green velvet sofa. Well, that wouldn't win us any points.

The man who had bitten me raised an eyebrow and sighed. Up in the room, I had been too angry to notice his face. Now I was too paralyzed to look away from the caked-on stage makeup he wore.

"Didn't your parents teach you that it is impolite to stare?" He glared down his aquiline nose at me, and I stumbled backward, wiping my mouth with a sleeve.

Ben stepped between us. "You scared her! You even scared me! Didn't we agree you wouldn't be scary?"

The tall, terrifying vampire drew his eyebrows together and frowned. "Yes, Ben. You are correct. I did agree not to be scary." He paused for a heartbeat too long and smiled. "To you. Grace, however, is another matter." His smile morphed into a leer.

Ben stomped his foot, which was no mean feat on the thick carpet. "If you are my friend, and I think you are," he said carefully, drawing himself up, "you will not scare my friends either." He crossed his thin arms over his narrow chest in a challenge. "It's easier to catch flies with honey, right?"

The vampire burst into a belly laugh. "Ben, I do so enjoy your company. I would miss you terribly if something were to—"

The point of an arrow exploded out of the front of the vampire's throat. I yanked Ben backward as thick clots of blood hit the same cushion I had just vomited on. That would never come out. I didn't wait to see who had shot the arrow. I grabbed Ben by the shirtsleeve and dragged him toward the front door, just as Elaine, Maria, and Felix appeared from behind the stairs.

"FELIX!" I cried. "How—"

"Run!" Elaine yelped.

I turned, grabbed Ben's arm, and flew to the front door, wrenching it open. We stumbled out and down the stone steps as a group. Ignoring a shriek from somewhere out on the lawn, we ran down the path for the iron front gate. I turned the handle and burst into tears when I found it locked.

"Aspetta, ho una chiave!" Maria pushed me aside and shoved a key into the lock. She turned it, and we practically fell onto the sidewalk. Maria pulled the gate shut behind us and locked it again.

"If we can get a couple of blocks away, I can call an Uber," Elaine said.

But I was staring across the street. I swiped tears out of my eyes and sucked in a lungful of air. "Or we can go with my mom." I pointed to the red Volkswagen Beetle, my mother at the wheel, Viceroy in her lap.

I jogged toward the little red beacon of hope, the others close behind me.

Viceroy saw us first. My mother was staring straight ahead, seemingly oblivious to the little dog leaping around in her lap. She jumped when I tapped on the window, flinging the car door open and leaping out to throw her arms around me. "Gracie!" was all I heard in English as she switched to a stream of Italian, ending with *"Sali in macchina!"*

She didn't have to tell us twice. We piled in, Maria in the front seat, and Ben, Viceroy on his lap, between Elaine and me in the back.

Felix stood on the sidewalk as my mother walked around to him. "Go," he said. "I have a ride."

"Mr. Belloquot, no. I am not going to leave you here. We can—"

"Call me Felix, please. I'll leave with my friends when they come out. Please, get them to safety, Mrs. Rinelli. I'll be fine."

They stared at each other. My mother finally extended a hand.

"I can never thank you enough, Felix. Thank you, with my whole heart, for saving my daughter."

Felix took my mother's hand, bent, and kissed it, lingering for a few seconds too long before releasing it and stepping backward. My mouth fell open.

"I did nothing," he murmured. "You need to go." He smiled with eyes only for her, then he turned and walked back toward the house without a backward glance.

My mother blushed, pointedly not looking at me, as she walked around the car, got in, and started the engine.

Viceroy jumped onto me and licked my face, forcing me to press my lips together to keep dog saliva out of my mouth and preventing me from uttering the expletive I had in mind. Viceroy immediately returned to Ben's lap, cocking his head and smiling at me—he'd done that on purpose!

I wiped my mouth on the same stinky sleeve I'd used after I'd vomited on the vampire's sofa. "Blech."

Elaine handed me a tissue, and I used it to scrub my lips.

"Wait a minute. Mom, I'm glad you're here, but *how* are you here?" I had to raise my voice above Ben's giggles as Viceroy began to lick him too. "And why do you have Viceroy?" I turned to watch Felix approach the front gate. "Who's here with Felix?" Though I wanted to yell at her for flirting with a freaking half-vampire, I couldn't unpack the weird scene I had just witnessed.

"Viceroy came with Felix, Lucy, and Ezekiel. I found you with Find My Friends—don't scream at me—and I brought Fay and Phillip, and they're all still inside the wall."

She pulled away from the curb, spun around a corner, and raced down a street with blessedly little traffic.

Out of sight of the house, I leaned forward, watching my mother through the gap between the front seats, my real questions and accusations too thick in my throat to verbalize. Even though it saved me, I was deleting that app as soon as I got a new phone. I shifted position to lean my head against the cold window and finally, safe, fell asleep.

I woke to the faint aroma of dead fish and the sound of the idling car, peering out the window to see a warehouse. "Mom, what's going on?"

"We wait here"—she held up a hand before I could interrupt —"until Ezekiel arrives."

"Who is Ezekiel?" My voice rose. "Mom!"

Before she could yell at me for yelling at her, a door in the side of the building opened. A man stepped out, pointing to a spot in front of a truck bay. My mother pulled into the space he indicated and shut off the engine.

"Mom! What are we doing here?" I demanded. She ignored me. "Mom! Mother!"

Without turning around to answer me, she got out and walked straight to the man. I fumed as he pulled her into a quick hug.

"What the ever-loving hell," I muttered when she hugged him back.

"Not hell," Maria said in stilted English. *"Penso che siamo in Paradiso."*

"What?" I asked, distracted by the show my mother was putting on.

Maria's next utterance jolted me. *"Quell' uomo è un angelo di Dio,"* she whispered and crossed herself.

"Heaven? We're not dead, and this isn't Heaven; it's a fish warehouse," I said, adding in an undertone, "And if Heaven is the Fulton Fish Market, no thanks." I shuddered. "And really? You think that man is an angel of God? Angels aren't . . ."

I stopped myself. She wasn't listening. She'd closed her eyes and was whispering the Apostles' Creed in Italian. Elaine and Ben watched me, Ben's eyes wide, waiting for me to say something. I was Catholic. There were vampires. "Oh, why the heck not." I glanced at Maria. "Angels. Fine."

We got out of the car while my mother chatted away, as

animated as a teenager, with a man who looked more like a barista than any angel I had ever seen in a Catholic school picture. He had a millennial beard and a denim jacket over a checkered shirt. Jeans and well-worn work boots completed the look of not-an-angel. When he turned to smile at us and wave us over, I saw a spacer in one ear. And worse, if that was even possible at this point, my mother was practically fainting with joy.

36

Lucy

I had told Felix not to watch, but now I couldn't look away. My stomach roiling, I watched as Phillip decapitated the last vampire. A man spattered with what appeared to be dark blood burst out of the house.

"Run! There are too many coming to fight," he shouted at us and veered toward the front gate. Stunned, we all looked at each other for a heartbeat.

"Hey! Is there a dark haired man inside?" I shouted at the bloody man.

"Let's go," Fay said and recalled her roots. We took off after him.

"He's a vampire—I can feel him. It could be a trap," I hissed to Ezekiel.

"It's not a trap." He fell into step beside me. "He's running for his life."

Phillip overtook us with long strides, reaching the wall beside the front gate as the bloody vampire was trying, unsuccessfully, to wrench the iron door off its hinges. Phillip stepped up to him, a ham-sized hand reaching for his head.

"Wait," Ezekiel bellowed.

Phillip froze, hand hovering above the man's head.

"Did you see another man inside? Dark hair? Camel coat?" I pleaded.

"He got out with the others." The man panted. "We have to go. NOW!"

"Which others? Who got out?"

He stared at me, his eyes bulging, makeup sliding down his cheeks to reveal a patchy network of darkening blood vessels. "My mother, Elaine, Ben, and a new woman. *Please!* Let me out!" He banged his fists on the gate, and I heaved a trembling sigh of relief.

"Phillip." Fay laid a gentle hand on the giant's waist. "Open the wall. We need to leave."

Phillip's grinned. "Okay, Fay." He curled his fingers into a fist and punched the wall. It exploded outward in a cloud of bricks, shards, and dust. A sharp pain tore at my chin as Ezekiel pulled me through after Phillip and Fay. The vampire followed.

Felix, leaning on the wall a few feet away, brushed a dead leaf from a sleeve. "Took you long enough," he said, raising an eyebrow. "We really should get the fuck out of here." He pushed off the wall and ambled toward my car.

"Go with him." The vampire put a hand on my arm. I flinched, but he ignored the involuntary movement. "I wounded Robert, but he is already healing and has called for backup." He looked back through the hole, then at each of our faces. "Your friend is safe. Please tell my mother, Maria, that I'm alive." He paused. "And that I've escaped."

"We'll tell her," Ezekiel assured him. The vampire turned on a heel and pounded down the street, away from us. He was out of sight in seconds, replaced in our field of vision by two black cars at the corner, slowing for a stoplight.

"I believe that's our cue," Ezekiel said, and we sprinted to my car.

The little red Beetle was gone. That could only mean one thing—Gracie was safe. I beeped the car open, and we tumbled inside, Ezekiel at the wheel. He started the engine and headed down the hill and toward Broadway.

My soul itched. It wanted me to sleep so it could sail free, back to the vampire stronghold, to listen and watch, gathering intelligence. Part of me wanted nothing more than to lean my head against the headrest and nap, but selfishly, I needed the camaraderie of these new friends.

Friends. How odd. I had met Phillip and Fay less than an hour ago. Felix, I'd met barely more than a day ago. Did I feel this fellowship because we had briefly fought a common enemy together? I checked my watch. We had been inside the garden for approximately twenty minutes, give or take a couple. Even though my sleep reverie had failed, and I hadn't done anything to help, we had escaped in record time and without personal injury. Did that constitute enough of a battle to warrant battlefield friendships?

Living for more than four hundred years, I'd had plenty of time to consider, well, everything. Often overanalyzing to the point of dissolution. If you take something apart down to the molecular level, it ceases to have any meaning at a material level. So I shut down my analysis before I reduced my new friends to a metaphysical argument.

"Does anyone else think that was too easy?"

I turned around at the sound of Felix's voice in time to see Phillip's eyebrows fold toward each other in a glower. Brick and concrete dust had settled in his beard and stuck to the wet splotches of thick vampire blood on his face, hands, and shirt. He was his pre-fight size again.

Fay let out a small sigh and frowned. She looked shrunken, withered, and yellowed, like she needed fertilizer. "Easy?" She coughed and cleared her throat with some difficulty before continuing. "No, that wasn't easy at all, Felix. I will need days to recuperate. I'm not as young or vital as I once was. And Phillip will have nightmares for weeks." She stroked his arm gently, and his face relaxed. "Gracie reminds him of his sister, killed by vampires. He'd do anything to protect her, including putting his own life on the line. If word of what he did gets out, and those dedicated to destroying his kind find him, he will die."

Felix flushed, and to his credit, he didn't press Fay for the details. "I'm sorry, I didn't mean . . . It's . . . it just happened so fast," Felix muttered. "I thought full-blood vamps were immortal. That's what they tell you. But after they were beheaded, they didn't get back up." He examined his hands. "I expected a battle to the death, but I thought *we* would do the dying."

"I can't help you with that, Felix," said Fay. "Vampires lie."

"Not all of us!"

"Oh, so you're the exception to the rule? You never lie to get what you want?" She snorted.

Felix turned his face to the window.

"That's what I thought," she murmured.

We hit Broadway and joined the flow of traffic, blending into a Bronx evening. I listened to the argument in the back seat peter out and watched people flow around our car at every stoplight. Mothers with babies on their hips and in strollers, older children tagging along behind. Teenagers and young people in couples and groups, laughing, pushing, kissing, arguing.

I darted a glance at Ezekiel. I wanted so badly to be one of them. Human, normal, one of the people going into the drugstore or the supermarket or the bakery, balancing my packages and checkbook, worrying about my daughter's science project or my son's graduation suit. I wanted a family. I wanted to age and experience creaky knees and reading glasses. I longed to feel Ezekiel's arms around me till the end of my days. I saw a woman carrying a tiny dog in a handbag, and an ache for Viceroy twisted around my heart. Felix had insisted I take him if something happened. But what if we all got out alive? Could I still have him? Should I even ask?

"At this rate, it'll take us thirty minutes or more to get there," Ezekiel was saying, shaking his head at the traffic. "At least Gracie and the others are already there."

"Do you know that for a fact?" I asked.

"Yes. I can feel them. Gracie's mother made it in record time."

"Where is 'there'?" Felix asked.

"Hunts Point. The Fulton Fish Market, to be precise," Ezekiel said.

"And we'll be safe?" Fay asked.

"Yes. Only the Church and angels have access to the place we are going," he said. "And from them, we have nothing to fear." His face tightened, but Fay, in the back seat, couldn't see his concern.

"Good." She leaned against Phillip, closing her eyes. Phillip arranged himself so that she was comfortable, leaned back, and closed his own eyes.

Felix tapped me on the shoulder. "So we're staying in a warehouse? In a fish market?" He wrinkled his nose at the mere thought.

"Felix." I couldn't hide my annoyance. "Do you remember the Celestial Parking booth?" I watched as his face morphed from quizzical into childlike delight. "Think better. Much better." I'd never been to the warehouse, but if Ezekiel had overseen creating it, the place would be splendid.

"Right." He closed his eyes.

I waited until I heard a chorus of gentle snores and turned to Ezekiel. "Did we do the right thing?"

He glanced at me quickly. After stopping for a traffic light and taking a moment to frame his words, he said, "We did what we had to do. No more and no less."

I put a hand on his arm. "I'm sorry I got you into this. I'm sorry you had to—"

"Lucy, stop. Do you think I'd have it any other way?" His voice caught, and he glanced at me again.

I trembled as his gaze consumed me.

"I've missed you so much," he whispered.

I swallowed, not trusting myself to answer. He huffed a quick exhale and turned his attention back to the street. Bereft at the loss of his hungry gaze, I leaned against the door.

Ezekiel had not touched a single vampire, but he had allowed Phillip to kill them. Did that make him complicit? What about

Phillip's soul? There were too many questions, and Ezekiel's tight face stopped me from asking them. My heart ached for him. For us. For all that could never be unless I could reclaim my humanity. But wresting my thoughts from our doomed love only brought me to the dead, soulless vampires.

They had once been human but had relinquished their souls in a mad lust for what they believed, what Felix had believed until less than an hour ago, would be immortality. But nothing, supernatural or not, survived decapitation. The only exception was me and others like me, indomitable spirits who had chosen to become reapers. The growing certainty that I would have to accept the Mantle of Death edged into my thoughts.

"Lucy?" Ezekiel prompted. "What are you thinking?"

He had sensed my deepening despair. I pushed it all aside to focus on the one problem I could at least attempt to solve now that Gracie, Felix, and Viceroy were safe. "I'm out of my depth, Zeke. How do we keep Deathy from forcing souls into vampires?" I twisted in my seat to face him.

He frowned. "Lucy, I wish I had told you that we knew what was happening with Deathy earlier. I may have been able to prevent Felix and Gracie's involvement."

I thought for a moment before answering him. "I think you have it backwards. If Robert Jameson, apart from Deathy's involvement, wanted Viceroy and Felix to try and determine how a half-blood managed to create a vampire dog, the same chain of events would have occurred, except you and I might not have been in the right place at the right time to save Gracie."

Ezekiel gave me a long look. "I suppose that's true. Thank you for putting it that way. As for the souls, we believe we can stop Deathy before it goes that far." He hesitated. "Lucy, perhaps you should go home. There's no need for you to endanger yourself any further. I'll arrange for everyone's safety."

I stared at him. "Go home? And do what? Nothing?"

I stopped abruptly. I could go home. Perhaps I should. My one contribution to the rescue effort had failed. I was just one more burden for Ezekiel to carry. Gracie and Felix weren't my responsibility, and if I had to accept the Mantle and become Death, I should talk to Marco and Patience and rest in preparation.

A panoply of emotions flickered across Ezekiel's face as he drove, and I knew I couldn't leave him.

"I'm not going home," I said. "Please don't argue with me. Whatever happens, I want to be with you when it does."

We stopped at a light, and he turned to gaze at me. "Your chin is bleeding." He reached toward me, his touch as gentle as a butterfly landing.

"'Tis but a scratch." I chuckled at my Monty Python reference. "Where were you this morning?"

"Reporting in. Your new information prompted an elevation of the threat level to Slate Gray."

"Slate Gray? Never mind," I said when he opened his mouth to explain. "I get the idea. I'll do whatever I can to help. Did you tell Them that?"

"I did. They said to thank you."

I nodded.

"Lucy, we will fix this. In due course, Deathy—although she no longer deserves that designation and should go by her human name, Isashkishu-Eshlesh-Inmeshlinzit—shall receive her just punishment for meddling in the ascension of souls."

I nodded again, hoping that "in due course" was soon enough to keep innocent souls out of vampire bodies.

37

Gracie

The man Maria claimed was an angel opened a door and motioned us inside. My mother entered the building, clearly expecting us to follow. I hesitated. The others, looking to me for guidance, stayed where they were. We had just escaped from a vampire prison, and some random guy expected us to walk into a dark warehouse in the middle of an industrial wasteland in the Bronx?

"Nope, no fish warehouse for me. I'm going home," I said over my shoulder as I strode away from them and toward who the hell knew where because I had no idea how to get home without a car or my phone. "I'm so done with this."

I was halfway to the fence when Viceroy blocked my path, ears forward, a soft whine vibrating from him.

I stopped and crouched down. "I need to go," I said into his earnest little face. "I need Bryan."

Tears spilled down my cheeks and fell into his fur. The little guy stood on his hind legs to lick them from my chin, which only made me cry harder. I scooped him up, turning at the sound of rapid footsteps behind me—my mother. She opened her arms, and I rushed into them, crushing Viceroy between us.

"Shhh," she soothed, stroking my head as I bawled on her shoulder. "You're safe. We're safe." She grasped my arms and pushed me gently back to peer into my face.

I set Viceroy on the ground. "You lied to me, Mom."

My mother froze midway to pulling an ever-present tissue from her pocket. "Who told you?"

"Elaine. Right before Robert Jameson bit me. And then she took the time to explain as much as she knew about my spirit. That sucked, Mom. It should have been you."

"Who bit you?" she whispered, her face pinched in anguish.

"Robert Jameson, Mom, not that it matters now."

"Oh, honey, I'm so sorry. But are you okay?"

"NO! I am *not okay*, Mom!" I shouted. "I'm not okay because you lied to me, a vampire bit me, and now we're hiding out at a fish warehouse! But mostly because you lied to me!" I stopped before my face exploded, taking a couple of deep breaths. "But I'm not a vampire if that's what you're asking."

She sagged in relief but stood her ground. "I deserve that, Gracie. I lied by omission. I didn't know how to tell you about yourself." She bit her lip, and I raised my eyebrows at her. "I'm sorry. I wanted you to have a normal life for as long as possible, maybe for the rest of your life. I didn't want you to . . . to feel different."

I pressed my lips together, not knowing how to answer that. She looked miserable, and part of me wanted to comfort her, to tell her I understood that she'd been trying to protect me, but the rest of me was boiling mad. So I tapped my foot and waited.

"Gracie, if that vampire Robert Jameson didn't bite you, you might never have known. You'd have married Bryan, gone to school or had your cake truck or both, and maybe had children and grandchildren. All without thinking you were odd. And you will still have those things, but—"

"But? But what? But now I'm the freak in the family?"

"No, now you're the blessing in the family. You've always

been the blessing in the family. Why do you think we all work so hard to protect you?"

That threw me. I opened my mouth to argue when a car rounded the corner of the parking lot to turn in our direction. My mother grabbed my elbow.

"We need to get inside!" she hissed, yanking me toward the building.

Mad as I was, I didn't want my life to end in a parking lot. I broke from her grasp, and we sprinted toward the open door and up the metal steps.

The car pulled into a parking spot next to my mother's red Beetle, all four doors opening simultaneously. A man and woman got out of the front seats, and Fay, Phillip, and Felix got out of the back.

"Felix! You're safe! You made it!" I yelped and rushed down the stairs, stopping just short of flinging myself into his arms.

"Of course I'm safe," he grumbled. "I had to wait for the rest of your rescue party." He jerked his chin at the others.

I felt my face flame. "You all came to rescue me?"

"We did," Fay said, reaching out to touch my cheek.

"Gracie, I'm—" Phillip's eyes flooded with tears. "I'm, you're, we—"

"We all made it," I finished for him. "Let's go in." I stepped aside to let them climb the stairs.

Felix took my arm to steer me up after them and inside. "It seems you have been gathering quite the coterie of protectors. Though, for the life of me, I don't know how you did it. I need a drink. Dare I hope there's a bar in this dump?"

Stepping inside the warehouse was like entering a castle. The effect was astounding. My mouth, along with everyone else's, fell open as we took in the soaring granite, arched ceiling, and massive staircases of a great hall.

My head buzzed as I turned to look out the door at the parking lot, then back into the medieval room.

Barista Angel smiled gently at our expressions. "The

doorway you just passed through is a liminal space. You are technically no longer in the Bronx," he said, closing the metal door, which morphed into a heavy wooden one as it clunked shut. He peered at me. "Passing through one affects some people oddly. You might want to sit down," he said, but not in time.

The buzzing increased until it echoed around my skull like bees in a jar, my knees buckled, and the last thing I saw was an enormous tapestry of God on a throne before blinking out.

I WOKE TO A WET DOG TONGUE SMUSHING ACROSS MY cheek. I moved Viceroy off my chest and sat up, a wet washcloth falling from my forehead and onto my lap. I was on yet another velvet sofa in a huge living room with gray stone walls, fancy red rugs, and more tapestries. I brushed my hand against the fabric. What was it with the velvet sofas and supernaturals anyway? I picked the washcloth off my lap and dropped it into a bowl of water on a coffee table before it could soak my pants.

Everyone was talking at once, in a circle, a few feet away from me.

"I called everyone and explained the situation. Bryan and Augustine have agreed to sleep at the hospital. Everyone else has left for a safe haven in the Catskills," my mother said to someone in the group.

Wait, what? My freaking family had agreed to go to the Catskills? My brother and Bryan were sleeping at the hospital? Just like that?

"What happened?" I croaked.

Everyone turned to me. My mother was at my side in seconds, smoothing my hair, not noticing the way I flinched away from her.

"You fainted. But you were only out for a couple of minutes. How do you feel?" she asked.

"Um, okay, I guess. What did I miss? What safe haven? Who are you three?" I demanded.

Voices erupted again until Ben plopped himself on the sofa next to my legs, Viceroy at his feet. "I'll tell you," he said and began pointing at people.

"That's Ezekiel. He's an angel. That's Raziel," he said, pointing at Barista Angel. "He's an angel too. That's Lucy. She's a reaper. That's—"

"Wait. A reaper? Like in *Dead Like Me*?" I examined the willowy strawberry blond.

Lucy chuckled. "Exactly like that," she said, her voice warm. "I'll tell you all about it once we get a bit more settled."

"Or how about right now? Why did you come to rescue me? You don't even know me." My head was starting to hurt, and I needed the bathroom. "Ben, I need to get up." I swung my feet to the floor as the little boy jumped out of my way. "Where's the bathroom?"

"They're just down that hall," Raziel said, indicating which door I should take.

"I'll go with you." Lucy separated from the group, and we walked down a gray stone hallway straight out of the 1400s until we reached a pair of modern illuminated restroom signs that looked like they still belonged to a warehouse—weird. Once inside, I slipped into a stall as Lucy did the same.

"So this isn't awkward at all," I said to her as we washed our hands, sneaking glances at each other in the mirror.

She smiled. "It will all make sense soon," she said, leaning over the sink to splash water on her makeup-free face.

I handed her a cotton hand towel from a stack.

"Thanks. A little cold water always makes me feel better," Lucy said, tossing the used towel into a basket on the floor.

She looked too young to be so composed. "Um, not to be rude or anything, but how old are you?" I asked.

That got me a grin. "This body is twenty-two. Gracie, we have a lot to tell you. You've already learned that vampires are real, angels are real, and now reapers. There—"

"Are others?" I finished for her, my stomach rising even though it was empty. I swallowed hard.

"That wasn't what I was going to say, but yes, there are others," she said, almost too quietly to hear.

I must have gone pale because she turned the faucet to cold and soaked a fresh towel, wringing it out and handing it to me.

"Put this on the back of your neck. It will help."

I swept my rat's nest of a non-hairdo up and laid the cold towel where she'd said, leaning against the sink.

"Better?" Lucy asked.

"Yeah, a bit," I said as the nausea retreated. I ran the towel over my neck, pressing it to my face to buy myself a minute. "But you're human?"

"I guess the best answer to that question is: mostly." She moved toward the door, but I didn't follow.

"What's the inhuman part?"

She pressed her lips together and held out her hand. I stared at it, tucking my own hands behind me.

Lucy burst out laughing. "I'm not going to hurt you. Take it."

I gritted my teeth. Nope.

"Gracie, take my hand. It will explain everything a lot faster than anything I could say to you."

I shook my head.

"Okay, if you're sure, we can go," she said.

"No! Wait." I grabbed her hand, electricity zinging through my palm, up my arm and shoulder, to light up my brain. I gagged and whirled to dry heave into the sink, leaning over to drink from the tap when nothing came up.

"That's what I thought," Lucy whispered.

I spun to face her. "You're indomitable like Ben and me!" I gasped. "So are we reapers too?"

"No, Gracie. You're very human. Becoming a reaper is a choice an indomitable spirit makes at the end of its human's natural life. A choice neither of you will have to make for hopefully a very long time." She smiled at my relief. "It's a good thing to have an indomitable spirit, Gracie. I'll answer all your questions, I promise. Can we join the others?"

"One more question. Are there werewolves too?"

"Nope. No such thing as werewolves," she said.

"Well, I guess Charlaine Harris got that part wrong," I muttered and pushed the door open to raised voices. By the time we joined the rest of our party, an argument was in full swing.

"What's happening?" I yelled into the din.

The tall blond angel left the group and strode over to us. "Gracie, it's a pleasure to meet you. My name is Ezekiel."

The man was gorgeous. Tall and blond, he looked like a Viking underwear model in a suede jacket. I shook his hand without a second thought, receiving only a gentle tingle of warmth.

My mother joined us. "Grace, before you can ask, our family is safe."

"And you know this how?"

"Ezekiel has arranged for them all to go upstate to an angel encampment sympathetic to our dilemma in the Catskills. Augustine and Bryan will remain at the hospital to care for their patients. A guardian angel will protect them. We, however, need to find a place to go, as we're . . ." She hesitated. I had noticed Raziel frowning at another doorway as we reentered the room.

"I'm afraid we can't stay," Ezekiel finished for her. "It seems we cannot trust some of our angelic brethren to safeguard us. Maria, Fay, Phillip, Elaine, and Ben are going upstate to join the rest of your family. I suggest you and your mother travel with them."

I bit a lip and looked for Felix, who was staring into space, frowning. I couldn't catch his eye.

I turned to Ezekiel. "I was in that house. The vampires know I don't have Viceroy. Why do my family and I have to hide?"

"Jameson might not be able to turn you, but you escaped. If

he is like any other full-blood, he'll want to make an example of you. He will certainly be watching your apartment, your mother's house, and Bryan's apartment. You and your family are all still in danger. You should go upstate."

I glared at him. "I'm not going. I need answers. Lucy is willing to tell me all about my indomitable self, and since no one else seems to care enough about me to—" I broke off, my chest burning with unshed tears, and turned to my mother. "I'm staying with Lucy. You should go and take care of everyone. I'll be fine."

It was as if I'd hit her with a sledgehammer. She rocked back but recovered as quickly as she'd faltered. The room fell silent, everyone staring at us.

"I'll stay with you if Ezekiel agrees?" she said, not taking her eyes off me.

"If that's what Gracie wants," Ezekiel said.

I had no idea what I wanted, but getting into a major battle with my mother wasn't it. A fight was coming, but not today, not here, and not at some summer camp for angels in the freaking Catskills. My chest loosened, and the incipient tears vanished with a growing sense of purpose.

"I'm staying, Mom, but you need to go. I want you to take care of the rest of our family. I'll feel better knowing you're with them." And it was true: I would worry about her, and them, a lot less knowing they were safe and together. "These guys will take care of me."

Her chin trembled. I still loved her, liar or not. I leaned in to hug her, and she wrapped her arms around me.

"I love you. Please be careful," she whispered in my ear.

"I will, Mom, I promise. I love you too."

I released her, stepping back, and bumped against Phillip.

"I am staying with Gracie." He crossed his arms over his chest.

I looked at Ezekiel and Lucy.

"Of course you can stay with us, Phillip. I was hoping you

would," Ezekiel said and clapped a hand on the big man's shoulder.

Phillip's brilliant blue eyes flashed with pleasure, and he smiled at me, lighting up the whole room. My mother looked relieved.

"So where do we—?" My stomach interrupted me with a growl loud enough to hear. "Whoops, sorry." I sighed. "I'm starving. I could so eat a bacon, egg, and cheese on an everything bagel from— Wait!" I snapped my fingers. "Manny!"

38

Gracie

"**M**om! I can call Manny." I pulled the neck of my T-shirt out to peer down at the number still imprinted on my skin. My mother stared at me as if I had grown horns on my head.

"What is on your chest?" she demanded. "Let me see!" Her face was in my neckline before I could back away.

"Grace Marianna Rinelli! What have you done?" She began to shout in Italian, and Maria rushed over to peer down my shirt, too, crossing herself as she listened to my mother raving about Manny and the Cosa Nostra.

"Mom, Manny's mafia? Bagel bakery Manny?"

She was pacing back and forth, Maria at her heels, sputtering at how I had gotten myself involved with the worst possible people.

"Wait a minute. *Mom!*" I shrieked. "STOP!" She froze at my tone. "I don't know who told you that. Maybe it's true and maybe it isn't. Either way, so what? You do realize that vampires are chasing us, right? And you're worried about Manny's family connections? Seriously?"

Her mouth fell open. You could have heard a pin drop. Everyone was silent, mouths agape, heads swiveling back and forth between us like they were watching a tennis match that no one was winning.

"Are you insane? You accept a favor from one of them—you owe all of them. And you tattooed that man's number on your breast," she said, wiping her eyes.

"It's not on my breast! It's on—" A hot flush reminded me we were in mixed company. "It's *not* a tattoo. The ink from the receipt Manny wrote it on transferred to my skin. It'll come off. Besides, the trouble we're in now is way worse than any trouble you think I could get into from Manny. Which, by the way, is none whatsoever. I'm calling him."

Her mouth snapped shut and flew open again. I threw my hand up in the universal stop gesture. "No. Don't say it. I don't care what club he belongs to. The man makes incredible bagels, he's a nice guy, and he'd want to help me."

Just the same, I'd tell Sylvie before she fell in too deep. In case, with her criminal justice leanings, she'd want to bail. Though it was probably already too late—I'd seen her moony-eyed, lovesick face.

My mother struggled to recover her equilibrium while Maria, glued to her side, murmured in Italian and rubbed circles on her back. I'd never seen my mother so hysterical, not even when she found out about Chris's motorcycle at the family dinner table, and that had been epic.

"Grace," she tried again. "Please. Don't call him. You cannot be indebted to them." She actually crossed herself.

"You never mentioned his mob connections in all the years we were buying bagels from him! Why is that, Mom? Manny owes *me*—he said so. Someone give me a phone. Lucy, please read me the number. It's backward."

Lucy stepped up, a grin fighting a frown on her face. The grin finally won as Raziel handed me his phone. Lucy peered into my shirt and began to recite numbers as I punched them in. Manny picked up on the third ring.

"Manny? Hi, it's Gracie. I could really use that favor. My friends and I are in a little trouble, and we need a place to hide."

T HIRTY   MINUTES   LATER,   AFTER   A   WATERFALL   OF warnings from my mother, and tearful goodbyes, Ezekiel, Phillip, Lucy, Felix, Viceroy, and I drove to Port Chester. We filed into Manny's Bagel Bakery just as he was about to lock the doors.

Manny pulled me into a tight hug, which I returned. He smelled like bagels with an undertone of cologne and shirt starch. "I'm glad you're safe, and it's good you called," he murmured and released me. "You'll all be safe here for the night. I think I've found a place for you to go tomorrow, but I won't have details until later." He slipped behind us to lock the heavy glass doors. "Are you hungry?"

My mouth had begun to water as soon as the smell of bagels wafted through the open door. "Oh yeah. Is the griddle still on?" I asked.

"I kept it on for you," he said and winked at me. I introduced Lucy, Felix, Ezekiel, Phillip, and Viceroy. Manny kneeled to shake Viceroy's paw, eliciting a grin from the little dog.

"Have a seat, everyone. What would you like?" He walked behind the counter to grab a pad to jot down the requests as everyone read the menu over the register. Manny looked Phillip up and down. "You get two," he pronounced and disappeared into the back.

"Need help?" I called.

"Get the drinks. I'll have a Vitaminwater, any flavor."

Ezekiel rejected the tables arrayed in front of the window, instead ushering us to a single long table hidden from the windows by newspaper and snack displays. I collected everyone's drink choices and got condiments and napkins from beside the cash register, setting everything in the center of the table. Manny was fast, and we had steaming bagel sandwiches a couple of minutes after that. He even prepared a plate of scrambled eggs and chopped-up sausage for Viceroy, who attacked his food with relish.

After a grateful round of thank-yous, intent on our food, we ate—the silence broken only by yummy sounds. But halfway through my perfect bacon, egg, and cheese, I started worrying about telling Manny about vampires, angels, and reapers.

I must have let a sigh escape because Felix, who had been weirdly silent for the entire ride up, finally spoke. "Just tell him, Gracie. He can handle it."

I searched Manny's face, thinking about my mother's hysteria. If what she said was true, he probably could handle it. "Okay, Manny, a vampire named Robert Jameson and his gang are chasing us, which is why we need to hide, at least until we can figure out what to do next. And Ezekiel is an angel, Lucy is a reaper, and Phillip is human, like us."

"Troll raiser. I am a troll raiser," Phillip announced, his chin high.

My chin practically hit the table. "What? A troll raiser?" I dropped my head into my hands, jerking it up just as fast. "Okay. Troll raiser. Got it." I looked him over for signs of horns or something weird I'd missed. Seeing none, I turned my attention to Manny while he chewed his last bite.

He took his time, swallowing and wiping his mouth with a napkin, before taking a long drink of his Vitaminwater and finally speaking. "I know the Jameson family."

This time everyone's mouth dropped open, even Viceroy's.

Manny pressed his lips together to keep from grinning at our collective shock. "Okay, look, I might as well tell you all, since Gracie probably already knows who I am."

He looked at me for affirmation, and I swallowed hard and nodded.

"It's like this. I am a member of a family. And a family's a family. What difference does it make what color their skin is, what language they speak, or what species they are? Italians, Russians,

Japanese, vampires, the dynamics are always the same." He scratched the back of his neck. "We've been fighting the Jamesons since they muscled their way into the vampire family hierarchy, displacing the Michaelsons. Robert Jameson is less amenable to our arrangement than John Michaelson was, God rest his black soul. Let's just say Jameson makes certain things difficult for us."

"Difficult how?" Ezekiel asked.

"There isn't much I can tell you, but among other problems they've caused, we've lost a few of our most profitable parking garages to them, and management is very unhappy about it."

"May I ask if you still control City Parking on Mercer?" Felix asked.

Manny chuckled. "I don't know. Parking isn't my area. What I do know is that we would be very grateful if Jameson were to disappear."

I swallowed hard and muttered, "Yeah, so would we."

Manny patted me on the shoulder. "Don't worry, Gracie. You're gonna be okay. I got you."

Once we'd finished eating and cleaned up, he led us downstairs to our temporary hideout. "So the bathroom is upstairs, as you saw, and I would leave the lights off in the bakery proper should you need it during the night. Of course, you can turn the bathroom light on once you've closed the door. You can't see the sliver of light from underneath it through the front windows in the dark."

Of course, he would know that. "Anthony will be here at three thirty a.m. to turn on the ovens and start the baking. Two more guys, Nick, and Alfie, come on at five in the morning. They all know you're down here, and they know how to handle themselves—just in case. Oh, I almost forgot." He pulled out a ring of keys and wrangled off a single key, handing it to Ezekiel. "This is for the back door in case the little guy"—he nodded at Viceroy—"needs to go out. It leads to the alley behind the building. Even if someone sees you from an apartment window, they all know me."

I shook my head at myself. How hadn't I known about

Manny's "family"? Why had my mother never told me? Oh yeah, because she'd never told me anything important.

"Is there anything else we need to know?" Lucy asked.

"Oh, how could I forget? There are cots. I'm sorry there are only three." He walked to a corner and patted one of three old narrow iron cots covered with a clear plastic drop cloth. They were already made up with sheets and blankets, pillows in plastic bags on top.

"Also, there's a loaded shotgun under the front counter, one behind the flour bin upstairs, and two behind this supply shelf, along with extra shells." He pointed to a rack holding baking ingredients against the wall. "But you shouldn't need them. You'll be safe here. Jameson's people wouldn't dare attack one of our properties directly. I'll see you tomorrow morning. Right now, I gotta run." He flashed a broad grin. "My youngest has a basketball game—the kid's a giant!"

He sprinted up the stairs, our thanks floating up after him.

"Shotguns," Felix sputtered. "Bakers who double as ninjas. This is just great. You have some interesting friends, Gracie. And he knows about vampires! *The entire mob* knows about vampires."

Lucy rolled out the cots and began unfolding them. "And apparently they've never revealed what they know to the general public," she said, shaking her head. "There's just so much to unpack there."

"Not really," I said, sudden exhaustion nearly buckling my knees. "Italians are superstitious. They believe in all sorts of legends, folktales, and myths. I took a whole class in belief systems at NYU. So learning of a new twist in something they already believe in wouldn't faze them. As for outing anyone? That would never happen. They don't talk. Talking is squealing, and we all know what happens to squealers in the family—we've seen the movies."

Lucy shuddered as Phillip moved to help her with the cots.

"Well, I guess it works in our favor," she allowed. "But do you think Manny's ever—"

"His soul is clean," Ezekiel murmured. "It was the first thing I checked."

I heaved a massive sigh of relief. I'd probably out Manny to Sylvie anyway, but at least I could tell her he wasn't involved in anything truly heinous.

"You must be tired, Gracie," Ezekiel said. "Why don't you try to sleep for a bit? The bakers will probably wake us early, so you might as well rest while you can."

"No, I can . . ." I looked around, dying to close my eyes but not wanting to take a bed from someone.

"Phillip and I will be fine. You, Lucy, and Felix will take the cots. And that's final."

Phillip's rapid nodding accompanied Ezekiel's pronouncement.

"Thank God!" Felix sighed, claiming the one farthest from the stairs. He stretched out, and Viceroy jumped up next to him, tucking himself against Felix's body and taking a full third of the narrow space. But Felix's eyes were already closed, and he didn't seem to notice.

I followed suit, removing my shoes and sliding under the blanket to curl up, facing Felix and Viceroy. It was barely seven p.m., but we were as safe as we could be, and I was emotionally, if not physically, exhausted. The last thing I heard was Lucy settling herself on the remaining cot and Ezekiel and Phillip pulling out chairs.

39

Felix

Wednesday, November 18

I woke to the aroma of coffee and the footsteps, thumps, and muffled voices of the bakers at the ungodly hour of five a.m. Gracie and Phillip had brought a pot of coffee and a large cup of hot water down the stairs. I managed to refrain from disparaging the two Lipton teabags Gracie dropped into the steaming water.

"Felix? Are you okay?" Gracie asked as she poured coffee for everyone else.

I shook my head. I'd dreamed that I was about to murder my soul to get Vampire Bob to turn me. My soul had screamed in terror, but Julianne Moore had appeared and laughed, offering me a lollipop as a consolation prize for killing my soul. The cold sweat I'd woken in had soaked my shirt. I shivered and pulled the blanket loose, draping it around my shoulders and clutching it against my chest.

Gracie turned a chair to face me and dropped onto it, angling it so that her back was to the rest of the group. "Tell me," she whispered.

I shook my head. It was just a dream, sheer nonsense. "I just need a shower, a shave, and a set of clean clothes." And a snack before I turned forty. Thinking of aging made me think of Gracie's mother, who looked to be in her mid to late fifties. She was small and fine boned, like Gracie, with an elegant sweep of silver hair that framed her face against the same dark brown as Gracie's hair, only without her curls. Mrs. Rinelli's warm brown eyes were wreathed in faint crow's feet, her full lips—

Stop it, Felix! You are not going to date Gracie's mother!

Gracie cocked her head and squinted at me. Thank God she couldn't read my mind.

"Where's Viceroy?" I asked to change the subject.

"He's upstairs, searching for mice. I found two dead ones laid neatly in front of the stairs when I went up to make the coffee. Manny's going to want to keep him." She chuckled. "Are you sure you don't want to talk about it?"

Manny pounding down the stairs saved me from insulting her to put her off.

"Good morning. I hope you all got a little rest. Again, I'm sorry there weren't enough cots. I got a call last night. Management is only too happy to help, and we have the perfect place for you."

"The enemy of my enemy is my friend," I whispered. "Even if that friend is—"

"Felix!" Gracie hissed at me. I glared at her but clamped my mouth shut.

The man was happy running a bagel bakery, meaning that anything he was so pleased with was bound to be subpar.

"Let's have breakfast and get going. I think you're going to like this," Manny said, rubbing his hands together.

"No. I am not hiding out at an abandoned amusement park!"

"Felix, this isn't just any amusement park—this is Rye Playland! And it's not abandoned; it's closed for the season. It's awesome, you'll see." Gracie tugged my arm, trying to get me to follow everyone into the park.

I pulled my phone from my pocket. "How on earth could that man think I would enjoy an amusement park?" I muttered loud enough to spark anger in Gracie.

She dropped my arm. "You'd rather take your chances without us and die alone?"

"At this point, I don't care how I die. I've had enough of this lunacy."

She forced a burst of air through pursed lips, flinging a tendril of hair out of her face and jamming her hands into her pockets. "Fine. I can't drag you—you're too heavy. If you want to leave, go. We'll take care of Viceroy."

The morning sun warmed my back as I watched the little shit trotting at Lucy's heels as they disappeared around a corner. Gracie spun and stalked after them.

I pulled up the Uber app, finger hovering over the screen. I didn't want to be alone in my loft waiting for Bob to find me, but I also didn't want to stay in a rundown wreck of a closed-for-the-season amusement park. Though, admittedly, it was probably better empty than full of the type of people who frequented such a place.

I shoved my phone back into my pocket hard enough to tear the lining. "This is just fucking perfect. You people are insane!" I yelled at Gracie's diminishing figure.

She turned. "Hurry up if you're coming. Better crazy than dead."

Fuming, with no one to vent it on, I stalked after her. "This place is a dump. How long do we have to stay here?" I muttered at her as we walked past several rides skeletally vacant of their cars, closed-up food and game stalls, and shuttered ticket booths desperately in need of dismantling, or at the very least, a tanker truck of cleaning solution and several coats of fresh paint.

"I don't know, Felix, until we figure out what to do. And the park looks better in the summer."

I raised an eyebrow.

"At night," Gracie admitted, shrugging. "But I love it here. I grew up coming to this place, and some of my happiest memories are of times here with family and friends. There was this one time—"

I shot her a look.

"Okay, fine. Maybe it's not as fancy as you're used to. Maybe you were a rich kid who went on expensive vacations, but you don't have to make fun of me because I love this place," she said, her voice breaking. Crap.

"Gracie." I grabbed her elbow and stopped. "I'm not making fun of you. My mother died giving birth to me in a bar. If the bar's owner hadn't taken me in, I'd have grown up in an orphanage instead of sleeping on a cot in the back room and working for my keep."

The color drained from her face. "Oh, Felix, I'm an idiot. I'm so sorry."

"Don't be. I didn't tell you so you could pity me. It was a long time ago. I've created a very comfortable life for myself, and I like it just the way it is, which precludes hiding out in amusement parks."

"Then you shouldn't have bitten me." I looked down to see Viceroy at my feet. "As usual, you're being an ass, Felix. And you shouldn't be such a snob—it's rude. This place is awesome. There are squirrels and rats here. I can smell 'em!" He danced around in a circle as I curled my lip at him.

"What?" Gracie asked. "Why are you giving him the evil eye?"

"Tell her, tell her, tell her!" the little nitwit insisted.

"SHUT UP! I'm not telling her anything. Go chase something!" I shouted at him. *Whoops.*

Gracie stepped back, fists on her hips. "Why don't you tell me exactly what the hell is going on between you two. Don't think I haven't noticed the looks passing between you."

"We should find the others." I strode past her but stopped short, realizing I had no idea where to go. I spun to see her immobile, hands still on her hips, Viceroy sitting at her feet. "Let's go!" I yelled.

Gracie shook her head slowly back and forth.

"Viceroy! Come!" I snarled. The damned dog turned his back to me.

"Fine. I'm going. You two can stand here as long as you like." The desolate park was beginning to give me the creeps. I started walking in a random direction.

"You're going the wrong way," Gracie called.

I spun on a heel and marched back to her.

"Come on, Felix, don't be an ass. Start talking," Gracie said, echoing Viceroy's insult.

"You do know that you sound like an old gangster movie when you use that phrase, don't you?"

"You do know you sound like my mother most of the time, don't you? Just tell me. Can Viceroy talk?"

The little moron yapped in assent, and Gracie's jaw dropped. She snapped it shut, teeth clicking, and focused all her attention on him.

"One bark for yes, two for no, Viceroy." She took a deep breath. "Can you understand me?"

"Woof."

"How do you— Wait, let's do yes/no questions. Can Felix read your mind?"

"Woof."

"And you can read his?"

"Woof."

"Is it because he's your, er, master?"

"Woof."

"Can you read my mind?"

Viceroy pawed at my leg. "Can you please explain it? I feel ridiculous barking at her," he thought at me.

"Fine." I harrumphed. "We can hear each other, he and Lucy can hear each other, and I think it's the same with Ezekiel." She opened her mouth, but I held up a hand. "I'm not sure why. Viceroy doesn't know why either, and frankly, I don't care. It's annoying as hell. Can we go now?" I started walking.

"Felix! You just told me dogs can talk—"

I spun around. "I never said all dogs can talk. Viceroy doesn't talk, he thinks, and some people can hear him. Maybe it's because he's a vampire, but again, I have no idea how he does it or why we can all hear each other. Ask Ezekiel. Maybe he'll know more. Now, can we go?"

THE SECOND-STORY TOWER ROOM, PART OF THE children's museum and bathhouse building at the end of the boardwalk, was empty but clean. There were two towers. We were in the one closest to the amusement park entrance. Manny had left us with a ring of keys, bits of masking tape on the ones we might need. Fortunately for me, the entire building, which operated independently of the amusement park according to Manny, was closed temporarily for repairs. I was allergic to children, and I scratched at imaginary hives just thinking about a building full of them.

But this unused space would do. It had a commercial kitchen and restrooms. Manny had also left several bags of groceries he'd purchased for us after the basketball game yesterday. Someone was going to bring bedding later in the day. I walked to a window. If nothing else, we had a water view.

No one had asked for my help unpacking the groceries, and Viceroy was off hunting vermin, so I was free to think. I watched the sun sparkle on Long Island Sound, lifting the sash to freshen the dusty air and listen to the cries of the seagulls as they wheeled, weaving patterns above the water. I'd never been a beachgoer, as I didn't know how to swim and hated the feeling of sand against my skin. But I loved the smell of salt air and the sound of the gulls. Come to think of it, swimming might be good, clean exercise. As an added bonus, salt water cleaned the sinuses. I might have to find a saltwater pool.

I wondered if full-blood vampires swam at night. Did they do anything for fun besides hunt? Did they have hobbies? Even I had a hobby—thieving. None of the full-bloods I'd ever met seemed like the type to take a dip or go to a movie or play a few hands of bridge. If you lived forever and needed minimal sleep, what did you do all day and night? This train of thought delivered me directly to Phillip's beheadings, and I shivered in the chilly air flowing through the window. Full-bloods didn't live forever. They'd never told us. They'd also omitted the fact that we would have to murder our souls to become like them. But why? To make the Turn seem more attractive? Or had I just heard what I wanted to hear?

"Felix, would you like a cup of tea?" Lucy asked from the kitchen doorway.

I turned to face her. "Manny sent tea bags?"

"No, I always carry some. I'm sorry I neglected to offer them this morning." She held a selection of tea envelopes like a geisha fluttering a fan in front of her nose and mouth.

I looked at my watch, an A. Lange & Söhne Zeitwerk I had lifted at a party last year, then shook my head at myself. What did it matter what time it was? I left the window to join her.

Ezekiel and Phillip were setting up a long folding table and chairs. I followed Lucy to the table, selected a tea bag from her outstretched hand, and took a seat. "I'll never make fun of what you stick in your purse in preparation for a rescue again," I said. I tore open the Russian Caravan packet and dropped the bag into the paper cup of hot water Lucy had placed before me. I could get used to people serving me tea.

"So you envision us together for another rescue." Lucy grinned at me, taking a seat.

"No, I only meant . . . Never mind, I don't know what I meant. Can we leave this building to walk around?"

Ezekiel lifted his head from his conversation with Gracie to answer me. "I don't see why not. The park is closed, and I can't imagine Jameson would think to look for us here. But can it wait? I'd like to talk options."

Viceroy, who had trotted over to me in anticipation of an adventure, heaved a sigh and collapsed his legs beneath him, resting his head on his front paws. He was asleep in seconds.

40

Gracie

Since Manny hadn't thought to include any coffee, I'd borrowed Lucy's phone to text him and ask for a jar of instant in addition to the bedding. I got a thumbs-up emoji in response. I texted again to ask for a burner phone, telling him I'd pay him back. This time I got a "crying with laughter" emoji.

We'd plugged in the empty refrigerator when we arrived, stashing cold cuts and a few other perishables inside, but it wouldn't be cold enough to chill soda for a couple of hours. I chose a warm can of cola instead of tea, making a face as I took my first sip. I carried it over to the table and sat between Felix and Phillip. Felix made a face at the can.

"What? It's caffeinated."

"And it will rot you from the inside out."

I shrugged. "Medicine will have evolved far enough by that time to take care of my rotten insides. I'm going to enjoy my poison now, thank you very much." I tilted the can to my face and took a long drink.

Felix grimaced. "Fine. It's your body. Now what?" he asked the table as everyone settled.

"Lucy and I should share what we currently know," Ezekiel said. "Lucy?"

Lucy cleared her throat. "Okay, Gracie and Phillip, I apologize in advance. I'm going to talk about things you were not aware of, and I'm going to be brief. Let me get through the whole thing, then you can ask questions."

Phillip and I nodded. Felix snickered, and I shot him a dirty look. Lucy pressed her lips together and eyed us as if she was about to assign detention. Finally, she composed herself and began.

"Death, my boss, has cut a deal with Robert Jameson, or Vampire Bob, as Felix calls him. To help fulfill Death's part of the bargain, I was to collect Viceroy and Felix and reap—meaning take Felix's soul—if he resisted. It would have killed him. Then, I was to give Viceroy to Death, who would, in turn, hand him over to Vampire Bob, along with—and we're only guessing this part— enough souls for Bob's family of full-bloods. In turn, he would fulfill his part of the bargain—"

"Which is?" I blurted.

"We don't know," Lucy said. "Ezekiel and I have been trying to figure that out. But what Death is getting in exchange is almost irrelevant. The horrifying part is that the only way to trap an innocent soul on this plane is to block its ascension to its final destination." Lucy held up a hand when Felix opened his mouth. "The only way Death can do that is to prevent reapers from guiding souls. That would mean that a soul would remain in its corporeal body until the body's natural death. Without the guidance of a reaper, it would then wander this plane, confused and unprotected."

"Ghosts," Phillip whispered.

"I know that's how most people think of them, but it's an unfortunate and demeaning label, and it negates the heartbreak a soul endures, sometimes for centuries. They're lost souls, not ghosts."

Phillip flushed, chastised.

I put a hand on his arm, whispering, "I always called them ghosts too."

Lucy cleared her throat again.

"Sorry." I shrugged.

"And we help those lost souls move on whenever we come across them," she continued, a crease forming between her eyes. "A soul who does not move on for one reason or another is disoriented and terrified, sometimes angry—easy prey for anyone looking to abuse them."

I glanced from Felix to Phillip as all the blood drained from my face. They were both pale.

"Like vampires," Felix croaked.

Lucy nodded. "So, there are two ways to interrupt the ascension of a large number of lost souls. The first would be hacking HELL, the software we use to allocate souls to individual reapers. But hacking the software would be virtually impossible for Death to accomplish, as only the demons who wrote it could hack it."

Demon coders? Now that was something I wanted to hear more about.

Ezekiel picked up the thread. "The second way would be if Death relinquished power, the Mantle of Death, without a succession plan. Should that happen, we'd first have to divine a successor, then transfer the Mantle to the new bearer. It would take at least a few days."

"So there would be a gap in the process for people who die during the transfer?" I said.

"Precisely. It wouldn't be for long, but long enough to create enough lost souls to fulfill Death's end of the bargain." Ezekiel drummed his fingers on the table. "Lucy and I believe that's the most likely scenario, though we can't figure out why Death would want to become human in the first place."

"Wait a minute," Felix said. "Why couldn't Death—I'm presuming we're talking about Lucy's boss here, the one she refers to as Deathy—just use souls that were already lost? Why the need for new ones?"

"First, because many of them hide," Ezekiel explained. "It would take a long time to round up as many as Vampire Bob probably wants. Second, souls that have been lingering too long are often the spiritual equivalent of insane, either from heartbreak or anger."

"Oh," Felix said, looking unconvinced.

All I could think of was how sucky it must be to have Death's job. "Wait a minute. Lucy, if Death doesn't collect the souls herself, what does she do all day? Are there other parts to her job?"

"She is supposed to train new reapers, but she's been delegating that task," Lucy said before Ezekiel could reply.

I caught Ezekiel's warning glance to her. She nodded at him to pick up the explanation.

"Through the ages, Death, the entity, has had many names and even more responsibilities. But the Angelic Council has rescinded those powers, one by one, as the current Death abused them to the detriment of humanity. For the last hundred years or so, Death's only task has been logging into the system once every twenty-four hours to authorize its continued operation. I believe the login is biometric. She has to provide a daily drop of blood via a finger stick."

"So the only thing she has to do every day is bleed? And she's been doing this for what, a hundred years?" I thought my eyes were going to cross. "That sucks! No wonder she's pissed off."

Ezekiel nodded. "The finger stick was the demons' idea of a secure system," he said. "I never thought about it from that perspective—what it would do to her over time." He frowned.

"She's bored," I said. "And pissed off. I would be. You guys took everything away from her, leaving her to poke a hole in herself everyday like an on-call blood-bank. Were you really *that* mad at her? No company today would be able to get away with doing that to an employee. I had an internship at a mental health clinic once, where, legally, I couldn't have access to patient information. The director had no idea what to do with me. I ended up sorting office supplies for a month. I wanted to make a noose out of paper clips and hang myself by the third day." I grabbed a lock of hair to twist, dropping it and picking at a spot on the table instead. "Of course she wants out."

Ezekiel sighed. "Well, that might answer that question. But how does becoming human, with a limited lifespan—"

Lucy put a hand on Ezekiel's arm. "Wait a minute, Zeke. Gracie, how did you know Death was a she?"

I wrinkled my nose at her sudden intensity. "Okay, so I had this weird dream last night. I dreamed that Julianne Moore, the actress who was in the second Kingsman movie, was Death." I spooled out the dream in my head as I said it aloud. "Vampire Bob called her Deathy, and he was telling her that Felix and Viceroy were not deal breakers, they were more of a curiosity than anything else, and he could easily collect them himself. Then he said that souls for immortality were more than a fair bargain for— oh shit—for a taste of her blood. He's going to make her a vampire!"

Lucy inhaled so fast she choked, coughing hard as Ezekiel pounded on her back. Felix was staring at me like I'd grown another head.

"What?" I asked. "What did I say?"

"Nothing," Felix muttered. "It's not important."

"Does my dream mean something?" I demanded.

At the same time, Felix asked, "Is that bad? What's one more vampire?"

Ezekiel stared out the window. "One more super vampire, you mean," he said, his voice barely audible. "If it were possible, she'd be virtually indestructible."

"Oh shit," Felix said. "She'd be stronger than Bob. I'm willing to bet a Borsalino fedora that Bob doesn't know that."

Lucy looked at me strangely and broke in. "I'm willing to bet he does, but since a vampire cannot turn an indomitable spirit, it's all theory."

"So let him do it. If he can't actually turn her, what do we care?" Felix said.

Lucy eyed him, bit a lip, and then turned her gaze on Ezekiel. "I'm beginning to think it's more complicated than that. It shouldn't work. The book says it won't work, but—"

"There's a book?" I couldn't help myself. "You mean like *The Handbook for the Recently Deceased* in the movie *Beetlejuice*?"

"I haven't seen *Beetlejuice*, but by the title of the book, I'd say that yes, it's probably similar. Though this book is ancient and written in Sumerian."

"You can read Sumerian?" Felix croaked, his eyebrows rising into his hairline.

Lucy blushed. "No. Well, just a little. Ezekiel translated some of it for me. Can I finish?"

"Sorry," I said, not sorry at all.

Lucy continued. "If Deathy just went about the business of being a human, she would still have an incredibly powerful spirit, perhaps enabling her to do some things humans can't do. But it wouldn't necessarily extend her lifespan, or at least I don't think it would. Make sense so far?" she asked.

Everyone, including Viceroy, nodded, now hanging on her every word.

"But if it's true, and Jameson can turn her, all bets are off." Lucy wrapped her arms around herself and shivered.

I drummed my fingers on the table. "Ezekiel?"

"I'll have to seek counsel before I can speculate." He glanced at the ceiling.

"Oh, come on, you must know something," Felix demanded. "Have you ever heard of an indomitable spirit turning vampire?"

Ezekiel was silent for a beat too long.

"Zeke?" Lucy touched his arm. "What aren't you telling us?"

Ezekiel placed both hands on the table as if to steady himself. "I can't be certain, but I believe it may have happened once before," he said, dropping his gaze.

I jumped to my feet, jostling the table enough to rock my empty soda can and set paper cups trembling. "What are you saying? That some of us can be turned? I wasn't, Ben wasn't, but Deathy could be?"

Ezekiel looked at Lucy, who leaned away from him, tucking her hands into her armpits. "Many years ago, I overheard a conversation amongst some of my brethren. I dismissed it as myth or superstition because none of them had any proof."

Lucy pulled her hands out of her armpits and massaged her temples with her fingertips. "So it *has* happened before."

Ezekiel reared back, but she glared at him and continued before he could interject.

"That's another conversation," she said to him before turning her attention back to us. "Deathy is no longer the altruistic personality she once was. The last two hundred years haven't been kind to her—she's become twisted and angry."

"And powerful. And angry and powerful is never a good combination," Ezekiel said.

Felix's shoulders slumped. "So you have no idea whether or not indomitable spirits actually can become vampires. That means we're either stuck with Bob, or if he manages to turn Deathy and she decides to take over, we could end up with a stupidly powerful Vampire of Death. Does that about sum it up?"

Nobody moved or spoke for a long few seconds.

I peered at my watch. "Guys, I know it sounds stupid, after hiding out at Manny's and all, and I hate to leave in the middle of this, but I've gotta go. Now. I have a date to meet Bryan's mother tonight. We're going to dinner. And while I'd rather stick needles in my eyes than meet the dragon lady, I'm not going to disappoint Bryan. And I need a facial and a mani-pedi, for which I have an appointment. Then I need a handful of Xanax, for which my mother has a prescription."

Everyone except Felix jumped to their feet, Ezekiel circling the table to confront me.

"Gracie, you're in hiding. Why would you think you could go wandering around in public where we can't protect you?"

"Look. I still have a life, right? And I have a hard time believing that the vampires know Bryan's mother is coming and that we're going to dinner. And they certainly won't be staking out every restaurant in lower Westchester!" My face was on fire. I took a deep breath. "I don't mean to be difficult, but—"

"Gracie, Bryan is sleeping at the hospital to stay safe—I'm certain he's canceled your dinner." Ezekiel held out his phone. "Why don't you call him?"

Canceled. I wouldn't have to meet Bryan's mother. At least not tonight. Relief at my reprieve warred with embarrassment at my delusional pronouncement and outburst, and frustration at my situation. I'd wanted to believe that my part was over, that I'd merely been collateral damage. But what Ezekiel said made sense. I'd wanna kill me too if I was Vampire Bob. I'd made him look foolish. So relief had to win if I was going to stay alive.

I heaved a sigh. "Fine. You're probably right. Thanks," I muttered, swallowing the lump forming in my throat and taking the phone. I was outside, down the stairs, and at the beach entry before I realized I'd fled.

"Wait, Gracie," Felix called to me.

"I was just going to call Bryan."

"Bryan's not going anywhere. Viceroy needs a walk."

I sighed and slowed to allow them to catch up, slipping Ezekiel's phone into a pocket. Felix fell into step alongside me. "Are you going to lecture me?" I asked.

"No. I don't want to stay here either, as you well know. I just can't think of an easy alternative, and believe me, it's not for lack of trying."

I stopped to stare at him. "Do you have a difficult alternative?"

He considered my question for a long few seconds.

"Well? Do you?"

"I have a house in New Orleans. I'd considered going there."

"You have a house in New Orleans? Why haven't you left

already?" And then a thought hit me. "And why haven't you told the others?"

He frowned at me.

"Oh, I get it," I said. "The get-out-of-jail-free card is only for you—not that I'm interested in leaving Bryan and my family."

"No. That's not it at all. There's nothing special about my house, though it is big enough to sleep all of us. The problem is that New Orleans is a pit of vampires, voodoo, and venality—the whole fucking city is supernatural central. Every creature under the sun, and some who have never seen the sun, wreak havoc there. It would be less about hiding and more about calling in favors."

I searched his face but couldn't read the emotions flashing across it fast enough. "Felix, do a lot of people owe you favors?"

"A few," he admitted. "I've been saving them up for a rainy day."

I peered at the cloudless sky. "I'd say this is a fucking monsoon."

41

Lucy

"I'm going for a walk, Lucy," Phillip said after refusing to let me help him tidy the table. The big man crossed the room with a surprisingly light step and disappeared out the door, leaving me alone with Ezekiel. I walked to one of the windows overlooking the boardwalk, the beach, and the water beyond. The view was lovely, with small clouds scudding across an otherwise clear sky above calm water.

"She can track me, you know," I said.

"I know. I thought of that. Back in the car on our way to the fish market, when I suggested you go home, I was planning on sending guards with you," Ezekiel said, coming to stand next to me. "Perhaps it's foolhardy, but I'm glad you didn't go."

"Me too, though it may have been a foolish decision. I'm putting everyone in danger."

"Perhaps, but I think we have a bit of time before we need to move again."

"Maybe, maybe not. I know I'm stating the obvious here, but we need to think about where we'd go next."

I turned away from the mesmerizing motion of the waves and put a hand on Ezekiel's arm. "And another thing. Have you noticed anything odd about Felix?"

Ezekiel nearly swallowed his tongue in an effort not to laugh. He coughed instead, tears springing from the corners of his eyes. "Other than the obvious, no. Why?"

"Because he remembered me over multiple sightings. And when I brought him to my house, and he saw my reflection in the mirror, he perceived me as I am."

Ezekiel furrowed his eyebrows and frowned. "I felt no indomitability in his spirit. It must be very faint if it is still alive. But I wasn't searching for it either. I'll delve deeper when he comes back." He took a step closer. I didn't move away. "Lucy, we need to talk about you."

I swallowed. I knew what was coming.

"If we want even a hope of subverting Deathy's plot and keeping as many souls out of vampires as possible, you're going to have to take on the Mantle. It's the only way." He was a foot away now. His breath stirred strands of my hair as he turned to face me. "I'm so sorry," he whispered.

If I returned his gaze, I'd be in his arms. I looked down at my feet. "I know," I said, careful to steady my voice. "I'm ready. And if Deathy does become a vampire, as the new Death, I may be in a position to . . ."

"No. I will never allow you to stain your soul by committing murder, no matter how dire the situation. We will handle Deathy should she revert to her human form as Isashkishu-Eshlesh-Inmeshlinzit." He glanced at the ceiling and rested a hand on my shoulder.

I drank in the warmth spreading throughout my body, taking what consolation I could from his touch.

"My brethren have already begun to prepare so that we can transfer the Mantle to you as soon as I receive it. If we're ready, the gap will be hours instead of days."

"And I can instruct a group to be ready to guide any souls that collect in Deathy's vicinity, providing I can find her in HELL." I bit my lip.

"What do you mean?"

"Assuming she shows up as a human in the software once she relinquishes the Mantle. And that reminds me, the battery in my laptop is nearly dead, and I forgot my charger." I pulled out my phone, which was also about to die, and texted Manny, asking him to add a charger for our phones and my MacBook to the growing list of things we still needed. I got an almost immediate thumbs-up. "Manny will send one."

"He's a good man," Ezekiel said and paused.

"What?" I asked, stepping back from the window. "What else, Zeke?"

"We should get a message to Vampire Bob, telling him that Deathy would most definitely usurp his position in the vampire hierarchy if he turns her. It's a long shot, but it might be enough to sway his decision."

"Oh! Good idea." I shook my head, chewing a lip. "How?"

"We can ask Felix when he comes in. And Lucy, we have another potential problem. Can we talk about Gracie for a minute?"

"I'm pretty sure this is what whiplash feels like, but go ahead. I've been thinking about Gracie too," I admitted.

"We should wake her spirit. We can do it here." He glanced around the big empty room then searched my face. "What do you think?"

"I think I'd like to hear more about why you want to force her spirit to wake rather than allow it to happen naturally."

He ran a hand through his thick blond hair, making it stand up in tufts. It took every ounce of control I had not to reach up and smooth it down.

"In short, she's more use to us, and better able to protect herself, if her spirit is awake."

I reared back. "Zeke! How can you say that?"

"There's no point in beating around the bush. If her spirit decides to wake in response to the stress we are all undoubtably about to undergo, she will not only be a liability to the rest of us, but in a comatose state, she becomes easy prey." He held up a hand to forestall my outburst. "But there's more. Gracie is barely aware of her indomitability. It still slumbers. But even with her spirit asleep, I could feel her through the walls of Jameson's house. Gracie is powerful, Lucy. It's been centuries since I've encountered such strength in a spirit."

My knees trembled, and I put my hands on the windowsill to support myself. "Damn it. You're right. And I know." I pushed off and left his side to pace. "I sensed it too. I was hoping I was wrong."

He watched me for several seconds as I regained my composure. "We have to tell her," he said finally.

I gaped at him. I couldn't fathom compressing a lifetime's worth of knowledge and understanding into a couple of conversations, much less telling Gracie that she was about to possess a spirit more powerful than mine and then perform the spiritual equivalent of inducing labor on herself.

"We tell her everything," Ezekiel said. "She's resilient. Look at what she's been through and had to process already. Not only is she still standing, but she's fighting mad. Grace Rinelli is tough, Lucy. She wouldn't have such a strong spirit otherwise."

I shook my head. "Zeke, young women bluster. It's a defense mechanism to cover uncertainty. We can't know how much of Gracie's 'resilience' is emotional armor."

"None of it. Her strength is who she is."

I was protesting out of fear. Fear that her provoked spirit would be unpredictable, and the last thing any of us needed was a super-spirit bouncing off the walls, drawing attention to itself and wreaking general havoc.

"She will be formidable, and the sooner we prepare her and wake her spirit, the better for all of us," he said firmly.

I sighed. I knew from working with Ezekiel in the past that once he'd talked himself into a course of action, I would not be able to talk him out of it.

We spent the next half hour talking through the mechanics of Mantle transference instead of Gracie. Neither of us wanted to talk about what it meant for us personally. We knew that I could transfer the Mantle to a better candidate should we find one, but we also knew how rare someone like that was, with the two main requirements being a strong spirit and a pure heart. People like that existed, but how many would be willing to give up their lives and families to become Death?

Felix and Viceroy came back first. Viceroy ran to me in greeting, and I bent to gather him in my arms and bury my face in his salt-air-scented coat. Sand drifted from his paws to dust my feet. They'd been on the beach. I put him down before he could lick my face.

"Where's Gracie?" I asked.

"There." Felix pointed toward the boardwalk. "She's on the phone with what's-his-name."

I crossed and peered out to see her pacing in front of the ticket booth, gesticulating in passionate conversation. I turned away. Watching her in such an unguarded moment felt like snooping.

"Have you and Ezekiel come up with a plan?" Felix asked, heading for the kitchen.

"Yes. But it's not the kind of plan I think you're hoping for," I said.

"So if you didn't figure out how to get Bob out of the picture so I can go home, what have you been doing?"

"Ezekiel and I have decided that I will be taking the Mantle as soon as, and if, Deathy releases it. Acting quickly will give Bob as few souls as possible. And if we can get a message to him now, perhaps we can prevent him from turning her at all."

Felix glared, open-mouthed, at me. "You want to *talk to him*?"

Ezekiel stepped between us. "Calm down, Felix. If we can talk to him, explain that she might very well be able to grab control, we might be able to convince him not to turn her."

Felix stalked toward the door, turning in the opening. "It's not your body he wants to vivisect—it's mine. And Viceroy's. If that's the best you've got, we're out of here."

Viceroy didn't move from his place at Ezekiel's feet but thought into the room, "Felix, wait. Listening won't cost us anything."

Felix trembled in the doorway. "You're a trusting idiot," he said aloud. "Ezekiel's only worried about Deathy and lost souls. He doesn't give a fig about keeping us safe. Let's go. I'll call us an Uber."

Viceroy didn't budge.

Ezekiel spoke, his voice low. "Felix, you need to understand something. Lucy, Phillip, and I are in no danger from Deathy and Vampire Bob. Phillip could go home, and Lucy and I could easily operate from anywhere—if we were willing to let the three of you go it alone. We're here, with you, solely to protect you all. Will you please come back into the room?"

"Then why don't we just . . ." Felix hesitated, then spoke from the doorway. "I was going to say kill Bob. But killing him won't solve the soul problem. Or will it? If there's no Bob, there's no deal with Death, and there's no one left to come after us."

Ezekiel nodded. "That's true. And it would most likely work for a time. Providing we can get to him."

"What do you mean 'for a time'?" Felix frowned and walked back into the room.

"We have to assume that Jameson has lieutenants. He would have advised them of his agreement with Death. If we somehow manage to kill him, his second-in-command steps up, and on and on." Ezekiel closed his eyes.

Felix sighed. "We'd have to kill them all."

"Correct," Ezekiel said. "But if we can convince Bob that turning Deathy would almost certainly mean the end of his reign, we might be able to negotiate a better deal."

"That and 'You know what you got; you don't know what you're gonna get,'" Gracie said from the doorway. She grinned at our confused faces. "My nonna used to say that about divorce. The devil you know and all that."

"Yeah, well, the devil we know wants to conduct experiments on Viceroy and me. So if it's up to us, I vote—"

"Not so fast," Viceroy interrupted Felix who shot him a dirty look. "The devil we don't know, this Death woman you're talking about, probably wants Lucy dead so she can't take the Mantle."

We all stared at the little dog lying at Ezekiel's feet, his chin on his paws. "I'm sure she does, Viceroy," I said, turning to Ezekiel to see his lips thin. "And she can find me easily through HELL."

"I thought it might be a possibility," Ezekiel admitted. "Knowing you as well as she does, she'd figure you would step up and accept the Mantle."

"So even though she can't kill me permanently, my having to find another body would take more than enough time to give her the souls she needs."

"Making it even more imperative that we talk to Jameson as soon as possible." Ezekiel strode across the room to stand in front of Felix. "Do you know how we can contact him?"

"Call the house," Gracie said, shrugging. "You can probably find the number online. And by the way, Bryan is coming to see me. And I don't want to hear it." She put up a hand at Ezekiel's expression. "It was his idea. He was too busy to talk just now, but he said he had to see me. I tried to stop him, but he insisted. He said he'd be careful." She tugged nervously at a lock of her hair. "Lucy, where's the bathroom? I need to freshen up, and the public ones are all locked. And do you by any chance have a brush or a comb?"

"Finally," said Felix. "I wasn't going to say anything, but since you mentioned it, your hair looks like—"

"Felix!" Viceroy and I yelped as one.

"What? Appearances are important." Felix shrugged. "If everyone paid as much attention to theirs as I do to mine, the world would be a much more attractive place." He heaved a theatrical sigh, and the sound grated on every last nerve I had.

I turned away before I said something inappropriate. By agreeing to accept the Mantle, I was giving up my last chance at becoming human, my last chance to be with Ezekiel. So as selfish as it was, I had little empathy left for Felix.

42

Gracie

"This way, Gracie," Lucy said, leading me down the hall after grabbing her enormous handbag on our way through the kitchen. It was deep blue and obviously cost more than I could ever afford.

"Wow. That's gorgeous." I stroked it with a fingertip. The leather felt like butter.

"Thanks. I forgot to change it for a casual one after dinner . . ." She hesitated. ". . . with Deathy. I have an old brown one that holds twice as much . . ."

She trailed off as she dug around inside the bag. I wondered how much bigger the brown one was. "Here!" Lucy handed me a wide-toothed comb with a flourish. "And I have these." She pulled out sealed packets of micellar water cleanser. "And these." She laid a blush, two shades of lipstick, eyeliner, and mascara on the counter in the rundown restroom. "They're not exactly your colors." She stepped back to examine my face. "But they'll do in a pinch."

"Holy crap! Thank you! You're a lifesaver." I picked up the comb and went to work on my hair. "What else do you have in there?" I peered over her shoulder into the bag's gaping maw.

"Some first-aid stuff, a spare phone—I always carry two after an incident on Tenth Avenue a couple of years ago." She glanced at me sideways. "You don't want to know," she said in answer to the question I was about to ask. Then she pulled out a pair of hand-knit wool socks. "A gift from a woman who recovered," she said, her voice low. "I can't seem to put them away in a drawer."

I drew my eyebrows together.

"Miss Eleanor was extraordinary—we became friends," she explained.

"She's gone now?" I asked.

"Yes, and I was the one who guided her dear soul at the end. I still miss her." Lucy shook her head. "Not knowing them is easier."

"But lonelier."

"Sometimes."

I could see she didn't want to talk about it anymore. "Can you do the back for me?" I asked, holding out the comb.

Her expression brightened as she took it. "We can braid each other's hair and show the men they were right all along about what we do when we go to the restroom together." Lucy chuckled and produced a selection of hair accessories from her bottomless bag. We giggled through arranging each other's hair into ridiculous configurations. Fifteen minutes later, we left the restroom with hair fit for either the prom or a zombie-fest.

"Lucy, can I ask you something?" I asked just before we reached the kitchen.

"Sure, anything." Her face was warm and open.

I chewed the inside of my cheek, stopping before I drew blood. "What was your life like before you became a reaper? You had an indomitable spirit, too, right? Was it weird?"

She stopped short, and I bumped into her. "Let's go outside," she said. "I'll tell you, but—"

"But not in front of Felix."

That got a grin.

"When is Bryan coming?" she asked as we crossed the board-walk to a bench facing the water.

"In about an hour. I told him to call from the gate so we could unlock it. I guess I should have told Ezekiel."

"He'll figure it out, don't worry." Lucy sat, tucking her hands under the hem of her sweater. It was cold despite the sun, but the air was clean and salty. We sat and stared at the water. I didn't rush her, sensing deep reluctance.

"Gracie, my experience was very different than yours will be, and I don't like to remember those days, but you deserve an answer." She gazed at me, concern in her green eyes. "Okay, here goes. I never knew, before my awakening, that I had an indomitable spirit. I was twenty-three and sleeping next to my husband, when my spirit woke. My husband was roused by the lights beneath my skin—a sign of an awakening indomitable spirit. The lights don't last long, just a few minutes or so, but he must not have been deeply asleep, and he saw them. He and everyone else in my village assumed I had been possessed by the devil."

"What? Wait, what? When did this—"

"In 1622. Back then, anything out of the ordinary—a mole, a funny walk, a talent, an odd laugh—was seen as evil. It was usually avarice, jealousy, or a desire to be seen as virtuous that would cause a neighbor or relative to inform on a so-called witch."

My face must have registered my shock, because Lucy squeezed my hand.

"It's okay, Gracie, I want you to know. People's under-standing of the natural world was limited. Superstition and conjecture instead of science," she continued. "Seeing someone light up from within was terrifying, which as we know from our current political climate, almost always translates to hatred. And we kill what we hate." She paused.

I gulped and squirmed, guessing what was coming. "Were you—"

"Accused and put to death? Yes. My husband accused me. I was burned at the stake, my unborn baby, still too small to be obvious, inside me."

"Oh god, Lucy. And yet here you are, helping people. The same kind of people who murdered you." I wanted to hug her, hold her, but my arms only managed to twitch, so I just sat there.

She put a hand on my shoulder. "It was a long time ago. I've forgiven those that accused and executed me many times over. And the assistance I provide, well, I'd argue it helps me more than it helps them."

I bit my lip. Lucy was a far better person than I'd ever be. I should have said something sympathetic, but there were no sympathy-card phrases for immolation. *I'm so sorry you burned to death at the stake?* Her expression was calm, but I was beside myself. "Where did this happen?" was all I could manage.

"Salem, Massachusetts. They were killing anyone suspected of being a witch long before they started recording the deaths for posterity."

My heart broke for her. Why did shitty things have to happen to good people? Why did the bad ones never seem to suffer?

Lucy leaned toward me to rub her hands up and down my arms. "Gracie, please, don't pity me. We all suffer in our lives, some physically, some emotionally—my version just happened to be a bit more dramatic."

I shook my head as tears slipped out. She dug in her magic bag and pulled out a small tissue pack before continuing.

"I told Ezekiel that I was worried about telling you everything, but just now, remembering how ignorant of the changes in my body I was and how knowing what was happening to me might have saved our lives—mine and my baby's—I've changed my mind. It's better if you know what you are, what's going to happen to you, and how it will or will not affect your life, depending on the choices you make. So let's talk about you."

I hiccupped. "This is going to sound crazy after all my bitching, but part of me is afraid, you know?" I whispered, then mentally slapped myself for sounding like a baby in light of what Lucy had endured.

"I do. But you need to understand that having an indomitable spirit does not change who you are. You are still human, still Gracie Rinelli, still able to live and enjoy a full and happy life. You can marry Bryan and have children or not. All choices are yours to make. You will choose to become a reaper or a guardian at the end of your life. You can also choose to relinquish your indomitable spirit and move on, though I've never heard of anyone doing it." She patted my hand. "Are you okay so far?"

"I am." That didn't sound bad at all. "Go on."

"Here's where it gets a bit interesting. Indomitable spirits have varying gifts, if you will. Some can see glimmers of the future. Others can learn anything easily. Some are deeply empathetic and can sense emotional states. Still others have enhanced powers of persuasion or manifestation. There are many possibilities. You will learn about yours as you come into your awakened soul."

"What's yours?" I asked.

"Can't you guess?" Lucy grinned. "You said it yourself. I'm here after what happened to me, and I rescued you without ever having met you. I'm an empath."

I gazed at her, knowing it was true. I could literally feel her kindheartedness. "Are there any bad ones? Like evil gifts?"

Lucy burst out laughing. "No," she said when she'd recovered, "but having an indomitable spirit doesn't necessarily mean you're a good person. A persuasive spirit could go either way, becoming a minister or a con man or both at the same time." She shrugged. "What you do with your gift is up to you, Gracie. From what you've told me, your lucid dreams are exceptionally clear. You may end up as a seer. You could go to the dark side, to borrow the phrase, and use it to game the stock market, or you could try to help those close to you by guiding them away from danger."

Half an hour later, after Lucy had answered most of my questions, my brain was on overload. And as mad as I still was at my mother, I had to admit that having a "power"—though Lucy was careful to explain that our powers were subtle, not superhero stuff—was seriously cool. I was on my hundredth question—"When does this all happen?"—when Ezekiel appeared behind us.

"Aren't you two cold?" he asked, eyeing our hair but smart enough not to comment.

On cue, I began to shiver. The wind had kicked up, and the temperature was dropping. Ezekiel chuckled as we rushed past him and hot-footed it up the stairs and into the kitchen.

I spied a box of instant hot cocoa I hadn't noticed during the unpacking. "Manny's a keeper," I whooped and filled the teakettle. "Lucy?" I waved the box at her.

"Oh, yeah," she said. "Make mine a double! Zeke?"

"I'm good, thanks. Chocolate isn't my favorite flavor."

"What?" I sputtered. "How is that even possible?"

"Lemon," he said. "And caramel." He peered at the ceiling in thought. "And pistachio. Yeah, pistachio."

I shook my head, dumping four envelopes of cocoa with mini marshmallows into two paper cups. "There's no accounting for taste," I teased.

"You sound . . . okay," Ezekiel said, watching me.

I leaned against the counter and stared at the kettle, willing it to boil. "My mother says that when things go wrong, it's okay to cry. Lay on the floor and cry and wail as long as you like. Eventually you'll have to get up to pee. When that happens, get up, wash your face, and move on. I've done a fair bit of moaning and crying. I guess I feel like it's time to get on with it. That, and from what I can tell, having this 'gift'"—I hooked my fingers in air quotes—"could be okay."

I glanced at Lucy, and she smiled in encouragement.

"I feel like I'm on an emotional rollercoaster. I love my mom, and I'd love nothing more than to grow up to be just like her. Maybe that's why it hurts so much that she knew about my spirit my whole life and didn't think maybe she should tell me. And I know I keep whining about it, but I can't seem to let it go." I trembled in sudden frustration.

"Try not to be too hard on her," Ezekiel said gently. "Parents do the best they can, to the best of their abilities, on constantly shifting ground. They do what they think is right for their children, day by day, decision by decision. But parents are just people with their own sets of baggage. They're fallible. So sometimes they make good decisions, and sometimes—"

"They make bad ones. But you're right. I know my mom loves me. I'll try," I said to end the discussion.

As a little girl, I had been glued to my mother's side, stirring sauce, learning how to make fresh pasta, baking my first cake under her watchful eye. We were so close and still did things together by choice. We shopped, went to Broadway plays and museums, had dinner together, just the two of us. I loved her to pieces, and maybe that was why it hurt so much.

"Hey, is boiling water one of my abilities?" I asked. "Because that could come in handy right now."

43

Felix

"I'll just be a minute, Felix. Please excuse me," Ezekiel said, his head bent over his phone.

Alone with Phillip, I had to ask. "So you raise trolls? What's that like?" I asked him. "Is it like raising ostriches, or—"

He snorted. "Not raise them from babies. Raise them like an army."

"Oh," was all I could think of to say.

Phillip didn't respond immediately, and I used the pause to try and figure out how to escape when he exclaimed, "If you want to raise trolls, you should wear a dress. And smear yourself with dung."

"Now, that's something I'd like to see," Viceroy snarked at me from under the table.

"Shut up!" I hissed at him in my head before answering Phillip aloud. "Why on earth would I want to do that?"

The big man considered my question. "Do you mean wear a dress and dung or raise an army?"

"Either. Both."

"Because that's how it's done, and because raising a troll army is a good skill to have under your belt." He tapped his belt buckle.

"In fact, it would come in handy right now. Do you want to learn how? I can go outside and collect a bucket of—"

"Uh, thanks, maybe later. I need to make a few phone calls." Viceroy at my heels, I was out of the room and down the stairs before he could start searching for dresses and dung.

I slipped past Lucy and Gracie to head for the park proper. I'd thought to call my New Orleans housekeeper to have her ready the house just in case. But my power indicator was red—it would have to wait. Viceroy and I walked for a couple of minutes in blessed silence until the hairy little ball of misery broke it with his inane chatter.

"Tell me about your other house in New Orleans. Does it have squirrels?"

"Stop snooping in my head! And not that you deserve an answer, but New Orleans has rats, not squirrels, and it hardly matters since you're not going."

Viceroy stopped as if someone flipped his power switch. "What do you mean I'm not going? I go where you go."

I kept walking. "You go where Lucy goes. We've had this conversation. It's all decided."

"I'll go with Lucy if something happens to you. But you don't get to abandon me because you're tired of me. Being my maker doesn't mean you're the boss of me," he muttered.

"You little moron, that's exactly what it means." Twitching the hem of my overcoat in irritation, I stopped in front of an ancient ride made up of a circle of weirdly tilted horses with metal rings instead of reins. "The maker is the boss," I said. "If my maker had cared enough to stick around and turn me, I would have to do whatever she said."

"Or what?"

"Or she'd kill me."

Viceroy backed up a couple of feet. "Don't be a shit, Felix, and don't get any ideas." He ended his thought with a soft growl and showed his teeth. "You'd bleed before I died."

I cringed. "I have no intention of harming you in any way. Physical violence is beneath me."

Viceroy lifted his leg and watered a patch of dead grass. "Yeah, and that's the whole problem," the snide little piss factory thought at me.

I didn't take the bait. Wrinkling my nose at the odor, I stalked away. "I came out here to get away from idiotic conversations, not to start one with you."

"Okay, fine. But just so you know, you're not going anywhere without me. Now we can change the subject. What do you want to talk about?"

I glanced down at him. What the hell—he was annoying as fuck, but he possessed an animal's intuition, and he wasn't stupid. He might have some insights. "What do you think about this whole Deathy/Vampire Bob problem?"

I'd never seen a dog do a double take. "Really? You want my opinion?"

"I asked you, didn't I?"

"Huh," he chuffed. "So you did. You might want to sit down."

"I think I can take whatever you have to say."

He dismissed my side-eye. "Felix, sit down."

Fine. It wasn't like I had anything better to do. Aiming for the next bench, I sat. "Okay, talk. Or think."

"So Lucy is going to take on the Mantle when Deathy—what a stupid name—releases it. And then Vampire Bob is going to make Deathy, assuming he can turn her, the most powerful vampire that's ever existed."

"So?"

He sighed. "Do you think she'll be satisfied with *less* power than she has now? What powerful person has even been satisfied with less power? Deathy will go for world domination, Felix."

I shrugged, not willing to ask how he came by this logic. "And?"

He shook his head and huffed. "You're exhausting sometimes.

Vampire Bob is the least of our worries, but he's not the only one who should be afraid of her. If she becomes the most powerful vampire, she'll want vampires loyal to her, not to Vampire Bob. She'll want to make her own army. She'll come after every single vampire in Bob's lineage. And then you and me, if only to find out how I exist in the first place, and how you were able to turn me. Just like Vampire Bob wants to know."

It took me a minute to catch up, but then it hit me. The little shit was right. "Fuck! When were you going to tell me?"

"When you took a break from being an ass, which turned out to be two minutes ago. I don't think Lucy and Ezekiel have run it out this far. We should tell them that if we don't get in between this before Bob turns her, we all end up dead."

"All?"

"Except for Ezekiel, of course. She'll kill Phillip because he's helping us, Gracie and Lucy because their spirits are strong enough to be a threat. Lucy will come back in another body, but not fast enough to help us fight Vampire Deathy. Gracie won't come back at all unless her spirit wakes before Deathy gets to her. And just so you know, I could eat."

The fast-approaching forms of Gracie and Ezekiel spared Viceroy my reply.

"Bryan's at the gate. We're going to let him in," Gracie said, slowing. "Wanna come?"

I rolled my eyes, but Viceroy barked his assent, and they were gone. It was just as well. I needed to think, and I didn't want the mutt listening in.

Turning right where Ezekiel, Gracie, and Viceroy had turned left, I wandered past a pizza stand toward another group of rides missing their cars, arms sticking out into the air. It was fucking creepy, the stuff of nightmares.

Rounding a ride called the Thunderbolt, I was on a path that looked to stretch back toward the water side of the park again. A locked gate stood between me and freedom from this creep-fest. Muttering curses, I spun around. I'd have to go back the way I'd come. I picked up my pace, brooding over the crow's feet I'd seen around my eyes earlier while I'd washed my hands in the restroom. I desperately needed a snack, and I wasn't going to get one hiding in a children's museum in an amusement park. I could ask Gracie to volunteer a couple of ounces, but I was pretty sure that would go badly. Slipping through a turnstile, I walked toward the water and peered left to see a restaurant.

I headed toward it. I was more curious than hungry. Manny's bagel sandwich still sat in my stomach like a lump of concrete. I wandered past the front and approached what looked like an outdoor music pier and venue when I spotted a tiki bar.

I strode up the couple of steps, and just as I was about to lean over the counter, a woman with hideous blonde streaks in her hair and a puffy jacket popped up in my face, scaring us both into shrieks.

"I'm so sorry for frightening you. I didn't know anyone was here," I said when I'd regained my composure, my voice purposely smooth and soothing. "I assumed that since the park was closed, everything was closed."

She gasped and forced a small smile. "Oh, no. The restaurant and bar operate independently of the park. We're not inside the gates. And no worries. I just thought I was alone out here, is all. There are usually runners, but the boardwalk's been pretty empty this morning. I'm just straightening up." She examined me, and seeing something that frightened her, she paled visibly and pulled out her phone. Punching in three characters, she held it, ready to hit send. "Can I help you?"

"I was just wondering what time you open." I stepped back. "I'm visiting my sister and wanted a break from crying babies. She has twins." I winked. That brought the smile back. I leaned in to read her name tag and spied a plain gold wedding band.

"Well, you found a great place to get away for a bit," she said, still holding her phone. "We're not usually open this time of year, but the owners are trying something new with a holiday music lineup and hot drinks. We open at eleven a.m. I'm on till five, and the music starts at seven. If you're around tonight, it should be fun. A band, lots of people."

Well, well, lots of people. At the very least, I should be able to get rid of these crow's feet.

"Thanks, Terri. I might come back for that." I would come back, but not for the band. "I'd better get going before my sister calls 9-1-1. Thanks for the tip, and I hope yours are good today."

Terri finally decided I wouldn't attack her and blushed, tucking her phone into her pocket. "They're much better at night, but my kid has a basketball game, and I promised him I'd go."

I wondered if her son played on the same team as Manny's boy.

"Thanks, though," she continued. "Come back anytime." She shot me a genuine smile, waved, and turned back to whatever she had been doing beneath the bar—probably restocking.

I left the bar and turned the corner, walking on.

Viceroy had said Deathy would want a loyal army of vampires. He'd also said she'd want us to experiment on. But the fact that I was able to turn a dog into a vampire meant I had something a little extra going on. Maybe enough extra to parlay into a position of power. If, and this was a big if, I could talk her into turning me, I'd be firstborn in her loyal army, and Viceroy, well, Viceroy would be the icing on the cake. The first-ever vampire dog, devoted to me and by extension to her.

All we needed to do was be in the right place at the right time, and if Ezekiel and Lucy were even close to being correct, Vampire Bob, Deathy, me, and Viceroy could be in the same place at the same time very, very soon.

I stopped to lean on the railing and stare at the water. I'd have to keep this from Viceroy until I thought of a way to convince him that joining Deathy was preferable to dying, which meant I couldn't think about it when he was around.

How the hell was I going to do that?

44

Gracie

I flew into Bryan's arms, knocking him back against the car door.

"Oomph. Hey, you," my hot-as-hell boyfriend whispered into my hair. "You're okay. Thank God."

He tried to press me back so he could look at me, but I clung tighter. "Not yet. Hug more," I said.

He wrapped his arms around me, and his stethoscope dug through his jacket and into my chin. I nudged it aside and closed my eyes, inhaling his clean, hospital-tinged scent.

"Whoops, I forgot to take it off," Bryan said into my hair.

"Leave it. I'm fine," I mumbled, my whole body tingling from his tight grip.

"What's wrong?" Bryan asked.

I looked up to see him wrinkle his sand-colored eyebrows, one of which was divided by a thin scar from a cut he'd gotten falling off a fence as a kid. I swallowed and shook my head. "Nothing. I'm just so glad you're here." I watched Ezekiel and Viceroy as they headed back toward the towers to give us some time alone. "Come on. I'll give you the grand tour and tell you everything." I tugged him into the park.

"I'm sorry I couldn't talk when you called. Your brother is a hard taskmaster."

I frowned at him. "You said my mother filled you in. What did she tell you?" I asked, steering him toward the rides.

"She said that you'd accidentally gotten mixed up with some dangerous people, but that Manny was helping hide you for a while and that you were safe."

I raised an eyebrow at him, but he was studiously looking away from me, examining one of the rides we were passing. Bryan was a terrible liar, and he had no poker face whatsoever, losing every time my brothers goaded him into playing.

"Bryan, look at me." I stopped, forcing him to stop. "What else did my mom say?"

He turned to face me, but his eyes slid sideways and down. "She said Auggie and I should both sleep at the hospital for a couple of nights, just to be on the safe side."

"And that didn't freak you out?"

Now he glared straight into my eyes. "Of course it did! Gracie, I'm terrified for you. And I'm mad as hell that you didn't tell me any of this."

I flinched at his vehemence, but he continued.

"I love you, and I trust you, but you can't expect me not to react when you're in danger."

I flushed. Bry was right. I often mistook his calm outward persona for detachment. He was anything but detached.

"Listen, Bry, I'm going to tell you everything. I would have told you earlier, but it all happened so fast." I started walking again, and he fell into step beside me, no mean feat since, with such long legs, he practically had to shuffle to match my short stride. "I'm sorry."

He looked away again. "Which is your favorite ride?" He was avoiding my eyes, which meant he didn't want to venture into the weeds. I was okay with that since I was the one who'd lied to him.

"This one." I pointed to the Derby Racer. "I've loved this ride since I was a kid. It's been operating at the park since 1928. Isn't it amazing?"

Bryan peered at the odd-looking horses. "It doesn't look like a regular carousel."

"It isn't," I crowed. "It's fast." I didn't add that it was even better if you and your friends were more than a little drunk, whooping and hollering like you were real jockeys.

"We should come here together," he said, his gaze rising to the framework of the Ferris wheel. "I wish it was open now."

I grinned. "I don't know why they haven't been removed for storage like all the cars and stuff, but do you want to sit on the horses?"

"Uh, won't we get in trouble?"

"I don't see how. There's no one here."

I walked up the ramp to the exit gate in the Derby's wooden fence, reached over the slats, and unhooked the latch from the inside. I slipped through, and Bryan followed, laughing.

"You've done that before?"

"No. I've been here for the skating rink, but I've never snuck into the park when it was shut down. This is just an easy latch." I headed for my favorite spotted horse. "Come on, chicken."

Bry threaded himself between the horses and climbed on the one next to me. "These are pretty awkward to sit on," he mused, trying all the rungs on the footrests.

"Yeah, it takes a little getting used to. The foot placement makes sense once the horses are moving. The carousel spins pretty fast, and the horses not only move up and down but back and forth." I pointed down to the felt covering on the mechanism that propelled them. "The music is 'Call to Post' like at the track. And then the sound of horse hooves hitting the dirt. The whole thing is pretty fabulous." I grinned at him.

"You used to go to the races with your dad when you were little, right?"

I warmed at the memory. "My dad loved the horses, but he never placed bets. He said gambling was for suckers."

Bryan was only half listening to me, fidgeting on his horse. "What?" I asked him as he slid off.

"Gracie, I want to ask you something."

I lifted my leg to slide off my horse.

"No, stay there." He reached into his pocket.

"Hey, I forgot to ask, was your mom mad that you had to cancel dinner?"

"Oh, no, she never came. One of her patients had an emergency embolism. She had to stay in Boston and operate. You're off the hook. And Alicia's party is postponed too."

I heaved a sigh of relief. "That's great—not for the embolism, I mean. Is the kid okay?" At least I hadn't shredded my potential relationship with Bry's demanding mother by ditching our first dinner together. The shitty thing was that I'd also missed my appointment to see the truck. My heart hurt just thinking about it.

"She caught it before it burst. Lucky kid," he said.

I shivered, thinking about how hard it was to be a parent. "Your mom's amazing."

Bryan's lips quirked into a wry smile. "She is, but I didn't come here to talk about my mother." He reached for my hand, and I looked down at him. His cheeks were pink, and his fine hair lifted in the breeze.

I leaned down to kiss him, our lips melting together like they were two parts of a whole. I slipped from the horse into his arms, and our kiss deepened until I wanted to rip my clothes off and climb on him.

The feeling was mutual because he broke away, panting, his jacket sticking out at the hem. "Damned scrubs," he muttered. "A man can't keep a secret."

"I guess not," I said, lifting the edge of his jacket to reveal his happiness at seeing me. Grabbing his hand, I drew him out from between the horses and off the platform. "I know where we can go," I whispered.

"Well, hurry up, woman, it's freezing out here, and I might just cool off."

"Right. Like that's ever happened."

THE KEY MANNY HAD GIVEN US UNLOCKED THE FRONT door of the museum building, and though we had so far confined ourselves to the vacant upstairs, the entire building was accessible. On the way in this morning, I'd noticed something that would be perfect for what I had in mind—tumbling mats.

Bryan's eyes lit up with laughter when he saw them. "So we're going athletic?"

"I'm in if you are."

I yanked him toward a corner out of direct window view. He shrugged off his jacket, laying it on the mat before removing mine and layering it on top of his.

He slid his hands under the hem of my sweater, one hand reaching up my back to unhook my bra and the other slipping a finger beneath the waistband of my pants. "These will have to go."

I pulled my arms out of my sweater sleeves and bra straps and let my bra slip to the ground. Bryan slid his icy hands up my rib cage to cup my breasts.

"Are my hands too cold?" he whispered in my ear.

"Yes." I moaned as he explored gently with his skilled surgeon's fingertips.

"And now?"

He increased the pressure, and the floor fell away.

Somehow, our pants and shoes were off, and I was lying on our coats, my sweater and T-shirt bunched around my shoulders, exposing me to the chilly air. But I wouldn't be cold for long.

Bryan lowered himself to rest on his elbows above me. I groaned as he found his target.

He bent to silence me with a kiss, but the fix was only temporary.

His hot breath against my cheek and the burning thrill building in my core would have me howling in seconds—silence didn't come naturally to me. I grabbed Bryan's shoulder and encouraged him to roll so that I could straddle him. It was easier to be quiet if I was on top.

Fortunately, he never minded. I took over, riding him until I drove us both closer to the edge. I rocked until my orgasm exploded. Bryan came immediately after me, his climax triggered by mine.

Panting, I grinned at him.

He reached up and brushed my hair out of my face. "You're incredible, and I'm the luckiest man alive."

"Truth." I giggled.

He slid me off him and pulled me into his side, hugging me close. I laid my head on his chest, listening to our heartbeats until the throbbing slowed, his breathing evened, and my hot flush subsided.

A baby screamed on the boardwalk outside. "Uh, I guess we should get dressed." I scrambled to my feet and pulled on my underwear and pants, wrestling my bra on last. "Bry, put your pants on."

Still half naked, he stretched out and closed his eyes. "Nope. I think I'm going to take a nap. I haven't gotten much sleep lately."

"Seriously, somebody could come. Don't you want to meet the people helping me?" I pointed at the ceiling.

"You weren't worried about that ten minutes ago." He snickered but got up and began to dress. "Yeah, I do want to meet them, and a better explanation of who they are would be nice, but I want to talk to you about something else first."

"Talk away." Still warm and fuzzy inside, I put my runners back on and tucked strands of hair back into the weird braid-do that Lucy had created.

"Who did that to your hair?" Bryan asked, touching one of the braids.

"Oh, Lucy and I braided each other's hair in the ladies' room —it's a long story. So you drove over here to ask about my hair?"

He blushed. "No. I came to . . ." He trailed off, fumbling in his pocket.

"What's in your pocket? Let me see." I reached for it, but he twisted away. "Bryan?"

He had his back to me. "This isn't the way I wanted to do this," he muttered. Spinning to face me, he dropped to one knee and opened a pale-blue jeweler's case. "Gracie Rinelli, I fell in love with you that day at Yankee Stadium. You laughed at me for dropping a mustard-covered hot dog on your new Yankees T-shirt when you could have been furious. I've never met another woman who comes close to you. You're funny and intelligent, brave, driven, and happy. You're my North Star, and I'm only half of me without you. Will you marry me?"

Shock waves raced around my body. I reached for Bryan's beautiful face. Cradling it between my hands, I dropped to my knees and kissed him, the ring box crushed between us.

"I love you, Bryan McLaughlin. Yes, I'll marry you," I whispered when we broke apart.

Tears glittered in Bry's eyes, making them appear crystalline. He took the ring from the box and slipped it on my finger. It was the Tiffany solitaire I'd loved since my friends and I had made wedding books in ninth grade, cutting pictures out of magazines. And it was a perfect fit.

"Oh my god, I love you so much more now." I giggled.

He dropped the empty box and, still on our knees, we clung together.

"I've dreamed over and over that you'd ask me to marry you, but I can't believe you just did," I said.

"You dreamed it, huh? When?" He leaned back to look into my face with a grin.

"Oh, lots of times, most recently a couple of days ago, but—"

A wave of dizziness overcame me. I wobbled, and he grabbed my arms.

"Whoa. Are you okay?"

"Yeah, I . . . I think I'm just in shock." I shook my head to clear it. "I'm okay." I scrambled to my feet and held out a hand to help him to his, the diamond glinting in the light. "It's gorgeous, Bry, but it must have cost a fortune. How did you—"

"Pay for it? I have an inheritance. I'm not allowed to touch it until I finish my residency, but I asked my mother, and she released enough money for me to buy a bigger stone. It was her idea. She said she could hear how much I loved you in my voice every time I talked about you, and that love wasn't a time to be fiscally prudent."

Wow. I guess I didn't have to worry about the missed dinner or what she thought of me. But I frowned. "Wait, what? You have an inheritance?"

He flushed a dull pink. "From my grandfather, a family trust. I was going to tell you after you said yes. Like now."

I cocked my head and put my engaged hand on my hip. "What else are you hiding?"

"Nothing, Gracie, I swear. I never think about the money and honestly almost forgot about it until I wanted to buy you a ring you'd love. Alicia told me you'd cut out a picture of this one when you were a kid," he said before I could ask.

"That rat. I'll have to kiss her," I muttered with a grin and held out my hand to admire the Tiffany solitaire, which was at least two carats. "Now what?" I asked, though I knew what came next. Visions of wedding dresses, bridesmaids, confetti, and our wedding cake raced through my head on fast-forward. I pictured my family. They would be so happy, helping us plan the wedding. I couldn't suppress an ecstatic giggle.

"Let's elope," Bryan said.

"What? Did you just say we should elope? Like run away and get married alone in some strange town with strangers as witnesses? That kind of elope?" I hadn't realized I was backing away from him until I tripped over a foam block and went down on my sore tailbone. "OW!" I yelped, rolling over as Bryan rushed to help me up. "We can't elope. My family would lose it if we denied them a wedding. Why would you even suggest it?" I looked at the ring on my finger. "We have to have a wedding."

"Okay, we can have a wedding. But let's get married first. Now."

"Bryan, what—"

"I was going to wait to ask you until I finished my residency, but now that you know about your indomitable spirit, and it's about to wake, I need to be able to protect you, and I can't do that if we're apart. Look at what just happened. You could have died." He put his hands on either side of my face and frowned, peering into my eyes, his blue eyes with their stormy gray ring suddenly serious. "Do you have any idea how much danger you were in?"

I stared at him, words forming and breaking apart in my brain, refusing to resolve into coherent speech.

"Gracie, you were in a goddammed vampire lair, for fuck's sake. Maybe they couldn't turn you, but—"

"You knew about me?" I whispered, finally able to form words. "How long?"

His face blanched. "I... when I asked your mother for her permission to propose to you at Easter. She started crying and said she'd been a bad mother. That's when she told me. She said she loved me like a son and that I was perfect for you. Then she asked me if, knowing what you were, I would be willing to take care of you." His face crumbled. "Of course I said yes. I love you, Gracie. I'll do anything for you."

My brain scrambled, trying to work out what he was saying.

"And you believed her?" I stared at him, my eyes about to pop out of my head.

"Well, no. At first I thought she was a combination of overprotective and crazy. But while your mother may be overprotective when it comes to you, she's not crazy. She'd never make up a story like that. And if nothing else, I figured *she* believed it, so I had to take her seriously."

"I don't know what's worse. That my mother still thinks I

need looking after, or that she lied to me. Why would she tell you and not me?" My throat began to ache. He reached for my hand, but I yanked it back as if he'd burned me.

"Gracie, please, listen. I've talked to her about it a couple of times since that night. I tried to get her to tell you, but she was afraid you'd be mad at her."

"And why didn't you tell me? I thought we told each other everything, but clearly I was wrong. You clearly didn't think it was important to tell me that you were rich, and you didn't think to tell me about myself."

"She asked me to let her tell you—"

"I can't even touch the money thing right now. But that explains why the two of you got so close. You shared a secret. A secret about me."

"Gracie, listen, they love you. They were worried that I couldn't—"

"They?"

"Your family. Your mom and your brothers."

"They all know? You all knew, and you didn't tell me? Wait a minute. That's why you tried to convince me to go back to school after dinner at Auggie and Alicia's. You thought it would be safer than having me on the street in my cake truck. You were all in on it."

I held out my hand and spread my fingers, tilting the ring so that the diamond caught the light, sending sparkling rays of my hopes and dreams around the room. I closed my hand into a fist, and the sparkles disappeared. What the hell good was an indomitable spirit if it couldn't keep my life out of the toilet? Where did I even go from here?

Something bumped on the floor above, and I looked up, my scalp tightening.

"Gracie, please. You have to believe me—" Bryan pleaded.

"Because you've been so honest with me all along?" I caught Bryan's hand and spread it open, palm up.

"Gracie, please, try to understand. We all love you. We're afraid for you. We just want what's best for you."

I shook my head. "We, we, we. What about me? Telling me the truth is what's best for me. And you lied. You all lied to me." I slid the ring from my finger and dropped it into his hand.

45

Gracie

"I want my spirit to wake up," I said to Lucy and Ezekiel, who were deep in conversation. I stood in the doorway, tears streaming down my face.

"Gracie, what happened?" Lucy and Ezekiel asked at the same time.

Phillip was at my side in a heartbeat, and I buried my face in his chest. He wrapped his arms around me, and I cried so hard my knees folded of their own accord. Phillip helped me to a chair, and I sank into it.

"Bryan proposed," I said, and Lucy's face lit up. "He bought me a ring, and I said yes, but . . . but . . . he *knew* about me," I wailed. "He knew all along and . . . and he didn't tell me. They all knew. My whole family!"

Lucy's face fell. "Oh, Gracie, I'm so sorry." She inched her chair next to mine and stroked my arm while I leaned on Phillip.

"Is he still here? Do you want me to hurt him?" Phillip rumbled.

I shook my head. "No, Phillip. Thanks, but no. I did a pretty good job of beating him up all by myself. He's gone." I sniffed, and Ezekiel handed me a red-and-white-striped handkerchief. I stared at it, confused for a second, then took it, wiped my eyes, and blew my nose before handing it back to him.

"Keep it, Gracie. I have more," Ezekiel said.

They tried to comfort me, but their platitudes only made me feel worse. I peeled myself off of Phillip to lean my head into my arms and sob on the table.

"Okay, let's give her some space," Lucy said. "You two need to go somewhere else. I'll make her a cup of tea."

I cried till my eyes were so swollen I could barely see. I got up from the table and paced, babbling under my breath about how much I hated them all. Then I threw myself into the chair and cried some more. Lucy brought a cup of tea, sat next to me, and put her arms around me.

I burst into fresh tears. "How could they lie to me all this time?" I wailed. "Alicia, Chris, Auggie . . . They all knew, they . . . they . . ."

Lucy rocked me awkwardly. "Shhh, Gracie, everything's going to be okay. You'll see. Everything will work out."

"No, it won't." I hiccupped and pulled away. I'd soaked Ezekiel's handkerchief, so I grabbed a napkin to blow my nose and another to mop my face. "I trusted them all, and they all lied to me, Lucy. How can that ever be okay?"

"You can't see it now because you're upset and angry." Lucy put up a hand as I opened my mouth to protest. "And you have every right to be. You feel that they've betrayed your trust. But they're your family. Aside from whatever they had wrong about overprotecting you because you have an indomitable spirit, you're the baby, the little sister. It's a double whammy for them."

I shook my head and blew my nose again.

"Maybe they went too far, but they risked everything to do it," she added.

I jerked upright. "What do you mean, *they* risked everything?"

"They risked losing your love. They risked you being so angry you'd never forgive them for doing the only thing they knew how to do."

"It's not just that they lied over this, Lucy," I whispered, exhausted. "My family fought me over everything, my whole life. I wasn't allowed to go anywhere alone as a kid. One of my brothers always had to play chaperone. And it didn't end as I got older. Dating was a nightmare. I wanted to go to the Culinary Institute, but where did I end up? NYU. I wanted to take pastry classes in Paris. What did I have to do? Sneak pastry classes I paid for myself in Brooklyn." I laughed and dabbed at my runny nose. "The only thing they didn't fight me on was Bryan. And then they ended up taking that away too by making him part of their lie. It's so fucked up, Lucy."

"Love is always fucked up," she said, her voice so soft I barely heard her.

I swallowed the whiny words I was going to say next. "You love Ezekiel."

She nodded.

"And he loves you."

She nodded again.

"But you can't be together?"

She shook her head. "It's forbidden for an angel and a reaper to mate."

I didn't think my heart could hurt any more than it already did, but it clenched at the sight of Lucy's bereft expression.

I bit my lip and, remembering my tea, I pulled it toward me, taking a sip. "Forbidden how, exactly?"

"Should we ever consummate our relationship . . ." Lucy paused and glanced at me.

I nodded in encouragement and took another mouthful of the strong, sweet tea.

"Ezekiel would be compelled to drive his flaming sword through my heart."

I sprayed tea across the table, catching Lucy on the side of the face. "*What?*" I yelped, staring at the tea dribbles tracking down her cheek.

She took a napkin and calmly wiped her face.

"He'd stab you with a flaming sword!" I croaked.

"Not by choice, by holy edict. Like a hypnotic suggestion, Ezekiel would be compelled—he wouldn't be able to stop himself." Elbows on the table, she put her face in her hands.

I gaped at her. I couldn't imagine loving Bryan as much as I did, and him loving me, and us unable to do what we just did. My heart clenched at the thought. Crap! Bryan had lied to me, and yet I still loved him. A trickle of relief found its way through the stone wall around my heart.

Lucy lifted her face from her hands, straightened, and turned to me. "It's old news. We deal with it."

"Maybe to you it's old news. To me, it's beyond cruel." I reached for her, squeezing her shoulders with both hands.

"It isn't meant to be. It has to do with the type of offspring we would create—a Nephilim, which is not *so* unusual. But because of my indomitable spirit, the Nephilim we'd create would have enough power to disrupt the world." She sighed. "It was our misfortune to fall in love."

"Uh, hello, *birth control*?"

"They created the edict long before you could buy condoms in every gas station." Her shoulders slumped, and the defeated posture looked wrong on her erect frame.

"Lucy, I'm so sorry I spit on you, but that's beyond the pale of messed up. There's nothing you can do?"

She shrugged and handed me a napkin before wiping the table with the rest of the stack as I patted my chin dry. "I can become human again. Angel and human mating *is* frowned upon, but it's not forbidden."

I stared at her. "Whose rule is this anyway?"

"God's, I suppose, though Metatron, God's scribe, probably wrote the edict."

I gritted my teeth as my anger at her situation flared. "What do you have to do to become human?"

"Deathy or whoever wears the Mantle must grant it."

I had to think about that for a few seconds. "But if you take the Mantle, you won't be able to—"

"That's right. I won't have another chance at my humanity until I find someone else to accept it." Lucy balled up the wet napkins and tossed them at a wastebasket in the corner. They sailed in without touching the rim.

"Fuck," I said.

"That about sums it up."

EZEKIEL AND LUCY HAD EXPLAINED THAT MY AGE, twenty-three, was around the time most indomitable spirits woke on their own. They said it would be better to wake my spirit before contacting Vampire Bob. Lucy had admitted she'd been reluctant at first, but having me strong and alert when we faced him was far preferable to having me sleepy and dreaming should my spirit pick the worst possible moment to arise.

Listening to them, I had to agree. Though I was nervous as hell, learning about waking an indomitable spirit was proving to be a great distraction from thinking about how pissed I was at Bryan and my family.

"So you're sure this isn't going to hurt?" I asked for probably the ninth time as Phillip paced back and forth.

"It shouldn't. I've heard it tickles," Ezekiel said for probably the sixth time. He had also claimed it could itch and another time said it could feel bubbly.

To his credit, the angel hadn't lost his patience with me yet, though I was beginning to sense I was pushing it. My coming change also distracted Lucy. She was back to her poised self. Felix, ignoring us completely, stood at a window, staring toward the restaurant as people filled the boardwalk. Viceroy slept in a corner on a beach towel Phillip had found and folded into a bed for him. Only Phillip was agitated, pacing back and forth, saying little but shooting warning glances at Lucy and Ezekiel.

"Phillip, please stop pacing. You're making me crazy, and I'm nervous enough already," I said to him as he passed.

The big man stopped and flushed furiously. "I'm sorry. I just don't want you to get hurt. I'll sit over here." He carried a chair to a window next to Felix's and sat so he could look outside. "Is this better?" he called over his shoulder.

Telling him he didn't have to take a time-out would only confuse matters, so I bit it back. "That's great, thanks."

"How much longer till the bedding comes?" Felix asked.

"Someone should be here in a few minutes," Ezekiel said. "Manny just texted."

We were waiting for air mattresses because the transformation would put me to sleep, and sleeping on a bed was always better than sleeping on the floor. I'd suggested the museum downstairs, but that wouldn't work, as there were now enough people on the boardwalk to make privacy impossible. Fortunately, there had been no walkers or runners passing by when I'd dragged Bryan inside a couple of hours ago.

There was nothing much to do without my phone, and to keep myself from pacing like Phillip had, I crossed the room to Felix. "What are you looking at out there?" I asked.

He sniffed. "It's appalling."

"What's appalling?" I peered around him.

"Do you see what those people are wearing? They chose those clothes on purpose. Did that woman get up this morning and say: 'Oh, I know, let me put on this ludicrously short green skirt, with this too-tight striped T-shirt, red Converse sneakers, and a black baseball cap.'" He glared at me. "Or that guy with the Members Only jacket, jeans, and black dress shoes with white socks."

I tried to jam my hands in my pockets so I didn't punch him, but they were too shallow—whoever designed women's pants with these ridiculous excuses for pockets should be forced to wear them. I crossed my arms instead. "Felix, these people don't have your money, and this is an amusement park and beach. They didn't dress for work."

"Poverty is no excuse for poor taste," he muttered. I wanted to tell him how cruel he was but couldn't summon the energy. I wrapped my arms around myself and stared out the window instead. After a minute, Felix tapped me on the shoulder. "Gracie, you're wound tighter than a violin string. In my experience, the only cure for anxiety is alcohol. The bar next to the restaurant is open. Would you like a cocktail?"

I brightened, pushing my irritation at his mean comments aside. "Lucy? Ezekiel? Can Felix and I go for cocktails? Do you guys want to come?"

Ezekiel looked at his phone. "No new messages. I don't suppose it would hurt, and Felix isn't wrong. It might take the edge off. Why don't you two go, and Lucy, Phillip, and I will wait here for the bedding."

I was at the door before he finished his sentence.

"Are you sure you're up for walking among *them*?" I asked Felix as we left the safety of the stairs to enter the thin flow of people strolling along the boardwalk.

"I can manage if there's bourbon as a reward for my suffering," he snarked.

"I'm surprised the bar is even open. I thought they closed at the end of September."

He didn't answer but made a beeline for his bourbon. There were no other patrons, and we chose stools with the best view of the water.

"Hey, you're back!" exclaimed the bartender, who looked about Alicia's age.

"Yes, as it turns out, both my niece and I could use a break from the twins."

I poked Felix beneath the bar, and he jumped.

"I'll have a double bourbon, your best. What would you like, Gracie?" He turned a brilliant smile on me. "You like sweet drinks. How about a piña colada?"

"Uh, s-sure," I stuttered.

"I'll need to see your IDs," the bartender said. "Sorry, we have to ask everyone."

"I didn't bring my wallet, *Uncle Felix*," I said and dug a knuckle into his thigh.

He ground his teeth through a pasted-on grin as he pulled his wallet out of his pocket. "Just bring her a Coke," he said, placing his driver's license on the bar.

"Will do." The bartender checked his license and hustled away to make the drinks.

"Your niece?" I rolled my eyes.

"I was here earlier. She thinks I'm visiting my sister. Don't judge me—I was winging it. Was I supposed to tell her I was hiding out from the vampire king of New York?"

Before I could reply, the bartender reappeared with Felix's bourbon and a Coke for me. She winked as she set drink coasters and napkins down in a smooth, practiced movement, then placed the drinks in front of us.

I sipped my Coke, heaving a sigh of relief. She'd added rum.

46

Felix

Two drinks later, Gracie's shoulders had fallen to their normal position, and I was feeling a great deal more confident in my decision. I'd managed not to think about it until Viceroy had fallen asleep. But staring out the window, not at the people wandering past, whom I couldn't have cared less about despite what I'd said to Gracie, I'd run the pros and cons of going full-blood. The funny thing was that I hadn't even thought there were any cons until I met Gracie, Lucy, and Ezekiel. I flipped bills out of my wallet and set them on the bar.

"You're leaving a fifty-dollar tip?" Gracie hissed.

"Don't tell anyone. I have a reputation to protect," I hissed back, exiting the bar area. Gracie followed me out onto the boardwalk.

"Hey, you're going the wrong way." She stopped.

"I need a walk. You go back. I'll be there in a bit," I said. *After I find a snack.*

"Okay." She nodded. "But don't be too long."

"One can only hope," I whispered under my breath.

The pickings were indeed slim. Most of the people walking the boardwalk seemed to be out of work. The few easiest targets, youngish women, were pushing strollers or dragging whining children. I turned to walk out onto the pier, having spotted a couple of people out at the end. One of them, a man in a canvas work jacket carrying a toolbox, left whatever he'd been doing and passed me as I walked, leaving a lone woman who was oddly well dressed for this crowd. She was probably in her late forties, sitting on a faded plastic chair, and sniffling, a tissue pressed to her eyes. Bingo!

Half-bloods didn't have the gift of the thrall in the same way full-bloods did. We were exceptionally persuasive. Some, like me, more than others. It was how I managed to talk marks out of their expensive outerwear or purchases. Our version of a true thrall was only activated via the virus when we bit someone, not before. I'd cursed lacking that ability on numerous occasions when up against men disinclined to be verbally persuaded but too foul to bite. With women, however, all I usually had to do was talk.

I walked up to my snack, staying several feet away—you had to be careful when approaching people these days.

"Excuse me, I don't mean to intrude, but I couldn't help noticing your distress."

She jerked her head up to expose a tear-ravaged face, and I stepped back a bit.

"Is there anything I can do to help?" I asked gently.

She took in my clothes and seemed to decide I wasn't a serial killer—a mistake that could get her murdered one day.

"Dismember my ex?" she muttered.

"Sorry, I'm not in that line of work. But I do have ears, and I'm particularly non-judgmental." Untrue. A woman I'd been involved with once briefly insisted I take a newly popularized personality test. I scored as an INTJ, the Mastermind. It was pure bullshit, but accurate in one respect: I'm judgey as hell.

She heaved both a sigh and herself out of the chair. "That bastard hasn't paid child support in four months. The fucker is punishing me for going on a date. My daughter will be kicked out of private school if I can't come up with the tuition." She leaned on the railing to stare out at the water, a sudden breeze whipping her expensively dyed hair around her face. "I'd use the mortgage payment money again, but I'm already two months behind on that." She gave me a side-eye. "Aren't you glad you asked?"

"Yes. Because sometimes it helps just to get it all off your chest. Do you have friends who can help?"

She barked a short, hard laugh. "My 'friends' would suddenly find themselves busy if they found out I was broke. My daughter would lose *her* friends. That's why I'm out here. No one I know comes to this park."

"Ah, that kind of situation. I'm sorry." I held out a hand. "Felix Belloquot, at your service." That elicited a genuine smile.

"Anne Jackman. It's nice to meet you, Felix."

As she turned, I gave her my most dazzling smile. This snack was going to be a cakewalk.

Since there were only two of them now, I convinced Anne that perhaps it was time to sell the big suburban house and downsize. She could find a lovely apartment in the city, closer to culture, save face, and save money. She was so grateful to not only have someone to talk to but someone who gave her sane advice. She hugged me and asked me about myself. It was easy to lull her into compliance with my story and take a few sips from her wrist. Thirty minutes later, I practically bounced my way back to the museum building.

I left her back in the plastic chair, sleepily surveying the empty pier. I hoped she'd at least remember my advice. No one in their right mind should live in Westchester when the city was so close.

I climbed the stairs to find that Manny had brought the bedding and extra supplies himself, and everyone was inflating mattresses and taking sheets out of packages.

"So this is going to the mattresses?" I asked. The first *Godfather* movie was one of my favorites, the wardrobes so stylish. I'd seen it in the theatre when it came out and several times since.

Manny burst a laugh. "I guess it is," he said. "Just without guns and Clemenza's sauce."

I grinned.

"Only one of the greatest movies ever made," Manny said, peering at me. "You look much better, Felix. It seems the fresh air is doing you some good."

"Seems so," I said. Fresh air and a lady in distress meant that if my plan worked and I was able to persuade Deathy to turn me, I'd be frozen in time, looking my absolute best. Maybe the whole Mastermind thing wasn't crap after all.

"Here, unwrap these sheets."

He handed me a package and, still high from my snack, I went to work on it without complaint.

Viceroy cocked his head at me from across the room and sauntered over to my feet. "What did you do, Felix?"

I glared at him. "I went for a walk. Can't a person get some fresh air?"

"A person can, but you're not a person." He stepped closer and sniffed my leg. "You bit someone!" he yelped in my head. And in Lucy and Ezekiel's heads. They both froze, staring at me.

Lucy recovered first. "Felix! You bit someone? Who? Where? Are they okay?" The room erupted in chaos as Lucy rushed to the window to peer up and down the boardwalk. Not seeing anyone slumped over, she whirled on me. "After what we talked about, why would you do that?"

"Felix, what the fuck?" Gracie was in my face, nearly stepping on Viceroy in her haste to get to me. The little traitor scampered out of the way. "Who was it? Do they need help?"

I backed up, my hands in the air, waving everyone back. Phillip had grown in size, his fists clenching and unclenching as he stepped up and pushed Gracie behind him. Ezekiel's face had turned to stone. And Manny? Manny was eyeing me with a speculative head tilt.

"Just hold on, people," I shouted. "She's not hurt. I never injure anyone I imbibe from."

That drew a fresh round of shouts. I shivered in frustration.

"You all know what I am, and you know what I do." I turned to Lucy. "I'm sorry to burst your bubble, but I'm a half-blood

vampire, not some kind of fanged Goody Two-shoes in training."
I focused on Viceroy. "And you. You dare to judge me? What do
you think happens to the animals you drain? And for that matter"
—I turned back to the room—"what do you think happens to the
animals which you all so gleefully chow down on? They die horrifying deaths before they hit your plates. At least I'm not a
hypocrite." I stalked to a chair and slumped into it.

"Eating a steak is not an offense of the same magnitude as
drinking human blood, Felix, as you well know," Ezekiel said.
"Don't try to subvert the discussion by bringing animal rights
into it. You bit a woman without her permission—"

"I never bite anyone without their permission!" I exploded.
"They can always back away from me. It has happened, and I
walk." That shut them up.

"Wait," Phillip said. "They know what you're doing?"

"Yes!"

"And they don't refuse?" Gracie whispered.

"Rarely. Since you're all so hellfire interested in me all of a
sudden, I'll tell you." I gathered myself. "I usually bite a wrist and
never take more than one or two ounces at most. The wound
heals instantly, they feel sleepy for a bit, and any memory of me, if
there is a memory at all, is foggy." I shook my head. "Though I do
hope the woman I just bit remembers the advice I gave her."

They glared at me.

"Suck it up," I said, "or throw me out. At this point, I don't
care either way." I cared a great deal, but telling them why would
be counterproductive. No one moved to heave me out the door.

"So that's why you look better?" Manny finally managed.

"Yes. The blood keeps me young. If I stop drinking—and
some half-bloods don't drink—I'll age normally."

"So it's like a fountain of youth for you?" Manny asked,
rubbing his chin.

"Except somebody has to bleed to make it work," Gracie
sneered.

"Don't get any ideas about infecting people to stave off

facelifts. It's a terrible business model that never ends well," I said, knowing where Manny's train of thought was barreling.

Ezekiel put up a hand. "Let's not diverge from the salient point: Drinking human blood is an inherently self-destructive act. Whether it's incrementally from drinking small amounts or all at once from draining a human to death, the end result is the same —your soul ultimately dies. And any conversation that suggests otherwise needs to end here. As for Felix leaving . . ." He paused, and I steeled myself. "It wouldn't be wise. Loose, he's a liability. Here, we can both watch and protect him."

Looking at everyone's faces, I had a hard time imagining that any of them wanted to keep me safe, except for Manny, and all he saw was a business proposition for the mob. Then he crossed himself. Well, scratch that. No one cared if I was protected.

Viceroy put his front paws on my knee. "I'm sorry, Felix, I didn't mean to out you. I was just surprised you found somebody to bite. You've been pretty good to me, and I was mean to you." His ears fell, and he dipped his head.

I heaved a sigh. "It's fine," I said aloud. "We are what we are, little man. People hate us and fear us—"

"But we're together, and it's easier together."

I rubbed his head, and he licked my hand. For once, I didn't immediately wipe it on my pants.

I looked around the room at the mattresses in various stages of inflation. "We haven't decided when to call Bob's house. Though it may mean we don't get to take advantage of Manny's exceptionally kind hospitality, I vote for calling him now."

47

Gracie

Lucy cleared her throat. "First, we need to wake Gracie's spirit, and I don't know how long that will take."

"Your spirit?" Manny asked me, his face creasing in puzzlement.

"It seems I have an indomitable spirit," I said, "which is kind of weird. It means that if I want, my soul can become a guardian angel or a reaper when I die. There's other stuff too, but one of the best things about having this kind of spirit is that vampires can bite me, but they can't make me a vampire, and their glamour, or thrall, doesn't work on me."

"That could come in handy. Does your mother know?" Manny would think of family first.

"Uh, yeah, which is why I'm not talking to her, or my family, or Bryan. Can we not do this right now?"

"Sorry, I didn't mean to—"

"It's fine. Just a sore subject," I said, hoping it would end his questions.

Lucy rescued me. "Gracie, are you sure you're ready? After what just happened?"

Just what I needed. A reminder.

"Okay, listen, everybody. I was engaged to the love of my life for about a minute. He broke my heart, and right this second, I hate him and my whole family. I need to become whatever the hell it is I'm going to become before I go batshit crazy worrying about it. I'm all in. Can we just do this thing?"

"Yes," Lucy said. "Let's get started."

Five minutes later, after trips to the restrooms, we were all back except for Felix, who had taken Viceroy outside. But thanks to Manny and Lucy bringing Bryan and my family up, I'd had second thoughts while washing my hands and staring at myself in the ladies' room mirror. Bryan's heartbroken face swam through my mind, making me want to climb out of the frosted glass window, withdraw my savings, and run the hell away from all of them. It took every ounce of willpower I had to walk back into that room.

"Um, do I have to do it now?" I asked Ezekiel. "I know I've asked this a million times, but I'm having second thoughts."

That was the understatement of the century. I had no intention of showing it, but I was miserable, and I just knew that forcing myself to be even more in tune with my soul would make it worse. I felt like a ping-pong ball bouncing back and forth between "I'm all in" and "I'm out of here."

Lucy put an arm around my shoulders. "No. You don't have to. But Gracie, it will happen whether we start the process now or not. Think of it like baking a cake for money. If you check to ensure you have all your ingredients beforehand, you can proceed with your baking and deliver your cake on time and stress-free. But if you find out halfway through your mixing that you're out of eggs, you have to stop everything and rush out to the store, delaying the whole process, making your delivery late, and potentially losing a repeat customer. It's going to happen to you one way or another. This way, we can make sure you're able to fend for yourself if something should go off the rails."

Her analogy was clunky, but she was right. And frankly, I had nothing more to lose.

"Okay, let's do it," I said.

Manny rushed to get a sheet on the one fully inflated mattress and slip a pillow into a pillowcase. I felt like an idiot, but I toed off my shoes and lay down. I stared up at the old rusty lights with cages over bare bulbs. I held out my hand to Manny, and he sat at my side, grabbed it, and squeezed.

I smiled up at him. "Thanks."

"No, thank you. For Sylvie," he whispered.

"Now what?" I said to Ezekiel, who was frowning in thought.

"I think it's best if Manny isn't holding your hand. I don't want to—"

"What?" I asked. "You don't want to do what?"

"Stop his heart."

Manny yanked his hand back. "Sorry, Gracie, but I got kids."

Felix picked that exact moment to reappear with Viceroy. The little dog raced to me, leaping onto my chest.

"Oof. You can't stay here, Viceroy. Ezekiel said it could kill you."

Viceroy stared into my eyes before licking my nose and jumping off. Lucy knelt on one side of me, Ezekiel taking the other side while Phillip hovered at my feet, clearly worried.

"I'll be okay, Phillip. They won't hurt me," I said to him. "You're sure, right?" I asked Lucy.

"We're sure," Lucy said, her voice firm. "And just so you trust us, I'm going to hold your other hand."

Ezekiel took one of my hands, and she took the one Manny had relinquished.

"Now, Gracie," Ezekiel said, "I'm going to glow with a little bit of power, then I'll send that power into you. You'll feel a tickle, like when your foot or arm falls asleep then wakes up. That's all it is. If it works, your power will awaken and bind to your soul. You may feel it happen, and you may not. But it takes a lot of energy to accomplish. You will tire, and you'll probably fall asleep. We'll let you sleep for at least a couple of hours."

I searched his face for any sign of worry or fear. Finding none, I nodded.

"Okay," I whispered.

"Ready?"

"Ready." I managed a weak smile. "Shock me." I held their hands tighter.

Ezekiel began to glow. It was the freakiest thing I'd ever seen. His skin looked illuminated from within, and I felt waves of peace and happiness flow through my hand and up my arm. Somewhere, Manny gasped, and I imagined him crossing himself again.

"Okay, Gracie, here it comes," Ezekiel whispered.

I closed my eyes, and it was a good thing I did because the next thing I heard was a loud whining sound and then a crashing boom from outside. Everything dropped away as my skin ignited with a boiling heat. I felt rather than heard myself scream as the room shivered with the explosion, and glass rained down on my face.

"What the fuck was that?" Felix shrieked.

"Don't open your eyes or your mouth, Gracie, you have glass on your face!" Lucy yelled.

Not only was I not asleep after a tickling sensation, I was freaking wide awake after catching fire. "Mmph, mmm! Mmph!"

"We'll get it off. Hold on." It was Ezekiel.

Someone was picking glass pieces from my hair, face, and chest, likely from the overhead light bulbs. I trembled as something stung my lip. One of the shards must have cut me.

"Does anyone have a light? I want to make sure there's no glass in her eyelashes and eyebrows." Lucy's voice sounded strangled.

I winced as a bright light seemed to pierce my eyelids—cell phone flashlights.

"Stay very still, Gracie, please," Lucy whispered. "I'm going for tweezers."

After what felt like an hour and several lost eyelashes later, she slid a hand behind my back and encouraged me to sit up. "Okay, you can open them now. Your mouth too."

Boy, was she going to wish she'd never said that. I struggled to my feet, stepping off the air mattress then right back on when I saw the glass-strewn floor.

I stared at the ring of concerned faces, my gaze finally resting on Ezekiel. "What in the hell did you do to me?" I practically yelled in his face.

He shook his head and ran a hand through his hair, jerking it back to reveal a red spot on a finger—more glass.

"The same thing I've done hundreds of times, Gracie. Your spirit is stronger than we imagined."

"She blew the transformer. That was the explosion," Felix called from the window. "You idiots could have killed her," he snapped.

I took a shaky breath. "Maybe now is the time to tell me the whole story, Ezekiel, and for Christ's sake, *stop lying to me!*"

Ezekiel winced but didn't flinch. Lucy trembled but was silent.

"Someone start talking *now!*" I bellowed.

"Gracie, can I carry you to the table to get you out of the glass?" the angel asked.

"Don't you touch me," I bit out as Ezekiel shrank back. "Phillip?"

He was at my side in a heartbeat, gathering me up into solid arms and carrying me to the table. He tried to set me onto a chair, but I clung to his neck. He hugged me tightly against his chest.

"I'll never let anything like that happen to you again. I was stupid to trust them," Phillip whispered into my ear before lowering me and moving to stand behind my chair, his hands on my shoulders.

I leaned against his tree trunk of a body, sure at least of *his* friendship. And Manny's.

The mob-affiliated bagel maker appeared at my other side.

"It's a good thing she's okay," he said almost too quietly. "I think you two need to explain yourselves."

"Well—" Ezekiel started.

"It seems—" Lucy and Ezekiel said in unison.

"You tell them, Zeke," Lucy said, falling onto a chair.

I got a glimpse of her hand, which was beet red. She tucked it into her lap before I could comment. But she needn't have bothered. Mean as it was, I was more interested in what Ezekiel had to say about me.

"Every couple of centuries, a fiercely indomitable spirit is born. We believe that it has to do with a coming disturbance in the balance of good versus evil. The emergence of the Soul has been a precursor to wars, pestilence, and . . ." He paused. "And a significant increase in supernatural activity."

"Wait just a freakin' minute here. Did you say 'the Soul' with a capital letter?" I yelped.

"Gracie, I sensed that you had an unusually strong spirit, but I had no idea how powerful it was. There hasn't been an omen—there's no way we could have known. Had we known, Lucy and I would never have attempted to wake it before it was ready. I'm so sorry." He dipped his head. "May I ask how you feel?"

I set my jaw in an expression my mother hated and debated refusing to answer him. But I wasn't a child, and I had agreed to let them shock the shit out of me.

I stood up, shook my arms, and bounced up and down on the balls of my feet. "I feel fine. No, better than fine. I feel—" I cocked my head, distracted by a commotion out on the boardwalk.

"What do you hear?" Ezekiel asked.

"Someone on the boardwalk must have called 9-1-1. There are police out there."

"You can hear that from in here?" Viceroy asked.

Wait. What?

I rounded on the little dog. "Viceroy? Did you just ask me if I can hear that?"

He wagged his tail hard enough to crack vertebrae. "Gracie can hear me!" He chortled.

Lucy stared at me. Everyone stared at me, a girl who wanted a cake truck. A nobody.

"As I said, a mighty spirit," Ezekiel muttered.

48

Lucy

I glared at Ezekiel, putting a finger to my lips as Phillip and Manny cleaned up the glass. Felix, Viceroy, and Gracie were at the window, watching the police chase people away from the downed power lines. I grabbed Ezekiel's elbow and steered him through the kitchen and down the long hallway past the restrooms, out the steel fire door, and onto a fire escape.

"Now what do we do?" I hissed, my voice barely above a whisper. I didn't want to chance Gracie overhearing us. "Do you have any experience with spirits like hers?"

"No, but I know someone who does."

"Who?"

"Camael—you don't know him. He's a teacher of sorts, and to some degree, a disinterested third party. I'll text him. If anyone can convince Gracie to at least listen, it's Camael. He's a literal voice of reason. And he'll be able to teach her how to guard herself moving forward." He massaged the back of his neck. "My phone should be charged by now."

"Since when do you guys text?"

"Since it was invented. It's a great way to leave a message if someone doesn't answer."

I couldn't argue with that logic, as reapers were now totally dependent on texting for reaping assignments. "What about Deathy and Vampire Bob?" I asked.

"We still need to contact Vampire Bob, and the sooner, the better. Camael can more than likely be here immediately. Hopefully, whatever time we have between his arrival and Bob's—if we can get Bob to come—will be enough for Camael to talk Gracie off the cliff."

"I know this is horrible to say, but for her safety, I'm glad she doesn't have anyone to run to," I whispered, pulling the door open. "And we'd better not let her out of our sight, just in case. Text Camael."

Ezekiel gave me a thumbs-up and followed me back into the hallway. I was relieved to find Gracie and Felix still at the window. Phillip was emptying the last dustpan of broken light bulbs. Manny was boiling water for tea and plugging in a coffee machine.

I smiled at him. "You thought of everything, Manny. I don't know how we can ever thank you."

He winked at me, and I stopped mid-stride.

"Just kidding," he said. "I don't expect a favor at some future unspecified date. You watch too many movies."

I wrapped my arms around myself, shivering from being outside in a T-shirt. Both Gracie and I had to remove our sweaters, as there was no way to get the glass out of them. Felix had given Gracie his overcoat, but I had only a long-sleeved cotton top.

"I have one of my son's jackets in the car, and it'll fit you. I'll bring it up before I go."

"Thanks. I'm a bit chilled." I walked over to the counter to open the bag of coffee.

"Seriously, Lucy. You don't owe me a thing. I've known Gracie since she was a kid in pigtails. She's like the little sister I never had. Did you know she helps me out at the bakery all the time, despite the fact that her mother never trusted me? And has never accepted a nickel from me."

I shook my head.

"And she just changed my life by introducing me to her friend Sylvie." His tone turned serious. "She is going to be okay, right?"

"Yes," I said without reservation. "She has to learn to deal with her newly awakened spirit, but she's strong, and she will. Ezekiel has another angel, a teacher, coming to help her."

Manny nodded. "Good." He leaned against the counter and angled his head at me. "Just so we're clear here: If she calls me for help, I'll come. Even if it means taking her far from all of you. Gracie is family. Do you understand?"

"I understand," I said. And I did. Like Phillip, Manny would do anything for Gracie. She was going to need friends like that.

"Good. I wish I could stay, but I have an appointment I can't miss. I'll bring up the jacket for you and say goodbye to Gracie, and then I gotta hustle."

I filled the coffee maker with water, put a filter and grounds into the basket, and stood there until the tantalizing aroma of hot coffee filled the room.

I glanced through the doorway to see Ezekiel talking to Gracie and Felix. Gracie wasn't frowning, and she didn't have her arms crossed over her chest, so Ezekiel must be saying something right. Too late, I realized that Gracie could have heard everything Manny and I had said. Fortunately, it wasn't anything that could upset her.

I watched the coffee drip into the pot. How many more pots of coffee would I get to make as a reaper? I poured myself a cup, grateful yet again for Manny, to find he'd also brought half-and-half. Sylvie, whoever she was, was a lucky woman. Fixing a cup for myself, I leaned in the doorway, watching Ezekiel, his head bent, listen to Gracie. Nearby, Felix stroked Viceroy, who snuggled in his arms. The serenity of the image soothed my swirling frets, and I took a deep breath, exhaling slowly and rolling my shoulders.

Phillip appeared as I took my first sip. "You made coffee!" His face broke into a wide grin. "Wait, how did you make coffee? We have no lights."

"Uh, I don't know. Perhaps the kitchen is on a separate circuit?" I stepped aside to allow him to pass. Manny set his son's jacket on the counter for me and walked through the opening I'd made for Phillip, patting my shoulder as he passed. He strode to the quartet at the window, said a few words, and drew Gracie into a tight hug. She wrapped her arms around him and hugged him back. He kissed her cheek, released her, and was gone.

The moment over, Gracie looked at me and, brightening, called out, "I smell coffee!" She touched Ezekiel on the arm and jogged toward me. "I'm still mad at you, Lucy, but you made *coffee!*" She twisted her lips, unable to hide a grin as Ezekiel and Felix followed her—Ezekiel to the coffee pot and Felix to the now-boiling kettle.

"Zeke was this you?" I stepped back to watch Ezekiel as he waited his turn at the pot.

"Guilty as charged." He said, his face solemn. "Don't tell anyone. I figured it was safe enough to charge up the circuit in here since you can't see this room from the boardwalk."

"Nice thank you." I offered him a warm smile. Once I became Death, our fates would be all but sealed. We'd never be together as lovers. But—and this was something—we'd work together. It was far less than either of us longed for but far better than the nothing we had now.

"Lucy?" Ezekiel touched my elbow with his free hand.

"I'm okay. Or rather, I will be. We'll get to work together," I said, sotto voce. "That's something."

"Yes. We will, and it is."

I shivered as he ran his hand up my arm, wanting nothing more than to melt into him. My breath hitched, and I stepped back instead. He nodded. We could do this. We could.

"Is Camael coming?" I asked, sipping from my paper cup.

"He should be here any minute." Ezekiel swung away from me to address the room. "Hey, guys?" Heads swiveled toward him. "I just wanted to let you know that Camael may not come through a door. He might just appear. I don't want you to be startled if he pops into existence next to you."

"Pops into existence? What does that mean?" Gracie asked between sips of coffee.

"Well, when a mass rapidly displaces air, it makes a sound—the larger the mass, the louder the sound. Angels can travel through space and time. So Camael can be in San Francisco one second and here in Port Chester the next."

"And he pops. Cool," Phillip said. "I wish I could do that. It would come in very handy at a troll raising." Our eyebrows all shot up. "There's a point where you have to run fast, or you become a troll's mate." He snickered. "It never happened to me, but I have a friend who . . ." He trailed off, flushing bright red. "Sorry, that's not a story for polite company."

Gracie patted his arm. "It's okay, Phillip. I think we get the gist of it." She reached for the coffee pot, flicked off the power switch, and poured herself the last half cup. "So, I—"

A loud pop from the other room interrupted her. "Zeke?" a deep voice called out.

"Cam! You made it! We're in the kitchen." Ezekiel stuck his head out the door and welcomed Camael with a one-armed man-hug.

"Well, finally," Felix said, "someone who can tell us what the hell just happened to Gracie."

Gracie's face lit up. Small as she was, Felix's overcoat made her look even smaller. I hoped Camael realized how young she was. Camael went straight to her and extended a hand.

"My name is Camael. I am honored to meet you, Grace. I hope you will allow me to help you navigate both your new soul and your new place in the universe."

Gracie looked up into his rough-hewn but warm face and took his hand. He closed his other hand over it for a long second.

"Shall we talk alone? Or would you rather have your friends with you?"

"You can call me Gracie. I want them with me. I wish Manny

was still here," she said, gazing raptly into Camael's eyes, her voice sounding almost dazed. Despite his prizefighter's appearance and build—he looked as if he'd lost more than a couple of fights—he radiated divinity like heat from a wood stove.

I moved closer. We needed all the divine help we could get.

49

Gracie

"Is it too much, Gracie?" Camael had just finished telling me about my newly empowered soul, and I had assured him that I wasn't overwhelmed. Despite all the drama of its awakening, my super-indomitable spirit didn't come preloaded with any superpowers. Though he did say I could develop them, it sounded like the amount of practice it would require would take time away from my cake-truck planning. So apart from enhanced senses and lucid dreams I would now be able to control, it didn't seem like much of an upgrade to me and certainly not worth all the trouble my mother had caused by keeping it a secret.

By the time we finished talking, it was late afternoon and growing dark. Because I'd apparently blown the transformer, we sat around the table, our faces illuminated by the thin light from a couple of candles Lucy had found in the kitchen. She hadn't located any matches, so Ezekiel lit them with a finger, which I had to admit was a pretty neat trick. We moved on to discussing Deathy's abdication, my spirit, soul, whatever, appearing, and other omens, portents, and signs that might augur the rise of evil and darkness in the world. You know, just another Wednesday afternoon.

Tired of the increasingly dense conversation, I wandered to

the window, Felix and Viceroy trailing behind me.

"The Con-Ed guys are still out there, and they're talking about being home in time for dinner. So we'll have power back soon," I said to Felix, beaming at being able to hear the men's conversations. "And hearing them talk about food is making me hungry. I'm starving. We didn't have lunch. Should we make sandwiches?"

Felix leaned closer to the glass and peered down the board-walk. "The restaurant has lights on, so we can get a real dinner. I won't vouch for its quality, but at least it'll be hot. The crew won't see us if we go out the parking lot doors."

"And we can get a drink," I said.

"Or nine," Felix added.

"And I can have steak, right?" Viceroy chimed in from the floor.

"If they have steak, you can have all you can eat. Felix is paying," I said, ignoring Felix's protestations and reaching down to scoop the little dog into my arms. "This is the best part of the new me," I whispered into his ear. "I love that I can hear you!"

"Me too!" Viceroy thought back. "Because I need to pee."

Felix stepped back. "Okay, since you can hear the little freak now, I'm putting you in charge of his pee breaks."

"That's fine. He'd rather be with me anyway, right, Viceroy?" I hid my grin in Viceroy's fur as Felix heaved a sigh.

"Can we go?" Felix raised his voice to address the room.

"We should try Jameson first," Ezekiel called from the table. "I didn't want to risk potentially alerting him before we'd woken your spirit, Gracie, on the off chance he'd show up or cause some other havoc while you were in the middle of it. But now, the sooner, the better."

"Listen, I don't want to rain on the vampire parade, but I need food," I said. "My stomach is growling loud enough to hear, and I can't think straight when I'm hungry."

Ezekiel rocked from foot to foot. "Okay," he sighed. "We've waited this long; another hour won't make much difference. Let's go." He swiped the ring of keys off the table, and we headed out the back way.

THE RESTAURANT, CHARLEY'S PIER, LOOKED PERFECT. Somehow, I'd never eaten here, only ever coming to the park for the rides, rarely venturing onto the boardwalk. The wind had kicked up, and a chorus of whistles and howls emanated from the park, presumably from the empty arms of the rides catching the wind. The lone lights from the boardwalk added to a horror-movie-set feel. I was glad to have a safe place to stay, but I peered back over my shoulder to the boardwalk, now rapidly emptying of the Con-Ed guys and trucks, searching for anything that might eat me.

Felix, who'd been leading us, stopped dead ten feet from the front door. "We have a dog. They're not going to let us in."

Viceroy flopped down and laid his head on his paws. "I never get to go anywhere," he grumbled. "This sucks."

"We can get the food to go and a drink at the bar while we wait," Felix said. "Let's get to it. It's freezing out here."

"Do you want your coat?" I asked.

"No. I'll survive until bourbon." He lowered his voice so only I could hear him. "Having a blood snack amps up my metabolism. I don't feel the cold for about twenty-four hours afterward."

I wrinkled my nose. "Blech. I can't even imagine."

"Well, aren't you fortunate to be you, then," he snapped.

Viceroy was right at our heels. "Don't forget, the best steak for me, and I want it bloody."

"You got it, little guy," I said aloud to him. The bar was empty despite the heat lamps arrayed around it, the lone bartender engrossed in something on his phone. We filled one side of the bar, and I took a seat next to Felix, Viceroy on my lap. The bartender perked up at the sight of a potentially hefty group tip.

We ordered a round of double bourbons and one Coke for me, which Felix promptly spiked from his glass. He convinced the restaurant to box up the higher-priced meals not on the to-go menu, and we ordered a second round while we waited. When the food finally arrived, Felix was on his third and apparently feeling no pain. He waved away Lucy's offer to split the bill and slid an American Express Black card across the bar.

I did a double take. "Felix. You're a man of means."

"Don't tell anyone," he hissed. "I have a—"

"Yeah, I know. You have a reputation to uphold."

"That's not all." He gave Ezekiel and Camael, seated on the other side of Lucy and Phillip, a side-eye. "I've heard that angels are notoriously cheap. I don't want them thinking I'll always foot the bill."

I tossed back the rest of my drink, which didn't seem to be affecting me at all, and heard voices from the darker section of the path.

Ezekiel and Phillip bolted from their stools the instant I made out words.

"Run!" Ezekiel hissed, yanking first Lucy, then me, off our stools and shoving us around the bar and down the steps in the direction of the museum.

Gripping Viceroy against my chest and without looking to see how close the voices were, I ran like hell through the stiff breeze off the water. We were at the stairs before I chanced a glance backward. A mob of people had just rounded the tiki bar. They weren't running. I strained to see who was in front but only caught a glimpse of a white coat before Ezekiel barked in my ear.

"Get upstairs." He pushed me, and I sprinted up. He was right behind me, moving through the crush of us to unlock the door. We tumbled inside, and he slammed and locked it after us.

Lucy was white as a sheet, silhouetted against the light coming in from the streetlamp. "Deathy tracked me," Lucy said, panting. "On HELL. I was afraid this might happen. I'm so sorry."

Camael peered outside. "And she brought vampires."

Felix joined him. "Well, I guess I don't have to call the fucker. Who's going downstairs?"

"I'll go," I said. "Bob didn't hurt me last time."

"No. I'm sorry, Gracie, we can't risk losing you," Ezekiel said, his face pinched. "I want you, Lucy, Felix, and Viceroy to hide wherever you can find a room, maybe one of the restrooms or a supply closet at the back of the building. Bar the door with whatever you can find. Phillip, you wait here in case we need you. Camael and I will go down and ask to speak to Jameson alone. He needs to know what will happen if he turns Deathy. Slim as it is, it's our only hope of getting out of this without a bloodbath."

"Gracie, let's go." Lucy took my arm to lead me after Felix, who was hot-footing it down the hall.

I looked at Ezekiel and opened my mouth to argue.

"This isn't up for discussion," he said and turned his back on me.

"They're at the bottom of the stairs," Phillip said.

"Gracie, come on." Lucy tugged my arm, but I was desperate to eavesdrop.

"Isn't it better if we know what they're saying? If they make a single move toward the stairs, I'll run."

"I'll protect you," Viceroy growled his thought at me. I hadn't even noticed him at my feet.

"No." Lucy shook her head and grabbed me with both hands, one still pinker than the other. "Ezekiel said to hide, and he's never wrong."

"I know. I heard him. Just let me listen for a minute." I shook out of her grasp and planted my feet.

"You're impossible!" She slapped her injured hand against the wall and winced. "If you won't go, Viceroy and I are staying with you."

"You three are idiots. I'll be hiding," Felix called from down the hall.

I turned back to the window, snippets of conversation drowned out by the sound of Felix's stomping. I turned to shush him, only to see him pass by the restrooms to open the fire door. He was gone before I could call out.

"Lucy. Felix went out the fire exit."

She spun on a heel and sprinted down the hall to yank it open. Viceroy and I were right behind her. From the fire escape, we saw Felix disappear around the corner of the building.

"Now what?" I said.

"Now nothing. I need to make sure you and Viceroy are safe."

"Ezekiel said to hide, but maybe we should run?" I ventured.

She bit her lip. "Deathy can find me, us, no matter where we go. Splitting up may be our best bet. Gracie, you need to take Viceroy and go without me."

"Leave you here? I don't think so."

But she wasn't listening. "Wait here," she said. She jogged down the hall to return with something in her hand. Keys. "Take my car. Start driving upstate—"

"No! I'm not leaving you here to die!"

"Gracie, I can't die. Not in the way you think of it. It will take me a couple of days, but I'll be back in a new body."

"So if I have a soul like yours, I can't die either. And anyway, I'm not leaving Phillip."

"It takes time to learn how to claim a new body, and now isn't the time to teach you. Your soul might get lost, and Camael would have to find it and assign it a body, which could take days, even weeks. If Ezekiel and Camael are right, your soul is necessary for whatever battle is coming. You can't die right now. I need you to take the keys and Viceroy and go. My car is right there." She pointed to it below us in the parking lot. "Gracie, please!"

"What about Phillip?"

"What about me?" the big man asked from the doorway.

"What's happening down there?" I asked. Not giving him a chance to answer, I pushed past him.

"They're talking."

"All of them?" I asked, heading back toward the window, Phillip and Lucy trailing me.

"Yeah. First, Ezekiel talked to one of the vampires away from everyone else. Now that woman Death is doing most of the talking," Phillip said.

"Did you see Felix? Did you hear anything?"

"Felix? He's not with you?"

I shook my head, pointing in the direction of the boardwalk. "Can you hear what they're saying?"

"No, they're talking too low."

I leaned my ear against the glass.

"Gracie, *wait!*"

Lucy's cry was the last thing I heard before the room erupted in a tornado of carnival-colored swirling lights that flung Phillip, Lucy, and Viceroy against the walls. The eye of the tornado swept me up into the center of the room, suspending me. I drifted toward the ceiling, thrashing against the force, but my arms and legs waved ineffectively.

Time stretched as I began to rotate slowly, the lights dancing over and around me. I stopped struggling to watch them. Some part of my brain knew I should be terrified, wondered if Lucy, Phillip, and Viceroy were okay, but cocooned in the warm lights, I couldn't force myself to care. I looked up to see the Milky Way arching overhead. If this was dying, I was okay with it.

I don't know how long I twisted in the lights, but after a while, they began to condense and wind around my body like plushy snakes. I heard myself laugh. This was fun!

Then I felt a pinch. Something had bitten my leg. A mosquito? Another one on my arm.

More bites. They got harder. I turned my head against the colors and saw one of the snake shapes burrow its way into my arm. I screamed in agony, screaming and screaming, as each color pierced my skin. A purple shape headed for my mouth, and everything went black.

50

Lucy

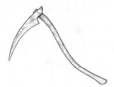

P inned to the wall, Phillip, Viceroy, and I could only watch Gracie scream as the blaze of multicolored lights ate their way into her body. Tears streamed down my face, but I couldn't raise a hand to wipe them away.

"Gracie! *Gracie!*" Phillip cried, struggling desperately to free himself. But he was as stuck to his wall as I was to mine.

"Open this door!" someone shouted, pounding on it.

"Viceroy?" I called. He must have been on the wall behind the swirling lights, but he didn't answer me.

Gracie's screams rose in pitch. The dawning realization, the horror of it, hit me like a cleaver to the gut. The Mantle was claiming her.

"Zeke! Stop this—" My voice cut off as if someone had pressed the power button on my vocal cords. "This isn't right. I'm supposed to take the Mantle. It's choosing Gracie! It's not possible! *Stop this! She'll die!*"

Gracie fainted as she absorbed the last color and fell to the floor. The force that had held us against the walls dissipated, and Phillip and I stumbled to her.

Phillip pulled Gracie onto his lap, cradling her in his arms. "She's alive," he whispered.

I stroked her face until she regained some color.

"Gracie, Gracie. Wake up." I tapped her cheeks, and her eyes flew open.

She creased her eyebrows and frowned at us. "Uh, what the hell happened, and why are we on the floor?" she croaked and pushed against Phillip's embrace until he loosened his hold enough to allow her to sit up. She shook her head as if to clear it, put a hand on her throat, and gazed blankly around the room. "My throat hurts. Who's banging on the door?"

"The force of the Mantle must have welded it shut," I said, as no amount of banging was budging it.

"What force? Will someone tell me what the hell happened?" Gracie hissed at me.

I stared at her. Granted, I had no personal experience with a Mantle transference, but according to everything I'd learned, what just happened wasn't possible. The Mantle did not possess self-determination. It was a blind power, and as such, it went to whomever the angels chose to bear it—it didn't choose its bearer. It couldn't. But it had. And it had picked Gracie. A wave of nausea swept through me, magnifying hot shame at the unbidden and unwelcome relief that the Mantle had not chosen me. A tidal wave of terror for Gracie just as quickly doused that sickening joy.

Gracie grabbed my arms and shook me out of my trance. "Lucy! Answer me!"

I opened my mouth to tell her.

"Wait, I remember. I was at the window, and there was a woman. Let me up, Phillip. I'm okay," Gracie said, her voice scratchy. She was far from okay, but she scrambled to her feet only to lurch sideways. "Whoa! I think that bourbon finally hit me." She giggled.

Phillip and I both sprang up to grab her as she staggered, smacking our foreheads together in the process.

"Ow," I yelped, stumbling backward.

"Sorry," Phillip said, undeterred from his focus on Gracie, who was now weaving toward the stuck door.

"You two are drunker than I am. What happened out there? And who's banging on the door?"

I grabbed her arm before she could reach it. "Gracie, listen to me."

"Ow. Let *go*. I'm just opening the—"

"No!" Phillip and I shouted, both leaping for her at the same time.

"Grace!" I shook her like a rag doll, and she finally turned at my use of her given name. "The Mantle chose you. That's what happened. You're Death!"

She stared at me as if I'd grown another head. "No, *you're* gonna be Death. I have an indomitable spirit. Remember? What the heck is wrong with you two?" She twisted around in a circle. "Where's Viceroy?"

I kicked myself for forgetting all about him. Hearing his name, he staggered toward us from the far wall, and I let go of Gracie long enough to scoop him up. "Are you okay?" I asked him aloud.

"Uh-huh. But I think I have a headache. Who's making that noise?" the rattled little dog thought as the banging on the metal door changed to clanging—someone had gotten hold of a crowbar or a pipe.

I handed Viceroy to Phillip and took Gracie by the shoulders. "Listen to me. We have to get out of here. Now!" I didn't know what would happen if whoever was on the other side of that door made it inside, but I didn't want to hang around to find out. I dragged Gracie toward the hallway when two loud pops from the kitchen signaled the arrival of Ezekiel and Camael.

"Thank God. Zeke!" I let go of her and ran to him, barely managing to stop myself from falling into his arms in front of Camael. "What happened out there?"

"What happened in here?" he shot back. "Do you have the Mantle?"

"No, I—"

"Lucy says I do," Gracie said, leaning in the doorway and

twisting a strand of her hair. Phillip was glued to her back, shooting murderous looks at us. "But I think I hit my head or something. I don't feel any different, except my throat really hurts and my ankle feels like I twisted it. Did I trip?"

"You tell her. She doesn't believe me," I said to the two angels as I struggled against conflicting emotions. "And how do we get out of here?"

"Camael and I can take you and Grace with us, but we can't move Phillip, Viceroy, and Felix." He looked around. "Where is Felix?"

"He ran out the back door. Didn't he join you in the front?" I asked.

"We didn't see him," Camael said.

"Okay, so maybe you two should at least get Gracie out, then come back—"

Ezekiel shook his head. "Only if you come too. I don't think it's a good idea to leave her unattended yet."

Someone started banging on the back fire door.

"Uh, hello? I'm right here," Gracie said, yelling over the racket. "And I don't appreciate the three of you making decisions for me. If we need to go, we should all go together. But first, we need to find Felix. He went—" She pointed to the fire exit, blowing the door off its hinges. Shrieks erupted from the other side.

Gracie's mouth dropped open. "Did I do that?" she squeaked as Phillip dropped Viceroy to the floor and pushed past her to thunder down the hall after Camael and Ezekiel.

I grabbed her hand and yanked it down to her side. *"Don't point!"*

"Okay, okay. You could have warned me. Are we in trouble?"

"Yes." I picked up Viceroy and handed him to her. "Hold him, and point at anyone who tries to take him from you. Just try not to hit any of us in the process."

"But you just said . . . Oh, never mind, I get it. Where are you going?"

"To fight," I said, reaching for my bag. "Stay here."

"Uh, maybe *you* should stay here, and *I* should go out there? Seeing as I'm the one with a weapon?" She gingerly put her finger in the air and blew pretend smoke off its tip.

"This isn't a joke, Gracie." Tears of frustration threatened to spill. "You're dangerous, and—"

"And they're not?" She handed Viceroy to me, and the little dog sighed in relief. "Listen, Lucy, I didn't ask for this. And you're going to take it from me as soon as we get out of this mess. But right now, I'm better off Death than dead."

I stared at her, conflicted, but I couldn't argue with her logic. She gave me a crooked smile and stalked down the hall, leaving me holding Viceroy.

"Wait!" I shouted, stopping her in her tracks. "I have an idea."

51

Felix

I rounded the corner in time to see Deathy lose her shit in a stream of twinkle lights. One second she was shrieking at Ezekiel and Camael, and the next, rays of colored light were pouring from every orifice I could see, and a couple I couldn't. The lights spun around her for a heartbeat before shooting directly up and into the same window I'd been peering out of not minutes earlier. The entire room lit up like a fireworks display.

Then Deathy collapsed, and Vampire Bob and his New York minions practically stomped her into the ground in their rush for the stairs. The angels tried to pull them back down without killing them, then abruptly gave up and popped out of existence. I ran past an empty swimming pool thinking to get back upstairs when I heard the horde behind me.

I hid in the deep shadow behind a tree trunk, watching vampires stream past me and up the fire escape. Whatever the fuck had exploded up there must have welded all the doors shut because the vampires tearing at the fire door were having even less success than the group pounding at the front door. I was congratulating myself for not getting caught in the melee when the fire door exploded outward, blowing several vampires out into the parking lot. Another couple fell from the now-creaking fire escape but scrambled quickly to their feet. Ezekiel and Camael stormed out the open door and down the stairs, shoving vampires over the railing. Phillip followed, cracking his knuckles loud enough for me to hear.

"Well, hello again, Felix. How nice of you to join us." Vampire Bob had his hand in my hair before I could blink. He put a knee on my ass and bent my head back until I gurgled in pain. "It seems I no longer have easy access to souls, thanks to that moron's inability to control her power. So you, that damned dog, and that girl will be my consolation prize." He pushed me forward, out of the concealing shadows, and I stumbled, dropping to my knees. "I'm going to release the pressure, and you're going to call them. Understand?"

"Glurgh."

"I'll take that as a yes." He righted my head but tightened his grip on my hair. "Call them!"

"No," I hissed.

He shook my head hard enough to rattle my teeth. "CALL THEM OR DIE!" Bob thundered in my ear, twisted my head and body in opposite directions until I screeched.

"Viceroy, Gracie," I choked as Ezekiel spotted us and sprinted in our direction.

"No closer, angel boy, or Felix gets the twisties."

Ezekiel skidded to a stop. "What's the twisties?" he asked conversationally. I was going to kill him if Bob didn't kill me first.

"Didn't you watch the Olympics gymnastics competition? You angels are all plebeians. It means his head . . . Why am I telling you this? Bring out the girl and the dog, and we'll be out of your hair." Bob leaned over to grin in my face. Still clutching a handful of my hair, he shook my head again, waggling my body along with it. "Literally," he added, chuckling at his joke.

"Ezekiel." I put up a hand. "Don't—"

"No one likes bullies, Bob," Gracie yelled from the fire escape. With her hands on her hips, silhouetted by the light over the door, she looked like a superhero. "You should let Felix go."

"As soon as you and the dog come down. Ah, there's the little man of the hour." He chuckled as Viceroy appeared at Gracie's feet. "Come, my lovelies. I'll take good care of you."

Gracie cocked her head as if considering his offer. "You know, I was getting tired of this place anyway," she said.

My bowels loosened.

Ezekiel and Camael spun. "NO!" they chorused.

Camael, closer to the steps, raced back up. Gracie whispered in his ear, and he peered inside. She scooped up Viceroy and edged around him to patter down the steps and stand between Ezekiel and Phillip.

"What guarantees do we have that you won't hurt us?" She smiled.

"Grace, don't—" I croaked.

Ezekiel grabbed her arm. She shook him off.

Bob reached around and slapped my face hard enough to split a lip. "Ah-ah-ah, Felix!" The lunatic wagged a finger in my face, his eyes blazing with acquisitive fire. I licked the welling blood before he could smell it and tear my throat out.

"Absolutely none, my dear," Bob said. "But as I do need to understand how this village idiot managed to turn a dog and why you are immune to us, I need you all to remain alive. So I guess you do have some sort of a guarantee."

"Well, you do have a nice house," Gracie said. "But I'll need a bigger room. With a river view. And I'll need some serious cheering up because I've just lost my boyfriend."

"He preferred another? Or is he dead?" Bob asked.

I whimpered as Bob remembered to twist my head.

"Oh, no, nothing like that," Gracie said. "He lied to me, so I had to end it."

"Without killing him? I would have killed him." Bob tilted his head to the side. "The only question would be how."

"Felix," Viceroy hissed into my head. "When Gracie scratches her nose, fall forward."

Bob didn't react, and I spared a second to wonder why he couldn't hear Viceroy. "What?" I thought back at him.

Then Gracie scratched her nose.

Bob spun at a sound behind us, wrenching me sideways and yanking out a chunk of my hair to erupt in a twisting, screeching whirlwind. I threw myself away from him, yelping at the fire in my scalp. The vampires that had gathered, presumably waiting from an order from Bob, charged.

I got my feet under me in time to see Gracie point her finger at Bob, shooting a blast of—

"*Oh shit!*" I dove to the ground as the tree I'd been hiding behind exploded into splinters. "Fuck!" I howled into the dirt as slivers of wood pierced my back and legs. I lay there, panting, as all hell broke loose above me.

"Felix! Get up!" Lucy clutched my arm and pulled.

"*Fuck!*" I struggled upright, my back and legs on fire, to see Camael, Ezekiel, Phillip, and Gracie back-to-back in a foursquare, Ezekiel and Camael slashing at the vampires surrounding them with flaming swords. At the same time, Gracie aimed her finger, blowing vampire after vampire into mushroom clouds of blood, gore, and bone shards. Lucy dragged me backward. I tripped over Viceroy, shrieking loud enough to cover his yelp as my splinters burrowed deeper.

"Felix, let's go. They've got this!"

I turned to her and gasped. Lucy, covered in blood from wood shards embedded from her face to her knees, was frantic. I took her hand, the only wound-free part of her, and risked a glance over my shoulder. The vampires were too busy dying to pay us any attention—our path was clear.

"What the fuck were you doing back there?" I moaned as we stumbled away.

"Everyone was in the back parking lot, so I went out the front and circled around the side to get behind you."

"Why?"

"Are you complaining?" Her voice hitched in pain.

"No, just trying to understand what the fuck just happened."

"Holy water. I threw it at Bob to distract him so Gracie could—"

"Yeah, great. I suppose I should thank you, but that was monumentally stupid. You should see yourself."

She attempted a chuckle, but it came out as a wheeze.

"Viceroy?" I called.

"I'm okay. Maybe I got a scratch or three, but I hid behind Gracie and the angels," he thought as we rounded the building.

"Well, good for you. I didn't have anyone to—" I stopped before I admitted that I would have hidden behind anyone.

"Hide behind?" he finished for me. "You could have hidden behind Death, who might have protected you if you'd had a chance to suck up to her. But she's gone."

How did the little fucker know about my plan? I gaped at him as he walked around the corner and onto the illuminated boardwalk.

"Because you're you, and you can't stop thinking about your-self," he muttered. "Don't worry. I won't tell anybody."

I glared at him.

"*Whoops*, except for Lucy."

"She's not gone," Lucy whispered, cutting off my retort. "There she is."

A disheveled woman sat hunched over on the bottom step, her hair obscuring her face, rocking slightly and singing to herself. Viceroy and I stopped dead at the corner, but Lucy kept walking.

"Sorry, Felix, I didn't think she was listening," the little shit thought up at me.

I glared down at him. He was lucky I was in so much pain.

"Deathy?" Lucy called to the woman. "Let's get closer, Felix. I can't feel any power in her."

Viceroy inched nearer, and I followed.

"Deathy? It's Lucy. Can you hear me?"

The woman kept singing. We inched forward another few feet. She was singing in what sounded like French.

"Deathy?" Lucy was now directly in front of her.

"Lucy?" the woman said, still not looking up. "Is that you?"

"It's me. Are you okay?" Lucy leaned forward, and Deathy lunged, wrapping her hands around Lucy's throat and squeezing.

Viceroy charged, sinking his teeth into the back of Deathy's ankle. The bitch howled but clung to Lucy's neck like an octopus. I ran to them and ignoring the agony of my splinters, pulled up Deathy's sleeve and sank my teeth into her forearm. The blood that flowed into my mouth was rancid. I gagged and sprayed her rotten blood all over her white coat.

Beneath her blood and splinters, Lucy's lips were blue, her eyes rolling up. I lifted my leg and kicked Deathy, flat-footed, in the ribs. Lucy crumbled to the boardwalk as Deathy flew sideways. Viceroy let go and tumbled head over ass as Deathy slammed into the building.

"That wasn't nice," Deathy mewled at me, patting her injured side as I tried to rouse Lucy without touching her wounds.

Viceroy licked her ear. "Wake up, Lucy. Gracie's coming; they've killed all the vampires."

Lucy coughed and moaned. I plucked some of the larger fragments out of her stomach and waistline to make it possible for her to sit up. She hissed in pain.

"Lucy!" Gracie cried, running toward us. "Are you okay?"

"Yeah, mostly," Lucy whimpered. "But I'm going to need more holy water." Then she fainted in my arms.

52

Grace

I sat in the car with Phillip and Viceroy while Camael and Ezekiel took Lucy and Felix into the emergency room at WestMed.

"Are you sure you don't want to go in?" Phillip asked again.

"Yes, I'm sure. I don't want to see Bryan. I need more time," I said, eyeing Viceroy, who had declined my lap in favor of Phillip's. The little dog snored softly as Phillip stroked his head.

"He's afraid of me," I said.

"He is," Phillip agreed. "So am I."

"You're afraid of me? Why?"

"You bear the power of life and death, Grace."

"No, I'm just holding it for Lucy. I'm not keeping it. And why is everyone calling me Grace?"

"Maybe you'll be able to give it to her, but the Mantle chose you for a reason. Ezekiel says that's never happened before, and—"

"And no one in Heaven can figure out why. I heard him." I sighed. Ezekiel and Camael had been walking on eggshells around me since the battle. It was like they expected me to burst into flames or something. And they'd all started calling me Grace, which was seriously annoying. The truth was, I didn't feel any different. I *wasn't* any different.

Okay, so I could disintegrate people and blow stuff up, which I kind of liked, and my voice sometimes took on a weird metallic vibration, which I didn't. And even after all the shit that had happened, I wasn't even tired. But I was still me.

"I'm still me," I said aloud. "And please stop calling me Grace. I like Gracie."

Viceroy grumbled in his sleep.

"No, you're not the same person as you were before, Grace. Even if it is temporary, right this minute, you're a Horseman of the Apocalypse, the Pale Rider. So even if Deathy used the familiar form of her title, calling you by your nickname now would be inappropriate. We could call you Death if you like that better."

"No!"

I stared at him, thoroughly creeped out, because Catholic school. I knew all about the Four Horsemen. They were the stuff of horror movies, and I did not want to be one.

"Listen, Phillip, this is all wrong. I'm just me, and I have a life. I'll take Bryan back. I'll forgive him. And my cake truck, I'm going to do that too. Lucy is going to be Death, not me," I grumbled, folding my arms across my chest and shivering despite Felix's coat. "Can you go check on them? And why did we need the emergency room anyway? Couldn't Ezekiel and Camael just heal them?"

"I don't know how angel powers work, and I didn't ask. But I'm not leaving you out here alone. Vampire Bob is still alive, and—"

"And I can fry him with a finger."

"And maybe a couple of innocent bystanders." Phillip shook his big head. "I'll call Ezekiel." He had Lucy's phone and her bag.

"Fine." I checked the burner Manny had given me to find a text from him saying his people would start the cleanup as soon as the sun rose and that they'd taken Deathy to a "secure location."

Grateful yet again at his unstinting friendship, I appreciated that he hadn't even hesitated when Ezekiel called him after the battle to explain what needed doing. I whispered a thankful prayer on his behalf. His second text asked me to call him when we knew how Felix and Lucy were doing.

I tucked the phone away and listened to Phillip's side of the short conversation, watching his face relax as he disconnected.

"They'll be out soon. The doctor wanted to keep Lucy overnight because some of her punctures were larger than Felix's, but she said she'd recover better at home." Phillip's gorgeous blue eyes lit up. "We're all going to Lucy's house." It was good to see him happy.

"Phillip, please don't be scared of me." I put a hand on his arm, and he didn't flinch. "You know I would never hurt you, right?"

He searched my face. "I know you would never hurt me, or any of us, on purpose. But the power you bear isn't something you take on and off like boots. I don't know how to explain it the right way, but you become it, sort of like going from child to teenager to adult, growing older. You're still the same person, even though you go through different aspects of yourself. Fay says that sometimes when she looks in the mirror, she doesn't recognize the wrinkled face that looks back at her because on most days, she still feels like a girl inside. We're all young and old at the same time no matter how bad we want it to be otherwise." He paused to clear his throat. It was the longest speech I'd heard him make.

"What makes you frightening is that you hold Death within you. You *are* Death. And Death is ancient. Ancient powers are unfathomable and unpredictable. So while I trust you, Grace Rinelli, I also respect the part of you that is Death. Does that make sense?"

Phillip's explanation sounded a hell of a lot scarier than Ezekiel's or Camael's, and it made me shiver harder.

"Do you want me to start the car and run the heater?" Phillip asked.

"No, I'm not cold. I'm just shaky. Delayed reaction, I guess." I looked at Viceroy. "So that's what Viceroy feels. The creepy, scary, ancient part of me."

He quirked an eyebrow. "I guess you could say that. Animals feel things most people can't. He'll be okay. He loves you. Give him some time."

"Can I ask you a question?"

"Sure, anything."

"Did you always know you were a troll raiser?"

Phillip tilted his head. "No. It isn't genetic. You come into it when you become a man."

"At twenty-one?"

He chuckled. "I was eleven."

"Oh. That kind of becoming a man. Were you okay with it?"

He thought for a minute before answering. "I wasn't. I wanted to be like my friends. I wanted to learn my father's trade. Instead, I had to spend a year in the woods with the old troll raiser, and he smelled. Everyone said it was good that our village had a new troll raiser, that it would help us defend ourselves, and they were right. I just didn't want it to be me."

"But you're okay with it now? You're happy with who you are?"

"I am. Without my power, I'd have died long ago. I wouldn't have been here or able to fight the vampires when we rescued you at Bob's house or today at the battle."

"But doesn't it make things harder, sometimes?"

"Sometimes I'm lonely. I've never married. I have no children. I would like a family."

My heart ached for him. "Is it too late?"

"No, but I'd have to find someone who understands what I am and what I do." He shrugged. "I haven't found her yet."

"Don't give up. When this is all over, I'll help you. I'm pretty good at matchmaking. I just matched Manny with my best friend, and they're perfect for each other." I didn't mention my legion of failures that came before it, as his face lit up.

"Whenever you're ready." I touched his arm. "I have a friend, a librarian. She's smart, tall, and gorgeous, and she loves fantasy and sci-fi. I think you and Rachel will be perfect for each other." I grinned at my sudden flash of brilliance.

"I would like to meet her when this is all over."

"You got it."

We sat in silence, listening to Viceroy's snorts and snores. Phillip, watchful and alert; me, running my brain at a thousand miles an hour until Ezekiel, Camael, Lucy, and Felix made their way toward us.

The two angels had arranged Lucy and Felix as comfortably as possible in the back seat before popping out to a meeting, presumably about me. They'd join us later. Lucy and Felix were out seconds after settling in, thanks to the painkillers. Felix was curled sideways to protect his back. He looked oddly innocent, his perpetual sneer softened by sleep. They were both wearing hospital scrubs, and butterflies and Band-Aids covered Lucy's face and neck. I cringed at the thought of what was underneath her clothes. If it hadn't been for her and the bottle of holy water she always carried in her magic bag, some of us might be dead.

I did that to them. The splinters were my fault.

This thing, this Mantle of Death that had chosen me, injured my friends. And Bob, the head asshole, had gotten away.

"Phillip, I'm dangerous to people I love." Tears welled.

"Don't, Grace. They don't blame you. Without your powers, we might not have been able to kill them all. We were four against at least a hundred."

I shuddered. The carnage we'd left in the parking lot and the dried vampire blood on our clothes were all too real. Felix had assured me that, once the sun rose, the dead vampires would turn to ash and blow away, so all Manny's people had to do was collect their clothing. There was no way I would let Manny write off this debt. I owed him big time.

Phillip drove carefully, glancing at me occasionally but leaving me to my thoughts. Viceroy had elected to settle himself between

Felix and Lucy in the back rather than sit on my lap. He'd claimed his bones hurt, and he wanted to lie on a flat surface, but it rang hollow.

I sat staring out the window, my heart aching for what I had lost. I needed to talk to my mother. I wanted Bryan to hold me in his arms, stroke my back, and kiss the top of my head. But would he, now, knowing what I was? And even if I did forgive them, I could kill them with the wrong gesture. I wanted myself back so I could stew for a while and then forgive everyone and go to family dinner. Was that too much to ask?

I turned to look at Lucy, who would take this curse from me in a heartbeat even though it would doom her to a loveless life.

I wished I could just be a little girl again, watching my dad shave, smelling the mouthwatering aroma of my mother's home cooking, wrestling with my brothers. But something told me it would take more than family to fix this mess.

Oh, Mom. What should I do?

53

Lucy

Thursday, November 19

Camael and Ezekiel had run their hands over Felix and me, radiating their particular brand of blessed energy to help speed our healing. Afterward, we apparently slept for hours. I woke to find Ezekiel sitting in the wing chair in the corner of my bedroom, a book open on his lap.

"What time is it? How are Felix and Grace doing? And what about Phillip?" I asked.

"It's about noon. Felix is feeling much better. He's downstairs having some lunch. Grace is fine. She had some breakfast and even took Viceroy out into the courtyard with Phillip for a bit. She's been talking to him, and he seems to have a calming influence on her, which is wonderful. And Phillip seems fine. Patience went out to get some clean things for him to wear, as you didn't have anything in his size. He's all set. How are you feeling?"

I flexed a few muscles before answering. "Better than I did last night. I imagine Phillip has seen battles far bloodier than the one we were in yesterday."

Ezekiel quirked an eyebrow. "That's what he told me. He said that as a troll raiser, he's been in more battles than he can remember. I think it's one of the reasons he emigrated, though I didn't ask directly." Ezekiel turned his gaze out the window.

"I can't imagine what his life was like. I'm glad he's with us now."

Ezekiel nodded and turned back to me. "I'm glad everyone got some sleep." He put aside the book and came to sit on the side of my bed. "Let me see how your wounds are doing." He gently peeled one edge of a butterfly bandage from my cheek and smiled. "You'll be good as new in a couple of days, though you'll have a few scars."

I sat up and breathed a sigh of relief. There was too much to do. I couldn't afford to be out of commission. "Did you learn anything about getting the Mantle from Grace into me?"

"No. We've never had to remove it without killing the bearer. The Council has suggested that we have her try to expel it on her own before . . ." He trailed off and ran both hands through his hair.

"Before what?" I asked. He looked at the ceiling, seeing far beyond it. "No, Zeke. We're not doing that. Grace doesn't want the Mantle, and we're going to work with her until we can convince it to leave her for me."

"It isn't that simple, and it isn't up to me. The Council has ruled that either she steps into the role or we forcibly remove the Mantle." He moved to the window. "Souls are trapped on this plane without Death to allocate them. They're already piling up. Look."

I got out of bed and joined him to see several souls wandering my street. "I can fix this. All I need to do is see the demons and gain access to administrator privileges in HELL. Then I can allocate them. I think."

"Or Grace can do it. You need to convince her to step up."

Ezekiel hadn't used that tone with me since our first disastrous job together, and I shrank from him.

"Lucy, please don't. I'm not in control of this. It's out of my hands. My instructions are to tell you that you have three days to get Grace to expel the Mantle or perform the role. If you can't, the Council will step in. I'm sorry." He reached for me.

I stepped back. He'd just told me that Grace would die unless she agreed to accept a role she hadn't chosen and didn't want. My head felt like it was going to explode. His face fell.

"Zeke, you know I love you. That will never change, no matter how many bodies I inhabit or how many centuries I live, but—"

"Don't. Don't say but. You're not alone. I'll help you. Camael is staying. We'll make it work—I promise."

He opened his arms, and I stepped into them, just for a minute.

My stomach grumbled as the smell of Napoli Pizza drifted up the staircase to meet us. Patience and Marco had ordered in. I'd have to remember to hug them for their thoughtfulness. They were busy setting out plates and silverware and fussing over drinks as I walked into the kitchen.

My gaze traveled from the exposed brick walls and hanging copper pots I had collected on a tour of Turkey many years ago to the plants, tended by Patience, crowding the windowsills, to linger on the cotton and linen kitchen towels hanging from the oven handle. This lovely, warm place was my home, and I had often forgotten how comforting it was and how beautiful I had made it. No. That was wrong. I hadn't forgotten. I simply had no time to enjoy it. My job consumed every aspect of my existence, dictating every part of my life until I had no time to savor, well, anything.

Deathy expected us to work our bodies until we wore them out and then took on another and did the same thing to it. She considered nurturing our indomitable spirits, the beings that made reaping even possible—a waste of time. I thought about the carriage horses ferrying tourists through the streets in the worst weather, quiet and compliant until they died of exhaustion.

But what if the horse couldn't die? What if it worked ceaselessly for eternity? An eternity without a green field to run in, without the wind combing its mane, eternally without a mate to love. A horse would go mad—as we did.

I sat at the kitchen table, watching my roommates at the stove and sink. They laughed and joked, thrilled that I was safe. My throat closed. Our souls were indomitable, but they were the essence of humanity, and like their younger brethren living in the bodies of ordinary people, they still had needs, needs we ignored.

I was an anomaly. Reapers never lasted as long as I had—living for an eternity drove one mad. I should have drifted into insanity and been released from service a hundred years ago to either reclaim my humanity or go to Heaven. But *did* Heaven heal us and restore our sanity? Or did we become patients in a celestial mental hospital for all eternity? No one knew, or if they did, they weren't talking. And now that I knew Deathy was a liar, I suspected that her tales of the glorious afterlife were inflated. But maybe having the Mantle would give me the power to address what happened to us at our end. That, and overhauling working conditions for my fellow reapers might make up for losing my humanity and Ezekiel. But I doubted it.

Patience interrupted my sudden descent into near tears with her bubbly cheer. "Pizza, a slice of each flavor, and a nice cup of chamomile tea." She was that person, the one who always made you feel better, the one whose presence in a room lifted everyone's spirits. And when I wore the Mantle, I could make sure she stayed that way as long as she was on this earth—and maybe longer.

I inhaled the swirl of pizza aromas, reaching for a random slice. "Marco, I'll have the tea after, but right now, I could use a Manhattan. With three cherries, please?"

"I'm on it, boss." He laid a hand on my shoulder as he slipped behind me to go to the bar in the living room. Boss. The lyrics of "Everybody Knows" by Leonard Cohen trailed out of the kitchen speakers.

Yep. I bit into the slice I had selected, now cool enough not to burn my tongue, and chewed before swallowing and sighing. The pizza was perfect. I took a long sip of the cocktail Marco placed at my elbow. It, too, was excellent. Marco would make a spectacular bartender.

"You two don't need to watch me," I said to them as they leaned against the sink, side by side, staring at me like worried parents.

"Lucy, are you honestly okay?" Marco asked, slipping onto the chair opposite me and leaning across the table to touch my hand.

"Yes, the pain is gone, thanks to the angels." Marco dipped his chin, a sign he didn't believe me. "Okay, nearly gone, but I'll heal completely and be pain-free in another day or so. Did you see Ezekiel when you made my drink?"

"He's in the living room with Camael. Grace is napping on the couch," Marco said. "The Mantle is very active in her."

"Oh?"

"You'll see. Eat a bit more, please?" He pointed to my plate.

"Yes, Dad." I grinned at him, despite the chill that raced down my spine, and took another bite. There was plenty of drama coming, but it would have to wait for ten more minutes. I was starving.

I fished a cherry out of my glass with the silver pick and popped it into my mouth, answering him around it. "Grace has a powerful spirit. She'll be fine," I said to reassure him as much as me. I chewed the cherry, savoring its tart sweetness, before swallowing. "Is Felix in there too? How is he?"

Marco barked a laugh. "He's an interesting character."

Patience turned from whatever she was doing at the sink and rolled her eyes.

"But I think he's as good as he can be under the circumstances. His mood improved when I handed him clean clothes and a new pair of Lorenzo alligator shoes in his size. He actually giggled." Marco chuckled.

I couldn't help the grin that pulled up the corners of my mouth. "Felix is easy that way," I agreed. "What about Viceroy?"

"He's here, somewhere," Marco said and called out, "Viceroy!"

I slid my chair back and patted my lap as he trotted in. He leaped up as if I were mere inches from the ground. I put him on the table and set a meat slice on a plate in front of him.

"Maybe you two can check on Grace?" I said to my room-mates, needing to be out from under their concerned watchfulness.

"Are you sure?" Patience asked.

"I'm fine. Viceroy and I will have a little chat."

Marco ruffled Viceroy's fur as they left for the living room.

"How are you?" I asked the little dog.

"I'm good, thanks." He examined his slice and selected a morsel, chewing and swallowing before choosing another. I watched him pick out chunks of sausage, meatball, and rounds of pepperoni before lifting the cheese and eating it without getting a lick of sauce on his face.

I finished my slice and drained my cocktail, eating the last two cherries as dessert.

Viceroy watched me finish before thinking at me, "But I'm worried about Gracie—I mean Grace. She doesn't look right." He swiped the back of a paw across his muzzle in case there were stray bits. Examining his foot and finding none, he added, "The thing you call the Mantle likes her too much." He rose on his hind feet until we were eye to eye. "She'll be okay, right? When you get it out of her?"

He'd been listening. I reached over to put my arms around his little body. He was trembling. I kissed the top of his head, and he tilted his face to lick my cheek. My heart turned over as he moved to sit, and I let him go.

"She'll be fine," I said aloud, as much to convince myself as him. "The Mantle goes where it's needed. Sort of like electricity. It doesn't take over; it just empowers."

He wrinkled his eyebrows. "Electricity can be in people?"

"Maybe that wasn't the best simile. I was trying to say the Mantle can't like or dislike things. It doesn't have a personality."

"But it chose her."

"It did, and though we don't yet know why or how, we're going to do everything we can to help her."

He looked far from convinced.

"Is everything all right, Lucy?" Marco had reappeared in the doorway, his eyes flicking between me and Viceroy.

"I'm fine, I promise. Can you three hear each other?" I asked.

"I can hear them," Viceroy thought. "But it's not polite to eavesdrop."

I raised an eyebrow at him.

"Well, I try not to, anyway."

Marco shot a glance to Patience, who added, "We can hear him too. We didn't say anything for the same reason."

"Good. That makes it easier." I gathered up Viceroy and lowered him to the floor. "Let's go see what's worrying you."

I walked to the living room, sparing a glance toward the front door. Souls were now milling about on my stoop, but they were quiet. I put a hand over my heart to signal to the ones closest to the glass that I would help them soon. I sensed an inaudible sigh from them. But was it a sigh of relief or frustration? It was hard to tell through the glass and wood. I entered the living room, and Ezekiel and Camael turned to me as one. My skin crawled beneath the waves of their anxiety.

"What's wrong?"

Camael pointed across the room to Grace sleeping on the couch. "The Mantle is openly defying us. That in itself isn't new, but the strength of its conviction is. I'm worried that she won't be able to expel it."

I took a step closer to Grace and Felix, who perched on the edge of a chair next to her, and then I saw it—the Mantle illuminated her. Features serene, she looked like an Orthodox icon of the Madonna, lit from within by the grace of God. Viceroy trembled in my arms, and I shook right along with him. I had known Deathy for four hundred years but had never seen the Mantle light up within her. Besides Deathy's human body of the day, the only visage I'd ever seen was a writhing, hate-filled, demon aspect.

Grace, on the other hand, was the epitome of her name. She was mesmerizing. Her internal light was far brighter than the light from an indomitable spirit. It raced about her face and neck, playing tag with itself, shades of pink, purple, yellow, and blue swirling and dancing, colors pooling and separating in joyous explosions beneath her skin.

I felt tears track down my face as I turned to Ezekiel. "What is it?"

He shook his head. "I . . . I don't know. I've never seen the Mantle light up like this. She said she wanted a nap. It began as soon as she was asleep."

We all stared at the light show playing beneath her skin.

Viceroy pawed at my chest, dragging my gaze from Grace's face down to his. "Like I said, that thing doesn't want to leave her, and I know she says she doesn't want it, but that's not what I'm feeling."

"What do you mean?" I asked aloud.

He was silent for a moment. "I can feel what's inside people. What they're made of. I can feel that thing in Gracie and how it's already changing her. She's getting used to it. I'm scared for her."

"I know, Viceroy, so am I." My thoughts raced on, hell-bent on catastrophe. He thought something else, but I had turned my attention back to Ezekiel, who still hadn't spoken. "We need to wake her."

54

Grace

"Grace, Grace, wake up." Felix was patting my shoulder. I opened my eyes to see him at my side and Lucy and Ezekiel leaning over me. Patience and Marco, Lucy's roommates, stood against a wall, whispering. They were talking about me.

"Don't bother whispering. I can hear you," I said, feeling rather than seeing everyone contract into themselves. I could feel Viceroy's fear leaking out from under the coffee table. "It's okay, Viceroy, I won't hurt you. Come out." I sat up and held out my arms, but he didn't budge.

"You're not yourself," he thought.

"Your voice still has a slight reverberation," Lucy said. "It should pass. How do you feel?"

"I had a headache, I think, and my skin hurts, and I had a bad nightmare. It was like I was telling my dream self that I had to go somewhere and see some horrible things. There was a—" I stopped, remembering that something bad had happened and I shouldn't share that.

Ezekiel motioned Felix up off the chair and sat in his place. "Grace—"

"You're all afraid of me," I blurted.

Crickets, until Ezekiel broke the silence, his voice warm, soothing. "We all have to become accustomed to our new shared reality, this new you. And dogs are more sensitive than people. Viceroy's behavior is natural. You shouldn't take it personally."

"Because you can explode things," came a thought from under the table.

"Shut up, you little wart," Felix hissed aloud.

I giggled, and there I was—Gracie.

"May I please have a glass of water?" I asked, and Patience peeled herself off the wall in a rush to the kitchen.

"I'll help," Marco muttered, disappearing after her.

I massaged the back of my neck. "I feel . . ." I paused and rolled my head, eliciting a crack loud enough to startle myself. "Drunk. Blurry. I know that sounds weird." Waving away offers of help, I stood and took the few steps to the window.

A street full of drifting souls turned toward me as one. I tottered back at the spectral sight.

"Souls can feel the Mantle in you, Grace," Lucy said at my elbow. "They've been here all night, waiting for the new bearer to help them move on."

The sight of the souls drifting about the street was unnerving. "Waiting for me?"

"Yes. You will need to assign reapers to them. As you are now the bearer of the Mantle, you'll need to log into the system and, for lack of a better phrase, push the button to approve the assignments for the day."

I slid my hands into my pockets. "Didn't you say Deathy had to use her blood to do it?"

"It's just a finger stick. No worse than being a diabetic and checking your blood sugar."

I bit my lip and gave her a side-eye. "And then I'm somehow bonded to the system or some other freaky sci-fi thing. When are you taking this thing out of me?" I turned to face her and blinked. I could see her indomitable spirit, a bright white light, glowing beneath a faint radiance illuminating her skin.

"Well, there are a couple of—" she began.

"Lucy, I can see your spirit," I yelped, leaning closer. "Inside you." I touched the hollow of her throat with a fingertip. "Right here. I can't believe I can see it. Who else has one?" I looked at Felix, Patience, and Marco. "You guys have them. Felix's is dim, though." I examined Ezekiel and Camael. "Yikes. You guys are all light inside!" I stepped back, blinking my watering eyes and bumping into the window. "It's really bright. Can I turn this seeing-the-lights thing off?" I asked, panic rising.

"Um, I don't know. Zeke?" Lucy turned to Ezekiel.

"The short answer is yes. The longer answer is Camael has to teach you how to do it. I suppose you could wear sunglasses if—"

Camael put up a hand. "Wait a minute, Grace. You said Felix has one?"

"Yeah, he does." I focused on Felix again. "But his is dimmer. Grayish, maybe?"

Crickets again.

"What's gray? Do I have something on my shirt?" Felix had been arguing with Viceroy, who'd finally emerged from under the coffee table. At the mention of his name, he tented his shirt front, examining it for stains.

Lucy broke the stunned silence this time. "I thought so. Felix, it seems you also have an indomitable spirit, though you've weakened it by drinking human blood. We'll need to talk about it, but we need to work through Grace's problem first."

Felix nodded, his face suddenly white.

"And there's our second sign," Ezekiel said. "What are the odds that we'd have two indomitable spirits appear at the same—"

"Three, if you count Ben, the little boy I was imprisoned with at Vampire Bob's," I said. "And where's Phillip? Maybe he has one too?"

Ezekiel pursed his lips. "He's sleeping in one of the bedrooms. He does have a type of evolved spirit, but it's not the same as yours. His type is found in the taxonomic family of Super Hominidae beings."

"Super Hominidae? Like super-human? That's not a real thing. It isn't on any of the charts I studied in school," I muttered.

"Just because it isn't on human-made charts doesn't mean it doesn't exist," Ezekiel said.

I shrugged. "Okay, fine. Go on."

Ezekiel quirked an eyebrow at me. "Phillip is human, but with enhanced abilities. There are many different species within the family."

I gawked at him.

"Like witches and leprechauns," Ezekiel added, nodding and lifting his eyebrows in encouragement at me as if witches and leprechauns should clarify the concept.

"I can't even think about leprechauns," I said, "and I have enough problems without adding witches to the crapload of supernatural things I have to worry about."

Felix frowned.

"Okay, I take it back," I said. "You're okay, Felix, mostly, and I like Fay, so maybe all witches aren't evil. To get back on track here, three indomitables and one evolved, making four. That's—"

"A sign, all right," Camael finished. "Something is brewing. We need to talk to the Council, Zeke."

Ezekiel sighed. "It's not safe to leave them. I'll go. You stay and help Grace at least log into HELL so we can get those souls moving."

"Uh, wait a freaking minute here," I said. "No. I am not going to bleed every day because some power randomly chose me. You know the old saying, if you know that job, you've got that job?" They all stared at me. "It's true. If I know the job, I'll be stuck with it. I have plans for my life, and they don't include being the Pale Horseman. Period."

Ezekiel stepped toward me. "Where did you hear— We don't want you to be Death permanently, Grace, but until we can get the Mantle to leave you, you have to learn to use it, or—"

I cut him off and put my hands on my hips. "Or what?"

Ezekiel pointed out the window. "These poor souls must be

allowed to move on. If you refuse to help, we'll have to take the Mantle from you by force."

"And that means?" I asked, my voice low and vibrating. Flushing, my skin fizzing like baking soda and vinegar in vegan chocolate cake batter, I flung my arms out in frustration.

Three lamps flew from their end tables and crashed against the walls. Everyone ducked, covering heads and faces. Pieces of ceramic bases, glass shades, and lightbulbs sprayed the room. Patience, who was pouring water from a pitcher into a series of glasses, took a slice to her cheek. A chunk of lightbulb flew into the pitcher, splashing water over the books and magazines arrayed on the coffee table. Viceroy yelped and disappeared back under the table.

"Whoa," I croaked.

"Whoa, indeed," said an angel, judging by the way he glowed through his overcoat from just inside the archway. Camael slipped between the new angel and me while Ezekiel moved to stand directly in front of him.

"Azrael," said Ezekiel. "The Council ruled we were to have three days. But you're not here on behalf of the Council, are you?"

I pushed past Ezekiel to confront the new angel. "He's not," I said, warily. "I don't know how I know, but he's here to kill me and take the Mantle so he can give it back to Deathy."

"Yes, that is correct," Azrael said, tipping his hat and smiling without teeth.

"Well, you've come for nothing. I'm not giving you the Mantle so you can give it back to her—she's evil. And I'm not handing it over to Lucy. She doesn't want it," I blurted to gasps from the room before clamping my hand over my mouth. Where the hell had that come from?

Azrael examined me as if I were a bug, and he was debating which foot to squash me with. "Yes. You will relinquish it, and Isashkishu-Eshlesh-Inmeshlinzit shall rule again. Though, to be frank, neither of you are fit to bear the power of life and death.

She, however, has agreed to work with us. Ezekiel, Camael, hold her!"

The fizzing in my skin caught fire as Azrael's hands snaked around my arms. Viceroy howled. He shot from under the coffee table to sink his teeth into Azrael's ankle, loosening the angel's grip on me just enough.

I jerked away from him and pointed a finger into his chest.

"Gracie, *no!*" Lucy crashed between us, knocking Azrael backward and spinning me around so that my finger targeted the wall behind the sofa.

I blew a hole through to the dining room and tossed everyone against walls like twigs in a tornado. Plaster, brick bits, and wood slivers rained down. Patience screamed as the force of the explosion shoved her into Marco's arms. I couldn't see Viceroy. Felix looked dazed, bleeding from his nose. Azrael came at me, murder in his eyes. Camael and Ezekiel flew at him, and the three popped out of existence.

Phillip came pounding down the stairs and flew into the room, skidding to a stop and surveying the wreckage. "I was sound asleep. What did I miss?"

55

Felix

Viceroy and I argued in Lucy's back garden. I wanted to go to New Orleans; he wanted us to stay and help however we could. As lovely as the garden was, it quickly got too cold for both of us, and we headed back inside, shelving the "discussion" for later.

"Oh, Felix, I was just about to go down looking for you." Lucy stood at the table, twisting the edge of the runner. "We need to talk."

Nothing good ever came of someone needing to talk. When she sat, indicating a chair across from her, I took it, listening for sounds of breaking glass or splintering furniture, but the house was quiet.

"Where is everyone?" I asked.

"Ezekiel and Camael aren't back yet. Everyone else is in the living room."

"So, what do we need to talk about?"

"I need your help."

"With what?" I peered under the table for Viceroy's "I told you so" expression, but he was nowhere in sight.

Lucy's solemn countenance faded into a troubled smile. "Felix, I know we haven't had time to talk about your indomitable spirit yet, but weak as it may currently be, you are still in a position to not only help me with Grace but to help in the coming war."

"Wait a minute, a war? Did I miss something?" A snort from under the table let me know the little rat was back. "Shut up. No one asked for your opinion. And stop eavesdropping." I bent to see him licking a paw, feigning ignorance.

"No, you didn't miss anything. It's a theory Ezekiel and I were discussing at Playland Park that now looks like more than a theory." Lucy studied me as I went from "unwilling to help" to "I need to get the fuck out of here before I die" in under ten seconds flat.

"Uh, can I think about it?"

Her face fell.

"No." Viceroy skittered from under the table. "He doesn't need to think about it, Lucy. *Of course we'll help.*"

"Hey! Did I ask you? Did anyone ask you?" I snapped at him.

"We are not leaving Lucy and Grace to deal with this alone, Felix. No, wait. Let me re-say that. I'm not leaving Lucy and Grace. You can do whatever your chicken-shit heart wants. But just know that if you go it alone, *you go it alone.*" He turned his back on me and walked into the living room. I turned back to Lucy to see tears sliding down her cheeks.

"Fuck," I muttered. "Fine. I'll help. But I am not dying in a fucking godforsaken supernatural war," I said, pitching my voice higher.

"Then at the very least you'll need to stop feeding," Lucy whispered, wiping at her tears with a napkin.

"Wait, what?" My mouth dropped open. It was a damned good thing no one but Viceroy knew what I'd tried to do at Playland Park.

"Felix, you're going to need all the strength your soul possesses. Your constant feeding has weakened it to the point that it has never been able to wake. It's the only way."

"You said 'at the very least.'"

"We can talk about other ways to strengthen your gift later. But for now, you should stop feeding. And there's one other thing."

I drummed my fingers on the table until she continued.

"Felix, the Mantle will drive Grace mad. And not in eons, we're talking months. Maybe weeks or even days. It's too much power too fast for such a young soul, her strength notwithstanding. I have no idea how long she has, nor do the angels. If it were up to Azrael, she'd be dead before we had a chance to find out."

"Did you tell her that?" I massaged the space between my eyebrows in an attempt to ward off the inevitable headache and heaved a theatrical sigh. "No. Of course you didn't. So, you expect me to help you talk her into stepping up while at the same time protecting her from angels that want her dead, and a massive case of insanity."

"Yes." She pressed her lips together.

"And?"

"And I think getting out of town will help," she barreled on. "We'll get Grace out of town, away from Vampire Bob, and away from familiar surroundings, which might enable her to see things differently. Then we can tell the Council we're making headway, and hopefully, they'll give us a little more time to—" She broke off. "Crap. Maybe I'm just trying to run from our problems." She lowered her head into the cradle of her arms on the table before lifting it again. "I'm clutching at straws here, Felix."

"What do you mean by getting out of town?" I asked, sudden suspicion flaring. I kicked out a foot hoping to connect with the little rat under the table. Fortunately for him, I missed.

"I think we go with your idea," she said firmly.

"My idea? Did I have an idea?" I feigned puzzlement. True, I hadn't told anyone about leaving town, though ever since I'd thought of it on the boardwalk, I'd been contemplating how to go without tipping off Bob. The sneaky little canine bastard had read my mind.

"Viceroy told you. Where is that little creep?"

She grinned broadly, revealing a small dimple in her left cheek. "He's in the living room. Don't be angry with him, Felix. He was trying to help. And I believe you're right—we need to leave town. New Orleans is different enough that it just might jog Grace's frame of mind." She searched my face for confirmation.

I hesitated long enough to cause her eyebrows to draw together.

"What? What are you not saying?" Lucy frowned.

"I wasn't planning on bringing you all with me. My thought was to go home with Viceroy, even though he doesn't deserve to go anywhere with me. If Bob continued to harass us, I planned to gather friends and go after him."

Lucy frowned. "You don't even know where Bob is. And why would you leave us now, when Grace is—"

"Look, Lucy, Viceroy and I aren't safe as long as Bob's after us. We won't have a moment's peace. You, on the other hand"—I waved my hand around above my head—"have everyone in this house, plus however many reapers and angels you can call in, to help you deal with Grace. Viceroy and I have only each other." I crossed my arms over my chest. "I made him. He's my . . . child. And like it or not—mostly not—I can't leave him with you. I owe him protection, as much as it galls me to admit it. So we're going tomorrow."

Lucy leaned across the table and held out her hands for mine. I sat, arms still crossed.

"Felix."

I sighed, uncrossed my arms, and placed my hands in hers.

"We've been drawn together—me, you, Viceroy, and Gracie— and now Phillip, Ezekiel, and Camael. It isn't a coincidence."

I attempted to tug my hands away, but she tightened her grasp and leaned forward, her eyes burning bright.

"We're together for a reason. And we need each other. We are better together, stronger together," Lucy said, her voice straining with urgency.

"No, I—"

"Not I, *we*. You and Viceroy are not alone." Her eyes glittered with unshed tears.

"Look, Lucy. It isn't safe for Viceroy and me to stay in my loft, and we can't move into your house. It makes no sense for you all to go with me to New Orleans. Going there from here would be like going from dangerous to suicidal. I have a connection to the rat-infested place because it's home, but New Orleans is number one on the hit list for madness, deceit, and supernatural malfeasance. If anything terrifying is going to happen, it's going to happen there."

"Not if we're together," she said firmly.

I shook my head. "You're delusional."

"Maybe, but it's the only solution that makes sense to me. We could go to the Catskills, but that might put Grace's family in danger. And I don't want to go anywhere without you. I won't take no for an answer." Lucy was behind me in a heartbeat, wrapping her arms around me in a tight hug. "We need to be together," she whispered in my ear.

I didn't have the emotional wherewithal to argue any longer. I leaned against her and into the hug, shoving the realization that she was right, and I was an asshole as far down as it would go.

56

Felix

Friday, November 20

I left Lucy, Phillip, and Viceroy to deal with Grace, and headed out the following morning to run errands, pack a bag, and have my car detailed. Over breakfast, Lucy had given me the address of a fabulous tea shop. She was right. It was marvelous, and I was able to purchase a few delectable new brews for the road, including a headache concoction and an apple-harvest blend that smelled heavenly.

I made a couple of calls from the car while driving from place to place. The first was to my housekeeper, who'd need to open the house and arrange for a thorough cleaning. The process would take a few days, so next, I'd called the Ursuline sisters to arrange a temporary place to stay.

The final but perhaps most urgent call was to an acquaintance who could broker a meeting with Marie Laveau. Contrary to popular belief and a tomb that allegedly held her bones, Marie Laveau was not dead. The vampire community suspected that one of us, and not voodoo, was responsible for her unnaturally long life. But whatever the reason, she still lived, and I needed to see her. Her price would be high, but she was the only person I knew who might be able to tell me whether I had managed to turn Viceroy because I had an indomitable spirit or if there was something else at work and how I had even contracted the virus in the first place.

Now close to Lucy's house, I stopped once more, looking for a parking space along Christopher Street. I finally found one a block and a half from my destination: a jeweler. The shop was tiny, sandwiched between a perfumery and a gourmet market. The dim, dusty interior was enough to frighten off all but the knowledgeable, as Allister and his wife Mary hadn't updated a thing inside since the building had gone up, and that might have been the last time they'd dusted.

Allister, a small, faded man of indeterminate age, looked up when the bell over the door tinkled. "Felix! It's been far too long." He came out from behind the worn counter with a grin and embraced me. I bent to clutch him tightly before releasing him.

Mary, his tall, thin but robust wife of too many years to count, was right behind him. "How wonderful to see you," she murmured in her soft voice, reaching for my hand. I pulled her into a hug.

"Mary, I'm happy to see you too. I shouldn't have stayed away for so long."

She stepped back to regard me carefully, making me glad I'd showered, shaved, and changed while at the loft. "You look well." Her blue eyes, level with mine, crinkled. "We've missed you," she said, then frowned past me and out the window. "But there's trouble afoot, and you don't have time to reminisce. What can we do?"

I spent a few minutes explaining the situation, though they were unsurprised. They had seen the souls wandering the streets and had already spelled a collection of possession-repelling pendants Allister said were selling briskly.

Mary disappeared behind the counter and pulled a tray from a cabinet beneath the glass display that showcased ordinary antique pieces. She placed the tray in front of me, and I bent to examine the selection.

"Your strongest?" I asked her.

"These." She indicated a row of unattractive russet-brown stones, explaining that this agate was a negative-energy repellant. Additionally, Mary had imbued them with powerful wards. "They will protect the wearer against most possessions, but only if worn next to the skin."

"Most?"

"Anything you are likely to encounter. There are, as you know, greater evils. But protection against them is beyond my skill set. So be careful; these amulets aren't infallible."

I felt her gaze boring into the top of my head.

"Felix, should we leave the city?"

I looked up, noted the amulets they both wore, then examined the room, spotting each freshly conjured charm, spell, and ward. Their shop, and their apartment just above it, were well protected. They'd be as safe here as anywhere.

"Not unless you have a remote place to go. Fewer people mean fewer souls on the loose. I think you've got yourselves covered." I pointed to a charm dangling above my head. "Can I carry anything for you?" I asked to be polite.

Mary brightened. She reached beneath the counter again and placed a small parcel on the glass, pushing the thing toward me. I picked up the small package, and it wiggled in my hand.

I dropped it back on the counter and withdrew my fingers. "It won't chew through the paper and eat me, or hatch, or explode, will it?"

They both laughed.

"Not for at least a week," Mary said with a wicked grin. "The sisters will be glad to have it back."

Ah. She knew I was going home. But then again, where else could I go?

I picked it up, stowed it in my inner jacket pocket, and blew out a puff of air. "You always could read me like a scroll."

I selected seven pendants in an overabundance of caution and one smaller stone in a flat setting that we could stitch to the inside of Viceroy's collar. Overkill, perhaps, but better safe than possessed. Slipping one on under my shirt, I paid for my purchases and hugged my old friends goodbye. I wanted nothing more from this city except to be shed of it and its freezing fucking winters. I was ten feet from my car when a hand landed on my shoulder.

"Hello, Felix. Going somewhere?"

I jerked away, a shout escaping my lips as I whirled to see Vampire Bob grinning at me. I stumbled back, banging against a plate-glass window that vibrated in protest. I opened my mouth, but nothing came out, so I shut it.

"You look like a fish caught on a hook. Can I buy you a drink?"

"No!" I spat, searching the street. "You've lost. Leave us alone!" I fumbled for my phone.

"I've lost? Is that what you think?"

"And you won't have us. Any of us. Ever."

Bob broke into a merry chuckle that congealed my blood. "Oh, Felix, all that is in the past. We're all going to have a bright new future. Together. Let's let bygones be bygones." He pulled a gold cigarette case from his breast pocket and opened it, offering me a clove cigarette.

I frowned.

"I know they're your favorite." He snapped the case shut, tucking it away when I shook my head. "I'm here because I have a gift for you," he said as if he were offering a fire truck to a little boy.

I slid sideways along the glass, adding a layer of filth to my coat, until I hit a shop door. My foot caught on the stoop, and I fell on my ass.

Bob stuck out a hand, but I scrambled up on my own.

"You have nothing I want," I said, biting out the words to hide the tremble in my voice.

But he heard it. "Now, now, there's no reason for you to be afraid. I am merely going to give you what you desire above all else. I am going to make you a full-blood."

My heart began to beat erratically, and a hot flush suffused my face. Bob held out his hand again.

I almost reached for it, sticking my hand in my pocket instead. "In exchange for what?"

"Now that's an interesting question. Walk with me."

"No."

"Felix, I'm not going to attack you on the street. There are too many people to enthrall. And besides, souls are sizing you up as a potential hotel." He pointed behind me, and I turned to see three pale shapes trailing us.

Momentarily forgetting that my protection amulet was more than effective against such simple spirits, I jerked sideways, jostling Bob, only to recoil as if he'd bitten me. "You know I'll never give you Grace or Viceroy," I said, regaining some of my wits as we put some distance between the souls and us. "What could I possibly have that you want?" I stopped at the corner, unwilling to go farther from my car.

An old woman carrying a cat in a ratty plastic Easter basket edged past us to cross as the light changed. "Don't listen to him— he's damned!" she hissed at me and took off, running jerkily across the street, trailing an unwashed miasma. She turned and flashed the sign of the evil eye before disappearing into a doorway.

"Witches. They just don't know when to stop," Bob growled, stepping into the street to peer up at the windows above her doorway. "I won't be damned for long." He turned back to me. "And neither will you, once I've turned you. You, Felix, are going to help me usher in a new era of vampirism."

I gaped at him. "What the hell are you talking about?"

"Are you sure you don't want that drink?"

"No. Say what you need to. I'm busy." I felt braver now that he wasn't about to kill me.

He grabbed my arm and dragged me down the cross street a

few feet. "I'm going to assume you know about Death relinquishing her Mantle."

I nodded.

"And you know about the souls wandering the streets."

I nodded again.

"But did you know that Death has the power to implant souls into soulless beings?"

"What? You mean possession?" Feigning ignorance seemed the safest path. "Souls don't need Death for that. They can jump us at will."

Bob sighed. "Souls won't willingly implant in vampires. We need Death to force them in."

"But how could she do that if, once she relinquishes the Mantle, she's no longer Death?"

"You ask too many questions. She doesn't need to be Death to do it. She just needs to know how."

"So why not just get someone else to do it? The old Death can't possibly be the only one who knows how to implant souls."

"Someone else? Who? Angels?"

"Oh, right. So what you're saying is that you think you'll get a soul."

Bob wagged a finger in my face. "I *will* get a soul. My fellow vampires will get souls—and you, once I turn you, will get a soul too."

"But I already have a soul," I said, continuing to play dumb.

Bob shook his head as if I were an idiot. "Yes, but once I turn you, it will die. You'll need a new one." He watched my face.

I stepped away from him and looked up and down the street. It was empty. "And how do you think I can help you?" I prompted.

"Because as insane as Deathy was, she still managed to disappear before fulfilling her part of the bargain, which was to ensoul us." Bob's cheek twitched. "And that means that we'll need the new Lady Death."

I massaged the back of my neck before dropping my hand. It

was a bad idea to show weakness of any kind to a full-blood. "She was Death, one of the most powerful beings in existence. What could you possibly offer her that she couldn't get for herself?"

Bob shook his head. "Eternal life without the tasks and responsibilities of her position."

"Are you telling me that Death hated her job enough . . ." I swept my hand out at lost souls trailing toward us, sweat gathering under my collar at their proximity. ". . . to relinquish all her power?"

"Don't be dim. Isn't it obvious? Deathy was a vain old cow, and—"

"And you lied to her. You said you could turn her, give her immortality despite her indomitable spirit. Which, now that I think about it, makes no sense whatsoever. But you were never going to turn her because she was most likely immune to you. Why did she believe you? Did she really believe you? Why didn't the angels figure it out?"

"You're giving me a headache, Felix. I don't care about the deep mechanics of indomitability, nor should you. You lack the mental faculties to parse it. As far as I'm concerned, she believed I could give her eternal life without the necessity of becoming a reaper all over again and trading bodies all the time. She believed because she wanted to. And because there was a minuscule chance that it would work. When you want something badly enough, you'll believe anyone who tells you that you can have it."

He pulled a different cigarette case from another pocket, extracted a tobacco cigarette, lit it, and took a deep drag, spiraling the smoke into perfect rings that floated above our heads and drifted apart. The man might be a monster, but he had skills.

"As for the angels, who knows what they're thinking or why they do anything. They don't have true brains, you know. It's all an illusion." He blew another perfect smoke ring. "Still, that silly bitch Deathy cheated me. I'm going to find her and have a little fun with her. Until she's dead." He brightened at my pained expression. "Come on. I'll walk you to your car. We don't want you possessed now, do we?"

He didn't need to know about my amulet. I hustled down the street, Bob at my heels. At my car, I turned to face him.

"Felix, just because Deathy is missing doesn't mean the terms of the concordat are null—the agreement is with the power, not the person that wields it. Deathy bet her power."

"But—"

"You really are a moron. Haven't you ever played poker? By losing her power early, Deathy folded. That means I win her pot without having to give anything in return. See what I did there? I don't have to turn her. And her pot is you, Viceroy, and those souls. I can have you and Viceroy anytime I want. The souls, I will collect now." He paused. "As Lady Death, Grace can and will provide them. The only question is whether she does it willingly. If she refuses, we will drain every member of her family, children first, so the parents can watch them die. Then we will move on to her friends."

"We? All your friends are dead."

"Do you think I was stupid enough to bring all the vampires at my disposal to Playland Park?"

"No. I suppose not." My nether regions began to frost over at the thought of another battle. But idiot that I was, I couldn't seem to shut the hell up. "Why do you even want them? Souls, I mean," I whispered. "You're immortal; you have everything."

"Not everything. It's a complicated answer you don't have time to hear—"

"Reapers!" I blurted. "You have the reaper problem. You've been around too long. You're losing your marbles, and you think getting a human soul will stave off insanity. But it doesn't work for reapers—"

"Because reapers have the same soul, you moron. The same ancient soul, which of course would go insane over time. We will get new souls."

Bob's eyes flashed, and I clamped my mouth shut.

"I'm done listening to you babble. Do I turn you? Or do I begin draining Grace's family until she concedes? Either way works for me," Bob said and flicked some ash from his lapel.

I stared at him and said the only thing I could to buy time.

"You turn me. Can we do it in New Orleans? I'm heading down to attend to some business, and Grace is coming with me. I'll need two weeks, but I can get her to comply. I'm certain of it." I beeped the lock, yanked the door open, and slid in, slamming the door in his face before he could answer.

Bob tapped on the glass, and I lowered the window. "Two weeks. Someone will contact you with meeting details. Oh, and by the way, I wasn't lying about the concierge job. Having someone who knows the finer aspects of a given city to help ease a vampire's transition to a new location is a capital idea. I would like you to at least consider training a few of them for me." He stepped back from the car and bared his fangs in a rictus grin. "Don't disappoint me, Felix. You won't like what happens if you do."

Night was falling along with the temperature when I parked half a block from Lucy's house. A small group of souls drifted toward me as I exited the car. One small spirit drew closer to watch me remove my purchases from the back seat—a child. Or it had been a child, once. My chest tightened. Juggling parcels, I shivered, the curious little soul trailing behind me as I made my way to the front door and rang the bell.

Patience answered in seconds. "Felix, you've been shopping!" She eyed the souls and frowned slightly upon seeing the little one. "Did you get anything for me?" She forced a smile and teased, yanking me inside before they could get too close.

"I did. I'll show you later," I said as Patience took some of the bags from my hands.

The household buzzed with activity. Patience ran ahead of me up the stairs, and we deposited everything on my bed. Viceroy ran in to greet me, Grace at his heels. It was hard for me to reconcile the flippant, cheerful young woman who had dragged me to the mall with this newly hesitant but frighteningly powerful person. While the unpretentious nickname "Gracie" didn't fit her anymore, I missed it.

"Is everything okay?" I asked.

"I don't even know how to answer that," Grace said.

She was wearing a pretty pine-green sweater over a crisp white shirt, jeans, and sheepskin slippers. I remembered the clothing Marco had brought me yesterday, though it felt like a month ago. Everything had fit perfectly.

"At least the house is well stocked with a multisized wardrobe."

Grace looked down at herself and grinned. "Yeah, I had my pick. It was the most fun I've had in days." She stood shifting from foot to foot for a few seconds, finally stuffing her hands in her pockets and backing out of the room. "I'll let you get cleaned up."

"Did you bring me anything?" Viceroy thought up at me.

"Not that you deserve a gift," I grumbled aloud at him. "But I did. I'll show you after I shower—the city is particularly gritty today." And far too full of killer vampires and wandering souls.

"Deal." He scampered down the stairs after Grace.

Shutting the door, I removed my jacket, mindful of the squirming package, and headed for the bathroom. I'd already had a shower that morning, but I needed to scrub Bob off. The high pressure and hot water relieved my chill and removed the layer of city grime but did little to steady my spinning head. Fucking Bob.

The thing I hadn't told him, the thing he apparently couldn't sense, was that if Lucy was right, I had an indomitable spirit. But then how had I been infected with the virus in the first place? Was it because I'd been a teenager and my spirit hadn't woken up yet? If I made my spirit stronger by abstaining from human blood, and Bob was unable to turn me, I would age and die.

Die? But did I have to die? Reapers had indomitable spirits, and they didn't die. They got to pick new bodies all the time. And maybe I was able to turn Viceroy because I was an indomitable half-vamp? Too much. It was all just too much. Marie Laveau would know. And Lucy and I would have a conversation—soon.

I pushed Bob out of mind. The immediate issue was getting to New Orleans. Flying was out for this new Grace. If she pointed at something, she'd blow the plane out of the sky, so we would drive. My car was roomier than Lucy's, making the more than twenty-hour drive over two days somewhat bearable. Three would be more comfortable, but no one wanted to risk a dangerously empowered Grace on the road for more nights than was necessary. I mulled over the difficulties of a car trip with Death in the passenger seat. What could go wrong?

I turned off the water and toweled myself off, peering at my deepening crow's feet and laugh lines in the mirror. I should have gotten a snack while out on errands, but Lucy's warning and Bob's new threat had turned my brain to gristle. I hadn't even thought of it, and maybe it was a good thing I hadn't.

Merry sounds floated up the staircase as I descended, drawn to the kitchen by the conversation, laughter, barking, and clinking plates. Something smelled delicious. I stopped in the doorway. Ezekiel and Camael had returned while I was out, and they must have gotten good news. They were practically glowing.

The big table was set with a starched linen tablecloth and Lucy's beautiful china. The double chandeliers cast a warm, convivial glow on the feast arrayed across the table, lighting the faces of the group, banishing the darkness outside the bank of windows, and drawing me in. I pulled out a chair between Phillip and Ezekiel. Everyone was talking at once, filling plates and pouring wine. I hesitated. The room was a bit *too* convivial, the cheer a bit too frenetic. It set my already shredded nerves on edge.

I opened my mouth to explain that this was no time for hilarity, but a shout of laughter from the end of the table interrupted me before I could utter a scolding.

Viceroy sat on the table, chewing each bite of his roast pork carefully before taking another. His tail wagged, and he smiled to himself between mouthfuls. Marco was talking soccer with Phillip. Ezekiel was regaling a delighted Grace and Patience with tales of angel antics.

Lucy searched my face, registering my concern, as I settled into my chair. "It's okay, Felix. We'll figure it all out once we get there," she whispered, glancing at Viceroy, who she knew was listening. "We'll be fine," Lucy insisted when I didn't answer, taking my hesitance for disagreement.

"Look." She pointed to a cake covered with white frosting and rainbow sprinkles. "Grace made a cake while you were gone. She said baking always made her feel more like herself." She chuckled. "We just happened to have leftover sprinkles from Patience's birthday party last year, and Grace said they were just what we needed."

Lying through my teeth, I reached across the table to squeeze Lucy's hand and echo her pronouncements. "You're right. We'll figure it out."

She nodded, satisfied with my apparent validation, and turned her attention back to the others. Viceroy was staring at the cake with soulful eyes, willing it to be for him.

In the mental silence afforded by the absence of his prattling, I took a deep, calming breath and surveyed the delectable choices on the platters before me. The camaraderie of our little band muffled my terror at what awaited us in New Orleans, and I began to fill my plate.

57

Grace

Saturday, November 21

My insides were trembling, but we packed Felix's Range Rover, a gorgeous car with plenty of room for everything, in record time. Felix had even rigged a dog bed atop the luggage so Viceroy would have a sleeping perch with visibility over the seatback. Patience and Marco had supplied us with lunches, snacks, thermoses of tea and coffee, water bottles, and parcels of meat for Viceroy.

Felix and Phillip were in the front, leaving Lucy, Viceroy, and me to take the back seat. The angels would travel by bubble wrap, popping from place to place, but they had promised to track us and join us whenever we stopped.

"Are you coming?" Felix asked.

I stood on the sidewalk, reluctant. Everything was about to change—had already changed, I supposed. But leaving New York meant I had to own it.

"Can I ask a favor?"

"Sure. Anything," Lucy said before Felix could pull the inevitable face.

"Can we drive past my mom's house?"

"You do not want to leave your mother?" Camael asked from the sidewalk. His deep but gentle voice lifted into the morning breeze, the word "mother" drifting down the sidewalk.

My voice caught in my throat. "I don't know when I'll be back, and I need to—"

"Yes, of course," Felix said. "It's practically on the way."

My neighborhood was in the opposite direction and would add an hour and a half to the trip, but it was kind of him not to point that out.

"Can you get in now?" Felix laid his forehead on the steering wheel. "Pretty please?" There he was. I knew nice Felix was a blip.

Five a.m. was early enough that we managed to avoid commuter traffic, arriving in Port Chester in just about forty-five minutes. Felix maneuvered the big car down the narrow residential streets, passing Manny's. Inside the bagel bakery, Sylvie wiped the counters as the first customers trickled in. Tears welled, hot and fast. I gulped, and Lucy laid a hand on my leg. I plucked a tissue from the box that had been affixed to the back of the driver's seat and pressed it against my eyes until bright sparkles appeared beneath my eyelids. I blew my nose, looking up at the street where I had grown up.

So many things hadn't changed over the years. The lumpy macadam that the city never managed to smooth out, no matter how many times they repaved, was still lumpy. Those lumps had knocked me off my bicycle, causing me to skin my knees more times than I could remember. When I was little, my brothers had bounced my sled over the moguls of ice and snow, leaving me with a sore butt more times than I could count.

And so many things had changed. My brothers moved out one by one, and then finally, I brought Bryan to the house for the first time to meet my mother.

Bryan. Could Death even have a boyfriend? Would he even still want me? My heart ached as I looked at each neighbor's home, knowing which would soon wear strings of Christmas lights.

My breath hitched as we pulled over. Trying to control the rush of emotions, I hiccupped, and the large fire agate pendant Felix had given me tugged against my skin. I had initially refused it, thinking I didn't need the protection he explained it offered, but Lucy had convinced me to wear it as she fastened one around her neck. I was glad she had. I liked the warmth of the stone against my breastbone.

"Do you want to step out?" Lucy asked, searching my face.

I knew that look. It was the same look my mother gave me when she was hoping I would do the right thing. They all thought I couldn't or wouldn't turn the Mantle over to Lucy, and they were right. I wasn't going to doom her to this fate even if I could.

They also thought I wouldn't assign reapers to souls. They were only partially correct. I would do it if the only alternative was death by the Angelic Council, but we hadn't even begun to look for other options. As a baker, I knew all about substitutions, and I had a hard time believing there wasn't one here. Except I had no idea where to start to search for it, being pretty sure Google wouldn't help. Lucy could temporarily handle directing the reapers to take on souls themselves, and if a couple of reapers got possessed, well, that was a risk I had to take to protect both myself and my new friend.

The house, with its windows dark, looked lonely. My mother's little VW Beetle was missing from its customary spot in front, and there were no lights on in the kitchen. Had I not gotten involved in all this, my mother, always an early riser, would be buried in one of the books she was currently reading, sipping coffee, and listening to the local public radio station in the background. But because of my choices, she was hiding out in an angel encampment upstate.

Felix turned the ignition off, and I sat, looking at our home. The gutters would need replacing soon. My mother would probably have them replaced in the spring. We had talked about painting the house and perhaps changing up the color of the shutters, trim, and the front door. We had even collected paint samples from Home Depot. I had voted for a gorgeous plum; my mother loved a pretty blue-green. I opened the car door, and Viceroy stepped onto my lap. I picked him up, got out, and set him on the sidewalk.

"Don't be sad. You're not leaving forever. You'll be back, and I'll come with you," the little dog thought up at me.

I gazed down into his face and nodded, not wanting to risk releasing the tears that welled by speaking aloud. Viceroy stiffened, his head swiveling towards a movement down the street.

A little girl skipped down the sidewalk from the library's direction, followed by a teenage boy. The boy carried a pile of books. A chill raced up my arms and through my scalp. My hands clenched of their own accord, and Viceroy grumbled low in his throat, stepping forward. Phillip, Lucy, and Felix were deep in conversation and didn't notice the pair of kids.

As they drew closer, a wave of love dispelled the chill. It was me. The little girl was me, the boy my brother, Auggie. He was carrying books we had checked out of the library. I hadn't been allowed to go alone at that age, so one of my brothers, usually Auggie, always accompanied me. I glanced into the car—no one was watching.

"Shhh," I whispered aloud to Viceroy as the threatening tears spilled down my cheeks. "They won't hurt us."

I remembered that day! Little me was wearing my favorite sweater, a red wool pullover with a white heart on the sleeve that my mother had knit for me. I danced up the steps, curly ponytail swinging. Without looking back, I twisted the doorknob and slipped inside. My brother paused on the sidewalk, his arms full of books, and scanned the street, a puzzled look on his face. We were less than twenty feet apart, and I stared at him. I'd forgotten how handsome he was, even as a teen. Finally, not seeing me or our car, he shook his head slightly as if to clear it, and ran up the steps and through the open door, kicking it shut behind him.

The Mantle rippled inside me.

"Thanks for that," I whispered. Swiping at my wet face with

my fingers, I drank in the image of our house once more as Viceroy relieved himself on the wheel of the Range Rover. The only motion on the street now came from two squirrels chasing each other around the trunk of a maple tree.

"Grace?" Lucy asked.

"I'm ready," I said. I wasn't, but there was nothing I could do about it here. Without looking back, I picked up Viceroy, climbed inside, and shut the door.

The End

Afterword

Thank you so much for reading! I hope you enjoyed Indomitable, and the travails of Gracie, Viceroy, Felix, Lucy, Ezekiel and their friends.

I started writing this book seven years ago, with Felix as the protagonist. I didn't get very far, and ended up throwing away hundreds of words trying to get it right, until one night, I dreamed of Gracie in the lead role. I guess prophetic dreams are infectious.

Viceroy was a huge part of the story from day one, as Toby, the beloved cairn terrier I lost years ago is never far from my thoughts. I couldn't think of a better way to immortalize him then by giving him a voice as Viceroy.

In Book 2, Incorrigible, our crew continues their adventures in New Orleans. Felix opens his home and pays the price, Grace gains the fealty of the angels, vampire Bob lays a trap, and Viceroy learns rats are as tasty as squirrels.

Finally, If you loved, or at least liked, Indomitable, please leave a review and share on social media. As an indie author, I rely heavily on the feedback and support of readers like you.

Thank you again!

Claudia

Acknowledgments

Alpha and Beta readers and believers in the dream, Anthony, Chandra, Holly, Susan, Christy, Lana, Chris, Kerri, and Sam. And Ziggy, who caught things no one else did.
Italian translators: Paola Martino and Chandra Dunitz
Editors: Kate Angelella and Crystal Watanabe
Chapter heading illustrator: Imre Jeneses

My small but mighty twitter community who folded me into their midst with acceptance and friendship. Finally, a hug to Chris Tullbane, author extraordinaire, who so generously shared his knowledge and experience.

It would never have happened without you.

About the Author

Claudia Brooke has been writing since she could hold a crayon. In addition to writing poetry and short stories, she was a corporate communications and investor relations writer and a copywriter for small businesses.

Her favorite number is two; she loves James Thurber, hot buttered toast, and coffee. She can find almost anything online and plays the accordion.

She has two talented daughters, three delightful grandchildren, and lives with her tolerant husband and muse in Maryland. Indomitable is her first novel.

She shares updates at www.claudiabrooke.com

twitter.com/ClaudiaLBrooke

instagram.com/claudialbrooke

CPSIA information can be obtained
at www.ICGtesting.com
Printed in the USA
BVHW080932290822
645757BV00004B/175